PRAISE FOR *INDIGO SPRINGS*
WINNER OF THE 2010 SUNBURST AWARD FOR CANADIAN FANTASY LITERATURE

"The theme here—the problems of power in irresponsible hands—is archetypal, but Dellamonica realizes it very well through characters you wouldn't want in your neighborhood but who certainly hold your attention in what becomes an edge-of-the-seat thriller." —*Booklist*

"I loved this. An original and terrific apocalyptic fantasy set in the real world, *Indigo Springs* is terrifyingly insightful, sprinkled with bits of humor for leavening. Newcomer A. M. Dellamonica has deftly crafted a book that is both literary and a very good read. What a fine storyteller Tor has discovered."
—Patricia Briggs, #1 bestselling author of the Mercy Thompson novels

"A psychologically astute, highly original debut—complex, eerie, and utterly believable. Stay tuned for the projected sequel."
—*Kirkus Reviews* (starred review)

"A fascinating and multilayered tale of people who get caught up with forces beyond their control. Not only is it a cracking good tale, it's also an insightful look into the consequences of using great power selfishly." —*RT Book Reviews* (four stars)

"A lyrical and richly imagined world with a storyline that encompasses both eco-politics and the vagaries of the human heart."
—Syne Mitchell, editor of *WeaveZine*

"This is an entertaining and terrifying tale of terrific characters who stumble into the practice of blue magic and find that it is neither simple nor safe. Astrid, Jacks, and Sahara will enchant you and lead you down unexpected paths of discovery and danger. A great read that will make you look for magic in everyday objects!" —Toby Bishop, author of *Airs Beneath the Moon*

TOR BOOKS BY A. M. DELLAMONICA

Indigo Springs
Blue Magic

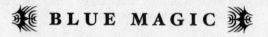 **BLUE MAGIC**

A. M. DELLAMONICA

TOR®

A TOM DOHERTY ASSOCIATES BOOK
NEW YORK

BLUE MAGIC

Edited by James Frenkel

A Tor Book
Published by Tom Doherty Associates, LLC
175 Fifth Avenue
New York, NY 10010

www.tor-forge.com

Tor® is a registered trademark of Tom Doherty Associates, LLC.

Library of Congress Cataloging-in-Publication Data

Dellamonica, A. M.
    Blue magic / A.M. Dellamonica.—1st ed.
        p. cm.
    "A Tom Doherty Associates book."
    ISBN 978-0-7653-1948-7 (trade pbk.)
    ISBN 978-1-4299-8719-6 (e-book)
    1. Magic—Fiction. I. Title.
    PR9199.4.D448B58 2012
    813'.6—dc23
                                            2011033199

First Edition: April 2012

Printed in the United States of America

0 9 8 7 6 5 4 3 2 1

For my sister Michelle Millar,
with my love

ACKNOWLEDGMENTS

Blue Magic is about physical, social, and magical ecosystems, and I could not have written it without my own serendipitous web of support. Always at its heart, and in mine, is my wife, Kelly Robson. I owe much to my parents—Barb Millar, William and Sandra Robson, and Brian and Lily-Anne Millar—my grandmother Joan Huffman, and my wonderful siblings: Michelle, Sherelyn, Susan, and Bill. My friends do everything from reading drafts to explaining tricky research concepts and providing moral support when I am flailing. Some of the most stalwart are Lisa Cohen, Ming Dinh, Denise Garzón, Nicki Hamilton, Liz Hughes, Benjamin Lewis, Elaine Mari, and Ginger Mullen.

I am deeply grateful to my agent, Linn Prentis; my editor, Jim Frenkel; and a host of editors, writers, and mentors who've guided me over the years, especially: Wayne Arthurson, Ellen Datlow, Gardner Dozois, Mary Hobson, Nalo Hopkinson, Doug Lain, Louise Marley, Bridget McKenna, Jessica Reisman, Nancy Richler, Harry Turtledove, and Peter Watts.

Even a book about magic needs the occasional fact. The hardworking environmental scientists of ESSA Technologies have inspired me, time and again, with their expertise and passion for developing solutions to humanity's climate change problems. Jason Tuell provided specific advice about meteorology and storms, while Ramona Roberts provided legal advice. My excellent copy editor, Eliani Torres, corrected my many mistakes, particularly with Spanish grammar. Any errors in what passes for science, language, or courtroom procedure within this book are mine.

You made it possible for me to write *Indigo Springs* and *Blue Magic,* and I will always be thankful.

BLUE MAGIC

THE GATE HAD BEEN stalking Will Forest ever since he arrested his wife. It grew into bare patches of wall in his various hotel rooms and his quarters at Wendover Air Force Base; it had taken over a discreet corner of the kitchen of the Oregon home he so rarely returned to. It turned up in his peripheral vision in restaurants, TV stations, and shops. An archway of brambles, seven feet high, it pushed through drywall and hardwood with apparent ease. Its slats were a blue-tinged wood; its handle was a carved ram's horn.

He touched it once, and his hand vanished into nothingness. Blue light bled from the boundary between his wrist and the absent wall. When he pulled back, his skin was chilly to the touch, like meat from a fridge.

He would go into restroom stalls and find the gate on the side wall, exhaling a cold draft that fluttered the toilet paper. He had seen it in the temporary courthouse the air force had erected at Wendover. It waited in the prisoner interview room, an unobtrusive witness to his attempts to get information out of captured Alchemite terrorists.

None of his colleagues noticed the thing. One of the prisoners tried throwing herself at it . . . and bounced. As far as anyone at Wendover was concerned, she had flung herself against an impenetrable wall. The suspects had done crazier things: shouting prayers through the pretrial hearings, faking seizures, pulling out their hair during jury selection.

"Daydreaming, Forest?"

Startled out of his contemplation of the gate, Will found General Arthur Roche neatly turned out in full dress uniform, his hair so newly cut that every salt and pepper strand lay in perfect, bristling formation. Even the hearing aid tucked into his left ear gleamed.

It wasn't a reprimand. In fact, Roche served up one of his carefully rationed smiles, a rigid upturn of the lips that froze as he took in Will's wrinkled shirt and unshaven chin.

"It's Monday morning," Will said. "My son and daughter should be getting ready for school."

Another man might have clapped Will on the shoulder. Roche, though they'd been friends since college, barely nodded. "Take another run at your wife today. Maybe when the trial starts, it'll sink in that this is serious."

"Yes, I'll try Caro again," Will said without much hope.

"Now Sahara's on trial before the whole world, the Alchemite movement will crumble like dried-out cake."

"Cake," Will agreed. He didn't point out that getting this far had taken a tremendous toll on both the government and the military.

"Today's the beginning of the end for the witches, you'll see." With that, Roche hustled Will into a glorified storage closet furnished with a cheap table and chairs, a space designated for witness interviews and small meetings.

One of Roche's tame journalists waited inside, dictating copy into her phone: ". . . opening arguments in the trial of Sahara Knax, head of the fanatical cult that sank the aircraft carrier USS *Vigilant* last fall. Knax and nine followers face charges of attempted murder, committing terrorist acts, and treason in connection with the attack on the carrier.

"Today I am talking to the two men responsible for bringing Knax and her so-called mystics to trial. Will Forest insists that he is an ordinary person, doing his best in extraordinary circumstances. . . . Listen, they're here. Call you back?"

Will stifled a sigh. Sahara's show trial was little more than a diversion from the magical catastrophe enveloping the country. The real power lay beyond the gate of brambles even now embroidering itself on the wall. It lay within a reservoir of spilled magical energy in the Oregon forest and with the woman who controlled it, Astrid Lethewood.

Officially, Astrid was a bit player in this mess. Sahara had embarrassed the navy when she sank its carrier, so quashing the Alchemites was the government's first priority. Oh, the air force was firebombing the magical well, and they were fighting to stop the alchemized forest from spreading. But as for recapturing Astrid? She would keep, Roche said.

Would she? Will hadn't pushed: Astrid was probably beyond their reach. And he'd liked her, more than was wise . . . which might be why he hadn't mentioned the gate.

The reporter snapped her phone shut. "I appreciate your talking to me, Mr. Forest."

"Call me Will." He shook the hand she offered.

"Minimal pleasantries, okay?" Roche glanced at his watch. "Trial starts soon."

"Okay, Will: We'll start with an easy one. Everyone remembers where they were when they learned that magic exists. How about you?"

"Home, watching the same news broadcast as everyone else." It had begun with a police standoff: Some guy with a shotgun, holding his girlfriend and her roommates in an old house in Oregon. A local fireman had blundered in and been killed. The gunman was holding off the sheriff's department. Sad stuff, but nothing peculiar.

Then . . .

"You saw the lawn and trees growing to giant size, the alchemized bees and songbirds attacking police?"

"Yes, from the comfort of my living room. I saw Sahara Knax escape on a flying carpet. Then the house collapsed."

Sahara had fled to California with a pillowcase full of magical objects, now known as chantments. She used them to set herself up as a goddess, scamming thousands of believers.

"Your wife was with you?" the reporter asked.

"My whole family saw it," Will said. "Afterward, Caroline became one of Sahara's followers."

"She left you and kidnapped your children?"

"That's right."

"And it was Caroline's departure that led to your capture of Sahara Knax?"

"Indirectly," Will said. "I got involved in the effort to contain the alchemical spill in Indigo Springs. My job included interviewing the survivors of the initial standoff—"

"Including the gunman, Mark Clumber?"

"Mark had been contaminated. He couldn't speak." Clumber, a supposed bad guy, had arrived in Indigo Springs to find Sahara Knax locked in a power struggle with Astrid Lethewood. Their house was sitting on a source of immense magical power Sahara wanted to control.

"He'd been in contact with this magical fluid?"

"Vitagua—that's right. Sahara had broken into a wellspring of the magical liquid. Astrid, Sahara, and their roommate, Jackson Glade, were trying to contain the spill when Mark Clumber showed up. He was something of a last straw."

"Things went from bad to disastrous?"

"Catastrophic. Sahara used a chantment to force Mark to shoot at police. They were trying to buy time, but the ploy failed. The magical spill triggered an earthquake. Vitagua contaminated the entire region."

"What happened to everyone in the house?"

"Clumber and one of the neighbors, Patience Skye, were doused in magic. The army took them and Lethewood into custody. Lee and Jackson Glade were killed." The press still didn't know that Jacks Glade had been shot by police. "Knax, of course, got away."

"And you caught her, three months later."

"That's right. I was interviewing Astrid Lethewood, and Alchemites attacked the facility where she was being held. Lethewood and Clumber escaped, and I arrested Sahara Knax."

The reporter leaned in. "Since then, you've helped arrest several key Alchemites, including your wife. But you haven't recovered your children?"

"No. If anyone knows where my children are, please contact the authorities. There is a reward."

The worried father stuff played well with the public; Roche was using him and the kids, but what could Will do about that? *Not* search for Ellie and Carson?

It wasn't working. A sense of pointlessness, time wasted, assailed him with the force of a riptide. The confidence he'd had in his old friend and the might of the army was fading.

"This trial is a step forward for America," Roche said. His plan to steer the United States beyond the magical crisis was simple: convict and execute Sahara; then subdue the remaining Alchemites. Last, sort out the contamination in Oregon.

Will tried not to stare at the magical door. Astrid had offered to help him.

Still. He'd give Caroline one last chance.

They finished the interview in time to watch as nine Alchemite prisoners, seven women and two men, were led into the courtroom. Caro was third in line. Her posture was upright, her golden hair ragged. Scabs and bald patches marked her scalp. Hunger strikes had diminished the curves Will had once loved, and her now-skeletal face was puffy and bandaged. She wasn't the only one: several prisoners sported black eyes.

Will shot an uneasy look at Roche.

"Self-inflicted," he huffed. "Marshals caught 'em smashing their faces into the cell walls last night."

The defendants were led to a side room for a last search, in case anyone had gotten their hands on a chantment on the way from the cells.

As Will followed Roche into the courtroom, the gate of brambles flowered into view behind the bench.

Sahara Knax was brought in after her followers were seated. Like Mark Clumber, she had been exposed to raw magic. Astrid had improvised a treatment for her condition: before her arrest, Sahara had been devolving into a bird. At present she looked human.

Her delusions of godhood were as strong as ever.

"Who's the new guy?" Will asked, spotting a lean black man, maybe thirty-five years of age, conferring with the prosecutor.

"Gilead Landon," Roche said. The man's head came up, as if he had overheard. He raised a hand in greeting, revealing a badly scarred palm. "Landon's been helping hold back the magical forest. He's got ideas about containment."

"Containment as in burning Alchemites?"

"It may come to that." Will darted a look at Caro, and Roche added hastily, "Landon wants to burn the contaminated and their magic toys. Just Sahara and the chantments, see?"

"How'd this clown find you?"

"I found him."

"What?"

"True or false, Will: Lethewood murdered that fire chief, Lee Glade, because he was in a competing magical faction. . . ."

"Fyremen."

"Correct."

"This Gilead Landon is a witch burner?"

"Will, if these people understand magic, I want 'em on board, not running wild. Anyway, he's with you on Lethewood. Says she's the one that matters."

"Oh, if he agrees with me, let's get into bed with him."

"Why shouldn't I reach out to a potential resource?"

"They're murderers, Arthur. A society of killers whose charter was written in the Middle Ages."

"Says who? Astrid Lethewood? She'd killed one of them, Will. She had every reason to claim they're bad guys."

"Didn't you just say this guy wants to put Sahara on a stake?" The Fyreman was studying Sahara as she sat at the defendant's table.

"Law says if Knax gets convicted, we'll give her a lethal injection," Roche said. "So what if we cremate the remains afterwards?"

"What if he wants to burn her alive, Arthur?"

Roche made a frustrated noise. "This isn't pattycake we're playing here. You want your kids back or not?"

Will was spared the necessity of a reply when a clerk called court into session. The assembly rose, and the Federal Circuit Judge, George Skagway, wheeled his chair to the bench.

"Be seated." His voice was a rich, resonant bass, the modulated boom of a seasoned speaker. Everyone obeyed him . . .

. . . except Sahara Knax.

"Poisoners of the world, lovers of the Filthwitch, I hereby mark your faces," she said. Her lawyer tugged on her orange plastic sleeve, but she shook him off. "You will drown in floods, freeze in blizzards, choke in the dust storms I bring down upon your Earth-hating heads."

Filthwitch: that was her name for Astrid.

"Praise the Goddess!" The defendants chanted, "Praise the Earth, praise the—"

"That's enough!" Skagway had the lungs of an opera singer; he drowned out the sound of his own gavel coming down, overriding the prisoners. "Defendants will quiet down or be banned from the courtroom for the day."

The Alchemites' prayers became shrieks of rage. Several banged their heads against the table. Others, Caroline included, curled so they could reach their hair with their cuffed hands and yank it out in bloody tufts.

The U.S. Marshal in charge of courtroom security, Juanita Corazón, already had her team jumping in to restrain the defendants.

Sahara feinted, stepping out to face the prosecutor. "You, Wallstone. You'll be first to feel my wrath."

The Fyreman, behind her, laid his scarred palm on Sahara's shoulder. She swayed, dropping into Juanita's arms. The gallery quieted.

"Move to dismiss, Your Honor." The defense attorney hopped up. "Prosecution's assaulted my client."

"Motion denied. Who are you, young man?" Judge Skagway asked.

"Gilead Landon, Your Honor." The Fyreman raised his eyes to the bench. "Consultant to the air force."

"I'll thank you to stay away from the defendants. The marshals have this in hand."

"Just trying to help."

"Help us again, you'll be banned from court." Judge Skagway said, "Defendants may watch the proceedings on closed-circuit TV. We'll recess to facilitate the transfer."

"See, Will? Gilead's got his uses." Roche covered a smirk with his hand. "The public sees how easily subdued Sahara is, it makes her less scary."

"You planned this?" Will said.

"It didn't take much imagination to know Sahara would want to disrupt the first day."

"But will you broadcast her threats?"

"We may edit the footage."

"And pretty up the Primas' black eyes digitally, while you're at it?"

"Not a bad idea," Roche said, ignoring his sarcasm.

"Won't people wonder how Landon knocked her out? Won't they say, 'Hey, wasn't that magic? Aren't you government types telling us that magic is bad?'"

"Officially, the point is terrorism, not magic," Roche said. "Now, do you want to talk to Caro?"

No, Will thought. "All right."

Minutes later, he was seated across from his ex-wife in one of the six-by-six booths the Wendover staff had dubbed "squirrel cages," watching a marshal cuff her to the table. A screen on the far wall offered a view of the courtroom; a keypad on the desk let her text her defense attorney during proceedings. No need for that now, though—a lawyer was present.

The newest raw spot on her scalp was oozing.

Caroline the Alchemite bore little resemblance to the Caro who had rappelled from the roof of a student residence tower to the deck of Will's apartment when they were undergraduates; the woman who'd climbed K2 without oxygen on her twentieth birthday. The woman who had shared his bed and dreams, who'd worked two jobs while he attended grad school, who'd soothed their son's night terrors while writing her bioethics thesis was gone.

These days, Sahara was first in her thoughts. "What did that bastard do to the Goddess?"

"Want me to find out how she's doing?"

"Still the negotiator, William? I'd have to do something for you, right?"

Never fight the subject on her own terms. Will produced a file, sliding out two news clippings: an account of an Alchemite's death in Wichita, first. Just after Sahara's arrest, her followers had taken to wearing orange jumpers similar to prisoners' uniforms. It made them easy to spot; this one had been beaten to death in his home, which had then been looted—the killers, naturally, were after chantments.

The second clipping was about a woman who'd had the bad fortune to resemble Sahara: she had been drawn and quartered in Bogotá. He let Caro read, saw her blanch. She passed the pages to her lawyer with a shaking hand.

"Caroline, tell me where Ellie and Carson are. Whoever you've left them with, she isn't safe; she can't protect them."

She shook her head.

"Sahara can't watch out for her flock. The army's chipping away at your leadership. . . ."

"We're coming out even there," she muttered. It was true. Hundreds of soldiers had vanished in the skirmishes of the past six months. A few had been killed; when desperate, the Alchemites powered their chantments by drawing the life out of the people they were fighting—and any unfortunate bystanders. *Vamping,* they called it.

Will fanned three last pages out in front of her. "You weren't the only mother in the cult, Caro."

"I am the Prima of Wind, Worker of Miracles," she hissed. "I am soft air washing away the sins of the technofilth—"

Her gaze fell on the pages.

It was the biggest weapon he had, a police report detailing the fate of a minor Alchemite and her three children. He had not spared her the photos. Caro let out a long keening breath. For the first time since her arrest, she was rattled.

"Caroline?"

Tears ran down her face, and Will felt a shred of hope. She tried to pray, stuttered, looked at the images of the bodies. Then her expression closed, shock bleeding out, hate brimming in. The fleeting glimpse of his kids' mother was gone.

She launched herself across the table, clawing at him with her free hand.

Will stood his ground. A gust of power from his enchanted ring heaved Caro back. Her arm jerked against the restraint of the handcuff and she teetered, pinned and off balance. Will had to fight not to slump. Magic was tiring; it would have taken less energy to step out of reach.

"Ellie and Carson, Caro. They're not safe out there."

"Filthwitch puppet," she bellowed, regaining her feet. "I'll cut their throats myself before I see them back with you!"

Will's hand flew to his gut, as if he'd been punched. "We're done, then," he heard himself say. Abandoning the papers, he walked out.

Roche had been watching through the glass. "You okay?"

"Did you hear her?" It was sinking in; the army couldn't get the kids back. He'd been wasting his time.

"Will," Roche said. "Snap out of it. I'll get the team on it, work up a new strategy. Try drugs on her, maybe."

Cut their throats myself . . .

"She's locked up; she can't harm anyone. Will, you listening?"

"I'm okay." He forced his numb lips into a smile.

"Trial starts again in five."

"Five." Six months, the trail cold, and anything could be happening to Carson and Ellie. They should be in school. . . .

"Where are you going?"

"I need a protein shake. The ring."

"Of course."

"Arthur," he said. "I know you're trying. Thank you."

"See you in there." Roche almost saluted, then turned the gesture into a weak wave before walking away.

Will took a last look through the one-way mirror of the squirrel cage, at the woman who had been his wife.

"She's bleeding," he said to the marshal on duty. "Can you get her treated?"

"Of course, sir."

He stumbled across the base to the officers' lounge, a dimly lit bar with big flat-screen TVs. Off-duty pilots crammed the place, waiting for more trial coverage.

Near the bar sat a fridge filled with protein shakes.

As Will opened the fridge, the magic gate formed silently beside him. He could write a note, explain his departure. He could send a text message and be gone before Arthur received it.

He fingered the shakes. He thought of stealing one, bearing something from the old world into whatever lay beyond the magical gate. He examined the plastic bottle, the stamped red expiration dates, the foil seal. . . . This faltering world of technology had been such a marvel. Would the land of the fairies have refrigeration, or hot running water? It seemed unlikely.

Closing the fridge, he slipped through the bramble-framed magical gate.

Nobody saw him go.

❊❊ CHAPTER TWO ❊❊

MORNING ARRIVED IN INDIGO Springs, but it did not bring the dawn.

The shattered remains of Astrid Lethewood's hometown rested beneath a dense thicket of magically contaminated forest. Earthquake-tumbled buildings lay in pieces in the understory, the concrete rubble interspersed with steel beams, plastic refuse, and the knotted roots of overgrown cedar and spruce.

Though daylight could not penetrate the matted canopy overhead, it wasn't dark: the glow of raw magic suffused everything it contaminated. The massive trunks of the alchemized trees cast a lambent blue-white light. Their glimmering, fast-growing roots eroded ancient bedrock and cement building foundations with impartial ruthlessness. Blades of grass and seed cones shone; motes of dust hung in the air, winking like stars.

The trees had crushed cars and shoved whole homes aside as they shot upward, like a thousand fairy-tale beanstalks . . . and then died. Even magical plants needed sunshine, and most of the affected trees had lost the race to the sky. Much of the luminescent tonnage overhead, as a result, was deadwood.

As the federal treason trial raised its curtain in Utah, as Sahara Knax threatened judge and jury and Will Forest finally lost faith in the system, Astrid was planting tomato seedlings.

She had erected a makeshift greenhouse atop one of the few buildings that had weathered the disaster—the Indigo Springs Grand Hotel. The hotel was the center of her world, in a sense: when she escaped government custody, six months earlier, she had found it standing here, stately and solid, defying overgrowth and tremors alike. Here, in the heart of the enchanted forest, she had begun pruning out the tons of sun-starved vegetation around the building. By reducing the dead trees to chips, she had carved out an open space at ground level, a clearing both supported and illuminated by the trunks of the surviving trees.

Beyond and above the perimeter of the clearing, the forest remained overgrown and impassable. The tangle blocked out daylight, but it also shielded them from ground assault and from Roche's planes.

As if summoned by her thought, a jet howled past, rattling the panes of the greenhouse.

"You could just make tomatoes using magic."

Astrid had not been alone, even in those early days. Mark Clumber had been with her ever since she got away from Roche. An ill-tempered sound engineer with mismatched eyes, Mark had always seemed like a big-city con man to her, not a hometown boy. In reality, they'd known each other since kindergarten.

"Gardening helps me think, Mark," she said.

"Plants won't grow without real light."

"I've chanted the helium tank over there—it'll make sunshine."

Mark frowned. "Government might pick up the heat."

"Then what? They bomb us? They're already bombing us."

"Astrid—"

"You've been keeping the air force out of here."

"Doesn't mean I want you making my job harder."

If they were mobile, protecting themselves would be simpler, a game of hide and seek. But Astrid was tied to Indigo Springs. The magical well was here, and they had to defend it.

"It's a teeny bit of sunlight, Mark."

The two of them had never liked each other: it was one of the reasons she trusted him now. Sahara had flattered them both—then lied. She'd agree to something, then do as she pleased. And that was before she'd lost her mind.

These days, Astrid preferred honest dissent.

"Today it's sunlight. Tomorrow you'll want to put in a landing strip for the jets and see if you can win the pilots over to Peace, Love, and the Magical Way."

"Think that would work?"

He covered his face in his hands, moaning.

Astrid relaxed. "You're not angry."

"The bombing runs have been off target, haven't they? Nobody's getting to the well as long as I'm around."

True, so true, a voice tittered. She shook it away, like a mosquito.

"So," Mark harrumphed. "Sunshine?"

With a magician's flourish, Astrid lay her hand against the rusty helium tank. Waxy drops of golden light wobbled into the air, filling a nonexistent balloon that shivered liquidly as it grew. It rose to the scooped-out ceiling of the clearing, splatting against the trees and coating them in light. The encampment brightened, and Astrid felt warmth on her skin.

"Waste of power—vitagua throws plenty of light to work by." Mark gestured at the glowing tree trunks.

"Cold light. Anyway, it's not extravagant. I'm just borrowing some of the sun shining on the canopy."

Mark gave her the look that meant he wished her priorities were in line with his. Thankfully, he seemed as tired of speaking the words as she was of ignoring them.

"Aren't you guys watching the trial?" Patience Skye appeared on the hotel roof, apparently from nowhere.

Patience, like Mark, had been in Astrid's house during their standoff with the police last September. Sahara had dunked both of them in vitagua.

The raw form of magic was cursed, and direct exposure turned people to animals—"Frog Princed" them, Mark liked to say. It stripped away their emotional armor, amplifying psychological weaknesses.

Astrid had found a way to arrest the process. It wasn't quite a cure; it hadn't cured Sahara's greed for magical power. But she had managed to keep Patience and Mark from going crazy or devolving into animals.

The treatment involved fusing chantments into their bodies, items that drew the contamination into themselves. It was an okay compromise, and someone thus treated could make use of the magical powers embedded within the chantment.

Patience had been the first attempt. Astrid had fused three objects into her: one gave her stunning good looks, while a second allowed her to pass through solid objects. The third had been a shape-shifting chantment. But three objects had been too many. Patience's appearance changed at random and entirely against her will.

"Patience, I need a favor," Astrid began. Then Everett Lethewood—Astrid's mother, sort of—appeared on the hotel roof beside them.

Like Mark and Patience, Ev had been exposed to raw vitagua. In his case, the contamination had revealed something he said he'd known all along. Ev wasn't female, hadn't been meant, he said, to live in a woman's body.

Her Ma, really a man? At times, Astrid still didn't quite believe it. But when she treated Ev's contamination, Astrid gave him the ability to change a person's sex. Ev hadn't hesitated: his body now was as male as he claimed his spirit had always been. He hadn't shown any inclination to change back.

Patience spread her arms wide, drinking in the sunlight. She was short-waisted and petite today, with Japanese features and a buzz cut. "These sunglob thingies work at night?"

"No. You gotta have sunshine to borrow sunshine," Astrid said. "And they burn out. Someone will have to make new ones."

"Good job for new volunteers, I suppose," Mark said.

"It's a relief to see daylight," Patience said, basking. "I'll do it if no one else will."

"I have something else in mind for you," Astrid said.

"That so?"

"We need someone to speak for us in the unreal," Astrid said. The magic she was restoring to the ordinary world was coming from a realm her father had called Fairyland. The trapped residents of that realm were demanding their freedom . . . and Astrid had promised to give it to them. "The pressure on the magical well is increasing."

"How much?" Mark demanded.

She shrugged. "They're pushing. Testing me."

Patience clucked, an old-woman noise that reflected her age more accurately than did her appearance. "They got every right."

"I'm committed to getting the vitagua back here where it belongs, you know that. But I need time."

"The question is how much time, sweetie?"

"However long it takes to get the body count down—"

"I'm for no body count at all," Ev said.

An awkward pause: it was already too late for that.

"You've seen the Big Picture," Astrid said. "We have to take it slow, equip people to deal with the emergence of magic."

"Fine," Patience sighed. "I'll go play ambassador."

"Pop? Would you go with her?"

"Me?" Ev's weather-beaten cheeks reddened. "I've got a job. I'm helping the trans folk coming through Bramblegate—"

"We can send 'em to you for gendermorphing," Mark said.

"Young man, I don't much care for the way you give cute names to every little thing, and that word especially—"

"I'll make a second chantment for the hospital, Pop," Astrid interrupted. "The medics can do gender transitions here."

"There's Two-Spirited people in the unreal, Ev," Patience said. "Some of 'em might want morph—transforming too."

Ev glowered. "Astrid's trying to get me out of here before someone drops a nuke on her head."

"Nobody's getting nuked, Pop."

"You're sure?"

"Yes." She knew the future—bits and pieces of it, anyway. There were disasters in the offing, terrible things, but nothing like that.

"Roche knows that if he lobs a nuke at us, we might manage to send it back," Mark said. Shortly after their escape, the government had fired missiles into town. Some had exploded harmlessly, far from the magical well. As for the rest, the four of them—with the help of a growing pool of volunteers—had sent them off course.

They detonated missiles above the forest, out at sea. They'd even sent one back to the Bonneville Salt Flats, where Roche was holed up, blowing it up a few miles from the Wendover air base just to make a point.

Sabotaging unmanned missiles had been no small feat. Magic took power. Diverting those first barrages had left them starving, kitten weak, and half frozen. But Roche got the message. Now he sent manned flights, planes with napalm. Will must have told him that Astrid wouldn't harm the pilots.

"The point of Sahara's treason trial is to show that the government is in control of the magical outbreak," Mark said. "They can't go nuclear on us without seeming desperate."

Ev relaxed. The chantment Astrid had embedded in Mark—his eyeglasses—made it impossible for him to lie.

Astrid took his hand. "Pop, I'm not coddling you. Sending you to the unreal shows I'm serious about keeping my promises. Please go. Remind the Roused we're on the same side. They have something I want, remember?"

"Jacks Glade." Pop nodded. "Okay. Patience can calm people down, I'll . . . gendermorph the transgendered folks there."

Astrid felt a surge of relief. The grumbles, those little voices she kept hearing, claimed Ev was going to survive this crisis. But knowing the future didn't keep her from worrying.

"Astrid?" Tuning forks hung around their necks quivered, projecting a lilting Irish voice. "There's a newcomer caught in Briarpatch. I think it's Will Forest."

"Is it Will day?" she said, pleased.

"Gee, I guess we're all saved," Mark muttered.

"Don't be a grouch." Astrid headed through the nearest archway of brambles.

She stepped out onto the intricately patterned marble floor of an old train station. Gleaming rose-colored stone stretched between its crumbled walls. Scarred oak benches with thick leather upholstery formed a gallery to one side of the gate, across from a big ARRIVALS board that still showed the time of day in cities around the world. Two dozen people were gathered on the benches, watching a glassed-in television that was tuned, naturally, to Sahara's trial.

Over where the departure platforms had been, columns of frozen vitagua rose skyward, casting their oceanic glow.

As Astrid crossed the marble floor, she became part of a small crowd flowing through the archway; the train station was their primary transportation hub. Anyone who passed through the gate of brambles ended up here.

Mark appeared at her side, hustling to catch up.

"You're coming?"

"Would I miss the big reunion?"

They crossed the plaza, stepping among the blue glowing columns and murmuring "Briarpatch" in unison. Blue light washed out everything . . . and then they were at the rim of a pit of blackberry canes. Will Forest stood in its midst, his hand—the one with the chanted ring—snagged in blackberry thorns.

A rotund Swede in a parka got out of a lawn chair, raising his hand in greeting. "I tried knocking him out," he said, breath misting in the chill. "Didn't work."

"He has a protection chantment," Astrid said. "You'd just be vamping calories off him."

"Don't worry; I stopped."

"Mark? You going to let him loose?"

Mark tsked. "There's security on Bramblegate for a reason."

"Come on, he's not dangerous."

"Yes, infallible one," Mark sighed, speaking to his security people. "Jupiter, pull the pin on Bramblegate."

The thorns entangling Will's arm curled back. Astrid brought them all into the plaza, into the semiprivate alcove near a bank of lockers.

Will blinked, adjusting to the changed light. "Mark, hi. Hello, Astrid."

Astrid fought an unexpected interior flutter. "What's the etiquette for this? I feel like we're friends, but the only time we met was when you were interrogating me for the Roach."

"Want to see how a hug feels?"

Mark grimaced, no doubt biting back a sarcastic comment. Will opened his arms, and Astrid stepped into the embrace. It felt more natural than she would have guessed.

"I guess you knew Arthur would strike out on finding Carson and Ellie," Will said.

"I'm sorry it didn't work out."

"Ever since we caught Caro and the children weren't with her . . ." He was hollow eyed and thin. "I need you to find them, Astrid."

"I can't do worse than Roche."

"More optimism, please. By now I'm probably wanted for treason."

"I can do upbeat." She gave him a smile, tried to seem steady, rock certain. "Remember the grumbles?"

A nod. "They tell you the future."

"They speak of a classroom of children, all learning how to chant. And your kids are there."

"A magic school? What if it's Alchemites teaching them—?"

"It's my class, Will. I hear me."

"You're absolutely sure?" He looked hopeful and apprehensive. "The grumbles have lied before."

"They withhold things, but they don't lie." It was something she understood better now. "And the longer we're in the Spill, the more I learn."

"In the Spill?"

Careful, she thought, take it slow. "Before, there was almost no magic. People like my dad made chantments and Fyremen hunted them, closing down the wells. I screwed all that up—"

"—by spilling tons of vitagua into the ravine, I know."

"Will, we're still spilling. The more magic we dribble out, the better it will be when the well pops."

"When it pops, not if?" He took that in, evaluating the information without seeming to judge her.

He had never judged her, Astrid thought, not even when she told him she'd killed Jacks's dad.

"When," she confirmed.

"I call it Boomsday," Mark said. "Astrid doesn't like that, so much—it rhymes with *Doomsday*."

"Which is why you do like it?" Will asked.

"Astrid prefers the Small Bang."

"Because the smaller the better," Astrid said.

"Yessir, boss, sir."

Will wasn't tracking their banter. "What does the well opening have to do with Carson and Ellie?"

"The grumbles say we have good days ahead, Will. They talk of magicians digging wells, feeding the hungry. A floating city in the Pacific, cleaning the water, repopulating fish stocks. The Roused free, the curse broken . . ."

"Meanwhile society goes down the toilet?"

"No! We figure it out. Will, there's still going to be cars and email and plastic surgery. It's just there'll also be magical cures for cancer and, you know, sea monsters."

"Happily ever after?"

"I don't know about *ever* after, Will, but it's going to be good. A long honeymoon. Lifetimes."

"Happy After doesn't have the right ring."

She tried a disarming shrug, realized she was aping a move of Sahara's, and ended up feeling self-conscious. "This is why I leave naming things to Mark."

"A good future." Will chewed this over. "You promised that my children would be fine. That they'd thrive."

She let the grumbles in, listening for the children. "I hear Carson. He's chanted a pair of magic . . . skates, I think. He's laughing. You're arguing with Ellie over homework. . . ."

As she spoke, she felt the shape of that future; she was cold, for some reason, chilled to the bone. Will was teasing her about being a permissive stepmother. . . .

Stepmother? Were they together, then? Her emotions surged, tangling: hope, panic, a pang of guilt for Jacks, who had loved her, an upwelling of nameless, unidentifiable grief.

"How soon?" Will's brittle tone brought her back.

She shivered. "They're young, Will, still young. It can't be long."

Mark shot her a worried glance from behind Will's back. *Soon* wasn't good: they were trying to hold off the Small Bang.

Will looked at the glowing columns, the people vanishing into the blue light. "I don't know how long I can wait."

"We get them back, Will. They're young, they're chanters, and we're all laughing."

"Har dee har." He took a ragged breath, turning to Mark, and began to extend a hand in greeting. Then fighter jets screeched overhead, and he froze.

Astrid covered her ears. Seconds later, explosives whumped a few miles away.

"Off target," Mark said with a smug grin.

"Mark's keeping the bombs off us," Astrid explained.

"All by himself?"

"Not at all. I have minions, underlings, cannon fodder—"

"Mark!" Astrid said. "He's kidding about the fodder."

Will smiled.

Mark said, "Speaking of my team, I should be with them. You giving Will the grand tour?"

Astrid nodded.

"Catch you both later, then." Giving Will a nettled look, Mark headed off into the glow.

"What now?" Will said.

There were so many answers to that question: she wanted his advice on a dozen different things. "I'll show you what we're doing here. It'll give you an idea of how we'll go after your kids."

It was the right answer: he brightened.

She led him among the columns of vitagua, saying, "Bigtop," as they stepped down the concrete steps and came out in front of the hotel.

Will's jaw dropped.

She realized anew how strange it looked. Even with the overgrown trees and brush cleared away, the forest floor was drenched in vitagua, dangerous and uninhabitable. They'd left it that way, a bright impassable lagoon of magical fluid and mulched forest.

Glowing mushrooms formed a carpet over the slime, toxic blue-tinged amanitas in fairy rings, clusters of gold-streaked honey fungus, fluted chanterelles and tall, porous morels all lending an exotic, fairy-tale look to the place.

Working up from the floor, she and her volunteers had created an island of fill by gathering the bones of the destroyed town, forming piles of concrete and steel among the enormous stumps of the dead trees. Abandoned cars, bits of highway, and garbage bridged the clearing; brightly colored silk tents were pitched on its main hub. New fill radiated from the central campground in spokes, raised pathways that expanded outward into the lagoon.

The fill bridged the space between the hotel and one other building they'd managed to salvage whole—the Indigo Springs hospital.

Sunshine globbed onto tree branches like paint, a camp built on rubble, vitagua-filled bottles hung from the trees, magic mushrooms, tinkling musical messages . . .

Will turned a slow circle. "This is your base of operations?"

Astrid nodded. "Let's start with the ravine."

Shaking his head in disbelief, Will followed.

"How much do you remember about vitagua?" she asked.

"Let's see . . . magic used to be a living cell. It allowed people to bend the rules of nature."

"Right," she said.

"Centuries ago, when the Inquisition began burning witches, the cells—"

"Magicules."

"Magicules, right, were driven into the unreal and they became vitagua."

"Blue in color, thick as blood, dangerous as hell," she said, quoting her father. The fluid had been drizzling back into the real world for centuries. Well wizards like Dad had taken it drop by drop, locking it within magic items like Will's ring.

The physical breach between the real and unreal was in the ravine. It had been concealed in the chimney of Dad's old house, and an irregular pile of bricks still marked the epicenter of the

Spill. Blue fluid oozed through the porous, cracked bricks, pooling in the ravine, forming a boxy lake.

Will peered down. "That's . . . a lot of vitagua."

"Barely a drop in the bucket," Astrid countered. "Remember the glaciers in the unreal?"

He nodded. "You're spilling it into the woods?"

"I'm also making chantments." She pointed at a line of shopping carts filled with junk: small carvings, combs, dishes, lampshades, books, tools, purses, plastic necklaces, jewelry boxes, flowerpots . . .

"Where's all that coming from?"

"There are crews out salvaging in the evacuated towns. See that work crew there, going through the stuff?"

"That's . . . what, twenty people?"

"It's a lot of work. They have to sort through everything. Broken stuff has to be mended. Glass and electronics can't be chanted at all."

"You must be making hundreds of chantments."

"Abracadabra." She'd had a gold barbell pierced through the web between her right thumb and index finger: chanting required a break in the skin. She twisted the barbell before bending to dip her fingers into the flow of vitagua from the ravine.

Liquid magic passed through her body, seeping from the piercing in the web of her hand and, from there, into the rescued objects. She'd shown Will how this worked before; she didn't need to explain that she was binding raw magic into the scavenged items so people could safely access its power.

Peace and a sense of vitality flooded her.

This was what she was meant to do. The personality juggling, the meetings, the planning and recruiting, the endless defense of the town—those were just by-products of the Spill. Item by item, she made the junk into chantments. Volunteers bustled in to take the carts away.

Will asked: "What'll you do with them?"

"Mostly, give them away."

"You're not hanging on to everything?"

"Only what we need. Being a well wizard is about sharing power." She pointed at a red silk tent. "Over there, we have a team of volunteers using chantments that make them psychic. They've been working on locating your children."

"What if they say the kids are in Timbuktu, surrounded by heavily armed Alchemites? Got a plan for that?"

"Of course," she said. "You think I've been sitting around all this time?"

A smile—a real one—broke across his face. "You are more of a go-getter than a sitter."

"What we're gonna go get is your children, Will." Astrid found herself wanting to hug him again. Instead, she led him toward the hotel. "Come on, I'll show you the rest."

CHAPTER THREE

"WE THOUGHT IT WAS a joke. I mean, here's a bunch of civilians in motorboats and flying carpets and they're trying to surround a carrier? A few of the women were dressed up like mermaids, and there was a guy with a trident—"

"Did you see any of the defendants?" Special Prosecutor Lee Wallstone brought up the Alchemites' mug shots on the courtroom media screens.

"Yessir. I saw Sahara Knax, Patricia Finch, and Arlen Roy."

"Thank you. What happened next?"

The televised trial had gotten off to a dramatic start, with Juanita and the other marshals hauling the defendants out of the courtroom bodily, like so many screeching sacks of laundry. Afterwards, things settled down. Wallstone had gone with a low-key opening; by the time he'd finished explaining the treason statute for the benefit of the jury and American viewing public, it was almost dull.

He'd save the verbal fireworks for his closing, Juanita guessed, working the theory that the last thing the jury heard was what would stick.

Defense counsel came out heavier, preaching the fire and brimstone of ecological disaster, claiming that Knax and her followers were forced to take action to reverse climate change. Necessity defense, it was called. Apparently they hadn't noticed it was the same tactic that failed to save Timothy McVeigh.

Now the prosecutor was examining a young sailor who had been aboard *Vigilant* when the Alchemites sank it.

As for Supervisory Deputy U.S. Marshal Juanita Corazón, she spent the day with Sahara Knax in her squirrel cage, watching it all on closed-circuit TV.

Deprived of an audience, Sahara slouched in her chair, toying with her restraints and pretending to listen to spirit voices. "You're a pet of Judge Skagway's, aren't you?"

"What makes you say so?" Juanita kept her tone neutral.

"He's fond, right? Perhaps . . . a sort of father figure?"

"Pay attention to the trial, Knax." She feigned boredom, hoping Sahara wouldn't see she'd struck a nerve: Juanita didn't want to think about the judge.

She'd run into him yesterday morning, wheeling his way out to the fresh air, his racquetball gear in his lap.

"Big show tomorrow, Corazón," he'd said. "I want spit and polish. Show these jarheads we civvies understand discipline."

"Jarheads are marines, Your Honor. These are airmen—"

He waved that off. "You think any more about after this? Law school?"

"The way things are right now—"

"Turmoil, shmurmoil. Life doesn't stop, Corazón."

"I don't know if I see myself as a lawyer."

"We get bad press, but it isn't as bad as all that."

"I can't imagine making the world a better place just by sitting on my ass all day."

It was an established joke between them, but it earned her a glare and a significant glance at the judge's wheelchair from a passing clerk.

"Spit and polish, Corazón." With a bass rumble of laughter, the judge rolled on, leaving her aching with guilt.

"I grew up without a father, too," Sahara said, tone nostalgic. "I was jealous of girls who had dads. . . ."

"Girls like Astrid Lethewood?" Juanita asked.

A curl of the lip. "She put a chantment in my chest."

"A bottle cap—I was briefed. Keeps you from running away."

"It's litter, Filthwitchery. An attack upon my divinity."

Can Sahara believe this crap? Does she really think she's a god?

"Astrid thinks she can contain me."

On-screen, the impossibly youthful sailor continued his testimony. "The mermaids were singing."

"In English?" Wallstone asked.

"No, some other language. Knax gave us ten minutes to get to the lifeboats. I remember that one of my buddies laughed."

Several sailors had recorded the sinking, using their phones and cameras. Wallstone brought up a shot of Sahara, hanging in midair off the bow of the ship, borne on gigantic starling wings. "Did you take action?"

"Yessir—we issued verbal warnings, then fired upon them."

"And?"

"My weapon malfunctioned. Other guys, their bullets turned to flowers. Patricia Finch was shot, but one of the others put a hand on her and she stopped bleeding."

"What happened next?"

"Knax, also singing, stabbed the flight deck with a rusty pocketknife. The air got cold, and the ship started falling apart."

"Falling apart?"

"Deck plates buckling, bolts popping loose, metal rusting. Like it aged a thousand years in five minutes."

"And you had to abandon ship?"

"Yessir. The *Vigilant* went down in about half an hour."

"Is that when you were injured?" The Alchemites made a point of rescuing everyone, but this particular fresh-faced boy had been caught by rapidly freezing sea ice that formed around the wreckage of the aircraft carrier.

"I lost a foot to frostbite."

In the cage, Sahara muttered: "I'd grow back his damn leg if they'd let me."

The electronic lock beeped, unlatching the door, and Roche poked his head inside. "Talk to you a minute?"

"Uh-oh," said Sahara. "Something wrong already?"

I haven't done anything, it's not too late. . . . Juanita quelled a rush of panic, switching places with her backup, Gladys, and followed Roche down the hall.

"Something going on?"

Roche eyed her with distaste. Sahara was right: Skagway had insisted that Federal marshals take charge of prisoner security during the trial. The judge was too important to hate openly, though, so Roche settled for resenting Juanita and her team.

"Will Forest is missing," Roche said.

"Abducted?"

Roche shrugged. "We're searching the base for magic items."

"Pardon my saying, but Forest's seemed . . . scattered lately."

"Yes, yes, his kids are AWOL, I know."

"When your family's in danger, General . . ." Roche gave her a dull stare, so she wrenched herself back on task. "Does this change my routine for tonight?"

"No. Shower Prisoner One, search her, put her in restraints. No black eyes tomorrow, you hear?"

Juanita winced. The previous evening, Sahara's minions had smashed their faces against their walls and sinks. She'd had them restrained, but they started the trial looking as if they'd been beaten. "Anything else?"

"No—wait, yes. I had a report. Your brother's MIA?"

"Alchemites attacked the contaminated forest near his station, sir—his squad's vanished. But my mother's seen him."

"In a dream, you mean?"

"Yes." Most of the missing soldiers who'd clashed with the Alchemites had turned up, apparently unharmed, in the dreams of their loved ones. "Any luck finding a way to rescue them, sir?"

"It'll happen—we just need to arrest the right Alchemite."

"What do you mean?"

"They must be using a chantment to turn people into dreams. Presumably there's a chantment that will bring them back. We just have to catch whoever's got it."

"Sounds simple." Lots of Roche's plans sounded easy.

He glowered. "Be glad he's okay."

Dismissed, in other words. Juanita returned to the squirrel cage.

"Court's adjourned," Gladys said. "Want me to take her?"

"No, thanks. Time to go, Knax." Juanita touched her radio. "Transporting Prisoner One to search and sanitation."

"All clear," came the reply.

Shadowed by armed soldiers, she led her charge down the hallway to a well-lit tunnel, past more guards and into a windowless bathroom. Sahara was forbidden personal possessions, lest they be switched for magical items. A brush and other toiletries were kept here for her use.

She uncuffed Sahara, waiting while her prisoner used the toilet and washed her hands.

"What's dinner tonight?" Sahara said.

"Thai tofu," she said, donning latex gloves. "Mouth?"

Sahara opened her mouth, visibly steeling herself for the indignity of the cavity search. "I'd kill for a steak."

You'd kill for less than that, Juanita thought. She wondered how long she'd be in jail if she broke Sahara's traitorous neck and solved everyone's problems.

Slap on the wrist, at worst. Roche might give her a medal. . . .

She finished the search and gestured for Sahara to step into the shower. As she washed, Juanita unlocked a cabinet, bringing out a fresh towel, underwear, and jumpsuit, all sealed in plastic to ensure that nothing had been smuggled into them.

"Time." She held out the towel. "I need to dress that scratch."

Unlike her followers, Sahara restricted her self-harm to one behavior—scratching her chest, digging so deep that the skin over her sternum was scarred. Trying to get to the chantment embedded there, the psychiatrists thought, the bottle cap that kept her from running away.

"It's fine, it's scabbed over."

"I'm not asking permission," Juanita said, hiding another surge of murderous rage.

"Oh, I forgot. It's national Humiliate the Goddess Day, isn't it?"

"You're no goddess." Juanita took out the first aid kit, preparing a pad of gauze. She slipped a postage stamp and a scribbled scrap of paper inside the dressing, taping the gauze over Sahara's chest. Then she handed over her jumper, cuffed her, and inventoried the bathroom supplies, checking each item off a printed list.

Shrapnel churned in her stomach.

Sahara's eyes had dilated and her breathing was shallow.

Juanita fumbled her radio. "Moving Prisoner One from S and S to Isolation."

The Alchemites had gotten to her three days ago.

She had been coming off shift when one of the cooks, a wispy blonde named Heaven, had pushed her way into her bedroom. "Your brother's name is Ramón, right?"

"So?"

"Ramón Alfonse Corazón," Heaven repeated. From the folds of her skirt she produced a digital camera, holding it screen side out. It lit up with a shot of Juanita's baby brother in uniform, patrolling the scorched frontier of the contaminated forest in Oregon.

Heaven pressed a button, and the video file began to play. A civilian in a long dress and head scarf passed Ramón, turning his head. She spoke; they laughed together. Juanita saw a scrawl of henna or a tattoo on her skin as she caressed his cheek. Something sparkled in her hand.

The woman walked away and Ramón stood bemused, staring after her. Behind him, another U.S. soldier sagged, as if drunk, then sat down in the street.

Then it was Ramón himself falling over, lying in a spray of glittering light. The camera zoomed in—his eyes were fluttering as he fought to keep them open.

A snore, a twinkle, and the soldiers were gone.

The video ended.

"That's . . . ," Juanita had managed. "It isn't real."

"Relax, he'll live." Heaven turned the camera, fiddling, and handed it over. The screen showed Juanita's niece, crossing the street in front of Our Lady of Sorrows School. The tattooed woman was in the frame.

A beep. The image changed—Mamá at the grocery.

Kill Heaven now, part of Juanita thought. *Kill her, take the camera, call Security.*

"What do you want?"

Heaven held out the postage stamp and the coded note. "Give this to the Goddess, that's all."

Coldly, like a dead person, Juanita picked it off her palm. And now she had done it, betrayed the judge, betrayed everyone. Passed over a chantment.

"Smells like antiseptic," Sahara said suddenly, with what could only be called a loving smile. Did she think Juanita was one of her followers?

At least it was over. She locked the prisoner in her cell and bolted, heading for the mess, where the aroma of frying beef and garlic made her stomach flip. To steady herself, she scanned the room. The jury was tucked in a glassed-in, soundproofed dining room that kept them from overhearing trial-related scuttlebutt.

Okay, cope. Unknot the shoulders, walk to the chow line. But relaxing was easier said than done, especially when Heaven slipped into line behind her with a chirpy, "Hi!"

I could still kill her, Juanita thought. She settled for thwarting Heaven's attempt at a hug—a hug!—by putting her tray between them.

"How was your day?"

"Did everything I needed to do." Of course. The betrayal wouldn't be a one-time thing. Heaven would cling like a tick, demanding more, waving the threat to Juanita's family. . . .

Fight her, she thought. "Sahara asked me for a steak."

Heaven blinked. "The prisoners are vegans."

"Prisoner One may talk the eco-talk," Juanita said. "I don't think she ever walked the walk."

"She preaches respect for life." Then, remembering she was supposedly against Alchemism, Heaven added: "I heard."

Juanita gave her a nasty smile. "Her followers won't know if she gets a juicy slab of Angus beef, will they? Just like they don't know she didn't create the sea monsters she's always bragging about, that her prophecies are self-serving bull—"

"I'll tell Chef about the steak," Heaven said hastily.

Juanita had hoped to drive her off, but Heaven was apparently determined to keep playacting at being friends. She followed her to a table near the jury room. Spilling packets of crackers, she bent to retrieve them. . . .

"You hear about Will Forest?" she asked from under the table.

"Kidnapped, apparently." Juanita glanced at her tray. She'd ordered lamb stew without even registering it.

Heaven tucked a lumpy something into Juanita's shoe before climbing into a chair. "Forest is AWOL."

"Says who?"

"Everyone. He's run off to Astrid Lethewood."

"They'll search the base for chantments, then." Juanita said, "To see how he got out."

Heaven's gaze flicked in the direction of Juanita's foot. "Everything will be fine as long as we all keep doing our jobs."

"A search might slow things down."

"Delays have consequences." Heaven tucked in to her meal, a pasta dish with heavily burned chorizo. It was a point of honor that, prisoners aside, there were no vegetarians at Wendover. "You've got an ex-girlfriend at Caltech, don't you?"

Juanita stirred the stew. "Roche questioned me about Ramón."

A twitch. "Did he?"

"Someone must be tracking our families, watching for patterns. Ramón gets sent to dreamland, my file gets flagged. Mamá falls down a flight of stairs tomorrow, they haul me in for a real interrogation." She was relieved to see uncertainty in Heaven's face. *That's right, bitch—you're not riding some tame saddle nag. . . .*

"You're right. If work slows down now and then . . ."

A trickle of triumph. Whatever Heaven had stuck in her shoe, she'd delay passing it to Sahara.

By now, the jury was filing out of its soundproofed dining room. Juanita tensed. If Heaven attacked the jurors, blackmail or not, she'd have to intervene.

But Heaven turned to her pasta.

After dinner, Juanita moved on to the gym. She ran the tread-

mill, then worked her chest and shoulder muscles until she burned
the rage down to a manageable level.

Delay, fight, push Heaven's buttons. It didn't help the gnawing
in her belly whenever she thought about that postage stamp, that
undoubtedly magical postage stamp, in Sahara's cell. It didn't stop
the recriminations: *Show some backbone, break their necks. . . .*

*If the postage stamp were enough to allow Sahara to escape, they
would never have asked me to pass on a second chantment,* she rationalized. And magic took power, didn't it? If Sahara tried anything too dramatic, she'd lose weight. A person had to use her own
physical resources to work magic—burning calories, they'd been
told—or she had to recite something aloud.

If Sahara vamps someone, I get to shoot her, Juanita thought,
indulging the fantasy with grim satisfaction.

Back in her room, with her curtains shut and her door locked,
she fished out the lump Heaven had stuck in her shoe. It was an
amber bead, no bigger than a marble. As she turned it over in her
hand, her vision shimmered. She dropped it immediately, skin
crawling, and shoved it in a drawer.

When sleep took her, hours later, she saw Ramón playing football with his squad on a flawless, palm-dotted beach.

Juanita almost wished they could trade places.

CHAPTER FOUR

AS WILL FOLLOWED ASTRID around the magical campground she'd called Bigtop, he saw magic in use everywhere. A black woman in a vivid red chador was directing a dozen mutated spiders as they spun thick silk sheets over a pile of mulched blue sawdust, trapping the particles beneath it, presumably so they couldn't be inhaled. A bandy-limbed, tattooed skatepunk, meanwhile, was using a big barrel to draw tainted pollen from the air, clumping it together in balls. Workers were planting carpets of vitagua-blue moss and mushrooms over the slosh, the crushed mixture of vitagua, dead vegetation, and wreckage at ground level. Others carved flutes from contaminated deadwood, or poured vitagua into glass vessels, putting its internal radiance to use by making lanterns.

Most called greetings as Astrid passed.

Clad in jeans, work boots, and a brown T-shirt, her red curls hanging every which way and a hint of mud under one fingernail, Astrid reminded Will of the Communist leaders of the mid-twentieth century, with their working-class garb and lack of pretension.

She paused to wave at a fair-haired family—a middle-aged couple and three children—who were carving planks from a dead cedar tree. Will caught a snatch of their conversation; they were speaking German.

Was she drawing volunteers from around the world? Will asked: "Why are you still clearing forest?"

"Lots of reasons. There are chemical spills we're trying to get to, to clean up. The ecologists say making space helps the animals."

"You have ecologists?"

"Ecologists, an ethics board, malaria-eradication team, salmon experts . . ."

"Malaria?"

"Curing malaria outbreaks overseas frees up aid money for other kinds of disaster relief."

"Who says?"

"We have a couple economists, and development experts."

"Only a couple?" His eye fell on a picnic, a circle of lunching townspeople seated on a blanket, passing around a set of barbecue tongs and clicking them together like castanets to create sandwiches from thin air.

"We call that spinning," Astrid said.

"What?"

"Making something from nothing. It's called spinning. It's another of Mark Clumber's words."

"Do I see Jacks Glade's mother over there?"

She nodded, murmuring something he didn't catch into the tuning fork hung at her neck.

Olive Glade had disappeared soon after Astrid escaped from government custody. Now she was presiding over what was obviously a working lunch—the picnickers were poring over a scattering of drawings spread out on their blanket. A bread box–sized crystal at Olive's side was throwing off tiny white sparks.

Will opened his mouth to ask what she was doing. A fluttering, like paper shuffling near his ear, interrupted him.

"Lifeguards," he said. The knowledge had simply dropped into his mind. "They rescue people endangered by the magic spill . . . get them out of harm's way."

"That's right," Astrid said.

He felt a thread of excitement. "I knew that. I just magically knew it."

"Yes. I connected you to the . . . Oh, what's the word?"

"A wiki," he said. "I magically know that, too."

"Right. It's a pool of information everyone adds to. . . ."

"I'm familiar with the concept. You made a wiki? You? Astrid, you don't even watch TV."

"Someone explained it to me," she said. "If you wonder who someone is, why they volunteered—"

"I wonder where my kids are," he said, bracing for disappointment as he spoke. He and Roche had run down dozens of fruitless leads after Caro's arrest.

But now he heard a flutter, and knew: The children were in hiding with a team of eight Alchemites led by Sahara's chief Prima, Passion. They were healthy, well fed, and a bit homesick. The Alchemites' focus was on avoiding arrest while turning both children into devout Sahara worshippers. It seemed to be working, on Ellie anyway.

The group stayed on the move, but just this morning one of the Indigo Springs seers had learned they were in Missouri.

"Will?"

"They're in St. Louis," he said, a little breathless.

Astrid nodded.

"Why haven't you gone after them?"

"And then what? Keep them against their will? The Alchemites are teaching 'em to hate me. I'm the Filthwitch, remember?"

"You thought if you grabbed them and I wasn't around . . ."

"I'm afraid of scaring 'em to death," Astrid said. "But now you're here, we'll go collect them."

"Just like that?"

"Sure."

"Today?"

"Tonight."

It was almost too much. He put out a hand blindly, felt her squeeze it.

Finally, by way of pulling himself together, he turned his attention back to Olive Glade.

Every inch the aging flower child, Jacks's mother wore an undyed wool cardigan and a denim skirt. The owlish glasses Will remembered from her "Missing" photo were gone. A pendant—an althame, symbol of her Wiccan beliefs—hung around her neck, along with a pennywhistle.

"Are you surprised to see her here?"

"No," Will said. "Her son's in the unreal. You could help her find him, if he's alive."

"Oh, Jacks is alive," Astrid said. "I see him again."

"How's that work out? Do you two rekindle your romance?"

"Me and Jacks?" She gave him a peculiar look, as if he'd spoken in another language.

"Or are you still hung up on Sahara?"

"Pah. Not a chance."

Yeah, right. Turning back to Olive, he allowed himself a hint of curiosity and heard another flutter. Suddenly he knew the names of everyone on the picnic blanket. Astrid and her people had saved them all, from illness and homelessness and impending tragedy, from mere bankruptcy in one case.

"You've got a lot going on here—I'm impressed."

"Job's too big for me alone," Astrid said.

"I never considered the logistics." Will had seen the vast frozen seas of liquid magic in the unreal. Astrid had promised to get it melted and into the real world.

"Dealing with large-scale contamination and its consequences . . . it's a lot, Will."

"So you've delegated. Olive's in charge of these Lifeguards?"

"Yes."

"And Mark keeps the government from bombing you flat."

"Bombing *us* flat. He's doing a good job."

"It doesn't hurt, I'm guessing, that the army's got so much on its plate."

She ducked her head. "War overseas, fighting the Alchemites, containing the forest . . ."

"So all Mark's coping with are the bombing raids?"

"That's plenty, believe me."

"Roche will come after you eventually, with more."

"After us. Yes, there's going to be a big battle."

Voice neutral, he said: "That's a scary prospect."

She poked a toe into the fill, turning over a hump of blue moss, and changed the subject. "Over there is Katarina—she's our Dean of Science."

"Science?" That fluttering sound again, and Will sensed a network of researchers studying everything from the atomic weight of vitagua to how much power that sandwich-making chantment of Olive's took.

He said: "Why does the wiki make that fluttering sound?"

"I chanted it out of a Rolodex."

"Of course you did."

"Let's see, what else? We're trying to find the Fyremen. One team's putting information about magic on the Internet. Recruiting, of course, lots of recruiting. We watch volcanoes and fault lines. . . ."

"Because when magic gets out, there are earthquakes and eruptions."

The scale of it was staggering. These were *departments*—research, intelligence, propaganda. Malaria-eradication projects and Mark Clumber as secretary of defense. What Astrid had here was a makeshift government. "And you're salvaging garbage, making—sorry, *spinning*—food, digging up the old town, and deflecting missiles . . . *all* using magic?"

"Mostly. Magic and computers don't play together. And we're bringing in food when we can. People give us money, things to chant."

"But where's the power coming from?" Using his ring wore him out: it burned calories. "You can't be drawing heat . . . we'd be freezing."

"We've made progress there." She drew him through the arch of brambles, back into the train station and then across its plaza. This time when they stepped between the blue columns, they came out into a hotel lobby. People bustled around them, moving under the glow of a chandelier whose lightbulbs had been filled with liquid magic.

"Boss," someone called, "they're putting Sahara's grandma on the stand."

"Okay," she called, voice cheery.

"You've been watching the trial?" Will asked.

"Oh, you know." She spoke in the same light tone. "I'm not much for TV."

"Astrid." He caught her, turning her to face him. "Don't hide from me. I risked everything, coming here, and I betrayed an old friend. I need to trust you. . . ."

Her expression changed, sadness leaking through the placid mask. She spoke softly. "Seeing Sahara like that . . ."

"It hurts?"

"I'm not hung up," she said. "It's not love."

"No?"

"Isn't it the same with your wife?"

"Astrid—"

"Sahara threw me away, like trash. Is it so weird I don't want to see her mugging for the cameras?"

It was important to her, Will could see, that the two of them share that—her sense of abandonment and betrayal ran deep.

"You're right," he said. "Watching just rips the scab off. What's say we avoid the trial together?"

"Deal." With that, Astrid led him to a marble-topped concierge counter covered in random junk. She hugged the fey and apparently genderless person standing beside it.

"Will, this is Pike."

Pike looked to be about twenty years of age, with black skin covered in gold tattooed words: *jigsaw, rats, leper, phantasm, gold, slate, worry, gelatin* . . .

"Seen you on the news, lad." Pike's accent was Irish. "Nice to finally meet you."

"Thanks," Will said.

"First things first." He or she held out a box of small musical instruments—panpipes, whistles, tuning forks, all hung on leather wrist straps. "You'll need a phone."

Will picked a tuning fork. "A phone?"

Astrid ran her hands through her curls, revealing the scars on her right ear. "Everyone's all, 'We need cell phones, we need email—'"

"We need communications, ye Luddite." Pike gave Astrid an indulgent glance. "Boss here drew the line at text messaging."

"You got your wiki thing," she pointed out.

Will hung the tuning fork around his wrist. "If I wonder how this works . . ."

An especially loud flutter interrupted him: the wiki was right here. A petite, nerdy-looking octagenarian sat in a recliner behind Pike, turning the Rolodex and seeming to read its cards.

The answer about the tuning fork came all at once—Astrid had chanted the big pipe organ in the old Lutheran church, creating a magical switchboard. Musicians played the organ around the clock, routing calls and taking messages. The whistles and tuning forks functioned as receivers, like personal phones. Bigger instruments, like guitars, served as loudspeakers.

"Got it?" Astrid asked.

Will nodded. "I say who I want to speak to, then I just talk."

"Good!"

"And you, Pike? You must do more than hand out phones."

Astrid said: "Pike tracks who's doing what, who has which chantments, which crews need help."

"Human resources?"

"No," Pike said. "Overall project management."

"So you'll be assigning me a job?"

"For now, we'll focus on finding your children," Pike said.

Will thought about everything he'd done for Roche: press conferences, interrogations, paperwork. "Thank you."

"That does mean you'll be on the strike team," Pike added.

"The what?"

Astrid winced. "We need a better name for them."

"Boss here don't like the armyspeak."

"I also don't like being called *boss*, remember?" Astrid said. "Before we move on, Pike, Will asked about powering the chantments."

Pike reached under the registration desk, coming up with a lambent crystal like the one Will had seen next to Olive. It was the size of an apple and glimmered like lightning.

"This is letrico—stored power." Astrid folded it into his palm, where it thrummed faintly, like something alive.

"Feel that?"

"That bit of a hum? Yes."

"Hold it firmly," Astrid said. Then, without warning, she threw a punch at his face.

Will was more startled than scared: his fists didn't even come up. A lick of electricity, as thin as a spider leg, tickled over his skin, sparking between the crystal and his magic ring. As the letrico crystal shrank slightly within his grasp, the ring blew Astrid backwards onto her butt.

"Are you okay?" he asked.

"Totally fine," Astrid said, picking herself off the floor.

He offered her the crystal. "Stored power, I take it?"

"Yes. Keep it. I've been worried that if you got attacked, the ring would suck you dry."

"I thought you made the ring so you wouldn't have to worry about me." The power crystal looked like compressed cobwebs, or fiberglass insulation. It smelled of ozone and fudge.

"I made it to keep you safe."

"Safety's good," he said. "Where does this letrico come from?"

"We weave it out of other energy. Heat, for example—"

"Vamping?"

"Theoretically possible, but we'd never kill people," Astrid said. "Mostly it's electricity. Remember Olive's boyfriend?"

"Thunder Kim?"

"He's an engineer. He scavenged up parts for a power generator, hooked it to a hot spring, and channeled steam through it. It took a lot of setup, but we have some cheap electricity now."

"Not enough," Pike put in. "More juice we generate, more we use."

"You'll learn how to weave letrico, Will. New arrivals take a class as part of the orientation process. Pike can set that up later. But for now, I want to take you to meet the—" Exasperation crossed Astrid's face. "Strike team."

"It's got a nice honest ring, darlin'," Pike said.

"Strike team," Will echoed, thinking first of the shooter games he used to play with Carson and then the reality of the hostage sieges he'd worked in Portland when he was still a cop.

But as Astrid led him down to the hotel's underground parking lot, the first thing he saw was a 1920s-era trolley car with peeling paint and a bit of a sag. An ancient-looking black man leaned against it, clad in a leather flight jacket and pilot's cap. A cane dangled from the crook of his arm as he fiddled with its engine. Beside him, a white woman with salt-and-pepper hair sat nearby in a deck chair, holding but not strumming a banjo. Two young men were working with hammers on something in the backseat.

"Spiderwebs and sticks won't hold out artillery." The old man waved a bony hand from under the hood. "Armed forces'll blast their way in—or it'll be these witch-burners Astrid told us about."

"Boss wants to release the magic gently, I say more power to her," the woman said. "You've seen the Big Picture."

"Casualties are unavoidable in war."

"Casualties, fine, but triggering a massive calamity . . ."

"You don't win these things by being touchy-feely."

"Sometimes you don't win them at all."

The old man grunted. "I want to know how long we're gonna wait for this Forest character to get sick of the army's kangaroo court."

Astrid nudged Will, winking. "Ask him yourself, Clancy."

Will felt a ripple of unease as the group took him in. The woman moved first, setting aside her banjo, rising to her feet.

"Good to have you here."

Astrid said: "Will, this is Janet. Clancy's the gentleman with the wrench—he's our driver." She indicated the young men, a serious-looking duo. They had dark hair and Polynesian features, but there was no family resemblance: one was tall and ascetic looking; the other rounder, with cheerful, fidgety energy.

A couple, maybe? A flutter of the wiki confirmed it.

"This is Aquino and Igme," Astrid said.

Will said, "You four are the commando squad?"

"I never said commando," Astrid protested.

"Don't laugh, young man," Clancy said. "I was dropping para-troopers on France when you weren't yet a rude thought in your daddy's knickers. Janet served as a nurse in Vietnam, which makes her tougher than all us put together."

"No offense meant." He eased his body language, consciously broadcasting warmth, openness. "If you four are going to help rescue my children, it makes you my new best friends."

Igme grinned. "Have a look at our bus?"

Will stepped aboard. Most of the seats were gone, and the interior walls were lined with Peg-Board and covered in chant-ments. "Looks like a cross between a dollar store and a carpen-ter's shop."

Unlike Igme, whose speech was colored with just a trace of California surfer, Aquino had a strong Spanish accent: "You tell us where to go, Clancy takes us there. Janet, she keeps people from noticing us."

"We're going to be invisible?"

"Just sneaky." Janet said, "Invisibility's a power pig."

"What if Sahara's people are expecting us?" Will fingered the chantments dangling from the Peg-Board. "Are these . . . for combat?"

"I'd rather calm people down than fight them," Astrid said.

"Casualties happen," Will said, echoing Clancy.

"Janet will heal anyone who gets injured."

"Okay, I believe you. Janet's doing stealth and first aid; Clancy's driving. The rest of us gently quell the opposition. Any-thing else?"

"We'll leak a bit of vitagua—spread magic beyond the forest," Astrid said. "But the primary goal is finding your kids."

"And after that, Pike will find me a job?"

"If you're willing," she said. "Nobody's obliged."

Will frowned. "Before you escaped custody, you asked me to be your apprentice."

"That's up to you, Will."

"Is it? You know the future—bits and pieces, anyway."

"Nobody can force you to take on the magical well."

"You're ducking the question, Astrid. You believe I'll do it, don't you?"

She nodded.

He could feel the eyes of the others on him. So much responsibility had fallen on Astrid's shoulders. As far as anyone knew, she was the last well wizard, the only one with access to the unreal and its seas of enchantment. It was up to her to return magic to the world.

Astrid was literally remaking the planet, and by her own admission struggling to hold off catastrophe. Expecting Will to be her backup . . . it was overwhelming, impossible.

But if it was the only way to recover Ellie and Carson?

He shook away the apprehension. Astrid wasn't asking for anything. He'd forgotten this: her generosity of spirit, her willingness to let people be themselves.

"Let's just collect the kids," Astrid said. "The rest of our plan—"

"Mission," Igme corrected.

"Raid," Clancy said. "Into enemy territory, no less."

"Oh! I'm really uncool with the word *enemy*," Astrid said.

"Operation?" Janet suggested, needling.

"Maybe we can leave the semantics for later," Will said. "According to the seers, the kids are in St. Louis, Missouri."

"Igme?" Astrid said. "You've been studying up on St. Louis?"

"You bet I have," the young man said. "They're okay for food and water. There's been power brownouts, looting. It's too hot, especially in the refugee camps. We could draw some heat—"

"Windstorms," Janet objected.

"Might keep people indoors."

"When you make things in a hot region very cold all of a sudden, Will, there's side effects," Astrid explained.

He had seen this when the army clashed with the Alchemites. Cold air took up less space than hot. When chantments drew heat, the air pressure dropped, causing the wind to rise.

"Katarina has a fancy weather model in Europe," Aquino said. "In Bern."

"Bern?"

"I'll make chantments for the locals." Astrid interrupted—hastily, he thought. "Will, I'd like to get you briefed on Alchemite activity in St. Louis."

"Temples, Primas, missing persons, that kind of thing?"

"Yes. We'll home in on the kids using magic, but preparation—"

"Knowledge is power," he agreed. "How do I get briefed?"

"Igme will take you to meet the seers. I—"

The tuning fork at her neck piped: "Astrid, are you still going with Ev and Patience?"

"Yes, Pike. Tell 'em I'm coming, please. Will, are you okay if I go?"

He nodded.

She reached out, as if to touch him. Then, instead, she turned, vanishing through a gate of thorns on the nearby wall.

Clancy clapped him on the arm. "We'll have your family back soon, sonny."

"St. Louis," Will said under his breath. It had been a long time since he had felt this much hope.

CHAPTER FIVE

THE UNREAL WAS A sunless expanse, lit by the glow cast by the glaciers of vitagua that lay atop most of its land mass. Its nature was poorly understood. Astrid, when explaining it to new volunteers, said that throughout human history there had been tales of other worlds—spirit realms, Hades, Asgard—and that the unreal was one or possibly all of those realms.

Albert had called it the land of the fairies.

The explanation satisfied many of the new volunteers, Ev knew. But it wasn't that simple: the fairies were long gone. In fact, the unreal's inhabitants were all aboriginal people, Native Americans who'd fled the European conquest. But Fairyland was a simpler concept to grasp, and a less thorny one.

The three of them—Ev, his daughter, and Patience—had stepped through Bramblegate and now stood on the gritty steppes of the unreal, next to a tumbled-down pile of concrete and steel beams commingled with bits of tree. A sharp breeze blew from within the wreckage, along with a wisp of steam—humidity, from the real, condensing in the cooler air.

"If I hear you're driving yourself into the ground working, kid, I'm coming back to the real."

"I feel great, Pop. As long as I'm chanting, I've got energy to burn."

"Don't think we won't find out if you're fibbing," Patience said. She was wearing a copper-colored silk dress, and its skirt snapped in a gust of breeze, billowing like a sail. "None of us can afford for you to collapse from exhaustion."

"I'm not gonna die of burnout, promise."

"I hate you shoving me out of harm's way like this," Ev said.

"It might not be as safe as you think, Pop. The Roused know you're my—" She paused, snagging on his gender. "—parent."

"Just take decent care of yourself," he said before things could get awkward.

"I don't remember there being a breeze here," Patience said, deftly changing the subject. She turned into the wind, which pressed the dress snug against her figure.

Ev looked away. "Vitagua's flowing into the real through the Chimney," he said. "Katarina figured something had to come into the unreal. Otherwise the whole place would collapse."

"Magic flows out, so air comes in?" Astrid said.

"A little water too, from the look of it. See the steam?" Patience pointed.

Astrid's expression became dreamy. "Thunder's going to put a wind turbine here. Cottages, a letrico mill."

"Let me check with the locals before you go putting up a suburb on their turf." Patience's father had been Native—Umpqua Nation, Ev thought, or Chinook?

"Good idea," Astrid said, missing her sharp tone. "Will you guys be okay if I get going?"

"Of course," Ev said.

"If everything goes well in St. Louis, they'll be in a good mood. We're going to release a lot of magic tonight."

"Beyond finding Jacks, what do you need me to do?" Patience asked.

"When I first came here, there were these ice statues," Astrid said. "One of Dad, and his granny. They had all the chanters, I think, going back to Elizabeth Walks-in-Shadow. I'm wondering if they're still around."

"Fine. The Roused will want to know how long it's going to take to get the magic thawed."

Astrid frowned. "I know it all goes—the grumbles say so."

"In five years time, or fifty?" Patience pressed.

"What if I ask Katarina about finding a . . . would it be a hydrologist?" Astrid said. "Someone who can measure how many gallons of magic there are and how fast we're moving it."

"It's a start," Patience said.

"Okay." Astrid's attention was elsewhere: Bramblegate had flowered amid the ruined pile of concrete. She stepped through and was gone, moving on to her next task.

Patience jerked her suitcase, trying to make it roll on the soft sand. "Here I am playing ambassador, and what do I get? No limo, no entourage—"

"Let me get that." Scooping it up, Ev began to march, glad to have an excuse not to look at her.

"I wasn't fishing for help."

"I don't mind." His transformation had given him the body of a fifty-five-year-old man and the libido of a thirteen-year-old boy. Around Patience, he felt desire that was nigh unbearable.

Knowing it was magic that made her sexy didn't help.

She has twenty years on you, Ev. Remember when she was just the dotty old crank on your Mascer Avenue mail route? "I doubt we rate an escort. It's not far, and we're no threat."

"I'd appreciate some VIP treatment. I liked being on TV—"

Ev said: "Having a million fans. What's not to like?"

"And you, you're the mother of their best shot at freedom. Definitely a red carpet visitor."

"I'm not the red carpet type. Do you think it'll be hard to find Jacks?"

"They'll know where he is," Patience said. Something must've shown in Ev's face, because she added, "You don't look happy about that."

"Astrid killed the Chief," Ev said. "And the Chief wanted Jacks to be a witch-burner."

"The Chief wasn't the best of fathers, maybe, but I wouldn't worry—Olive raised Jacks to be a peacenik. Besides, Ev, the boy is mad in love with your daughter."

"Look what contamination did to Sahara," Ev said.

"Sahara was a self-centered half-crazy brat before she got anywhere near magic."

"It warps you, Patience. I thought I was someone else, remember? Near took Astrid's head off once, for trying to set me straight." Ev shuddered, remembering the rages that had over-taken him after he'd been exposed to raw vitagua.

It started on his mail route; he had suddenly *known* that the envelope in his hands was a vicious attack on the woman receiving it. Hate had boiled through the paper . . . and he had been unable to cope. Such things didn't happen, he had rationalized, and something in his mind gave.

Scared and grasping at straws, he'd decided he wasn't psychic—he'd just deduced what was in that envelope. An ex-husband, a bitter breakup. It was a small town, and he knew all the local gossip.

But the insights kept coming, intimate details of strangers' lives. To cope, Ev had adopted the persona of his favorite fictional detective.

Since Astrid had learned to treat vitagua sickness, Ev felt sane again. Now that his body was male, he felt more sound than he'd ever been during his early life. Daughter, mother, wife—all those Evs had been costumes. All of them fit wrong.

But even now, he wasn't quite himself. Traces of the detective persona remained: a fondness for hats, hokey chivalry.

Patience didn't get this. She had been exposed to vitagua, but Astrid treated her within minutes, before her sense of self could fracture.

"Say for the sake of argument we find Jacks alive," she said now. "Say he's insane and looking for revenge."

"You think he died?"

Patience shrugged. "No. Astrid promised the Roused that if they saved Jacks, she'd thaw the unreal. There's a lot of magic here: they can pull it off."

"Can we afford to turn him loose?"

"Not our call, Ev."

"Sahara broke Astrid's heart. If Jacks was nuts too . . ."

"Astrid is going to risk it."

He found that it was a relief just to have given voice to the fear. "You don't think Jacks is a danger?"

"Nope. If you want something to worry about . . ."

"What?"

She sighed. "We are all of us, especially Astrid, inventing a very dangerous wheel here, Ev. We could destroy both worlds—"

"Her grumbles say it doesn't happen that way."

"And you believe— Hey!" She stopped. "Where's the city?"

On their previous visit to the unreal, the Roused had been living beneath the ridge the two of them had just climbed. Their settlement had been a sprawling bundle of giant seedpods, each as big as a room, stitched together by translucent stems big enough to walk through.

Now the gritty white plains below the ridge were empty, a bare expanse stretching to the edge of a vast frozen sea.

"There, on the horizon!" He could just make out structures rising from the surface of the ice.

"That is a hell of a lot farther to walk," Patience said.

Bubbling erupted from the bleached grit at their feet; a pair of human hands scrabbled up through the dust. They were suspended from the ends of the two slender antennae, and followed by an enormous cricket.

"Hi, guys!" he chirped. "Enjoying the stroll?"

"You uprooted the whole city?"

"The People move as we must. Action's out on the glacier, so we are too. But I got a shortcut, if you want."

Patience's relief was obvious. "We definitely want."

"Okay!" The cricket spat a stream of green juice onto the white grit. It clumped together, forming a line of ivory stalagmites that curved inward as they reached a height of seven feet. The cricket spat again, forming a second, parallel line about a yard away. Laid thusly, they formed a structure that resembled a giant rib cage. Its floor curved like a bridge, a low arch on the sandy soil.

"You have gates here in the unreal?" Patience said.

"Gates are ours, always were," the cricket said. "Spirit realm's everywhere. You step through Astrid's blackberry arches in the real, you slide over us on your way elsewhere."

Does Astrid know this? Ev would have to ask.

"Gonna take the bridge?" the cricket asked.

"Yes, thank you," Ev said.

Stepping through, they emerged on the surface of the massive glacier. The cluster of seedpods that had formed the city rose above them, organized into a freestanding honeycomb, skyscraper high, with roots sunk deep into the ice. Human–animal hybrids moved along its walkways.

The scent of cooked food—roasted vegetables, refried beans, and something eggy—rose from a long dugout canoe parked at the base of the honeycomb. Remembering his first visit to the unreal, Ev inhaled slowly. Sure enough, his belly filled.

At the foot of the honeycomb was a pit, a melted chasm that yawned within the frozen vitagua.

Ev stared into the hole. Magic had mutated from its original, relatively benign form about seven hundred years earlier. That was when the witch-burners of Europe launched their effort to corner the market on enchantment. In the process, they had driven magic into Fairyland—to use Albert's term—where pressure compressed the magical particles into vitagua.

In their last battle with the Fyremen, the people of the unreal had frozen it all. They had saved themselves, but they'd also been trapped by their own defensive move—the ice had formed instantly, capturing everyone on both sides.

Vitagua was naturally luminescent; staring into the pit was like being underwater on a sunny day, seeing the sun shining down at you through several feet of ocean. Half-transformed people were frozen in the ice, a profusion of animal and human faces, all with aboriginal features, most caught in attitudes of surprise or terror. Here and there, a body part stuck out; in one case, a girl's head had melted free. She keened at Ev with the voice of a Siamese cat.

"She has been freeing about ten people a day."

Ev turned. The speaker was a raccoon with long black braids, dressed in a nineteenth-century dress and glasses that made her look like something from a kid's book, a raccoon granny.

"Hello," Patience said. "I'm Patience Skye. This is Ev."

"I'm Eliza," the raccoon replied.

Ev was about to ask if Eliza was in charge, but Patience cut in smoothly. "You were saying something about Astrid?"

A man with dragonfly wings flew over the lip of the chasm. He had someone in his arms, a coughing, blue-slimed bullfrog from the pit. He passed the frog to a waiting quartet of Roused, who sponged off the new arrival, their movements as tender as if they were nurses attending a birth.

"You spoke of measuring the ocean in gallons," Eliza said, indicating the bullfrog. "What matters to us is how many of our people remain trapped."

"Astrid has melted more of you folk loose than any chanter since the freeze," Ev said.

The raccoon eyed him. "Promises have been made."

"They're being kept," Patience insisted. "She's picking up the pace."

"Each person freed is a gift. But the more of us there are, the more impatience we feel." Eliza smoothed her apron. "Asking us to have faith in your daughter's commitment—"

"Astrid has her own reasons to want the job done," Ev said.

"The Fyrechild."

"Jacks Glade, that's right. Is he alive?"

"After a fashion," the raccoon said. "When all the others are freed, *all*, he will go."

The glacier trembled. Ice melted, sending liquid magic down the chasm wall. The cat-girl tumbled free, twisting in midair as she fell. A wolf spider with human eyes skipped up and over the edge of the pit, into a waiting blanket.

Cries, human and animal, rose from below.

The dragonfly appeared, laboring under the weight of the cat girl. Dropping her, he chattered at Eliza before power-diving back down.

"What's happened?" Patience asked.

"A large melt," the raccoon replied. Roused were rushing out of the city, hurrying to the pit.

"St. Louis," Patience said. "Astrid and the others must already be there."

Ev asked: "Can we help?"

"Dry people off as we bring them up." The raccoon pointed at a pile of blankets, then rushed downward with the others, vanishing into the impenetrable blue light.

CHAPTER SIX

VOLUNTEERS SET UP A banquet in Indigo Springs that night, amid the silk tents and vitagua lanterns of the Bigtop. They spun picnic hampers laden with baked squash, poached trout and salmon, curried chickpeas and eggplant, and cranberry custard. The food was served on scavenged glassware, a motley collection of bowls and plates. Cups of a light mead were passed round.

Afterwards, a steel drum band set up on the giant blue stump of one of the mulched trees, playing fast-paced Caribbean music while the feasters danced.

Astrid's gaze kept returning to Will Forest. He was on the fringe of the crowd, observing, taking everything in. He seemed calm, but he must be eager to get going.

She made her way to his side, passing a pair of volunteers bent over a small video player. On its palm-sized screen, the former editor of the *Indigo Springs Dispatch*, Aran Tantou, was giving evidence. "Before the magical disaster, I'd been working on an article on the ten worst polluters in Oregon." The player's small speaker made Aran's voice tinny. "Afterwards, Sahara came to me. She wanted my research; she wanted to go after the companies and their executives."

"Did she say why?"

"She was going to reveal their inner monsters."

"Contaminate them, in other words," said the prosecutor.

"Yes."

"Did you give it to her?"

"Of course he did," one of the viewers muttered.

"Weasel," added another: Aran had been unpopular in town. In trying to please everyone, he'd come off as mealy-mouthed.

"I had everything on a flash drive; the Alchemites took it,"

Aran said. He looked nervous. The camera angle switched: Sahara was giving him her shark smile.

Astrid put her hand over the player. "Give the newscast a rest for a night, guys. Join the dance?"

"Too tired." One, a pixie-faced kindergarten teacher from the team of seers, pocketed the player. "I spent all day in Marseilles, trying to figure out what'll go wrong there when Boomsday comes. Now I just wanna kick back with a little TV."

"Couldn't you find a good show?"

The pixie's medic boyfriend smirked. "Trial's got the best ratings in America—it must be good."

"If you say so." She left them to it, moving through the crowd to Will. "Want to say a few words?"

"Me?" He frowned. "Surely that's your job."

"I'm terrible at speechmaking."

"Comes with the job, Astrid. You may not like that they call you boss, but it's you they need to hear from."

"Stand up with me."

"My mind's far away, Astrid," he said. His tone was gentle. "Maybe after St. Louis, okay?"

Feeling absurdly crushed, she turned away, climbing up beside the band.

The murmur of conversation didn't wane. She hadn't developed Sahara's knack for getting everyone's attention. Finally Mark started banging a couple wooden bowls together, breaking into the chatter.

Where to start? "I want you all to remember this isn't an attack. We're not going to St. Louis to hurt anyone."

The words had a sobering effect.

"We're going to make things better," she continued. "Yes, we're going to leave vitagua there, but we're also going to leave behind water weavers, food spinners. We'll cool the air, clean up garbage, patch up busted houses. The government will call it terrorism, but people will see the magic improved things."

"They'll all live happily ever after!" someone shouted.

"Yes." She raised her cup. "Um, to the Happy After."

"The more, the merrier," replied the group, raising glasses. Will looked perplexed; she'd have to explain the toast to him.

Right now, what he needed was a successful mission. She walked to the Chimney, with its dripping rills of vitagua.

Astrid had been reluctant to shoulder this burden. Her father taught her to chant when she was a child, but when she realized how much responsibility it meant, she wimped out. She'd made a chantment that wiped out all her knowledge of magic.

Then Dad was murdered. Astrid inherited the magical well— and thanks to her self-inflicted amnesia, she got Jacks killed and let Sahara run mad.

"Stop," she murmured aloud, as she always did when her thoughts started running this track. "No regrets."

The world had been in trouble before the well ever broke open, she reminded herself. The goal now was to steer everyone to that happy ending the grumbles kept talking about.

Happy endings. Her and Will. Could she have misunderstood? The idea had a certain allure; he had Jacks's steadiness, and he was so fair, so kind. . . .

The vitagua pool in the ravine was glass smooth. A slow trickle lipped its edge, leaking into the swamp surrounding the camp, saturating the forest floor.

Under Astrid's direction, the blue magic roiled. She warmed it into mist, gallons of it, raising a blue fog above her head. As much as she dared, as much as she could hang on to . . . she all but emptied the lagoon surrounding the Chimney.

Fluid gushed out from the gap between worlds. It would fill up fast.

Drawing the magic around her like a cloak, Astrid took Bramblegate to the plaza.

A cluster of volunteers was waiting, debating who should break a champagne bottle over the front bumper of the trolley.

"Who's newest here?" Astrid asked.

"Amber," Pike said.

A young woman stepped up, reaching for the bottle. She christened the trolley *Overlord:* Clancy's choice, in honor of all his dead Normandy invasion buddies. More warspeak, Astrid thought. Excitement crackled through the gathering.

Mark punched the air. "Kick ass and take names!"

Olive frowned. "The gentle path."

To Astrid's relief, most of the volunteers echoed Olive.

The others were waiting. She could delay no longer.

She pulled vitagua into herself, into the empty spaces within.

Voices assailed her. Grumbles, she called them, the voices of the frozen people of the unreal, with all their opinions, resentments, their knowledge of past and future.

They spoke of the future, of Sahara escaping, of Alchemites committing atrocities. Or maybe she'd misheard—without Sahara, the Alchemites were relatively harmless. Astrid had seen to that.

The grumbles mumbled about her first-grade graduation ceremony, Dad's death, the night she lost her virginity.

She reeled, dizzy and disoriented. When was now?

Flames licking skin, smell of burned hair . . .

"She's spacing out," a voice said. Someone caught her before she could step off the trolley.

"Jacks?" Jacks was the one who always caught her. She burst into tears: his blood was on her skirt. Her fault. Was that now?

"Go, Clancy," Will said. It was him holding her steady, not Jacks. She felt the gut-deep pain of his children's absence, his gnawing fear they'd be harmed, the exhausting effort of holding it together. . . .

"St. Louis," Clancy said, driving into the glow. Hot, syrupy air lolled over them as they rolled out into nighttime.

"Where are we?" Astrid said.

"Missouri," Will said.

"I think it goes well here," she said.

Car alarms were blaring—their arrival had displaced a shock of air. People were going to their windows.

Janet raised a tin watering can, spilling water onto the street. As it pattered on the pavement, people shrugged, closing their curtains. The alarms quieted.

Aquino crossed himself quickly, then raised an elaborately

painted lampshade over his head. Letrico flickered up his arms and hands, and countless twinkles of light boiled from the lampshade, swarming out into the city like fireflies. "Invitations to new volunteers are away."

"And here goes nothing." Igme held out a plastic turkey baster filled with vitagua. Soap bubbles blew from its tip, each the size of a tennis ball, each containing a trace of liquid magic. Some drifted upward; others rolled in the street, vessels of microcontamination that would spread enchantment when they broke.

"Boss? Boss?"

Astrid twisted the barbell pierced into the web of her hand, breaking the skin so blue magic could steam out. Leaning out of a trolley window, she looked for objects—tricycles, dog toys, laundry, anything that could hold a benevolent charm.

"Will—your children?"

The magical well would be vulnerable until she had a successor, and the grumbles said it would be Will. But he wouldn't do it if she couldn't produce the kids.

He will bend, he will see . . . , the grumbles murmured. They told the truth, but they laid traps with it; you couldn't entirely trust them. Would he really love her one day? *Could* he—could anyone—love someone who was destroying the world?

She had chanted him a spinner from a kid's game, a plastic compass whose needle pointed east. "Turn left, Clancy," he said.

Astrid kept chanting. Their route took them past a derelict shopping mall that had been turned into a temporary camp for evacuees from Oregon. FEMA trailers lined its parking lot. Astrid made food spinners for the refugees, healing chantments, items that would mend broken tools and teach new skills. It wouldn't be long before the camp realized they had magical items on their hands.

Igme kept sending out vitagua-contaminated bubbles, using the baster.

Astrid was chanting hundreds of things at once now: a rain barrel that purified water, a stuffed crab that cured cholera, air scrubbers, hole diggers, roof patchers, a shoemaker enchantment, a fireworks generator—anything a person might use to help, supply, even entertain others. . . .

A snap—one of the vitagua-contaminated bubbles had broken on a nearby willow. The tree wasn't shooting skyward like the vitagua-drenched trees at home. Its leaves were stirring, and one of its spreading roots had broken through a nearby sidewalk.

"Trace contamination, just a little growth," she murmured. The world would end up like this, covered in magically tinged vegetation. People had to learn how to coexist with enchantment.

They turned onto Market Street, and an inhuman cry rose around them. Starlings blanketed the roofs all around the buildings, cheeping and trilling so loudly, her teeth buzzed.

"They're here!" Will said. Clancy brought the trolley to an abrupt halt in front of a yarn store.

"So much for catching them by surprise." Aquino went into action, handing out chantments. He slapped a grocery pricer, disturbingly gun shaped, into Astrid's palm.

Igme dropped the turkey baster, tightened his grip on a hunk of letrico, and cranked a pepper mill. The yarn store shivered, then blew away in a cloud of fine dust. In the space where it had been, a circle of men, women, and children was murmuring, as if in prayer.

"Carson!" Will's kids were here, all right. "Eleanor!"

Chilly air gusted toward them—a heat draw. Four of the Alchemites broke ranks, putting themselves between the children and their father. Chunks of rock pelted the trolley.

Clancy yanked on a dog toy on the dashboard, squeaking it, and the missiles bounced away. Janet threw a hula hoop over one of the women. The hoop contracted, pinning her arms. She fell on her rump, dazed but unharmed.

Little Ellie Forest spotted her father.

She began to scream.

Carson Forest had stepped toward the trolley, but now his sister clutched at him, visibly panicked. The boy turned, the frown on his face so like his father's.

The cold was spreading.

"They're drawing power for something big," Clancy said.

"On it," Igme said, but the Alchemites were raising their faces to the sky. One had a whistle in her teeth.

Will sprinted toward the children, ignoring the flying knitting needles, batting aside a net thrown by a barrel-chested Alchemite. A chunk of letrico in his left hand powered his ring.

Astrid grabbed a set of carved wooden salad spoons. *Open up a path,* she thought, chanting the spoons and then sweeping them outward. The Alchemite circle broke, adults tumbling aside, clearing the space between Will and his children.

One of the defenders threw a beanbag at Will's feet. A pit of muck opened up in front of him. Quicksand? Will stumbled, arms pinwheeling. The ring kept him from plunging in.

The children turned into starlings.

Now the Alchemites were all birds, shrieking in triumph as they flapped up to join the flock above. Thousands strong, it swirled upward.

Astrid scooped up an old purse, thinking of nets—

There was a boom and all the birds were gone.

Will let out a frustrated cry as he recovered his balance. He whirled, grabbing the Alchemite Janet had entangled. "Where are they going?"

The woman thrashed, straining to escape.

"Nobody's going to hurt you," Astrid said.

"Filthwitch!" she shouted.

"It's okay, Will. We'll get the truth out of her." Snatching a small wooden turtle, a toy, out of the crumbled remains of the store, Astrid chanted it swiftly, thinking of truth serums and lie detectors. Drawing letrico, she held it to the woman's face.

"Where are the children?"

"Among the flock."

"Where'll they go?"

She grinned, gap toothed. "They'll scatter."

"Astrid," Igme said. "We're running out of juice."

Will held out his spinner. The needle turned in slow circles. "It doesn't know where they are."

Among the flock. Astrid bit her lip. "We need to go home, regroup."

Will scowled at the woman they'd caught. "What about her?"

"Knock her out." Janet pressed a gooey plastic eyeball to the woman's forehead. Letrico flowed; she fainted.

"We should take her with us."

Astrid shook her head. "Leave her for the police."

"Astrid, she might know more."

"I'm sorry, Will—I promised the volunteers we wouldn't take captives."

"Some of us have been locked up," Clancy put in.

"But—"

"Will, Sahara's people move on. When they lose someone, they abandon them. She won't be able to tell you."

Will glared at her, furious, then at the unconscious woman.

"We can't become a jail," Astrid said again.

Under the hot umbrella of the St. Louis night, sirens were wailing. Here and there, alchemized trees were getting bigger as the contaminated soap bubbles began to pop.

"Will?"

"Fine, all right. I see your damned point." They boarded the trolley and Clancy floored it, bringing them to the nearest VA hospital.

"What are we doing here?" Will asked. He was upset, but Astrid could see he was struggling to calm down.

Aquino held out a plastic model of the human heart, offering it to Will. "This is one of our more powerful healing chantments," he said.

"It'll fix anything physical—cancer, broken bones, chapped lips, diabetes," Astrid chimed in. "It's a power pig, but the idea is to cool off the city, give everyone a break—"

"Heal everyone we can, it leaves a good impression," Janet said. "Frees up doctors and nurses too."

"Fine." Will stepped clear of the letrico lines, murmuring the heat cantation Astrid had taught him, and held it out. The plastic flexed; the heart started to beat.

"Temperature's ninety-two Fahrenheit," Igme said.

A low thump—*buh dump, buh dump*—issued from the heart. As the humid air around them cooled, fog pooled at Will's feet, blowing outward, wisping out to caress a clutch of smokers crouched in wheelchairs beside the hospital's glass door. The magic reached them too; one screamed as his amputated legs grew back. He jumped up, then tripped. Others scrambled to catch him.

Mist enveloped the hospital. The wind blowing from the trolley got stronger.

Spreading fog, a grumble said.

"Eighty-six degrees," Igme reported.

Vitagua, spreading in a fog when the well opens . . .

Astrid shook away the murmur, imagining the surprise inside the hospital as the sick and injured recovered. The heartbeat *buh-bump*ed, louder in the increasingly murky air. The chantment would cure common colds and undiagnosed tumors, fix bumps and bruises, restore failed organs, mend bones.

"Seventy degrees," Igme said. Their sweat-damp clothes were chilly on the skin now. The air around them was gusting outward, and a warm wind was blowing in and getting cooled in its turn. Aquino caught Astrid's eye, a question on his face.

Will was occupied; she nodded.

Quickly, Aquino hefted out an acorn-shaped trunk filled with chantments, tucking it under a lamppost. The acorn spun like a top, burying itself in the shallow soil. Will, focused on the hospital, didn't notice.

"Sixty seconds to freezing here at the hospital." Igme said, counting down, voice raised. "Greater metropolitan area's falling to a nice habitable fifty."

"Three. Two. One."

Will lowered the heart and climbed back aboard the trolley.

"Let's go," Astrid said. Bramblegate had bloomed on the hospital wall; Clancy drove toward it.

Leaving the city colder, healthier, and unmistakably enchanted, they went home.

CHAPTER SEVEN

JUANITA HELD ON TO the next chantment for three long days.

In court, the Alchemites, looking ever more brutalized as their bruises yellowed, got tossed back into the squirrel cages for biting their tongues and spitting blood at the bench. Wallstone had the jurors experiment with a chantment, a child's finger-puppet, a glow-in-the-dark ghost that allowed its wearer to create pockets of darkness in broad daylight. The lapsed Alchemite who'd surrendered the puppet, a sculptor, testified that he'd used it to obscure their movements during robberies.

Gilead Landon watched the demo with a look of pained forbearance on his face.

Special effects, Wallstone argued, nothing divine here. Court had adjourned then, so the jurors could rest up and bolt a protein shake to offset the calories they'd used making magic.

The kitchen had sent Sahara her steak, but Sahara refused to eat it. Heaven shot her a look of triumph when it came back untouched; next day, the prisoners began refusing food. A few reporters questioned whether the court was abusing the prisoners or simply incompetent, but the story didn't get much play; the networks weren't interested.

Sahara declined to join the hunger strike, so Juanita slipped a teaspoon of sesame oil into her soup. She had a mild allergy; within an hour, she was shaking, sweaty, and cramping up. Petty revenge, yes, but it also made a good excuse to conduct her to the infirmary, cuff her to an exam table, and leave her in the able hands of the medical staff.

Finding holes in allegedly secure systems was something Juanita had always been good at, and medical staff were often casual about protocols. It took a bit of doing, but she managed to slip into the pharmacy and get the keys to the drug cabinet.

Court staff and other civilians had submitted their medical records before coming to Wendover, allowing the pharmacy to lay in a store of prescriptions. On-site storage was part of a general strategy to limit the flow of material—and possible chantments—in and out of Wendover. Heaven's antianxiety medications for the next year were in the cabinet, neatly labeled and dated, along with everyone else's.

Juanita had entertained fantasies of switching sugar pills for the drugs, sending Heaven into a panic, but medication was designed with exactly that kind of tampering in mind. Tempting as it was to imagine Heaven was too flaky to know one pink pill from another, Juanita knew better.

Instead she flushed the prescription, leaving a conspicuous gap in the cabinet. Heaven would go for her refill, they'd find it gone, and hopefully the hassle involved in replacing the meds would bring the cook to Security's attention.

As resistance went, it wasn't nearly as satisfying as throttling Heaven unconscious and dragging her to Roche, but it also wouldn't get Juanita's family killed . . . she hoped.

Destroying the pills took about five minutes. Strolling back into the exam room, she gave Sahara a conspiratorial wink and passed over the magical amber bead. With luck, she would think the detour to the infirmary had served an Alchemite purpose.

"Looks like a food reaction," the doctor said. "Someone in the kitchen must have gotten mixed up."

"On purpose?" Juanita asked. Anything that drew attention to the kitchen staff might also trickle down to Heaven.

"Impossible to say. I'll report it."

"Thanks," she said, taking her prisoner back to the cells.

That night she was dreaming of Ramón when Sahara turned up, stepping directly between Juanita and her brother. Birds fluttered around her, gold-marked starlings with razor-sharp talons. Her feathered gown was low cut, and a bottle cap shimmered, like a star, on her breastbone. "Time we had a chat."

"I don't want to chat with you."

"Come on. I can make you happier with the situation."

"Situation? Meaning your threats to my family?"

Sahara's eyes blazed with righteous fire. "I'm not trying to hurt anyone."

Juanita pointed at her brother.

"Relax. It's paradise here: anything he wants, anytime he wants it. Nobody can hurt him, not even me." Sahara laid a hand on Ramón's shoulder. The Nevada desert formed around them: sagebrush, red rock, tumbleweeds. "Looks like he's homesick."

"He gets anything he wants except his freedom."

"You'd rather I'd thrown him in a prison? He could be sitting in a rat-infested hole."

"I thought you were above petty human rights abuses."

"Of course I am. But without me to temper their impulses, a few of my followers may be inclined to do something impetuous to your other loved ones. . . ."

"Oh—so it's them threatening me, not you?"

"I need you on my side," Sahara said. "Having a little leverage . . . I know it's unpleasant, darling, but—"

"Don't 'darling' me. What I am is your bitch. You got me giving you God knows what. . . ."

"The amber bead lets me talk to people, like we are right now. Is that such a big deal?"

"And the postage stamp?"

"Hides my chantments from Roche. Little perks, basic civil rights I'm being denied—"

"Stow it. I'm not a lawyer and I don't care."

"Roche's new buddy, Gilead Landon, wants to burn me alive on a stack of dry wood. Do you care about that?"

"You made a choice. If you'd told your followers to surrender, if you'd fought the contamination . . ."

"Are you that naïve? Maybe I could save myself from the fire, but I'd be locked up forever."

"You sank an aircraft carrier!"

"Pooh. Nobody was hurt."

"You call me naïve? You picked a fight with the United States of America. Now you're surprised we got our game on."

"It wasn't you that caught me," she purred. "Juanita, Roche can't win. And you've been looking for a new direction, haven't you? A fresh start, a purpose?"

Dammit, how does she know these things? "Right now I'd settle for not being blackmailed."

"Darling, when I take Indigo Springs, you're at my side—"

Juanita laughed.

"There's going to be a battle." Sahara ran a finger over one of the birds. "My voices . . . I hear Gilead Landon, burning a path into Indigo Springs. I'm holding him off—"

"All by yourself, I suppose," Juanita said.

"You kneel before me, hands upraised—"

"Yeah, that'll happen."

"Show some respect. The Goddess has done a great thing tonight." The voice came from behind them; turning, Juanita saw the tattooed woman who'd attacked Ramón. Passion flowers adorned her ankles, peeped out over the collar of her dress.

"A great thing," Juanita repeated. "Like what?"

Sahara clucked. "Heaven's going to give you another chantment, darling. I want it tomorrow." With that, she put her arm around the new arrival, leading her away.

Juanita strained to catch a few phrases of their conversation: ". . . back to Missouri. Seek my gifts in the usual places."

Twenty feet away, Ramón had dreamed up a coyote, was amiably walking around the desert with it, picking through flakes of obsidian, looking for Paiute arrowheads, the way he and she had when they were kids.

Juanita stepped past Sahara, and her brother smiled.

"Look—," he said.

Banging. She was awake, at Wendover. Someone was rapping on her door.

"Yeah?"

"Something's up—come to the TV room."

Throwing on a robe, she padded down the hall into a crowd of base personnel, automatically scanning for the judge before she remembered he'd be with the higher-ups.

"What is it?"

"Windstorm in St. Louis," said a pilot.

"*Contamination* in St. Louis," someone corrected.

"Shut up." A dour-looking lieutenant with a hearing aid grabbed the remote, turning on the TV's captions.

". . . a number of trees have grown to gigantic size . . ."

The contamination wasn't following the same pattern as in Oregon. There, the whole forest had sprung skyward, destroying everything on the ground and forming a solid mat of vegetation. In Missouri, the effects seemed spottier: mutated fish in the Mississippi were capsizing small boats. Tangles of contaminated vines grew within stands of healthy ones. Compared to Oregon, it was small stuff.

That hadn't kept people from panicking. Helicopter cameras showed refugees jamming the motorways, trying to get away.

"Alchemites," someone said. The newscast agreed: Sahara's disciples had already taken credit, promising to assist anyone who stayed to live "in harmony with the reclaimed Earth."

"Will they napalm?" Juanita asked. *Sahara said something to that woman, about seeking gifts in Missouri.*

"Like that's helped in Oregon," a law clerk snorted.

"Fire has kept the forest from spreading." That was the new guy, Gilead.

"Capturing Knax was supposed to put an end to this."

"Knax is a symptom of the disease," Gilead said. "Kill her, let her go tomorrow—it won't change a thing."

The clerk bristled. "So everything we've been doing here has been pointless?"

"Uncle Sam needed spin control. This trial's just a big show."

"Who asked you?" Juanita asked.

"Yeah, if Wendover's such a joke, why are you here?"

Landon's eyes flared like coals. "To do whatever needs doing."

"Very ominous. Answer the question." What was she doing? Provoking this guy would lead to trouble, and she needed to keep her head down. Gilead might sniff out her treachery.

To her surprise, he relaxed. "Sorry. I did some acting in college. Penchant for the dramatic, you know?" He launched into *Henry V.* "We few, we happy few . . ."

"Shakespeare, just what we need." Juanita turned back to the news.

Maybe Sahara's people could get rid of him, she thought.

A jolt went through her at the idea. Cooperating meant knuckling under. Crawling like a dog—and to save her own skin. She turned abruptly to the soda machine, getting a drink she didn't want, drowning a tar-rotten rush of self-loathing with a burning swallow of bubbles and artificial sweetener.

CHAPTER EIGHT

WRONG BED.

Will Forest drifted up from sleep, trying to place himself.

A whiff of antiseptic threw him back to his one on-the-job injury. He'd been cracked on the head by an especially agile junkie, had awakened in the hospital with his family around him.

Good days, before magic, before Caro metastasized into a stranger.

Groaning, he opened his eyes to confront his present self: sprawled, grimy, and unshaven, on a king-sized mattress in the Indigo Springs Grand Hotel. The room was cold; a draft blew under the door.

They hadn't saved the kids.

"Can't fall apart," he muttered. "Keep it together, keep it together. . . ."

An inner voice tut-tutted. Squeezing back the pain, refusing to deal, would eventually cost him. But what could he do? Nobody else would save Carson and Ellie.

He stripped, got in the shower, and only then discovered the bathroom had no running water. Standing there naked, filthy, and furious, it was all he could do not to punch the wall.

Struggling back into the previous day's clothes, he took the stairs down to the lobby. Teenagers were serving breakfast in the hotel café: he grabbed a boiled egg, a piece of toast, and a tomato and chewed automatically, tasting nothing.

"Thirsty?" chirped a floppy-haired skatepunk.

"Yes," Will said. As their eyes met, the magical wiki fed him information: The boy's mother had died giving birth to his younger sister. He'd asked Astrid to help him save women who might otherwise die the same way.

A chunk of letrico glimmered in the kid's pocket, powering a chantment that spun cups of steaming coffee.

"New arrival, right? How you feeling?"

My children are missing and I'm probably wanted for treason. He faked a smile. "All right, I guess . . . Paolo."

"Things get easier." He handed him a cup that got heavier as it filled itself.

"I'm okay." Will sipped. It was espresso—strong, scalding, and bitter. "Thank you for this. Any idea where Astrid is?"

"Greenhouse, maybe?" Paolo indicated the tuning fork on his wrist. "Ask Pike."

"Okay." Will headed across the lobby. A trio of researchers bubbled past, debating quantum entanglements, dark energy, and human willpower as they merged with a second clique, this one a handful of those who'd been gendermorphed by Ev. Both groups vanished into Bramblegate. Six engineers sat on two love seats near the hotel's revolving door, dividing their attention between the glassed-in TV playing trial coverage and a set of blueprints on the floor at their feet.

"Reporters are asking about you, Forest," one called. "Roche told 'em you're in the field."

"Uh . . . they buying it?"

"Nah—sightings of you are coming in across the world. You're the new Elvis."

"Just what I wanted." He glanced at the screen. Judge Skagway had a plastic toy in his massive hand. Wallstone was explaining what they knew—what Will himself had told them—about how chantments worked.

"William!" Over at the concierge's desk, Pike beamed out from behind two women in lab coats who were absorbed in a tin globe. "What can I do for ye this fair morning? Want to update your wiki entry? Merle's right over there with the Rolodex."

Will eyed the chantment and its elderly operator without enthusiasm. "Doesn't that waste power?"

"Helping everyone get to know each other?"

"Everyone knows me already. I'm the new Elvis."

"You have an unhealthy sense of your own importance, lad. How about a sample of the day's headlines?" The lab coats had moved on; Pike handed him the globe.

Will pushed it in a languid half circle with a fingertip . . . and immediately saw hundreds of newspapers.

"Focus on what you'd like to read."

"It's all the same, Pike." Magical contamination in St. Louis was front-page news worldwide. The president was calling it a terrorist attack, but insisted the damage was minor. The last desperate gasp of Sahara's cult, he called it.

"They're saying last night was Alchemites?"

"Age of Miracles," Pike replied. "Sahara's brand, not ours."

"Roche will go after them."

"So? Boss didn't ask 'em to claim responsibility."

In Missouri, the effort to burn contaminated plants and wildlife had been hampered by the storm and the gridlock on the highways out of the city. People would start ripping out their gardens and taking flamethrowers to their lawns, Will knew; in the early days of the catastrophe, he too had succumbed to that species of panic.

Dispersing the magic was a mistake.

He let go of the magic globe. "How do you know this thing is safe, Pike?"

"Medics put a couple of the news junkies through regular PET scans. No brain tumors."

"Yet." Could Astrid's so-called volunteers really know what they were doing?

"They can scan you too, or hey—don't use the globe. There's a stack of papers in the plaza, near the TV."

"No, it's fine."

"Good. Then why don't ye ask for a map of town?" Pike pointed at Merle again.

"A map?" Merle fluttered the Rolodex, and the geography of Bigtop snapped together in Will's mind. Astrid had given him a general tour, but this provided details: who worked in each tent, how the hospital was divided between Katarina's various science types and Janet's medics, the topography of the forest where the scavengers were currently working.

"What I want to know is where's Astrid."

"Power station," Pike said. The hospital's generator room, in other words. "Are you in a hurry?"

"Why?"

Pike handed over another chantment, a soap on a rope. "Shave and a haircut, if you know what I mean."

"Shave and a haircut," Will repeated. The letrico in his pocket fizzed, and the sense of being grimy, which he'd been stubbornly ignoring, dropped away.

Taking the soap back, Pike pointed at a mirrored pillar. The phrase was literally true—the shadow on Will's chin was gone, his hair was short, and his clothes were not only clean but also pressed. "You were getting a tad ripe. Next time—"

"Showers on the fourth floor here in the hotel, new clothes in the hospital laundry," Will said. "Got it. Thank you."

Crossing Bigtop, he went into the hospital. Down in the generator room, he found Olive's engineer boyfriend, Thunder, overseeing a group of new volunteers. He was teaching them to convert electricity into thin fibers of letrico, weaving up powerful balls of lambent fluff and then compressing them—Will thought again of crushed cotton candy—into crystals.

The training group was working with a small generator. Across the room, a second group was constructing a letrico boulder the size of a minivan.

When Will caught his eye and mouthed Astrid's name, Thunder held out both hands, waggling his fingers in an imitation of the gesture she used when chanting.

Will headed for the Chimney, but Astrid had already been and gone: volunteers were loading newly chanted items into shopping carts, hauling them to Bramblegate.

"Will!" That was Janet, the strike team medic. She and Clancy, the driver, stood at the edge of the vitagua reservoir. With them was a woman with tightly curled black hair, olive skin, and the huge eyes of a newborn infant.

"What's up?" Will said.

"New project," Janet replied, brandishing a set of dog tags inscribed with her name.

"You're not giving up on the strike team, are you?"

"Your kids are priority one," she said. "But the seers haven't found 'em yet."

"Priority one," he repeated.

"We'll go again as soon as we have a location."

"Yeah, right." Yesterday's optimism had leached away. They'd come close, true, closer than Roche had ever gotten. Will had seen with his own eyes that his son and daughter were healthy, unharmed.

But Ellie's terror at the sight of him . . .

Fury with Caro and Sahara warred with anxiety for his daughter. What had they done? What if Ellie never recovered?

"Igme and Aquino have restocked the trolley for another rescue attempt. In the meantime . . ." Janet jingled her dog tags. Rocky bits of rubble from the destroyed town began tumbling upward from the forest floor. With each jingle, the pile grew— until it was the size of a largish house.

"My turn." Grinning, Clancy pressed a beribboned Easter basket against the rockpile. It softened like clay, reorganizing itself into an imposing pyramid of concrete, brick, and asphalt champagne flutes.

"I'm Katarina." The curly-haired woman stuck her hand in Will's direction. She had a faint Russian accent.

"Will Forest. Astrid called you . . . Dean of Science?"

She guffawed. "Lofty title, yes?"

"Isn't it difficult to conduct research in a campground? Limited electricity, no water—"

"No computers," she agreed. "We only do easy stuff on-site."

"Easy?"

"How much does vitagua weigh, measure the freezing and boiling temperatures. Is it radioactive, does it carry electrical charge?"

"That's easy?"

"*Da,*" she said. "More complicated experiments I give to scientists outside the forest, people with real labs."

"Complicated like—"

"Oh . . . calculating the carbon uptake of the alchemized forest. Video of cell division in contaminated bacteria, how fast do embedded chantments absorb magic from the infected, why does this not work the same on everyone, what happens to blood glucose levels of people using chantments?"

"PET scans for the news junkies."

"Medics handle that, but I get copies of the scans. Everyone studies, everyone gets results. Then we figure out what it means." She beamed. "Which is the fun part."

"Ready," Janet said, and Katarina held out a hospital IV bag. She pointed the business end of the tubing at the champagne pyramid, and vitagua arced out of the ravine and into the bottommost glasses, flowing upward, filling the cups and, as far as Will could see, not spilling a drop.

"How does Astrid come up with this stuff?"

"This is my project," Janet said, voice a bit sharp.

"Sorry." Blue fluid oozed upward to the topmost champagne flute until they were all brimming. "What now?"

"Watch," Clancy said. The champagne flutes shivered. Their bases stretched and broke into sections—petals, really—that furled tightly over the open top of each "glass," sealing the vitagua inside even as they tumbled out of the pyramid formation, becoming a disorderly pile of eggplant-shaped rocks.

"Okay," Clancy said, satisfied. "Cart 'em up, give 'em to volunteers to scatter, and we're done."

"You're going to disperse them?" Will said.

"All round the world."

"Then what—they're timed to break, spreading alchemical contamination?"

"No timers," Janet said. "The natural process of erosion will random it up nicely without wasting energy."

"Isn't dispersing vitagua Astrid's problem?"

"You expect her to do everything?" Janet said.

"The more, the merrier," Clancy said.

That phrase again: it was some kind of inspeak, Will realized. "Speaking of Astrid, I'm trying to find her."

"Phone her," Clancy said.

"Pardon?"

Katarina raised her hand and spoke to a whistle hung round her wrist: "Astrid, where are you?"

The answer came back immediately: "Limbo."

"Limbo?" Will asked.

"The Grand Ballroom," Katarina said, even as the wiki dropped the same information into his mind.

"The ball—" He sighed. "Back to the hotel."

"Gotta move fast to catch the boss lady," Clancy chortled.

By now, Will had gotten the hang of getting around Bigtop: Pass through the nearest Bramblegate, step out in the plaza of the train station, and cross from there to the blue columns of vitagua. He stepped between them, murmuring "Ballroom."

He found himself in a hallway floored by antique flood-stained carpets and lined with ornate Victorian armchairs. Vases full of liquid magic lit the corridor, illuminating brass signs that named the conference rooms for flowers: ORCHID ROOM, LILAC LOUNGE.

A sound drew him to a set of open French doors. Beyond them was a patio, its safety rails broken and twisted, hemmed in by alchemized foliage. Olive Glade was out there, smoking a joint and staring at a black-and-white sketch of a woman. One of Jacks's pieces, Will thought, recognizing first the work and then the subject—a figure skater, from the U.S. national team.

Ellie had a similar poster up on her wall. She and Caro loved figure skating. . . .

Olive waved the card. "Tell me, Will. If the medics fix her wrecked ankle and she wins another gold medal, is it cheating?"

He shrugged. "Sports organizations regulate themselves, don't they?"

"You're saying leave the dilemma to the Olympic commit-tee?"

"They're going to have an opinion anyway."

"True enough." She added the card to a small pile.

"We're treating sports injuries now? Isn't that . . ."

"What, trivial?"

"A colossal waste of resources."

"The ankle injury's just a way in. We approach people with something they want, and then we ask for their assistance."

"You're bartering miracles?"

"Magic's fun, Will. Helping people, changing their lives—it's a rush. Most recruits end up volunteering full-time."

"What do you want with a figure skater?" he asked.

"There's a cluster of people from her skate club at risk." She fanned out a series of the pencil sketches. "The seers say that on Boomsday, they all die."

"Die how?"

"Dunno yet. If we can find out if it's a bus crash or avalanche—well, they're not skiers, that's not likely—or an outbreak of chol-era, we'll equip the skater so she can protect the group."

"Sounds a little like you're creating superheroes."

"Why not?"

"Isn't that dangerous?"

She shrugged. "We screen the recruits pretty carefully."

"Olive, what are you doing here?"

She blew skunky smoke into the thicket. "You know those old-looking women who turn up on the news now and then. . . . My kid's in jail, I worked twenty years to prove he's innocent, DNA evidence overturned the conviction, I knew it all along. . . ." She started to offer him the marijuana, then seemed to remem-ber he'd been a cop. "I think I've become that mom."

"Because Astrid thinks she can get Jacks back from the brink of death?"

"She'll do it." Her belief was rock solid.

Somehow, that made his own doubts more painful. "In the meantime, you save others?"

"It was find a purpose or wallow in despair," she said, tone pointed. "Not a tough choice."

He fingered the skater's portrait. "Jacks did these?"

"Yep." Reaching into a satchel, Olive produced a magic paintbrush. It was the first chantment Will had ever seen up close. The paintbrush was wrapped in a coil of fine copper wire, and it had a small plastic nub over its few remaining bristles.

"It's falling apart." He touched it gently. "I thought Astrid had toughened it up."

"She did what she could, but heavy use wears them out. Theory is it's the energy. Katarina's got a physicist in Santiago trying to figure out if electrons are actually moving through the objects, if it's friction or heat . . ."

"We saw wear and tear with a lot of Alchemite chantments," Will said. "Arthur complained that by the time he confiscated anything, it was too frail to use."

Olive's eyes darkened. "Rotten luck for him."

"Not a fan of Arthur's, I take it?"

"I take the napalm runs personally."

It was awkward: until yesterday, after all, Will had been with the people bombing the town. He turned to the skate club pictures. "So . . . thirty people at risk? That's not bad."

She gave him a strange look. "You were looking for Astrid, right? Boss," she told her pipe whistle, "Will's on his way."

He took the hint, continuing down the hall, wondering if she'd "phoned" Astrid out of courtesy or to warn her.

The ballroom was a long rectangle with an arched, coffered ceiling and alcoves that ran the length of the dance floor. It was gloriously ablaze with blue light—glasses, jars, even test tubes filled with liquid magic hung from the chandeliers.

The room was full of people, the biggest concentration of volunteers Will had seen yet, grouped around tables that lined the parquet dance floor, poring over more sketches. As his eyes roamed the crowd, the wiki filled in biographical data. One woman was contaminated; she'd been turning into a llama until Astrid treated her. The guy beside her, a doctor, had been cured of a drug habit that cost him his license. A trio nearby, lifelong friends, had come so that Ev could gendermorph them.

This was Olive's crew: the Lifeguards. Unsettled, he tried counting heads. There were hundreds of people.

"Morning!" Astrid passed a silver bracelet to a gangly man with dusky skin and facial tattoos before drawing Will off to the bandstand, out of the way. "How you feeling?"

If Olive had been warning Astrid—if she was hiding something—it didn't show. Then again, she'd always had a decent poker face. "Overwhelmed. What we did in St. Louis . . ."

"It's going good there. The windstorm didn't do much damage, and the rain and the break from the heat seem to have been appreciated. Power grid's mostly restored. The mass healing earned a lot of goodwill."

"Which is going to the Alchemites."

She shrugged.

"Astrid, about this agenda of spreading contamination willy-nilly—"

"Honestly, Will, it freaks me out too."

"Does it?"

"Of course," she said. "But we all went over and over it. The consensus was people should get used to living with magic before the Small Bang."

"It was a group decision?"

She nodded. "Also, some of the volunteers accused me of hoarding magic in America."

"Hoarding? Who would want to live this way?"

If she was insulted, it didn't show. "There's lots of personalities here, lots of opinions. Some of the volunteers are afraid of a future where the United States controls most of the vitagua and everyone else makes do."

"Is that likely?"

"No, it's not what happens," she said. "But let's talk about your kids. Your daughter didn't look happy to see you."

"She was terrified."

"It has to be magical," Astrid said. "Sahara did something to her."

"Or Caro did," Will said. He heard her again: *I would cut their throats myself.* "If we get our hands on Ellie, can you cure it?"

"We must, at some point. She's not scared in the After."

Predestination again. "Astrid, I'm not prepared to just rely on your prophecies."

"They promise your kids end up here, Will, with us."

"That couldn't be a lie?"

"They don't lie outright. Sometimes they withhold things, but every day, I learn a little more."

"How? You're scrambling from the hospital to the Bigtop to here, running like a maniac. You've got people filling rocks with vitagua and dumping them. It smacks of desperation."

"We save your kids," she said, irked. "They survive, they learn chanting. I hear 'em laughing in the forest and you, giving me a hard time about being a permissive stepmother—"

"Excuse me?"

She snapped her mouth shut, looking sheepish.

"You believe we're getting involved? Romantically involved?"

"The grumbles—"

"Astrid, as far as I'm concerned, your grumbles are full of it. They hold out on you; they got Jacks killed."

"I believe them," she said. "What else have I got?"

"Do you even like me?"

They had been speaking in low voices from the start, but now they were scrunched against the wall, as far from the volunteers as they could get, all but whispering.

"Well, I—," she said. "You're a good guy."

"High praise. Jacks was a good guy. You didn't want him."

"Could you stop smacking me in the face with Jacks?"

"You didn't want him, because of Sahara," Will said.

A dismissive huff: "That's over now."

"Is it?"

"Will, this is ridiculous."

"I'm ridiculous? I abandoned the law for this rinky-dink operation, and now it turns out you're grooming me to be your successor *and* your concubine."

She giggled a little, covering her mouth: it was her usual reaction to shock. "Look, some things are bound to happen. Like the sun burning out one day. Is that destiny? Science says it's inevitable. Or everyone dies—mortality."

"You're saying it's not if it happens, it's when and how."

"When and how are a huge deal, Will!"

"Even if the end result is the same?"

"Think about the Small Bang. We're releasing vitagua into the real as fast as we safely can."

"So that less of it comes when the well opens?"

"Less of it? No, Will. This isn't about another minor spill."

"Minor? Are you kidding me? Astrid, nothing about what's happened so far is minor."

"It might look that way when the well pops."

"The scale of contamination will be larger, I get that—"

"No, Will, you clearly don't," she said. "All the remaining magic is going to come out, into the real, all at once."

"All of it?" His breath caught. "The whole of the unreal?"

"Every last frozen drop." A bead of liquid magic welled up from the gold barbell pierced through the web of her thumb, misting into what looked like a mushroom cloud.

"Boomsday," he said, remembering Mark's word. "Small Bang. You said the smaller, the better. I thought that meant limiting the size of the next spill."

"Not the size, just the damage," Astrid said. "Will, I'm stomping the brakes on a runaway truck."

Will's mouth was dry. "Close the well."

"The Roused would freak. They might already have enough force of will to bust out."

"Because magic is desire," he said.

"Exactly. They seriously *desire* their freedom."

He grappled with that. All that magic. The first spill had been a catastrophe. Releasing it all . . .

"So we're back to predestination," he said at length. "Booms-day comes, I'm getting my kids back, you and I find true love, and I should just . . . what? Lie back and enjoy?"

"I'm not dumb, Will. I don't expect you to just assume the children will fall into your lap. Why do you think we're pursuing them?"

"Then what are you trying to say?"

She shook her head. "The sun burns out, everyone dies, the well blows . . . that's big, unstoppable. But we can have an effect. Shrinking the Small Bang by releasing vitagua up front. Giving people chantments so they can deal with the disasters."

"Deal how?" he asked.

"I'm making things that heal, stuff to dig through rubble, find survivors . . ."

"Rubble? Good God, Astrid—"

"We can reduce the casualties, Will. The Small Bang can be a stupid mess instead of a . . ."

"A what?"

"Horrific. A calamity." She swept an arm out, indicating the whole ballroom, and now he let himself really see the boxes on the dance floor, the snowdrifts of pencil sketches.

"Jacks made a picture of everyone who's going to die?"

"Everyone we can save, Will," Astrid countered. "And before you ask, your children survive, I know that. I know it."

Pictures in the thousands. Tens of thousands? His legs felt watery. "How many people are at risk?"

"Focus on this," she said. She led him past the bandstand and up a curving flight of stairs to the mezzanine. On the back wall, a collage of faces rose to the ceiling. He saw Olive Glade first, then Katarina. Unlike the pencil sketches, these were paintings, colored in and vibrant.

"This is the Big Picture," Astrid said. "It's everyone we saved already."

Will looked at the faces, thousands of them, lacquered to the wall. "There's more down there—is that Limbo?—than there are up here."

"That's why we need time. To get more vitagua out, more magicians in place."

"The more, the merrier. The more you save—that's what it means?"

"Yes."

"And these?" A few portraits were still black-and-white sketches. But before she could answer, he saw: "There's your dad. And Chief Lee."

"It's everyone who's died already."

He looked from one set of images to the other: the colored pictures of people they'd saved, the black-and-white of the dead and, below, all those people at risk. There must be some way to make it stop, stop it all, bring the old world back. Make his daughter whole, halt this insane runaway train and let all these endangered people off.

The tuning fork at his wrist hummed, not forming words, just wailing, like an air raid siren.

Astrid frowned. "That's weird."

Will pushed her to the floor, shielding her with his body. Jet engines tore the air, and molding fell from above, bouncing harmlessly off his back. A tickle rippled through him, the ring, protecting him from the impact, drawing energy from his chunk of letrico.

A shout: "Get Astrid to the plaza!"

"I'm okay," she called.

A second explosion jolted the building. Will dragged her to Bramblegate.

Within the ruin of the train station, the roar of planes was even louder. Hundreds of Astrid's volunteers were crossing the plaza, moving swiftly but without apparent fear as they vanished into the glow.

"Is there a bomb shelter?" he asked.

"We dig one," Astrid said, with that faraway look that meant she was listening to the grumbles. "Cave of wonders."

"Astrid—"

"Don't worry." She pointed at a muscular Latino—Jupiter, the Rolodex told him, one of a pair of formerly conjoined twins from Nicaragua—who stood atop a letrico boulder. He wore a catcher's mask and asbestos gloves. "Jupe's on Mark's defense team. There's no danger."

"Then where's everyone going?"

"Some volunteers go out to heal people or disperse chantments. Some go home."

He blinked. "You evacuate?"

"It's no fun getting bombed, so why not skip it?" She crooked a finger. "Come on, let's put this time to use."

She led him between the pillars, murmuring "Green Gate One," as they stepped into the glow and out into . . . a bank vault? Yes, definitely a vault. Its back wall was a gridwork of safe deposit boxes, all full of cached letrico. A steel door, slightly ajar, revealed six-inch steel walls. Bramblegate filled the corner, its thorny canes hung with hollow glass ornaments filled with vitagua. They gave the room a cool, oceanic glow.

Eight people sat around an eight-sided blackjack table. Mark was among them, as was Aquino, one of the gay guys from the strike team. A scattered selection of grenades and model airplanes were at hand, along with other chantments.

"Let me guess—a defense center?" Will asked.

Astrid nodded. "We call it the Octagon."

"Which is a secret." Mark shot Astrid a glare.

"It's not in the wiki," Will said.

"Yeah. Because it's a secret," Mark repeated.

Astrid ignored this. "What've we got?"

"The usual," he said. "Fighters with napalm."

"If it's the usual, how come they almost hit the Grand?"

"I guess the air force got itself some magic," Mark said.

Will thought fleetingly of the guy who'd just come to Wendover. *Gilead, he's called.*

"Can you send them off course?"

Aquino shook his head. "Pilots aren't falling for it."

"I don't want anyone hurt," Astrid said.

"God forbid we should curl one hair on their heads—they're only trying to kill us." Mark flicked Will a exasperated look. "Boss here wants a bloodless war."

"'Boss' is standing right here and wishes you'd stop calling it a war."

"Tell that to the USAF."

"It's okay," Aquino said. He was rolling a beeswax candle between his hands. "The planes aren't protected."

"Ready to drain their fuel tanks," said one of the others, a middle-aged Englishwoman who looked like she should be teaching grammar school.

"How's my rainstorm coming?" Mark said.

"Canopy's good and wet. Thunder sent out a team to draw some heat, so it's all fogging up. Temperature's dropping, wind's rising. Flying conditions are getting worse."

"Fires?"

"Eyes on the reservoir." A bamboo mat in the center of the blackjack table resolved into an image of a burning tree near the dam. "One blaze, almost out."

"Okay, damage the planes," Mark said. He shot an annoyed glance at Astrid. "Take it slow, so the pilots can break off." He scooped up one of the grenade chantments, drawing letrico.

"What's with the grenades?" Will asked under his breath.

"They're models," Astrid said. "Mark used to collect them. We found his house in the forest, practically intact."

"And military toys fit with the general theme of the Octagon?"

"They're his grenades, this is his project." Astrid's face held that listening look. "It's handy, Will . . . you use the Bramblegate grenade to bluff . . . someone?"

"Astrid, I need a break from the futuretalk," he said.

Jupiter's voice thrummed through a bass guitar hung over the blackjack table. "I've caught five incendiaries and parked 'em at the old fairgrounds. Where are we sending them?"

"Astrid?" Mark asked. "You spacing out, or what?"

"Empty out the bomb casings and fill them with vitagua," she said. "We'll leave them in a big leaky pile somewhere on our next run."

"You're doing another run?" Mark said.

"If we move faster, we might catch the kids. . . . Will, are you ready to try again?"

Was he? He could do one more run with the strike team, Will thought. If he got the kids back, he could go back to Wendover and throw himself on Arthur's mercy.

Fantasy or not, the idea that he might yet step back from this madness steadied him. Speaking to his tuning fork, Will called the seers. "Do we have a location on my children yet?"

"Saskatoon, Will," came the reply. "They're in Saskatoon."

CHAPTER NINE

DURING THE ST. LOUIS RAID, Astrid and her strike crew had freed about four dozen of the Roused from the glacier. Ev spent that night in the unreal drying clumped, icy vitagua out of their fur before turning them over to Patience, who was spinning up rose hip tea and strong black coffee. From there, the rescuees moved on to one of the few truly warm places in the unreal—a marble-lined pool filled with heated water.

It was crucial to warm them as fast as possible; having been frozen within iced vitagua for centuries, the newly Roused were at risk of hypothermia.

Centuries ago during the magical war, the Fyremen had laid a curse on vitagua, making it a contaminant. Anyone who came into contact with the raw magic got Frog Princed into an animal, usually losing their mind in the process. Astrid had found a way to reverse the effect, by taking a magical object and embedding it directly into the person. Embedded chantments drew contamination into themselves. It was a treatment, not a cure—like giving insulin to a diabetic.

A dime thus embedded in Ev's hand had arrested his devolution into a goat. The coin also let him turn people into whoever they might truly be, regardless of the body that nature had given them at birth. Gendermorphing, Mark had dubbed it.

Most of the Roused had opted to wait on getting a chantment embedded in them. They didn't consider themselves mad.

It had been something of a relief, as far as Ev was concerned—Astrid had more than enough demands on her time, and even though she was making chantments by the hundreds, they were precious, rare, and needed in the real.

He was helping the newly awakened—and struggling to keep

himself from mooning too obviously over Patience—when a nude man, seven feet tall, red of skin, with shaggy black hair and no visible signs of Frog Princing, pulled himself onto the glacier.

Ev stepped forward with a towel.

The newcomer whisked it out of his hand, drying himself efficiently. "Who are you supposed to be?"

"Ev Lethewood," he replied.

"Ah, father of the Savior. Our very own Virgin Harry."

Ev tried not to bristle. "Astrid is my daughter, yes."

"She send you to spy on us?"

"No."

"What, then? A show of good faith? Hey folks, I trust you—here's my mama."

Ev had not gotten used enough to being male to appreciate being reminded that he'd spent fifty-five years as a woman. But he was here as a diplomat, so . . . "You got a name?"

"Call me Teoquan," the newcomer said.

"Tay oh kwan," Ev repeated, trying to get the odd vowels right. Judging from the contempt on Teoquan's face, he'd messed it up. "There's tea over there, and hot baths. . . ."

"Yeahyeahyeah. Tell your brat that if she's expecting gratitude, she'll have to do better than drinks and a pool party." With that, he strode over to Patience, kissing her hand. She laughed, tipping a curtsy.

Ten hours passed before the last rescuee was out of the Pit. As the effort wound down, Patience brought Ev a cup of tea. Everyone was drooping. The raccoon granny, Eliza, curled around a cedar branch poked above the level of the ice. Her open eyes were glazed with exhaustion.

"We'll ask about seeing Jacks once everyone's rested," Patience murmured.

"Think they'll say yes?"

"We've earned some goodwill by pitching in," she said. "What you figure, Ev? Fifty people tonight?"

"Yeah. Fifty new mouths to feed. There's no resources here: Astrid was right about their needing a letrico mill," Ev said.

"I'll talk to Eliza," she said, yawning.

"She can free up some bodies, I have other ideas on—"

"Please, Ev, rein in the Lethewood work ethic until I've had some sleep," Patience said. "They'll be just as impressed—or not— tomorrow."

Feeling his face warming, he took refuge in a gruff nod.

She raised her voice: "Where'd our stuff end up?"

A field mouse with glossy black hair piped at them. Rather than translate, Patience just gestured: *Follow me.*

Ev fell into step beside her, tracking the mouse up through hollow, bamboo-textured stems that served as corridors, to a suite of egg-shaped rooms halfway up the honeycombed skyscraper. Their things had been unpacked into silk hammocks that hung from the ceilings. The walls were gold wax, and mattresses of moss lay on the floor of each room.

Ev fished out his old dulcimer and plucked a string, dictating a quick report for Astrid: Arrived safe, Jacks won't go free until everyone else is loose. He struggled to summarize what the cricket had told them about the unreal being key to how Bramblegate worked. He wrapped that up with: "Maybe Katarina could send someone to talk to them about it?"

With that, he staggered to bed.

"Night, Ev," Patience's voice wafted from the next room.

"Good night," he echoed, falling into dreams of turtle girls and winged boys and an endless glare of blue light.

CHAPTER TEN

CHASING WILL'S KIDS WOULD have to wait until after the bombing raid was over, so Astrid decided to try distracting him.

One of her volunteers was a TV actor. He'd opened up his apartment in Los Angeles to anyone who wanted a comfortable place to wait out the bombing raids.

She and Will arrived to find a dozen volunteers in the home theater, watching Sahara's trial. They sprawled on the couches, enjoying the air-conditioning, munching chips, and following the coverage while waiting for Mark to declare an all clear.

"Defense lawyers promised the Alchemites would behave if they could come back in the courtroom," a volunteer explained. The prisoners were filing in now. Sahara was last, accompanied as always by the woman who seemed to be her personal guard.

"What do you know about that marshal?" Astrid asked Will.

"Why, boss? Got a crush?" Pike crooned.

"I know I do," someone said. "Sista looks like a cross between a flamenco dancer and Buffy."

"I'd do her," one of the engineers agreed.

"I don't have a crush," Astrid protested, her face warming.

"A woman like you should be using her power to get laid, lass," Pike said.

"I'm ignoring you all," she said. "Will? The marshal?"

"Juanita? Army brat, from a big family. She was handpicked by the judge, I think; they're both from Nevada Federal Court. Are you thinking of recruiting her?"

"Would it work?"

"I doubt it. She's loyal to Skagway."

She filed away the information. Juanita Corazón was important, a piece of the puzzle.

Sahara was on-screen now, pursing her lips at the camera, *smooch-smooch-smooch.* Acting insane, Astrid thought. There had to be something, even now, didn't there? Some core, buried deep, that could be touched by reason or compassion?

The camera panned the defense table, homing in on Caro Forest. Will flinched slightly.

Astrid slipped out to the patio, looking out at the Pacific Ocean and listening for the grumbles. She could hear Will's children, somewhere up after the Small Bang, laughing.

She should never have told Will that they'd become lovers. It sounded deranged.

The thing was, she did like him. He'd always been so kind to her, so gentle and fair.

That was just his job, argued one of her interior voices. It was the nasty one, the voice of doubt. *Getting you to trust him was something he did for Roche. It was an interrogation, remember?*

No, it was more. He was decent.

Yeah. Decent. That's sexy.

She pushed away the whirl of skepticism. Taking out a rubber stamp and some letrico, she pressed the stamp repeatedly against the wall. Each impression created a glowing white outline of a caterpillar. They moved, nibbling at the letrico, forming chrysalises, then breaking out a minute later, as real-looking butterflies—mourning cloaks.

Astrid cupped her hand, allowing vitagua to well from the piercing in the web of her thumb. The magical butterflies lapped tiny drops of the vitagua, then fluttered off. They would lodge in trees, land in gardens, or get eaten by birds and spiders. Each would transmit a microscopic bit of enchantment.

She worked for an hour, hoping the whole while that Will would join her, maybe say something to ease the awkwardness.

What's keeping you from going to find him?

"I'd just make matters worse," she said aloud.

You want him to believe you care for him? You gotta show it.

Maybe it would be easier if she just shelved the romance idea. He wasn't wrong: The grumbles had misled her before.

Someone tapped at the patio door—Pike. "Mark says it's safe to go home. Want to come check out the damage?"

"Coming," she said, rejoining the group as they filed through Bramblegate.

It was the first time the napalm had gotten close. Rainwater poured in through an ugly burn in the canopy, and there was a scorched-looking crater in one of the islands of rubble. Dense lilac-scented smoke hung in the air. Singed remnants of a silk tent blew to and fro.

Astrid said: "Mark's right. They're fighting magic with magic now."

"Arthur's got a new consultant," Will said. "A Fyreman. Guy seemed to understand that you're a bigger threat than Sahara."

She felt a thrill of fear. "And I guess Roche is angry that you defected."

"Yes. I'm sure my desertion hurt him."

Broken friendships. She sighed. "At least everyone's okay."

"They aren't," Will said.

She turned, following his gaze. A body was lying just under the sawdust-and-vitagua surface of the lagoon.

Parting the vitagua, she exposed the corpse: a girl of maybe sixteen years. She had the features of a fox, and her red-furred face was slack, almost serene. She might have been sleeping, but for the torn clothes and the deep gash in her leg.

"She must've been hiding in the forest." That was Olive; she had appeared beside them, holding Jacks's card-sized black-and-white portrait of the girl.

Astrid took the body's still-warm hand. *Jacks bled out,* she thought, fighting tears.

"Is it too late to save her?" Olive asked.

"Yes, she's gone." She was crying now.

A grumble whispered: *Red blood, blue magic*—

"You didn't kill her," Will said, drowning out whatever it might have said. "You're trying to minimize the carnage."

"So many planes, all those explosives, only one death . . ."

"Exactly."

It didn't help. "Poor kid. She must have been so scared."

"So what do we do?" Olive's voice was harsh.

"Clean up, get everyone back to work?" She wiped at her face.

"Not enough." Olive jerked off her cardigan, covering the body.

Will let out an odd, incredulous bark of laughter. "Are you accusing Astrid of slacking?"

There's that fairness again. Will might be angry with her, but he was defending her anyway.

She had the weight of the world on her shoulders, so many people expecting her to be politician, priest, big sister, boss. Olive furious about every death, Roche and his bombers, a Fyreman involved now, and the Roused pushing her to speed up the contamination. She thought of the Ballroom, the room full of pictures of people she hadn't yet saved . . . or lost. Small wonder the volunteers had taken to calling it Limbo.

"Pike?" she said.

"Aye, boss?"

"Have the medics set space aside in the hospital for a morgue, and schedule a funeral."

"Done."

"Olive, find out who she was, get her cleaned and dressed, see if she has family." Standing, she took in the crowd of Springers forming around the body. "Okay. Time we started dispersing the vitagua faster. Suggestions?"

"Freeze it in chunks and tuck it into glaciers?"

"What's your name?"

"Dorrie."

She said, "Put a crew together, Dorrie, get on it."

Thunder coughed. "There's a new guy, Ilya, on the letrico crew. He thinks we can build a pipeline underground."

"How would that work?"

"He's a coal miner, geologist . . . something. Says if we dig an underground river, we can tunnel out of the contaminated zone. Vitagua can flow through the shafts. Digging's energy intensive, but there'd be no air release, comparatively few contaminated animals. Magic could just seep into the stratum."

"Tunneling—that's a lot of displaced rock," Astrid said.

"We'll find a use for it."

Four young men had eased the girl's body onto a sheet of silk from a shattered tent. Now they each took up a corner, lifting her. The crowd fell silent, parting as they bore the corpse to the hospital.

Olive brandished a bloodstained wallet from her pocket. "Libby Wilson. Fifteen years old."

Fifteen. "Who dropped this bomb? Where's the pilot from?"

One of the seers replied: "Maryland."

"Find me a beach in Maryland, Pike." She reached out to the ravine, scooping up as much vitagua as she could and stepping through Bramblegate.

Will rushed after her. "What are you doing?"

"Got it, boss." Pike's voice buzzed. "Assateague Island National Seashore."

"Stop calling me boss." She stomped into the glow. Sea air embraced her, and a herd of wild horses spooked, fleeing north. Bramblegate grew out of the beach, spraying sand.

"Astrid . . ." Will appeared beside her. "Don't do this."

Vitagua was vulnerable to seawater, but there was plenty of life on the beach. She sprayed liquid magic into the salt marsh grass, into kelp thrown up by the tide. She brushed the birds: egrets and herons, gulls without number, a peregrine falcon roosting in a nearby tree. She contaminated a copse of small wind-blasted shrubs, a stand of pine, and then sent the rest of the vitagua rolling inland as a glowing blue fogbank to the limits of her sight, over the surface of the sand.

Clouds of contaminated ticks and mosquitoes rose from the grasses. Clumped starfish in a tidal pool began to bloat and stretch. Ghost and horseshoe crabs by the hundreds, unseen when she had begun, grew into dog-sized monstrosities.

"Astrid, stop! This is retaliation. You're acting like a terrorist—"

"Why not? I'm a murderer, aren't I?"

"Does this make you feel better about the dead girl?"

"It's not about . . ." But it was: she was angry, out of control. "I'm sorry."

He understood: She could see it.

"This was stupid." The horses had doubled in size. Blue patches of hair marked their coats and manes. "We hit St. Louis, Roche hits us, I do this. Tit for tat. Stupid, stupid."

"You can't afford to lose your temper, Astrid. Too much is riding on you."

The understatement made her burst into tears. Will hesitated just a moment before he opened his arms. She let herself lean in and cry.

He's kind, she thought again.

"I know you're having a tough day," he said eventually. "But I want to go after my kids before the Alchemites move on."

Of course. It was the interrogation all over again. He wasn't comforting her because he cared; he was keeping her on task.

Buck up, she told herself. *Of course he's tunnel-visioned on the kids. Forget the romance prophecies and get to work.* "Canada, right?"

"Saskatoon, Saskatchewan."

"Astrid." Their tuning forks were abuzz. "Come back, lass, or we're sending the strike team."

"We're on our way," Will said. He dried her eyes, then gestured at Bramblegate. "After you."

Bracing herself, she stepped into the plaza. A crowd waited, volunteers packed around the trolley. For once, nobody was glued to the big TV with Sahara's trial on it.

Mark spoke for them all. "You can't take risks like that."

"She's not hurt," Will said.

"This time," Mark insisted.

Astrid reined in an impulse to run back into the glow, to flee all this attention and the burden too. Instead she met Mark's mismatched eyes. "I didn't mean to scare anyone."

"You're the key to this whole operation," Clancy huffed.

"I'm sorry," Astrid said. "Let's just get back to work, okay?"

Mock groans and laughter rippled across the plaza.

"Come on," she said. "Are we saving the world or not?"

"More the merrier!" someone shouted back.

"Good!" She reached for Mark, giving him a friendly squeeze, showing solidarity. "We're heading out after the kids. But I want a plan for that idea about hiding vitagua in glaciers. Was that Dorrie's idea?"

"You want it right this second?"

"First thing in the morning."

The woman gave her the thumbs-up and waved to a trio of volunteers, leading them away.

"And Thunder, set up a meet with this guy who says we can dig an underground river."

He nodded. "It'd help if someone could teach him English."

She picked a Frisbee off the nearest bench, chanting it while concentrating on the idea of language lessons, instant fluency. "Presto. Go learn him up."

"Abracadabra," he replied, cheerfully, twirling the Frisbee as he headed for the glow. Around the plaza, she could hear the tuning forks buzzing, transmitting her orders.

"It'll be enough," she murmured. "It has to be."

CHAPTER ELEVEN

"IS SAHARA KNAX A god?"

A couple days had passed since Juanita slipped Sahara the latest chantment, a ladybug, bringing the total number of chantments hidden in her cell to three. Three crimes, three betrayals. So far, Wendover hadn't crumbled to dust or been obliterated by a plague of locusts. The trial was continuing in almost humdrum fashion, bound up in procedural arguments.

Today, though, the atmosphere was tense.

The Alchemite lawyers had petitioned to get their clients back in the courtroom, and so far they'd behaved. Sitting in a double row at the defense table, they looked vulnerable and beaten down. Some slumped in their chairs like bored schoolchildren. Caro Forest kept scanning the galleries, presumably looking for her husband.

Lucius Landon, today's witness, was a nerdier version of the firefighter, Gilead, who now shadowed General Roche's every step. He dressed like a young academic, someone you'd expect to see teaching chemistry labs to university freshmen. When he was introduced as a magical expert, Sahara leaned forward, lips slightly parted.

In response to Wallstone's question, Landon said: "Sahara Knax is not divine. She's David Koresh, Charles Manson . . . but on a different scale."

"Meaning?"

"Knax escaped from Indigo Springs with a collection of magical objects. Using these items to create an illusion of godlike power, she developed a following of gullible believers."

A hiss from the defendants' table. Skagway shot them a glance that could've frozen blood, and they quieted.

"So there's no spiritual foundation for the Alchemite religion?"

"Knax has drawn her so-called prime lessons from legitimate sources," Landon said. "She's pilfered Wiccan teachings and exploited widespread public concern for the environment. But her disciples, the religious practice—it's Sahara-worship, pure and simple. The people she's attracted aren't interested in profound spiritual practice. She's offering easy answers and magical power. That's what these snake oil vendors do."

"Sahara's followers claim she has guided them to troves of holy artifacts," Wallstone said. "Items she laid aside decades ago for use in their rebellion against the government."

"Decades ago?" Landon repeated. "When she was . . . what, ten?" The gallery chuckled, and the witness shook his head. "As long as magical objects—chantments—have existed, there have been chantment thieves. Knax is a gifted thief. It doesn't make her a deity."

"And the sea monsters she claims to have created?"

"Raw magic befouls living things, afflicting them with giantism and mutations." Using a remote control, he brought up a time-lapse sequence of an ant blundering into a droplet of luminescent blue fluid, and subsequently growing to the size of a handbag. "Imagine what would happen if you exposed a blue whale, or a giant squid."

"The monsters are alchemically contaminated sea life?"

"That's all they are."

Wallstone asked: "What about the icebergs created when the Alchemites destroyed the *Vigilant*?"

"Using a chantment to work magic requires energy; it's no different from technology in that regard. The Alchemites drew heat out of the ocean near the carrier. The icebergs were a side effect of the sinking. Anyone could do the same."

"So her powers aren't special, her philosophy is hollow, and her so-called miracles are a side effect of chantment use?"

"That's about the size of it."

"Is what Sahara Knax has done against the law?"

"Objection," defense counsel said laconically. "Witness isn't a lawyer, Your Honor."

"Sustained."

Lucius locked eyes with the attorney. "It's morally wrong. Isn't that enough? As for unlawful, that's a no-brainer."

"How so? It's not illegal to propogate magic," Wallstone said.

"There are laws against contaminating the environment and poisoning people, aren't there? Against terrorism? Knax openly boasts of having caused earthquakes and wildfires. Tens of thousands were displaced by the contaminated forest. They lost their homes, lost everything. And maybe I'm no lawyer, but sinking the *Vigilant* was certainly against the law."

Sahara snorted, too softly for the judge to hear. Juanita resisted an urge to flick the back of her head.

"Let's move on. The defendants are using a necessity defense. They claim their crimes are justified because they demonstrate magic's potential to reverse climate change."

"And Sahara Knax knows how to carry that off? She's a radio deejay. How much sea life died as a result of her actions?" Lucius Landon clicked the remote, bringing up a shot of the wreckage of the carrier, surrounded by ice floes, a fuel slick, and dead gulls.

"Still. Drawing heat from the sea, right when the oceans are heating up and the Antarctic ice sheet is shrinking—"

"Randomly creating massive icebergs could make things worse. What if they cool things down so much that it affects the North Atlantic current?"

"Is that possible?"

Landon directed his response to the camera, to the viewing audience. "A large enough casting, unchecked, could trigger an ice age."

"Earth survived the ice ages," Wallstone said, pressing the point further.

"How well do you think humanity will do if one hits us all at once?"

"And global warming?"

"Sir, we know how to slow climate change. We knew before the magical spill."

"Is there no way magic can be used to restore balance to the world?" Wallstone said.

"Objection." The Alchemite lawyer rose. "Calls for speculation."

"Your Honor," "Wallstone said. "This witness has experience with vitagua and magical chantments, as well as a master's degree in physics."

"I'll allow it," Skagway said.

"False prophets like Sahara Knax prey upon human weakness," Lucius Landon said. "It's natural for us to wish for a painless way out of the world's ecological problems. But if there were a quick fix, she'd have done it already."

False prophet, Juanita thought. The archaic-sounding phrase struck a chord. She remembered Sahara's prediction from the other night: *You'll be a believer, you'll be in Indigo Springs with me at the end.*

False prophecies. Garbage, in other words. The words were comforting. They cut Sahara down to size.

Wallstone continued playing devil's advocate: "Magic shouldn't be used to feed people, cure epidemics, relieve droughts?"

"Since when do we allow churches and amateurs to decide what society's problems are, or how to solve them?"

"Ever hear of a soup kitchen, man?" one defendant called.

"Order," Skagway said. "Young man, I won't warn you again."

"All right," Wallstone said, "what if governments and experts wanted to employ magic in taking on society's problems?"

"There are responsible ways to channel magic."

"Such as?"

Landon produced a vial of coffee-colored fluid. "This is a potion."

"A magical potion?"

"Yes. It was produced in a controlled environment and produces a limited magical outcome."

"Now who's the false prophet?" Sahara rose, sliding Juanita a wink. "Sorry, Your Honor—I can't let this pass."

The ladybug chantment was in her hand.

Juanita was on her feet, weapon drawn, safety off, adrenaline pumping.

Suddenly the room was full of starlings, hundreds of birds whirling above the ceiling. They were shrieking, their characteristic *snnk-snkk* noise rasping through Juanita's skull like a hacksaw.

"It's all right, my darlings," Sahara said. "Everything is absolutely fine."

And it was. Juanita hesitated. Her arm fell to her side, and she relaxed. For the first time in weeks—months—she felt safe. Looking at Sahara, she felt an upwelling of love.

"Gladys, dear," Sahara said. "Unlock my friends, will you?"

Gladys scurried to comply. The Alchemites raised their hands to be uncuffed; they had their heads lowered and their lips were moving. *We should all be praying*, Juanita thought, but she couldn't take her eyes off Sahara.

She was getting woozy.

That was all right. Sahara would take care of everything.

"Stay with me," Sahara ordered the camera operator at the back of the courtroom. She sauntered to the witness box, plucking the potion from the hand of the witness.

Landon didn't object. He looked a bit green. *Good*, Juanita thought; now she hated both of them, these two Landon men with their Goddess-hating rants. . . .

Sahara spoke: "Children of the technofilth, you have done me great harm. Here I sit, chained, beaten down—"

Cries of outrage rippled through the courtroom.

That's a lie. Juanita felt a tickle of defensiveness.

"You foul my air, burn my sacred groves, devour my creatures, and persecute my followers."

We never beat you, Juanita thought. Her head cleared a little. Her knee trembled with the effort of holding her weight. Her right hand, her gun hand, was getting heavy. One of the older lawyers had sunk into a chair.

"Let me finish what I have begun. I will return to my sacred

grove and bestow enchantment upon you all. This man lies! I
can end food shortages, fix the weather, eliminate racism and religious strife—"

Juanita's heart fluttered, captivated by the sight of Sahara,
aglow, divine. Yet . . .

False prophet, the inner voice repeated.

"I offer peace of mind, good health, and prosperity," Sahara
said. Birds settled in a carpet around her, covering the floor, the
tables, soiling the paperwork of the trial.

She's weeping, Juanita thought. *We made her cry, we broke her
heart.* She gasped for air, chest aching with every breath. The old
lawyer had lost consciousness.

"My oppressors will pay." Sahara wiped a hand over her teary
face, creating a blue-red smear on her skin. She placed her palm
against the cheek of the prosecutor.

Wallstone staggered back, clawing at his face. Feathers sprouted
from his jaw.

Blood and vitagua in Sahara's tears, the rebellious, unbeliev-
ing part of Juanita whispered. *She's infected him, and she's killing
us, vamping our life force to power the ladybug.*

Wallstone choked, a deep anguished sound.

A familiar, gut-deep tearing within Juanita's psyche: She
wanted to believe . . . she'd been rudderless for so long. . . .

Sahara wiped her face again, starting toward the judge.

No. Juanita strained to move the only muscle she could. She
pulled the trigger on her service weapon. The ear-shattering bang
startled everyone. She felt the shock of the bullet hitting the floor.

A few of the defendants faltered in their prayers.

It was enough. Judge Skagway wrenched his chair back, beyond Sahara's poisoned, outstretched hand.

Glass tinkled, barely audible over the prosecutor's shrieks. Then
there was a loud *whump*, like a gas stove igniting, a rush of heat.
Juanita's stomach flipped; she gagged, expecting to inhale a reek of
burnt feathers—but the birds were gone.

And Sahara was just Prisoner One again. Red plastic slag—
the ladybug chantment—dripped from her fingers.

"Thank God," Juanita muttered. For once, saying it didn't make her feel like a hypocrite.

She crossed the floor to Sahara, who was shouting at the camera. "You will release me! It's only a matter of time!"

"It's over, Sahara, cut it out," Juanita said.

The observers in the viewing gallery were pale; a few had fainted. Roche was performing CPR on the fallen lawyer.

"Damn," Sahara said. "I thought we'd got to my big escape."

"No such luck," Juanita said.

"Fireworks ain't quite over." Sahara grinned.

The prosecutor, Wallstone, wheeled suddenly on the witness. "Tell me, Mr. Landon—"

Judge Skagway broke in. "We're out of session, Counsel."

Wallstone bulldozed on, "Do you believe you can oppose the will of the Goddess?" His voice, Juanita realized, was Sahara's. He stepped toward the jury, provoking cries of fear.

Gilead Landon put himself between them, sparks sizzling on his burned palms.

"You are Befouled," he said, looking past Wallstone, addressing Sahara. "You're sick."

Wallstone lunged at him. His rapidly growing hair had starling markings. "I am everywhere and nowhere, I am the mountain and the grain of sand, I am—"

Gilead threw the prosecutor, deftly laying him out on the floor, where, pinned, he continued to twist and change. His features were shifting, his face becoming like Sahara's.

The witness, Lucius Landon, stepped out of the box and put a hand on Sahara's neck. She swooned. The courtroom fell silent.

"You saved our asses there," he said to Juanita, sotto voce, as the two of them lowered the prisoner to the ground.

Juanita's heart sank. What would the Alchemites do to her family now?

"You must be real fond of that old man." Gilead Landon had joined them. "Nobody else managed to resist the spell."

Juanita's eyes dropped to Sahara. Definitely unconscious. What to do? "We need to talk," she whispered.

Gilead held out a cheap-looking glass pendant—a flame—on a steel chain, waiting until she put her hand out, palm up, and then dropping it into her grasp.

"What's this?"

"Sea-glass," he said. "Reacts with vitagua. If you'd been Befouled, it would burn."

"Do I pass?"

He nodded ever so slightly. "I have an office in the old hangar. Meet me there after this mess is all sorted. Keep the pendant." With that, he drew his . . . cousin? brother? . . . aside.

"Corazón!"

"Coming, Your Honor." She handed Sahara over to Gladys and headed for the bench. "You all right, sir?"

"Yeah." The judge didn't look okay: he looked sick. "They vamped us. We need a round of the high-carb milk shakes."

"Maybe someone here has a protein bar for you—"

"Those things are foul, Corazón. I'm hitting the stash of cookies in my chambers."

"You judges and your perks."

"I'm an important guy, Marshal."

"Yeah," she said, "you are."

His eye fell on Wallstone. "That could've been me."

Juanita nodded. "We got lucky."

"That's another of your nine lives." He gave her a fond grin. "Get these troublemakers locked up, will you?"

Locking up the prisoners, getting calories into everyone who'd been vamped, and moving Wallstone into medical isolation took over an hour. Getting her station covered and freeing up some time took another. When Juanita finally crossed the hangar to Gilead's office, though, he was waiting.

He had an office in the administration building. It had a churchy smell of incense and burnt wax, and its door was encrusted with dull glass tiles. Sea-glass, Juanita guessed, like the pendant he'd given her.

"Watch your step," he said as she came inside. A thick chain of glass lumps had been nailed in place around the perimeter of the room. "I don't have long. Roche has called a meeting to see if anyone can figure out how Sahara got that ladybug chantment."

"What are the chances of that?" she asked.

"Hard to say. Someone's helping her. That much is obvious."

She eyed the crystals. Black and white powder clung to the irregular beads, dulling their surfaces. "Is that salt?"

"We call it rosarite," he replied. "It's a holy chain made of sea salt, sea-glass, and gunpowder."

"What's it for?"

"Creates a sacred space. Magic won't work here."

"Could you do this to the courthouse?"

"Sanctify it?"

"Is that what you call it?"

"Ah, you're offended. Disenchant, then."

"I'm not offended," she lied.

"You Catholic?"

"Ex. Can you?"

"I could do the whole base."

"Why haven't you? If it would've prevented Sahara's outburst."

Gilead let out a long sigh. "Nobody consulted us when they set this place up."

"Sahara got the drop on us all." And it was her fault, Juanita thought.

"We looked like bozos," Gilead agreed. "Lucius was meant to present alternatives to Alchemism."

"To the jury or the viewing public?"

"Both. Sahara's stunt blew our whole show."

"She has a great sense of theater," Juanita said. "So . . . about this rosarite stuff."

"The problem is I'm here in an unofficial capacity. The general's taken a few of my suggestions, but . . ."

"But?"

He seemed to weigh whether he should go on, and then grimaced. "I screwed up. Suggested a precision strike on Indigo Springs, told him I could protect the air force."

"And?"

"Astrid Lethewood has been messing with the pilots, sending their planes off course. It's a parlor trick—it doesn't take much power. She's squeamish about killing people, you see."

"Gosh, that's rotten of her," she said sarcastically.

"Oh, she's no saint. I gave each pilot a potion, to protect them. But I underestimated her power resources. She had enough juice to sabotage the planes."

"Couldn't you protect them too?"

"Wrapping a precision flying machine in rosarite's not really feasible."

"Anyone die?"

He shook his head. "She did millions in damage to the hardware. Roche is in trouble with the joint chiefs, so I'm in trouble with him."

"Well . . . Lethewood's not going anywhere, is she?" she said. "Seems to me Sahara's the bigger problem."

"You saw what happened in St. Louis."

"That was Alchemites."

He shook his head. "Sahara's just taking credit."

"Why are you telling me this?"

"You're tight with the judge. If he tells Roche to disenchant the base . . ."

He might be willing to order it. "The chantments would stop working?"

"Yes."

"Sorry, I'm missing something. I get that Roche is pissed at you, but to the extent of leaving the base vulnerable? Wouldn't he want the place magic-proofed?"

"You forget—the government's in the chantment-stealing business too. Roche has confiscated magic from the Alchemites. They're useful; he likes them."

"So if I convince the judge and he orders you to . . . disenchant the base, the magic stops working?"

"That's it in a nutshell."

And with the chantments out of commission, maybe Juanita could report Heaven. Something could be done to protect her family.

"Well?" Gilead asked.

"If I put my neck on the line for you, I want something."

"Like?"

"Teach me how you fight them."

He winced.

"Problem?"

"There aren't any women in the Brigade."

"You have got to be kidding me."

He sighed, leaning on his desk. "Our prophets say that when the End of Days is upon us, our fate passes to a Lady of Lies."

"Sahara?"

"No, Astrid Lethewood," he said. "Knax is merely a hand-maiden."

"Handmaiden? Sahara hates Astrid Lethewood."

"Yet she serves Indigo Springs, in her way."

"How so?"

"She's spreading magic, isn't she?"

"She's not doing it for Lethewood."

"America's watching the rook and ignoring the queen."

"I'm not much for chess, and it shouldn't stun you to hear that I'm in favor of bringing criminals to trial," Juanita said. "It was Sahara who sank the *Vigilant,* after all. What's this about a Lady of Lies? Why can't I learn to fight chanters?"

He pulled an ancient-looking book from a locked drawer, reading: "The Lady will strike down our greatest warrior, thereby sealing the fate of the world."

"Because of this, you don't let girls in your club?"

"Medieval, huh?" He had the grace to look embarrassed. "Lee Glade is dead. Lethewood killed him. It translates, 'he is blind to her nature, and she strikes him in a moment of weakness.'"

"Does that fit with what happened to Glade?"

"As far as we know. Lee was—" He lit up. "You should've seen him. Greatest of us all, no doubt in my mind."

Gilead was sure the prediction had come true. For centuries, he explained, his Brigade had excluded women, assuming the threat would come from within. It was typical biblical sexism: Eve and the serpent, women as the root of sin.

"It's an old society, Juanita. The men of the Middle Ages weren't feminists."

"I suppose you are?"

"I've been wanting an opportunity to talk to my uncles. If the prophecy's come to pass, why not recruit women? You're perfect. Having a member of the Brigade close to Knax and—"

"And who?"

"I'll see what I can do. It won't hurt that you're a good Catholic girl. Sorry, ex-Catholic."

"Mamá would be so proud," she said dryly. Knax and who? The only person at Wendover she might be called close to was . . .

The judge.

That night she made it to Ramón, in dreams, for a scant minute. He was wandering an old-looking version of Paris, watching horse-drawn carriages clip-clop past on a stone bridge. He raised a hand in greeting.

Then Sahara turned up: "So, darling, you're buddying up to Roche's new best friend?"

"He gave me hell for letting you pull that stunt in court today," Juanita said. "I asked to learn his brand of magic."

"Sounds like you've forgotten which team you're on."

"Me, forget?" She looked at her brother pointedly. He was flirting with a woman Juanita recognized from his unit.

"Being surly won't change your situation."

"You made me look bad today, Sahara. I took an opportunity to cover my ass."

"Opportunity? To cozy up to a guy who wants to burn me?"

"What was I supposed to say: 'You're right, I'm incompetent, fire me'?"

"You won't be fired, darling. We're together at the end—"

"Whatever that means."

"As for your consorting with the enemy—"

"Aren't you curious about those potions they were waving around in court, Sahara? Gilead's the one who knows about them."

Sahara pursed her lips. "All right, see what you can find out. And Juanita?"

"Yes?"

"I haven't forgotten that it was you who broke my spell today." With a sound of wingbeats, she was gone.

Sahara's departure jolted her awake. She sat up in bed, taking deep breaths, fingering the sea-glass pendant as she battled with the fear.

CHAPTER TWELVE

THE NEWS WAS ON, as it always was, in the old train station, the oak benches facing the glassed-in television occupied by an assortment of volunteers who were taking a break from saving the world to catch up on developments at Wendover.

As Will stepped out of Bramblegate, he paused behind the benches. On-screen, Sahara's outburst was replaying in slow motion. "Any word on Wallstone?"

"He's contaminated and compromised. The junior guy's replacing him at trial. The show will go on."

"That's all they're saying?"

"Pretty much. That marshal who saved everyone is hero of the hour," added a familiar-looking stranger. With a jolt, Will recognized him—he'd starred in a hit sitcom, back when the world was normal. "You might say she's the new you."

"Juanita Corazón?" *Poor woman. Bet she's hating the attention.* "Roche put her in front of the press?"

"Not so far, but CNN has a pretty good profile running. Bio, school, family pictures. She's got a brother MIA, and they're interviewing her saintly old ma in Reno in—" The actor consulted his watch. "—eight minutes."

"Has Astrid seen any of this?"

"Astrid's a news avoider. Why?" the actor said.

"She thought Juanita might be important."

"Cool—I'll get up a briefing and give it to Pike."

Continuing across the plaza, Will ran into a bottleneck of people backed up in front of the gateway. The wiki fluttered, explaining: Astrid was conducting a graduation of sorts, saying thank you and good luck to the newest volunteers.

For a moment, he braced himself for a typical ceremony,

something formal and speechy. But Astrid, Mark, and a handful of the other team leaders were simply hugging the departing volunteers and sending them into the glow.

He was struck again by the scope of Astrid's operation—there had to be fifty people exchanging good-byes and last-minute advice—and the folksy informality of it.

The last to go was a sun-worshipping beach boy from Tofino, on Vancouver Island. Mike, the wiki told him: Astrid had chanted his surfboard so that it could hold back incoming tidal waves . . . assuming, as always, there was enough power available.

"The shark's-tooth necklace lets him breathe underwater," she told Will as Mike took his leave. "If he's swamped . . ."

"Seems like a good plan."

She shook her head. "I haven't got him onto the Big Picture yet."

"There's still a portrait of him in the hotel ballroom—in Limbo?"

"A sketch. If things change so he's safe, Jacks will let us know by coloring it in."

"Does Mike know he's still supposed to . . ."

"Die?" She nodded, eyes shadowed. "We got the body count down a lot this week. The raids on Saskatoon and Manila—"

Will smothered a pulse of guilt. "Saving people's good, but spreading contamination . . ."

"I know you're not crazy about that part of it. We can talk about it—"

"No. What I want is my kids." They had outrun him last night in Manila, Ellie sprinting away, screaming in terror, Carson loyally following. "Not soon, not in some happily ever unreal after. Today."

"How do you want to go about it?"

Her agreement caught him off guard. "Chasing them isn't working. Their escort just whisks them away."

"Yes, we've struck out there. What, then?"

He intercepted one of the scavengers, a delicate-featured drag king who was rolling a cart full of ready-to-chant objects across the plaza. "Make something that'll bring them here."

Astrid thanked the volunteer and then sorted through the cart, examining each scavenged item in turn before selecting a striped fleece blanket. She bled magic into it, brow furrowed. "Okay. Lay it out, like a picnic blanket. Stand on it and wish."

Will snatched it, laying it on the uneven marble floor and pinning its corner with his feet.

The blanket began to slurp letrico, flapping like a flag in a strong wind as the power ran through it.

Cries rang up and down the plaza. Pike's voice hummed through a hundred different musical instruments. "Someone's draining our power reserves."

"Will, hold up."

He waved her away.

"Tombe reports a spreading chill in Madagascar—" That was Pike again.

"The Alchemites are fighting you," Astrid said, voice low. "Give me a second, let them—"

"I am *not* letting go." Threads of lightning flickered across the plaza, jolting through the blanket. It frayed, falling apart in puffs and tufts of fiber.

"Mark, find the Alchemites drawing heat in Madagascar," Astrid ordered. "Mute them—steal their voices before they start vamping people."

"Nice in theory, boss, but we haven't got the juice—"

A last rush of power, and the blanket disintegrated completely. Carson and Ellie appeared on its remains.

Predictably, Ellie began shrieking at the sight of them.

Fatigue rippled through Will, a sign that his ring was drawing power. It would protect him for a while, but he'd burned out the town's letrico reserves.

Astrid and the other volunteers pitched over.

"Dad," Carson managed. Then he fainted too.

Ellie turned to flee, only to trip over Astrid's prone body.

Will caught his daughter's arm. "Ellie, it's me, it's Daddy."

She wailed. "Don't touch me!"

Exhaustion burned through him.

"Ellie," he pleaded. He'd have to sedate her, he thought. A few yards away, Olive tried to get up; Ellie let out another yelp and she collapsed.

"Nobody's going to hurt you," he said, fighting to seem unaffected. Ellie was pale, exhausted; she'd drain them both at this rate. "Give me whatever chantment you're using, before you pass out."

Behind them, Astrid was stirring.

Will focused on his daughter. She'd grown a couple inches, and her crooked tooth had been straightened . . . magically? Her hair, fine gold just like Caro's, had grown to her shoulders. "You need to give us that chantment."

Astrid's hand drifted to the shopping cart full of junk, bleeding magic into its dirty rubber wheel. Carson groaned, pushing himself upright. Ellie jerked in Will's grasp.

"The chantment," he said firmly.

The look she gave him was so like Caro's, that last day, laced with contempt and malice. "Around my neck," she said, lifting her chin. A whisper of chain lay against her skin.

He reached for it, and several things happened at once: the shopping cart clattered softly; Carson pushed himself upright, rasping, "Wait—"

Ellie twisted in his grip, fluid as a salmon, and almost broke free. She scrabbled in her pocket, tossing something bright and sparkly into the air. A diamond necklace, he realized, as flecks of light filled the air, blinding him. . . .

Then he, Astrid, the kids, and all the volunteers from the plaza were lying in a flower-strewn meadow, and Ellie was sprinting away.

"Take that, Pipeman!" she shouted. In a blink, she put a hundred yards between them.

"Don't chase her, Will," Astrid said. "We're in dreams—no matter what you do, she'll slip away."

"Car-car, come on!"

Carson made a show of staggering to his feet, keeping his face turned from his father's. "They used a chantment on her—a padlock. Sahara made Mom put Ellie's hair in it."

"It makes her scared of Will?" Astrid asked.

"No!" Facing them, he backed away, hands out as if he was afraid. "Dad, no, not you. She sees the Pipeman. I gotta go—she won't trust me if she thinks I'm on your side."

Anguish tore at him. "I'll fix this, son."

"Sorry," he said, pelting off after his sister and vanishing over the hill.

"Pipeman?" Astrid said. Her voice was raspy, weak.

"I got hit on the head, on the job, a few years ago. Ellie had nightmares about the kid who'd done it."

"Someone hit you with a pipe?"

He nodded.

"I'm sorry, Will."

Sympathy made it worse: he stepped away before she could touch him. "Dammit. What's it gonna take? What do I have to do?"

Astrid touched the tuning fork at her throat. "Pike, you there? Pike? I guess we don't have enough juice for communications yet."

"Are you surprised?" That was Olive—the unconscious volunteers were stirring. "Will's little stunt sucked us dry."

"I had to do something," he said.

"I know how you feel, but—"

"You know *what*?"

Olive stiffened. "I lost my son, remember?"

"Just because you have the patience of a saint doesn't mean I should have to wait forever. Carson and Ellie—"

She cut him off. "What happens if there's a bombing raid before we rebuild our reserves?"

"Yeah, Will," Jupiter said. "And those Alchemites damn near froze Madagascar, trying to hang on to the kids. There's bound to be a huge storm."

"Don't everyone start pecking at him," Astrid said. "Olive, you'd have done the same for Jacks."

"Astrid . . . ," said Jupiter.

"We're not doing blame," Astrid said. "Move on."

"We have time to do a little blame," Jupiter said. "We're just twiddling our thumbs here while we wait for the phones to come back online."

"Or we could work," Astrid said. "Did you notice Will was able to draw all our reserves? The letrico crystals aren't connected."

Everyone was quiet for about five seconds. Then Olive said, "Yeah, that is interesting. Did the letrico jump because he wanted it so bad?"

Will turned to face them. Astrid was sitting cross-legged in a circle of flowers, enjoying the dream sun, looking as though everything were okay. She'd effectively defused the situation, distracting the volunteers from what he'd just done.

Which was, if he wasn't mistaken, to land everyone in the same prison the Alchemites had been using for all their enemies.

"I—," he began, and they fell silent. "I owe you all an apology."

"Save it for when we get home," Astrid said.

"Home? But—"

"Abracadabra." She gestured at the hillside, and Bramblegate began to grow, slowly, on the lawn.

"We can get out?"

"We're just waiting on power," Olive said.

"Gate will take you back in, though," Astrid said. "You can talk to your son, maybe, while Ellie's back is turned."

"If people can just walk out of dreams—"

"The Alchemites can put people here, but they can't pull them out again."

"Or hurt them," Olive added. "Everyone's nice and safe."

"You can get them out?" Will repeated.

Something seemed to pass between Astrid and Olive—a debate, perhaps?

"Astrid?"

A shrug from Olive—go ahead?

"It was us," Astrid said. "We arranged for the Alchemites to steal the diamond bracelet that Ellie used to slide us into dreams."

"You did what?"

She rose, pointing. The horizon shifted and Will saw a beach, crowded with hundreds of the missing—soldiers, reporters, a few Alchemites who'd tried to leave Sahara's fold, several dozen police officers. "Sahara's followers would have killed all those people, Will, if I hadn't given them an alternative."

"You're helping the Alchemites?"

"That chantment saved hundreds," Olive said. "Their families can visit and they can't be abused, by Alchemites or anyone else."

"And they can do anything they can dream of," Astrid added.

"Except cause trouble for you," Will said.

"Will, think: The Alchemites can't hurt your kids if they're here. You can visit your son. All we have to do now is break the spell on Ellie."

He didn't want to concede she was right, but Sahara's people could have murdered the children out in the real. "What about the padlock chantment Carson says they used on Ellie? Did you arrange for the Alchemites to steal that?"

"No. Sahara stole a stash of pretty nasty stuff early on. It must have come from there."

He shouldn't be angry, Will knew. All Astrid had done was keep the fight between the Alchemites and the government from getting bloody.

"If we break the spell on Ellie, Will, the kids will step through Bramblegate on their own."

"When?" He knew this voice, knew he was on the edge of falling into bottomless rage. "Years?"

Astrid pressed her lips together. Fury had a tendency to silence her, Will thought. She wouldn't say anything that might provoke him further.

Jupiter interrupted: "Bramblegate's open."

"I'm gonna go ask the seers about the padlock chantment." Astrid led the others through the gate.

Soon it was just him and Olive.

The landscape darkened, the grassy hill changing to pavement. He was on a street about three blocks from home, looking up the street at the shop where he used to take the kids to buy shoes.

Behind him, a baker was arranging cupcakes in his window, creating a pyramid of pink-and-chocolate-capped confections.

Cars drove by, pausing for jaywalking pedestrians.

"Nothing magical here," Olive said. "This must be your dream."

He was still angry, but he also knew what grown-ups were supposed to say: "I shouldn't have snapped at you."

"We all blow occasionally, Will."

"I'm sorry anyway." It didn't feel true, but it would be.

She cupped her hands, staring at her interlaced fingers. "You know, the day we started on the Big Picture, we drew down lightning to power the paintbrush. Jacks made those sketches of everyone we have to save. Piles and piles of cards. We were hysterical. So many people, you know? The worst was knowing that some of us would be in the stack. But you know who Astrid looked for first?"

"Carson and Ellie?"

"Nothing mattered to her, none of us, not Mark, not even . . . She was determined to confirm your kids were safe."

"If Astrid wants me on board, she needs my children."

"Yeah, she's such a Machiavelli. It's all a big game to her." With a disgusted snort, Olive stormed off.

Dreams. Will thought of his children, and suddenly he was at the edge of their school playground. Ellie was crying on the merry-go-round. Carson had an arm around her. He caught his father's eye, then mouthed a word: *Later*.

Will nodded.

The tuning fork at his chest buzzed.

"Astrid says we can't hang you for burning our power reserves, lad," Pike purred. "Come on back, will ye?"

"Be right there." Bramblegate had followed him: he took a last look at the kids, then stepped out onto the plaza. People were sitting in groups, eating and chatting, waiting out the power shortage and catching up on trial news.

At his appearance, a round of boos—gentle ones—broke out.

"Way to go," Mark said. "You've slowed down the rescue in the unreal *and* our work on reducing the body count."

He ought to be contrite, Will knew, ought to offer to go do some grunt work, join the power-spinning circle. Instead, something Olive had said about the Big Picture tugged at him. "I'll make it up to you all, I promise."

He strode across the plaza, thinking of the ballroom as he stepped into the glow. The room was empty but blazed with light—the vessels of vitagua glowed whether anyone was there to see them or not.

He stepped into the midst of the dance floor and turned a slow circle, examining Limbo's cartons of cards. A number had place names hand-lettered on them: *Cincinatti, Paris, Argentina, Swaziland, Delphi, Alberta, US, Peru.* A trio of crates nearest the bandstand were marked: *Soon, Sooner, Soonest.*

Wait—had that been *U.S.* or *Us?* Will reached for the container, a bright orange laundry basket . . . then fumbled it as he recognized a sketch of Mark Clumber on top.

This is what Olive had begun to say. Astrid didn't care about anyone but his children, she'd said. Didn't care about—

The basket tipped, spilling cards across the floor.

Will knelt, heart slamming. He gathered up the pencil sketches of familiar faces: Mike the surfer; the strike team medic, Janet, who'd been a nurse in Vietnam. There were volunteers and Wendover workers and even the Alchemite Prima, Passion. Boomsday might engulf most of its authors, killing them as it had Albert Lethewood, Jacks Glade, and the fire chief.

His hands trembling, he scooped the cards into the basket. He'd go to the letrico factory, spin energy. He'd work harder, apologize. He'd been selfish, but he'd make it right. . . .

He froze, his hand hovering above the last two portraits on the floor as he recognized Sahara Knax and Astrid Lethewood.

CHAPTER THIRTEEN

"ELIZA'S ARRANGED FOR US to go see Jacks." Patience was extraordinarily tall this morning, almost seven feet in height, with generous, curvy proportions, skin the color of soot, and a cap of short, tightly curled black hair. She was clad in a dress woven from blue-tinged grasses. Her feet, which were massive, perfectly shaped, and oddly bewitching, dwarfed the sandals she had crammed them into.

"They make fabric here in the unreal?" Ev asked.

"Had to. I failed to pack anything for a giantess," she said without a shred of humor. "What I wouldn't give to be myself again."

Ev knew what it was like to be trapped in an ill-fitted body. Before he could say so, Teoquan sauntered into their rooms, wearing a knowing smirk.

Swallowing his words, Ev settled for a cool nod.

"Teo's going to be our guide."

"Thanks very much," Ev said, feigning enthusiasm.

"I agreed before I knew *you* were coming," Teoquan said.

"I appreciate it, whatever your reason."

"My reason's nothing to you. Let's hit the road."

"Fine," Ev said. "Where to?"

An evil grin. "Off to bone bridge."

He led them out to the Pit, whose edge, since St. Louis, had become a seeping waterfall of vitagua. Slush flowed downward into the brightness, thick, slippery, and dense with contamination. "Ready to go?"

Ev peered over the lip, blinked at the glare, and fished out a pair of tinted glasses. "Ready."

"Cute," Teoquan said.

"We playing whose is bigger, or we going?" Patience asked.

"Sorry, darlin'." Parallel bridge rails, brand new, made of white grit and encrusted with ice, waited at the edge of the chasm. Ev stepped out over the edge and found himself in a low-roofed corridor of blue ice, standing beneath tons of glacier.

A thick stream of vitagua flowed from the ceiling, blocking their path. It twisted away from Teo, its movements snakelike.

Patience whistled, impressed. "Did you use a chantment to do that?"

Teoquan shook his head. "Vitagua responds to passion. I happen to be very passionate."

"By which you mean stubborn."

"You say tomato, baby."

"I've never seen anyone but Astrid manipulate vitagua."

"Eliza seems able to push vitagua around," Ev said.

"Eliza used to be a chanter, back before she was murdered by the witch-burners," Teoquan said. "She's got a few of her old chops, even if she ain't married to the well no more."

"Married?" Ev said, disliking the sound of it.

"Till death did her part." He grinned.

Ev looked at Teo's teeth. They were big, but like everything else about him, they looked human.

"Shouldn't the vitagua be Frog Princing you?" Ev asked.

"No," Teo said. "I'm special."

They stepped out of the tunnel, passing the sunken face of a child with the features of a stork, and into a cathedral-sized cavern supported by irregular columns. The chamber was aglow with orange light.

Patience strode to the base of the first column. Each of them was an ice sculpture of someone. There were dozens of them, hundreds, maybe. "These are former chanters?"

"These can't all have been from Indigo Springs," Ev said.

"Eliza sent out search parties. The Indigo Springs guys are all here, but she found other chanters too, from other wells."

"Other wells—are any of the wells open?"

"Nope. Far's anyone can tell, your kid is holding the last well. All our chicks in one fragile hatchery."

"Astrid is working on finding . . . an apprentice, I guess you'd say," Patience said.

"Will Forest," Teoquan said. "Am I right?"

"If he agrees."

"A white guy. *Quelle* fucking *surprise.*"

Ev opened his mouth, but Patience spoke before he could: "Where's Jacks Glade, Teo?"

"Follow the fiery brick road," he said, pointing in the direction of the orange light before vanishing amid the chanter statues.

"You've made such charming friends here," Ev said.

She laid a hand on his arm. "The better Teo likes me, Ev, the less likely he is to make trouble."

"You think you can defang him with a little flirting?"

"Courtesy ain't flirting. Teoquan and Eliza have something in common. The Roused respect them."

"But you like him?"

"I'm here to play ambassador, remember? Teo speaks for the Roused who want everything melted tomorrow, regardless of the consequences to the real, or to Astrid."

They started toward the light, following an unusually warm breeze. Fire, Ev thought as he gave Patience a hand around a geyser of ice and caught sight of Jackson Glade.

Jacks was caught in a massive frozen wave of vitagua, a rising wave of fluid with a crisp curl at the top. Vitagua dripped from above, freezing on its upper edge, forming icicles. The ice was intensely clear and the boy was upright within it, arms outstretched as if he were swimming for the surface of this peculiar sea. His open eyes were glowing coals, and his face was lifeless. He wore the clothes he had been shot in, that terrible day of the siege at Albert's house. The belly of his shirt was torn and blood soaked. Veins had grown from the wound into the substance of the glacier, pulsing minutely.

Ev stared. Astrid had spoken of Jacks's death, but to find him here, torn open and preserved like a pickle in a jar . . .

Memory struck, crystal clear: Jacks at two in the playground, wearing a saggy diaper and nothing else, chubby baby legs churning as he ran away from the Chief.

The glow—the heat—was coming off Jacks. Under his skin was the shifting orange light of embers. At his feet, vitagua bubbled into a brick-lined canal.

"That's the Chimney," Ev said, but Patience wasn't listening. She had one hand on the wave and the other over her mouth. She was sobbing.

"Hey," he said, reaching out, feeling helpless. The touch was awkward. But pulling away would probably make it worse.

Patience turned to mist, passing through Jacks, through the wave. She solidified on the other side, changing into a short Latina beauty. The huge dress billowed around her.

"Stupid damn kids," she said.

"It wasn't your fault." That was Teoquan, gliding out from elsewhere, his face wet with blue magic.

Ev had enough time to think that this wasn't the point before Patience dissolved completely into grief.

Teoquan opened his arms and with a step, Patience was in them, crying. "You told them not to be idiots. What could you do, jump in front of a bullet?"

There was no room for Ev in this scene. "I'm going to go find Albert," he said, leaving them together, slipping into the forest of statues.

From earliest childhood, for as long as he had been able to remember, Ev knew the world had him wrong. He'd refused to wear skirts, tried peeing standing up, took absurd pride in being labeled a tomboy. He had outplayed the boys in sports . . . when he'd been allowed on the field at all. He joined the town's bagpipe band, boycotted Girl Scouts, and flirted with enlisting in the army.

Albert Lethewood had been the only man he ever felt any kinship with, any attraction for, and to this day Ev—who through his teens had had crush after crush on girls, made vows to be celibate, and periodically fantasized about becoming a priest—could not say why. Had it been the magic within Albert? Had young Ev gotten tired of fighting a battle he couldn't even name? Had Albert come along just as he was giving up?

It was his life—if anyone could know, it was he.

Albert had been thought an alcoholic or gambler; he'd been beneath the notice of most of town. Playing the town bum had been his way of concealing the magical well: a façade, an attempt to avoid the death that had finally claimed him.

Here, in the unreal, Albert was a hero.

His statue was huge, his pose noble, his expression brave. Ev gazed upward, cast back to the seventies when they had married—Ev wearing a kilt and poor Albert in a borrowed suit.

Albert had courted Ev, chased her in his way, but it was she who had chosen him.

Now, of course, it was obvious why the sex, even with her in charge, had felt slightly off. Why the experience of pregnancy had been so awful. His body had tried to reject the life, Astrid's life, within him.

In hindsight, it felt as though he must always have known what was wrong, but nothing was ever that simple. Ev had loved Albert; he couldn't deny it. And Indigo Springs wasn't the kind of place where you met other transgendered folk. Astrid was ten before Ev even heard the term. Those days, if the subject came up at all, the phrase you heard was *sex-change surgery*. In small-town America, that meant self-mutilation; it was something sick men did. Ev was over fifty the first time someone told him about female-to-male transition.

You grew up. You got married. You had kids.

Vitagua contamination had been clarifying, almost a relief. Curse or no, exposure to magic had battered down a locked door in Ev's mind. At first he'd reached for a delusion, the most comfortable fantasy he could find: a fictional detective who delivered mail, as he did, a detective who shared his name. Of course he was Everett Burke, and of course Ev Burke was male.

Madness—for madness it had been—had been preferable to wrongness.

Here in the unreal, Albert's statue was upright, clear eyed, all the things he'd pretended not to be in life.

"Married to the well, hmmm?" Ev said. Teo had a gift for sticking the knife in.

Part of Ev hated himself for caring at all. He'd tried to have a woman's life—to marry a man, have a family. Seen from this side of his transformation, the attempt felt like a lie.

But he had tried. Had loved Albert. Had resented, *still* resented coming second.

Albert gazed down at him with infinite compassion.

"I'm not coming second again," Ev told him.

That brought his thoughts back to Teoquan and Patience. And, just like that, they reappeared.

"Hey, Virgin Harry, you done moping over your ex?"

"Teo," Patience growled. "His name's Everett."

"It's all right," Ev said.

"Honey, you've seen Jacks. Now we gotta shake."

They returned to the bone bridge, stepping out atop the glacier and heading in three different directions.

Ev went in search of Eliza. "I've been wondering if there are any crews working outside the city."

Eliza peered at him over her granny glasses. "We've been thinking about Astrid's offer to set up a letrico mill. We need the power."

Relief washed through him. "On the hill where the wind's blowing in? I could work on that, yeah."

"Didn't your daughter send you here to be a diplomat?"

"Patience has that covered, and I like to keep busy."

She nodded, seeming to understand. "I'd like to start soon, before . . ."

"Yes?"

Her eye fell on Teoquan. "My power here is diminishing."

"Maybe we can do something about that," Ev said, almost carelessly.

They let that sit between them, the raccoon fiddling with the cuffs of her long dress.

"I'll talk to your daughter," she said, and he shook her warm, tiny hand as the sound of Patience, laughing at something Teo had said, rang like chimes on the chilly air.

CHAPTER FOURTEEN

EAT, SLEEP, SAVE THE world. Not the kind of job where a girl
got vacations. Not that Astrid had ever taken one. Jacks was always trying to get her to ease up. . . .

They were in *Overlord*, sliding through the gateway in pur-
suit of the padlock chantment the Alchemites had used on Ellie
Forest. It was in Atlanta, according to Astrid's seers, so now they
were rolling down a street in Georgia, Igme blowing barely magical bubbles out to vitalize the city and the Chattahoochee River.

The raids had almost become routine. Astrid made chantments;
Janet kept them from attracting too much notice. The panic afterward had even become minimal. Two nights ago they had chased
the Alchemites to Britain. They failed to recover the chantment
that had turned Ellie against Will, but they did contaminate Manchester. Afterwards, barely five hundred people had fled the city.
The rest stayed, adapting to the slight magical changes to their
landscape.

Now it was Georgia's turn.

Before the magical well had blown open, Astrid had barely left
Oregon. Now she was crossing the world, seeing its great cities . . .
and altering them irrevocably. All she remembered about Atlanta
was Ev watching the Olympics on TV, and studying about Sher-
man burning the place down in the Civil War.

Her head was spinning. So much vitagua, so many voices.

They had materialized in a neighborhood called Cabbagetown,
near an old mill that had been converted into loft apartments.
Galleries and funky restaurants lined the rain-damp street.

"Up ahead," Clancy said. Smoke hung in the air ahead, lit from
within by red and white flashes: a fire, and firetrucks.

"He burned them out," Astrid said, quoting one of her grumbles. "Three dead Alchemites, and he's got their chantments."

"Who?" Will asked, voice taut. "Who, Astrid?"

They crested a hill, looking down on the fire. Ambulances and police outnumbered the fire trucks; the house was gone, the ruins smoldering. Paramedics were working on three or four limp forms. One was a figure with bird wings.

Pieces of Sahara, bits of you, the voices murmured.

Will squeezed her hand. "Astrid, focus."

"He's not supposed to go out alone," she said. "Since Lethewood murdered Uncle Lee, they're supposed to work in teams. Big bro's busy in Utah, Alchemites on his back doorstep, what's he gonna do? He can't handle a bunch of girls?"

Janet had been pouring water on the road using a magic watering pail that made them inconspicuous. Now she switched to the plastic heart, healing the surviving Alchemites from afar.

"What the hell's she talking about?" she asked.

"I think Astrid's saying a Fyreman burned these women," Will said.

Astrid said, "Clancy, turn north. Now's when we go to his house."

"You sure?"

"The grumbles say so."

Igme coughed. "Begging your pardon, but when the voices get helpful, it's usually so they can screw you over."

"Lying with the truth," she agreed. "Turn right up here."

"She said 'Uncle Lee,'" Aquino said. "Jacks Glade's father was named Lee."

"Clancy, stop here!" The trolley brakes whined; they coasted to a halt in front of a colonial-style bungalow with a stone fence.

"This is it." She hopped down, touching the mailbox, and found herself remembering her mother at about thirty, in her mail carrier's uniform. She tried to shake the impression away, but there it was: Ma, female, fluffy hair more blond than gray . . . carrying mail that originated from this house.

"Uncle Lee *was* Chief Glade," she said. Someone had asked that, hadn't they?

"He knew whoever lived here?"

"He sent letters . . . pictures of Jacks, but only as a baby. The letters stopped in the eighties."

"They probably got fax machines or something," Janet said.

Astrid stepped closer to the house, and the grumbles fell silent. She flinched back; the murmurs rose again.

"Magic's not working."

"How can we check the place out if our stuff doesn't work?"

"Go in and look?" Will suggested, sounding amused.

Walking to the corner, farther from neighbors' prying eyes, Astrid extended her hand again. There was a dead zone of sorts, just outside the perimeter of the fence.

Then I made a hole. She reached for a shovel propped against the fence. Instead of chanting it, she simply dug. *Remember when this was all you did—turn up soil, plant seeds?*

Was that her own thought, or another grumble? The longer this went on, the harder it was to be sure.

We're starting to sound like you.

The shovel crunched against something.

"Careful." Will knelt, brushing loose soil away. He unearthed a length of heavy chain, coal black in color, buried in a line that ran parallel to the fence. Crystals of salt and sea-glass crusted its links, and a twisted nylon cord was wound through. He teased up a loop of the cord with a stick, so Astrid could lay a finger on it.

"Primer cord," she said.

"Explosives?" He let it fall, pulling her back.

"It's called . . . rosarite. It's gunpowder, glass, and sea salt." Vitagua died when exposed to salt water—you could contaminate living things, but it wasn't like when it got into the rivers— and it could not pass through glass. Gunpowder meant fire— "I bet this runs all the way around the house."

"That's why the chantments don't work?" Will said.

"Let's find out how tough it is," Astrid said.

Driving the shovel into the soil outside the magical dead zone, she bled vitagua into it. She thought of gardens and weeds, grassroots boring holes through softwood, trees splitting mountains apart, roots insinuating themselves into cracks in the rock and growing, pushing outward . . .

Willow roots and cottonwood—stubborn, tough, destructive. Green shoots unfurled from the blade of the chanted shovel. As they met the buried chain, they burned. Smoldering, poisoned by the salt and sliced by the edges of the glass beads, the shoots hesitated, curling.

"More power?" Will held out a fist-sized chunk of letrico.

"Thank you." New shoots knotted around the chain, smoking as they were burned back. Then two glass crystals sheared off the links, leaving naked iron underneath. A root expanded between them.

Power sizzled through the shovel. One link of chain twisted, stretched, and broke. Roots overwhelmed the small hole she'd dug. The grass around the little bungalow charred in a straight line, burning a scorch mark that followed the perimeter of the fence. A lumpy braid of willow branches churned up from underground.

Will extended the magic turkey baster over the fence, blowing a contaminated soap bubble out onto the lawn. "So much for the magical dead zone."

"That took a lot of letrico," Clancy said.

He was right. And the shovel was still drawing power, pushing roots eastward—toward more rosarite elsewhere? Astrid yanked it free, breaking the connection. "Search the house. . . . Oh, too late."

A clunking sound—the garage door opening—made them jump.

A car turned the corner, a cream-colored convertible driven by a young black man. He braked sharply, gaping at the Springers with their chantments, the trolley laden with letrico.

"Do I know that guy from TV?" Janet asked.

"Duh. He's a trial witness," Igme said. "Lucius something?"

"He's a Fyreman," Astrid said, and froze. The last time she fought a Fyreman, she'd smashed his brains in.

Jacks's dad, dead on the living room floor . . .

The man scrambled out of the car. There were test tubes in his hand—by the time she recognized them, he'd drunk them: all at once, like shooters. He extended his arms, and flames boiled toward her. The trolley shivered.

Astrid drove a stream of vitagua toward their attacker. It sputtered like grease, emitting the smell of scorched lilacs.

It's flammable, she remembered: *It won't douse anything.*

She misted the yards to either side, making the grass and trees grow wild, burying the neighborhood in an explosion of growing plant matter.

Will dragged her aboard the trolley. "Clancy, get us out of here."

They glided away. The man sprinted after them, his body ablaze, keeping up easily.

"Chill, everyone," Igme said. "It's just one guy."

"I got him." Janet tossed the hula hoop. It soared out over the street. Then it boomeranged back, contracting around her.

Still running, the man crushed the test tubes in his fist, flinging the debris underhand. Something stung Astrid's abdomen. She started to burn as the vitagua inside her boiled.

Sea-glass, reacting with liquid magic. She blew the vitagua out of her body, through the piercing in her hand, a fast billow of steam that shot out, contaminating more of the boulevard, more of Atlanta's Cabbagetown. Oh, the pain was incredible; she had forgotten how much this hurt. . . .

Aquino was on fire. He was screeching.

Will was yelling: "Don't use chantments on him, he's protected!"

Scorching wind blew Janet from the trolley; there was a crunch as she hit the road.

Heat singed Astrid's hair. The abdominal pain had lessened as the sea-glass found less vitagua to burn.

Jacks had a belly wound too. Was that a thought, or a grumble?

Their chantments were melting, leaking vitagua down the trolley walls.

"Igme, wait!" Will shouted.

Igme had jumped off the back of the trolley. After bounding down the road, he scooped Janet into his arms. Bramblegate awaited on a nearby storefront; he dragged her through, vanishing.

"Can we go faster?" Will asked.

"We're running out of power!" Clancy shouted.

"Where's the healing chantments?"

"Janet had the heart," Will said. "Stethoscope's burnt."

"Bramblegate's ahead," Clancy said. "Get this guy off me for a second. . . ." The Fyreman was catching up, bolting along at inhuman speed.

Will shouted: "Brake, Clancy! Stop now!"

The trolley brakes squealed. Will had thrown an arm around her.

And we escape, Astrid thought with rising dread. *But . . .*

The Fyreman, running behind the trolley at about sixty miles an hour, ran straight into it. He slammed into their back door, throwing them all forward, crumpling metal. Then he bounced, the impact hurling him back onto the road.

"Did we kill him?" Astrid asked.

Will shook his head. "Go, Clancy!"

"Can you check?" she begged.

"We have to get you and Aquino to the hospital," Will said.

"Just check—"

"We're going, Astrid," Will said.

They were rolling. She'd been outvoted.

"Alchemites," Astrid said, holding her belly.

Through the hole in the back of the trolley, they saw a minivan pull up beside the fallen Fyreman. It disgorged two of the women they'd healed, a woman with the flower tattoos and the one who had Sahara's corkscrew hair and wings.

"They hurt him," Astrid said, pleading. "They hurt him and it's bad. Will—we have to—"

The winged woman looked at her then; their eyes met. It was Sahara—and yet it wasn't.

Mouse magic, whispered one of the grumbles.

A blast of cold air. They were through Bramblegate, and it was too late to save him. Will lifted her off the trolley.

"You're not going to die," he told her.

"Not by poison."

He squeezed her hand. "You're not leaving me."

An unexpected rush of hope glimmered through the pain.

The first thing she'd ever said to Will was, *You're going to fall in love.* She'd thought she meant Patience—everybody loved Patience.

"It's not just prophecy," she said. "I do like you."

"Astrid, now's not the time."

"I'm bad at this. I've never been a flirt."

"You're injured." He walked out into the hospital, into Emergency, and laid her on a gurney.

He wasn't listening. She caught his collar, pulling herself up—and kissed him on the lips, hard.

For a moment, apprehension wiped out the pain. If he pulled away in that wooden awkward way, if he rejected her, if he coughed and said it could never happen between them . . .

But with contact came first a little thrum, a nervous jolt, because she'd caught him—caught them both, really—by surprise.

And then, then he was kissing her back. He wasn't wooden at all, but flesh, alive and responding. *We might be,* she thought. *We might happen.*

The voices of the unreal rose in a confusing babble.

"Will," she said. "You don't have to cave in."

"Whatever you're talking about now . . ."

She heard Dad: "You're very brave, Bundle."

When had that been? Her magical initiation?

Dad was a maker of well wizards, she thought. *The sun burns out one day. Will caves. Boomsday comes. Sea-glass doesn't kill me.*

Now she was looking into a pool, and the original Indigo

Springs chanter, Elizabeth Walks-in-Shadow, was looking back, peering at Astrid through her granny glasses.

You're Jacks's obsession, not mine, she tried to say, but Eliza didn't go.

"I'm losing my grip on the people here," Eliza said. "Your mother suggested you might swing things my way."

"Sure," Astrid said to the dream or hallucination.

"What we're considering isn't ethical."

It's not a dream, Astrid thought. *I'm hurt, maybe dying. Will kissed me, and Eliza's decided it's time to take a meeting.*

Maybe dying. She rarely let herself think about the sketch of herself in the ballroom, but the image rose now.

"It's Teo," Eliza said. "He means to attack the real."

"Teo? You mean that hothead pain in the butt. . . ."

"He's building a following. If I could selectively thaw certain Roused, moderates, it would buy time."

Time. *Drag this out,* the voices kept saying. The more magic they dispersed, the more people they could add to Big Picture.

Including me, Astrid thought, and the grumbles laughed.

"I'll send a chantment," she promised, fighting up through smothering blankets of torpor, back to a world of heat and pain.

❄❄ CHAPTER FIFTEEN ❄❄

BACK WHEN THE WORLD still made sense, Juanita had been training for a triathlon. She'd been a competitive swimmer going back as far as high school, and later, when she'd begun work at the court as a newly minted baby marshal, she'd biked to work rain or shine. Swimming and cycling came naturally to her. Running had been a bigger challenge; she found it monotonous.

Growing dissatisfaction kept her going. She was thirty-five, single. Her life felt off-kilter, subtly broken, but she wasn't sure what to fix, let alone how.

In the meantime, she might be in a rut, but she could run inside it. She'd worked up slowly, completing her first half marathon a week before the magical outbreak changed everything.

Rounding the last corner of that course, seeing the finish line ahead, had given her a deep sense of accomplishment, the first in years. Looking back, she remembered it as the last time she'd had any peace of mind.

Now she was leading a triple life, running an endless track of pretense. By day she was in court, playing the role of faithful guard to Sahara and praying Judge Skagway wouldn't see through her. She spent her off hours trying to pry Fyreman secrets out of Gilead and her nights caught up in Sahara's invasions of her dreams, dancing to the Alchemites' tune.

But it was almost over.

She was outside the courthouse with the judge and Gilead Landon, watching a trio of men lay rosarite into a shallow trench dug into the sandy ground surrounding the building. The operation had been carried out under a pretext: plumbing upgrades, Roche said when Skagway insisted on the experiment.

Speaking of whom . . . "Where is the general?"

"On the horn with Washington," the judge replied. "There's been a magical spill in Atlanta."

Juanita had gleaned a few scraps about potion-making from Gilead. She'd told Sahara the core ingredients of their supposedly stable magical formulas were burnt vitagua and prayer. She'd reported the Fyremen were rigidly patriarchal, that Gilead needed permission to induct her into the Brigade. The only thing she'd held back was about rosarite and disenchantment, as Gilead called it.

Finish line: she clung to the memory of that half marathon, the feeling of impending achievement.

Skagway spoke: "So we do this, son, and any chantments they've smuggled inside the courtroom stop working?"

"That's the idea," said Gilead. "Magical influences won't affect the protected area."

I'll report the Alchemites' threats to my family, Juanita thought, *and begin disentangling this awful situation.*

"Once we show it works on the courthouse, we'll sell Roche on doing the whole base. . . . Sorry, that's my phone." With an apologetic wave, Gilead walked off, speaking Latin.

"Think this'll do it, Corazón?" the judge asked.

"We have to try something, Your Honor."

"True that," he said, like a kid.

The man unloading rosarite had taken advantage of a lull in his crewmates' rhythm, bending to tie his shoe. Now, as Gilead disappeared around the corner of the building, a shimmer of greenish fog rose around him. Winking at Juanita, he unzipped his pants.

"Roche thinks this is risky," Skagway said, reacting not at all as the worker urinated onto the rosarite, as the metal hissed and smoked. "He says Sahara's stayed where she is because of the chantment Lethewood put in her chest. It keeps her from running off. I told him that was your job. . . . Something wrong?"

"I—," she said. The stink of burning metal and steamed piss was overpowering. "Gilead should be supervising this."

"Relax, Corazón. Guy's entitled to a five-minute phone call."

The workman zipped up, gave her the finger, then flourished his arms in a ritual gesture—*Praise Sahara*, it meant. He handed over the length of dripping, corroded rosarite, and his coworkers bundled it into the pipe without a second glance.

"Tell me the truth," Skagway said.

"Pardon?" Juanita said.

"You falling for that guy?"

"Gilead?" She laughed a little hysterically. "He's more dangerous than Sahara."

The smile lines around his eyes deepened.

"I'm not looking for a relationship, Judge."

"You should be. You're lonely, kid."

To fight off the rush of tears, Juanita forced a smirk. "If you want me to put the moves on Gilead—"

"The moves?"

"He's not my type, but if it'd make you happy . . ."

"Oh, find yourself a nice woman," he said, playfully stern.

She saluted, pleased. She'd assumed he knew she was a lesbian, but Skagway's position as a judge charged their mutual affection with a certain formality. Outing herself fell well outside Juanita's comfort zone.

Gilead returned from his phone break.

"Everything okay?" the judge asked.

"Trouble at home," he said in a tight voice.

"Sorry to hear it," Judge Skagway said.

"Thanks. We're done here—the courthouse is encircled."

Except the Alchemites had gotten to it. "Can we test it?"

Gilead produced a chantment they'd seen before—the plastic ghost. "Want to do the honors, Your—"

On impulse, Juanita reached to intercept it, catching his hand before he could touch the judge. She caught a fading glow on Gilead's fingertips—embers, like cigarette cherries.

"Your Honor?" she asked, holding out the ghost.

"You go ahead," he said.

Dropping Gilead's hand, she held the ghost up, remembering the instructions Wallstone had given the jury: Imagine turning out a light. She looked across the compound, and a few of the safety lights vanished, creating a pool of pitch darkness.

She dropped the chantment before it could exhaust her. "Is there a time delay?"

Gilead was befuddled. "No. It should have worked."

"Maybe it isn't installed right," Juanita said. "Is it something we can . . . check? Debug?"

"Debug?" His voice was incredulous.

The judge snorted. "I'd call that strike two, son." Shaking his head, he wheeled away.

Gilead paced the trench. "It always works. The Alchemites, they must have . . ."

Still screwed, Juanita thought, *and Sahara knows I was in on it.* Tears threatened. "What were you going to do to the judge?"

"He wouldn't have been hurt."

"That's all you got to say?"

He was staring at the trench. "You're not in the club yet, Juanita—I can't tell you everything."

"To hell with your club. Go near him again, I'll break every bone in your hand." With that, she strode back to her quarters and sat up until late, fighting sleep.

When she finally drifted off, Sahara was waiting. "Disappointed, darling?"

"Sahara, I—"

"You didn't think I'd put anyone else close to our Burning Man? Darling, you told me he wouldn't share his secrets with a mere girl."

A dream coalesced around her: They stood in a basement that hadn't been renovated since the days of disco, a dusty hole with mildewy windows. Underfoot was a shag carpet; the walls were gold-flecked mirror. Birds—starlings—perched everywhere. A pretty young man sat, legs dangling, on a vinyl barstool, petting a moth-eaten fur coat and sipping a milk shake. Next to him was Passion, the tattooed Alchemite who'd sent Ramón to dreamland. She was toying with the boy's hair.

"She's here," the young man reported.

Passion crowed softly in exultation. "Beloved Goddess, we welcome you."

A groan, and Juanita saw Sahara lying on a couch and surrounded by Alchemite fugitives. Her heart raced into panic—had she escaped? But this wasn't Sahara—it was the nerdy black guy, Lucius Landon, who'd given evidence at her trial. Nude and bloodied, he lay on the frayed cushions, tied tightly, breath rasping in and out. Red and blue scratches marked the dark skin of his cheek. Starling-patterned hair coiled out of his scalp.

It was the same thing they'd done to the prosecutor, Wallstone. Sahara had effectively possessed him, contaminating him with a mixture of vitagua and her own blood.

Gilead and his "Brigade" can't stop Sahara. Could anyone? Juanita had a fleeting memory of Gilead saying that Astrid Lethewood was the real power.

"Juanita," the dream-Sahara purred. "Be honest, darling—when did you know they were going to disenchant the courthouse?"

"Too late to say anything. Gilead told me this afternoon."

"Lies," Passion sneered. "'Darling' Juanita doesn't understand her position, beloved Goddess."

"Why don't you spell it out for her?"

"You do as we tell you, Juanita, when we tell you. You don't withhold information. No playing mind games with poor little Heaven. You think we're stupid?"

"If you hit my family again so soon after vanishing Ramón to dreamland, someone will notice."

"Lots of soldiers get vanished." As Sahara spoke, the prisoner on the couch also mouthed her words. "Passion?"

The tattooed Alchemite smiled, moving languorously as she lay her hands on Juanita's shoulders, turning her to face an open doorway. "Dream your heart," she whispered, and the hallway morphed into the courtroom at Wendover. Skagway was behind the bench. In the gallery sat Juanita's family: Mamá, dressed for church, her brothers and sisters, her nieces, two aunts . . .

"Know what magic has taught me, Juanita?" Sahara—both of them—asked.

. . . *but not Tía Corina,* Juanita thought even as she lifted her hands in supplication, ready to give up, to beg.

. . . *not Corina,* the inner voice repeated. *She'd seemed sympathetic to the Alchemite cause. If Corina's not here because she's an Alchemite . . .*

"Please don't hurt them, Sahara."

"The soul exists, Juanita," Sahara said. "How can it not? I've taken root within the bosom of my foe. I'm in jail, I'm in a government hospital looking through the eyes of Lee Wallstone, I'm here in this Fyreman. Will you deny the Age of Miracles?"

"No." Juanita scanned the gathered, beloved faces . . . then looked beyond them. Most of the Wendover staff was here. General Roche, clerks and lawyers, the other marshals, the jury . . . "The soul exists, Sahara. I do believe that."

"My soul, being divine, can be spread infinitely," Sahara said. From her tone, she was nearing a point.

Heaven wasn't here. And two jurors were missing from the dream court.

"I'll do whatever you say, Sahara," she begged, thinking hard. Who else was missing?

Sahara smiled. "Tell me about tonight."

Juanita swallowed. "If Gilead had disenchanted the courthouse, the whole base would have been next. I could have reported you for blackmail."

"I am profoundly hurt by that, darling."

"He tried to do something to the judge," Juanita added. She described Gilead's attempt to touch Skagway, the lit embers at the tips of his fingers.

"Ruination," Lucius Landon whispered from the couch. "The Ruined seek their own destruction. Their strength becomes weakness."

"Another Fyreman curse," Sahara sighed.

Landon bared his teeth. "You are thrice-Ruined, Sahara. Lee Glade laid hands upon you, then my brother, then me—"

"If anyone's ruined me, it's the Filthwitch." Laughing, Sahara kissed his forehead. "Why the judge?"

"The unfinished work of the Brigade," Lucius gritted. "Wipe out the open wells, break the people of Raven."

"You went after him because he's Native?"

"It's them or us."

"How very binary of you," Sahara said. "Got anything else to share, Juanita?"

Juanita racked her brains. "Tonight, Gilead said . . . he had trouble at home."

"Ah," Sahara said, gazing fondly at the writhing, bastardized copy of herself. "That we knew already."

A lump rose in Juanita's throat: "I don't know anything else. I swear, I don't."

"Shhh." Sahara's hand mimed drawing a tear off Juanita's face. "You ordinary mortals. Your souls are more fragile than mine. Why is that, Juanita?"

"Because you're divine?" Juanita mumbled.

"Exactly."

Passion was wandering the dream courtroom, peering into the faces of Juanita's hostages: Mamá, Benita, the judge.

"Sahara, I'll do whatever you say. I'll avoid Gilead—"

"Oh, I want you to keep speaking to Gilead—he'd get so curious if you went cold on him now."

"I'll convert," she offered.

"Hold on, Passion," Sahara said.

The tattooed woman all but snarled.

"I'll convert," Juanita said again. "I'll accept the Age of Miracles. I'll pray to you. I'll stay with you to the end, as you predicted."

After an interminable pause, Sahara nodded. "All right, tell you what. Give me your faith, and we'll sacrifice someone who isn't too dear to you. What do you say?"

"I—"

"Juanita?" A purr, in stereo—it came from the Fyreman too. "Mamacita, or a coworker?"

"Coworker," Juanita said. *No, oh no, please . . .*

"Coworker what?"

"Coworker, beloved Goddess," she said, clumsily sketching an Alchemite gesture in the air.

"She's lying," Passion said. "She doesn't believe."

"Just pick someone, my bloodthirsty angel."

Passion pursed her lips, assessing the Wendover staff before laying her hand on one of the junior marshals.

"Oh, brilliant—she's guarding my cell," Sahara said. "I can watch her go. Juanita, your first task as a faithful Alchemite is to pay close attention."

"Yes, beloved Goddess." Stomach churning, Juanita stood, eyes wide, still trying to identify people who were missing from the dreamed hit list, silently reciting names. But the basement faded, and now they were in the cell block, standing in the hall as the youngest of the Federal marshals put a hand on her chest and then doubled over.

"Don't you dare shut your eyes," Sahara said.

The guard's mouth opened, but she did not scream—she chirped. Birds were coming out of her mouth in a rush, and her skin was shifting and rupturing as beaks broke through, fluid-slicked avian heads cutting their way out through her arms, neck, chest, a flock that soon obscured their victim.

"Now you say: 'Praise the Earth, praise the wind, praise the sun,'" Sahara said over the cacophony of cheeping.

Shakily, Juanita stumbled through the phrase.

A Klaxon buzz-sawed the nightmare apart and she jolted awake, lunging for her wastebasket, belly heaving. She retched, mentally clinging to her list of suspected Alchemites. She was afraid to say the names aloud.

CHAPTER SIXTEEN

WILL HAD BEEN SURE Janet would be dead when he got back to Indigo Springs. He'd seen the medic's portrait in the ballroom, and she'd landed hard when she fell off the trolley in Atlanta. But as he reached Emergency with Astrid in his arms, Janet was the first person he saw. She was whole, dirty, and holding another of the healing chantments, a mitten.

"We need help here," he called.

"Lay her down." Letrico frisked along her arms in little spikes of lightning as Janet placed the mitt on Astrid, pouring power into her. The belly wound closed; Astrid's color returned.

Janet reached out, and Will pulled back.

"Your wrist, Will."

Dumbstruck, he followed her gaze. His hand was hanging at an odd angle. With Astrid hurt, it hadn't registered.

"I must've—when that fellow hit the trolley . . ."

"Take your ring off." He obeyed, and Janet placed her mittened hand on his. There was a pop, a disturbing sensation of bones jerking into place, puzzle pieces snapping together. Pain he'd been ignoring went away, and his mind cleared.

His tuning fork buzzed: Mark. "Is Astrid okay?"

"Yes," Will said.

"No. She should be awake." Janet drew more letrico into the mitten. Another medic, a wiry Latino whose arms were covered in prison tattoos, rolled a plastic ashtray over Astrid's abdomen, apparently using it as an X-ray—Will could see her insides through it.

Astrid's eyelids fluttered. She mumbled something—

"What?" Janet said, leaning close.

"Was that . . . did she say vote-rigging?" Will said, perplexed.

"No," Astrid said, voice stronger.

"How are you, kid?" Janet asked.

"Hurts." She tried to rise, moaned, and collapsed.

"Let us look," Janet said, waving Will away. They wheeled the gurney into a treatment room and pulled a curtain.

Will stepped back to give them some privacy. He needed time to think about what had just happened. . . . Kissing Astrid had felt more natural, more right than he would have guessed.

The idea of blindly following a prophecy into a romantic relationship, of all things, rankled. *But there was something between us almost from the start,* he thought. *An energy . . .*

Instead of solitude, he found the foyer crowding with anxious volunteers, all looking for him.

"Is she patched up or not?" Mark headed up the pack.

Will shook his head. "She must have sea-glass inside her."

A worried murmur.

"Janet will think of something," Will said.

"Glass killed her dad," said Mark.

"She's not going to die."

"You think I'm overreacting?"

"I didn't say—"

"What happens to us if she dies?" Mark said. Volunteers were showing up by the dozens, all of them angry or scared.

"She's going to be fine," Will repeated.

"Just one of those thugs almost took you all out," Mark said. "What if they get into town?"

"They'll burn us alive," said one of the scientists, a pale, spindle-limbed blonde with a South African accent.

"What do you expect me to do?" Will said.

Mark said: "Astrid's been handling you with kid gloves, Forest. But she has this idea that you're the guy who takes over for her."

"That's my choice to make."

"It's not fair to the rest of us," Spindle-legs said. "She thinks she's going to bind you to the well, and in the meantime there's no backup for her."

"Your kids are in dreams now—they're safe."

"I'm not going to apologize for wanting my daughter cured," Will said.

"You're putting us at risk, Will."

"I'm not stopping Astrid from choosing someone else."

"She's not even looking," Mark said. "She's convinced you're the one."

"That's not my fault."

"If Astrid dies, the well closes. Then we die," Mark said. "What happens to your kids after that?"

"Yeah, man, who'll help you if not us?"

"Stop it, all of you." It was Olive, as it often was, who broke into the clamor. "Will, wouldn't you have a *better* chance of curing Ellie if you could make chantments yourself?"

He groped for an argument.

"This is about you being afraid to truly join us." Her tone was stern. "As long as you aren't initiated, you might walk away. Shop for a better deal. Go back to Roche."

"Or join the Alchemites," someone muttered.

"I'd never—" The disbelieving faces silenced him.

Olive said, "You abandoned the government. Why not ditch us for the people who actually control the padlock chantment?"

It was logical. He had never given the volunteers any reason to think he'd be loyal. But part of him was hurt by the suggestion. "Sahara Knax is a lunatic."

Olive said, "Will, I sympathize with the position you're in, I do. But you need to buy in to what we're doing. Show us you want to save the world . . . or tell Astrid you're out."

With that she left, taking most of the crowd with her.

"Will?" That was Janet, calling from beyond the curtain. Her hands were bloody; behind her, Astrid was unconscious. "We can't pull out the sea-glass. The fragments are resistant to magic."

Will swallowed. "Is she dying?"

"We'll keep healing her, pouring in letrico," Janet said. "It should work until we figure out an alternative."

Just what they needed: another problem. "Okay."

"What are you going to do?"

"You overheard that?"

"Did I overhear a shouting match happening ten feet away? I'm old, Forest, not deaf."

"Janet, my children are out there. I have every right to be a self-involved wreck."

"It's unfair, I'll give you that."

"I'm no more a god than Astrid." His family was in flames, and they expected him to take the world on his shoulders. "I don't relish the idea of playing one."

"You don't have to," Astrid said, opening her eyes.

He straightened her blankets. "I think I maybe do."

She searched his face. "And . . . us?"

Commit, Olive had said.

He caressed her cheek. "You're not still in love with Sahara, are you?"

"How many times do I have to say it? No."

"Jacks Glade?"

"I love Jacks, but getting involved with him—no. Fire and water."

"Then we'll see, okay?"

"The gentle path," she murmured.

"Gentle," he agreed.

Her eyelids fluttering, Astrid groped for his hand as she fell back into sleep.

CHAPTER SEVENTEEN

IT WAS TEOQUAN WHO christened the wind point Pucker Hill. As in "pucker up and blow." He'd said it with a little Jiminy Cricket singsong, leaving Ev to wonder why someone who'd spent centuries under a glacier could know music from *Pinocchio*.

Never mind that. He wasn't thinking of Teoquan. Or Patience. He certainly wasn't thinking of Teoquan *and* Patience.

Fortunately, there was plenty to occupy him at the Hill.

He had imagined that salvaging the pile of concrete and steel and turning it into a letrico mill would be something like an old-fashioned barn-raising. Get supplies, make a plan, erect a functional structure. One, two, three.

Eliza had recruited about twenty of the Roused, most of them Two-Spirited or transgendered, people he'd gendermorphed, to join him at the hill. Of the Roused, it was they who came closest to accepting him. Even so, they started by gently disabusing Ev of any notion that he—that anyone, really—might be in charge of this operation. They'd mounted an elaborate ceremony, complete with singing, dancing, speeches, and a modest feast, to pave the way, spiritually, for the construction.

Ev knew better than to say so, but as far as he was concerned, ceremony was no substitute for getting things done.

The Indigo Springs engineer, Thunder Kim, showed up shortly afterwards, carrying a metal footlocker filled with construction chantments and blueprints for the turbines. He'd hit the same wall: instead of just building something, the Roused picked his designs apart, butting heads with one another over architectural issues. For a long time, the only thing they seemed to agree on was that Thunder's design was plain wrong. Their discussions were passionate . . . and maddeningly unhurried. Ev had despaired of them ever reaching consensus.

Now, though, the crest of Pucker Hill was home to a terraced pyramid, Meso-American in its general outlines, but clad in sculpted West Coast masks. The turbine was within, out of sight; letrico weavers stood on a parapet atop the pyramid, converting electricity from the plant into nuggets of letrico.

Thunder had imagined building cottages to house the settlement, but they were building a communal home, an enormous, circular earth lodge supported by scavenged steel beams.

The breeze that powered the turbine wasn't the only thing blowing in from the real: there was moisture in the incoming air. Filtered water drizzled down the pyramid steps, carving out a little streambed that inched toward the city. It was little more than a drainage ditch, and it ran dry about a mile from the hill, but that hadn't deterred the unreal's peculiar vegetation—chalky grasses and reptilian flowers had taken root on its banks. There was even a sapling the color of ivory, with stiff, lapis lazuli leaves.

Ev was helping pack dirt over the earth lodge when Astrid and Will Forest stepped into the unreal with another load of letrico and chantments.

"Hey, Pop." Astrid wrapped her arms around Ev, like a kid. Her skin was clammy.

"Hey, kid. What brings you here?"

"We're initiating Will."

"You found your kids, son?"

Will shook his head, giving Astrid a significant look behind her back.

"What is it? What's happened?"

"It's nothing," Astrid said.

"Astrid has sea-glass poisoning," Will said.

Ev's breath caught. That was how Albert had died: Lee Glade shot him full of ground sea-glass. He'd lasted a week.

"I have a healing chantment, Ma," Astrid said, waving a plastic bangle on her wrist. "It'll be okay. Right, Will?"

Will nodded, looking more hopeful than certain.

Albert had died and he'd lost Patience to Teoquan. Now his daughter . . . Ev was going to lose everything.

"Pop," Astrid said, eyes glittering. "Nothing's changed. It all works out, remember? I don't know how and when, but . . ."

"Happy after," he said. His voice seemed far away.

"We're going to the Pit to initiate Will. Want to come?"

No, he thought, but some impulse spoke for him: "Sure."

They took a bone bridge down to the chamber filled with statues, and Ev led them to the vitagua statue of Albert.

"Ready?" Astrid asked Will.

"As I'll ever be," he said, and Astrid gave him a sharp look. "Yes. This is me, committing."

Astrid handed him a scalpel. "My father knew more about initiating chanters than anyone—it was his particular gift."

"You told me."

"Remember how it worked?"

"He dropped vitagua into your eyes."

She lay a hand on her father's leg. "Look up, Will."

Will raised his gaze to Albert's carved face. Two motes of magic dropped to within a hair of his eyes . . . and bounced.

"What the—?"

"Your ring," Astrid said.

He slid it off, and this time the blue specks dropped right into his eyes. He doubled over, groaning. Astrid produced a golden bowl and caught the rush of fluid from his eyes. "Saline," she explained, and her voice was deeper, masculine—

Albert's voice. Ev shivered.

"Not water, not seawater," Astrid continued. The fluid in the bowl rose in a fog, coalescing around Will's hair.

"Finally, blood," Astrid said. Will nicked his hand with the scalpel, dripping blood into the ice of Albert's feet. It twisted into the statue like blood pulsing through a vein.

"Will?"

He was panting. "Feels weird, that's all."

Clapping made them turn: two dozen Roused had turned up to watch, including Teoquan. "Good for you, whitey. Come to save us all . . . hoping we'll be grateful?"

Ev coughed, "Astrid, Will Forest, this is Teoquan."

"Hi," Astrid said absently, staring up at Albert.

Forest straightened, stepping closer and putting himself in front of Astrid. "Something we can do for you, Teoquan?"

"What, no handshake, no pleased to meetcha?" Teoquan bared his teeth in something that might, if one were nearsighted or obtuse, be mistaken for a smile.

"That isn't your style, is it?"

"Nope. I'm more the in-your-face type."

"Here's my face. Why don't you tell us what you want?"

Astrid's attention seemed to snap back. "I have a satchel of chantments with me, Teoquan. I could—"

"What? Bind some pitiful trinket into my flesh to stop the vitagua from turning me into a raving animal?"

"That's the idea."

"Do I look like I'm suffering?"

"You don't even look contaminated." She examined him closely. "If you know something about the curse—"

That wolfish not-a-grin again. "If I did, Miss High and Mighty, why would I share it?"

"You didn't come to say hello," said Will, "so I'll ask again. What do you want?"

He ignored Will, focusing on Astrid. "How much longer?"

"To melt—?"

"Everyone. All of us, all the spirit water. How long?"

"We're moving faster every day. I can't give you a date—"

"You can give me any date you want. You could pop the well like a champagne cork right now."

"How many people would die?" Will objected.

"Blah blah blah. When are you going to initiate one of the People as a chanter?"

"The People—," she said. "Oh. That's a good idea. Will, what do you think? Whoever we pick would inherit it from you."

"It can't be any of the Roused, am I right?"

"They can't have prior vitagua exposure." She looked back to Teoquan. "Unless you know a way around that."

"Believe me, sister, if I did, I'd be first in line."

Will frowned. "Darlene Lelooska, the hydrologist from . . . Edmonton? She's Cree, I think."

Teo made a disgusted sound. "How about Lilla Skye?"

"No!" Patience wafted up beside them, alarm stamped on her features. "Lilla's on a sketch in the ballroom."

"Don't fib, Patience. You dislike the girl, that's all," Teo said.

"Teo, she's—"

"Headstrong? Radical? Find Lilla for me, Lethewood."

"There's no harm in looking," Astrid said.

"That's what you think," Patience groused.

"Your boss is being magnanimous, sweetheart," Teo said. "Don't spoil the moment."

"You seem to think Astrid has something to apologize for," Ev said. "She didn't stick you here, Teoquan."

"So I'm supposed to let her dick around as she pleases, dishing out freedom by the teaspoon?"

"I'm hearing that you're angry, but—," Will said.

"Oh, let the well wizard speak for herself," Teoquan said.

"I'll look for Lilla, and I'll speed things up as much as I can," Astrid said. "Anything else?"

"Yes. When do you start letting us out?"

"Out?" Ev coughed.

Teoquan laughed. "What? You thought we'd stay on this barren little reservation forever? Locked away and cozy?"

Astrid drew in a slow, whistling breath, and Ev glanced at the shrinking pebble of letrico powering her healing chantment. "Bramblegate's right there. From what I hear, you control it, not me."

"Don't you have enough problems, kid?" Ev objected. "Letting this . . . hothead into the real isn't going to help matters."

"You may not like his attitude, Ev, but this ain't no Garden of Eden," Patience said.

Ev blushed. You couldn't fault her loyalty.

"No prisons, Pop," Astrid said. "Remember?"

"I got every right to want out." Teo strode to the edge of the gate, easing his arm through, then cursing and backpedaling. His hand reemerged, covered in icicles, frozen solid. "You've booby-trapped it."

Astrid shook her head. "Not me."

Teo turned, taking them all in—and then he bellowed: *"Eliza!"* The roof of ice above them shivered and cracked. Blue snow drifted down. Sprinting to the bone bridge, Teo vanished. Moments later, they heard shouting in the Roused tongue.

"What's that about?" Ev said.

Patience squinted, translating. "Eliza's afraid the Roused will be hunted down in the real. And she needs people for the rescue effort."

"It's up to her?"

"The strongest faction of Roused is holding the gate shut. Teo's saying she won't be in charge for long."

"It's true." Astrid rubbed her gut. "Grumbles say that when Teo has enough allies, he'll push through the Chimney. There's a fight. Fire, murder, Bramblegate burning—"

"Don't worry," Ev said, suddenly bitter. "It'll all be okay, re-member?"

"Pop." Unexpectedly, Astrid hugged Ev again. This time, she slipped something into his palm. "For Eliza," she whispered.

Ah, Ev thought. She hadn't told Will about their scheme.

"I'm going to go see Jacks now," she said, walking into the golden light. Will followed, leaving Ev standing uncomfortably close to Patience, with nothing to say and every reason to wish he'd stayed on Pucker Hill.

CHAPTER EIGHTEEN

ASTRID PRESSED HER HANDS against the massive vitagua wave.
Jacks was there, hands burning like embers, just under the ice.

The grumbles of the unreal rose around her. The glacier and
the people trapped within it were in some sense a consciousness:
a linkage of spirits and the knowledge their thousands of minds
contained. It held an incomparable body of knowledge, and it
knew its future as well as its past.

That mind's sole goal was to get all those people out, and it had
misled Astrid more than once. To the unreal, she was both ally
and jailer, someone to be indulged but never trusted.

"If I die, the well will close," she reminded it now.

That's not how it happens, the grumbles replied. *Not by poison, not by flame.*

"But I *am* poisoned," she insisted.

Her memory shifted, her sense of time lurching so hard, her
stomach bumped. Suddenly it was the terrible day when she'd
killed Jacks's father. He had stuck her with a sea-glass knife.

She tried to push the memory away—she couldn't relive
Jacks's death, Sahara's betrayal.

The knife fell, immolating when it struck the spilled vitagua
on the mantel. *It won't be poison. Death is sharp, a blade, drawn
fast . . .*

Old news. The Chief had stabbed her ages ago. "I don't want
to die, Jacks. How can there be a Happy After for me if I'm in
Limbo? Can I save myself—is there time?"

An ice cream headache blew down her spine, and she remembered the false Sahara again, back in Atlanta.

Someone muttered—oh, it was her. "Mouse magic."

It was too confusing; she broke contact.

"Sorry, Jacks. I know you've got your own problems." She kept talking: about Sahara's trial, about Olive, the volunteers. "And . . . I'm supposed to be falling for Will." She looked for some reaction, any reaction.

Nothing. He might as well have been dead.

The pain in her side worsened—she was running out of letrico. She found Will, who was waiting at the edge of the wave, out of earshot.

"You get any answers?"

"I don't die by poison or by fire."

"That's all he had to say?"

"Mouse magic."

"Meaning?"

"I'm not sure. Something to do with the people Sahara's been contaminating with her blood."

"Mouse magic," Will echoed. "Very helpful."

"Let's just focus on showing you how to make chantments." They headed back to Bramblegate. "How do you feel?"

"Strange," he answered. "Like I have a new lung, some organ meant to fill and empty . . ."

"Yeah," she said. She pulled a drop of vitagua, suspending it in midair, and said, "Can you feel this?"

He reached out, not touching it, and the droplet shivered. His fingers twitched, miming the action of pulling a string, and it followed. Astrid held on too, like a parent balancing a kid on a bike, as he practiced making it circle.

"Good," she said. "Ready to make contact?"

He eyed the blob, as if it were a venomous spider, then closed his fist around the droplet.

He opened his blue-stained hand. "I don't hear voices."

"It's a tiny amount," she said, relieved.

"I'm officially on the magical mystery tour, no going back now." He looked her in the eyes, seeming to consider it, and then kissed her.

Happiness glimmered, brighter than the growing pain in her side. "Thank you, Will."

They continued on to the Chimney. A traffic jam of filled shopping carts was waiting, each piled high with unchanted objects: plastic bottles, cutlery, hats, ski equipment.

Will frowned. "You can chant while you're injured?"

"It hurts a bit."

He gave her that keen interrogator's look.

"Okay, it hurts a lot. But this stack of things is for you. When you're starting, look for things that are receptive to magic. With Dad it was antiques. He called it—"

"Sparkle. I remember." Will looked over the pile. After a second, he picked out a baby's wooden block. Next it was a rag doll, a music box, a plastic tiara, and a dirty rake and pail.

Toys, noted Astrid. Toys, his kids trapped in dreams . . . how much room was there for romance, for either of them? She wondered how Will's children would fit into After. They would be chanters one day, the grumbles said. What about ordinary life, the part where she was their father's . . . girlfriend? Their mother loved Sahara—the Alchemites called her the Filthwitch.

Will hefted the kid's block in his hand. "I need to break the skin, right? Let the vitagua out?"

"You cut yourself during the initiation," She pointed to the slice he'd made with the scalpel. "Pull the magic here."

He frowned, concentrating, and after a second, the small puncture turned blue. He pressed it to the block. Then his back straightened.

"You okay? Will?"

"I wasn't ready for the rush."

She threw her arms around him. "You did it!"

He held up the block. "Any idea what it does?"

She grazed it with her fingertip. "*B* is for beluga . . . it emits whalesong."

"*B* for bizarre," he said. "Not very useful."

"Time and practice, that's all it takes." Pain made her gasp. Will gave her a fresh letrico crystal, and she healed herself, beating it back.

"Astrid? Sorry to interrupt." That was Pike, calling from the base of operations at the hotel.

"Go ahead," she said.

"Someone's been dumped in the forest, north of Bigtop."

"We'll be right there."

They arrived to find a crowd of Springers gathered at the edge of town, at the base of a massive poplar. Two volunteers were descending from the canopy, rappelling down with a large bundle.

"It was Alchemites. They dropped him here," Mark said.

The volunteers set the bundle down gently. Kneeling, Astrid opened the sheet with shaking hands.

He wasn't one of the volunteers. It shouldn't have been a relief, maybe, but it was. He was black, and his face was clawed to ribbons. His hair was long, curled, starling-patterned—Sahara's.

Mouse magic, the grumbles repeated.

"Madre de Dios!" Aquino pulled her out of reach. "It's that Fyreman!"

"From the trial?" Igme said. "Landon something?"

Astrid felt a pang of remorse. "It's the guy from Atlanta, who attacked us. We knocked him out and the Alchemites got him."

He wasn't quite dead.

"Alchemite atrocities," Astrid said. She'd hoped the grumbles had misspoken.

"Can we save him?" A curly-haired woman with a Bronx accent and the first hint of a whiskered seal's snout cut off the babble of the volunteers.

"We're gonna try." Janet pulled letrico into her magic mitten, pressing it against the shredded flesh of the man's shoulder.

The Fyreman began to scream.

CHAPTER NINETEEN

HEALING THE FYREMAN WASN'T working.

The obvious signs of torture cleared up fast enough: the knob of his dislocated shoulder popped back into place, and the rope burns on his wrists and ankles disappeared. As his torn face knitted itself back together, Will saw it was indeed the Fyreman from Atlanta, the one who'd poisoned Astrid.

His head was clear for the first time in months. He felt rested, calm, in control of both body and mind, filled with a pure, inexhaustible energy he remembered from childhood. And so far, he had made only a single chantment.

Small wonder, Will thought, that Astrid has been able to run the town, oversee the volunteers and their projects.

He turned the new acuity on his own problems: curing Ellie, seeing that Astrid recovered from the poisoning, and now, dealing with this new arrival.

The Fyreman was badly contaminated. Spiral horns jutted from his forehead, and a mane had grown under his chin. Starling pinfeathers sprouted from his temples; he seemed to be turning into two animals at once.

Seeing Astrid, the man stopped shrieking. "If it isn't my dearest, most loyal friend."

"Sahara? What have you done to him?" Astrid reached out. The man thrashed, trying to head-butt her. "Listen," she pleaded.

Janet did something and the guy went limp. "How many times do I have to tell you? Don't touch the homicidal zealots."

"Will?" Astrid beckoned. "Put your hands on him."

He obeyed, laying a palm on the guy's forehead between the still-growing horns.

"Sense anything?" Astrid asked.

"It's like touching a stove."

Astrid ran her fingers up one of the twisting horns. "Sahara's gang infected him with vitagua—and with her blood. He's cursed, turning into some kind of . . . antelope?"

"Kudu," one of the volunteers said.

"Kudu, thanks," Astrid said. "Sahara's in there too, trying to make him over into herself."

"Possession?" Janet asked. She was binding the unconscious man's hands with a strip of fabric. "That's a world-class sick thing to do."

"We'll have to euthanize him," Mark said.

"No!" Astrid was visibly horrified.

"I get that you want to save every last man, woman, child, barn owl, bumblebee, and plague flea if possible—"

"Can the sarcasm, Mark. You're talking about murder."

"Astrid, he almost killed you. If you can't muster up some resentment, at least recognize that he's dangerous."

Astrid's lip curled. "Are you gonna execute him? Or were you going to ask Jupiter to do it?"

"You're accusing *me* of not doing my own dirty work?"

"What's that supposed to mean?" Will asked.

"Nothing." Astrid waved the question away. "This is what Sahara wants. Us fighting, another Fyreman's death on my hands."

She was evading again, Will thought. He looked to Olive, and her gaze skittered away.

Olive and Mark had been among Astrid's first recruits. There was an inner circle: these two, maybe the project manager, Pike? Even now, Will thought, she was keeping secrets from him.

"Part of him is Sahara," Mark said. "It's creepy. We can't have him around."

"There's gotta be some way," Astrid said.

"To do what?" Will asked. "Get her out of his head, or reach the Sahara within?"

She made that infuriating gesture of dismissal, her standard response whenever he raised the issue of Sahara.

"Why infect him?" Olive asked. The sober cast of her face showed, suddenly, how much Jacks Glade had resembled her.

"They wanted Fyreman secrets." Astrid still had a hand on the man's horns. "With Sahara in his head, he had to tell them."

He had to go, they all agreed on that much. There was a babble of suggestions from the group: Put him out of his misery, flash-freeze him and send him to the unreal, exile him to dreamland, give him back to the Alchemites. Clancy, the old man who drove the strike team trolley, kept insisting they'd agreed not to keep prisoners.

"Let's talk to Wendover about returning him," Will said.

That triggered a chorus of dismay: "Excuse me?"

"Hand the guy over to the government?"

"He's a Fyreman," Will said. "His name's Landon. There's another Fyreman named Landon working with Roche. We have to contact them."

"That sounds like a fantastic way to get captured," Mark said.

Stifling exasperation, Will said, "If Roche starts taking us seriously—"

"We don't want him taking us seriously," Pike said. "The more of a joke we are, the fewer bombs they drop."

"What are we, people?" Will asked, hiding impatience. "Roche says terrorists."

"No," protested a half-dozen volunteers.

Will faced them squarely. "Who believes what we're doing is right, believes in Astrid's Happy After?" Hands shot up everywhere. "So everything we do is driven by prophecy. Does that make us a cult after all, like the Alchemites?"

No answer.

He took a breath. "Well? What are we doing?"

"We're rescuing people," Olive said. "In the real and the unreal."

"Preventing a catastrophe," Astrid said. Her voice rang with confidence. "The well is open, the magic is spreading. We're just holding back the flood."

"Delaying Boomsday," agreed Mark.

"Will's right. We'll return this man to his family." Astrid looked straight at Clancy. "No prisoners."

Will said, "So we call Wendover?"

"We'll approach that marshal," Astrid said. "The cute one."

Igme said, "You just want the woman's cell number."

"Try one eight hundred hot butch," said Pike.

The tension eased a bit.

Mark sighed. "Astrid made a chantment so Katarina and the off-site science teams could teleconference. We'll use that."

"Perfect," Will said.

"What'll we tell 'em?" Mark said.

"The truth, of course," Will said. "Alchemites dumped the Fyreman here. We want to return him."

"And then?" Mark asked. "Load up the strike team and roll into a trap?"

"One problem at a time," Will said.

"That's another thing," Mark said. "Astrid, you're off the strike team. We can't afford to lose you."

"I'm not the only chanter anymore," Astrid said. "Will's learned how."

There was a collective murmur of relief.

Mark crossed his arms. "Yeah, Astrid? Is he as good as you?"

"It's his first day."

"You know how the president and the vice president never get to fly together. . . ."

"In the first place, I'm not the president of anything, and in the second place, the two of us may be becoming an item, Mark—so you can just give up on keeping us separated."

"Becoming an item," Pike said. "Does that mean what I think it means?"

Janet clucked. "What'll that cute marshal say?"

The last thing Will wanted was to have the meeting devolve into public discussion of his love life. "Folks! Calling Roche?"

"Am I allowed to make phone calls, Mark?" Astrid asked.

"Only if you look healthy," Mark said. "They can't know you're wounded."

"We'll all clean up," Will said. "Legitimacy, remember?"

"Meeting the Roach," Astrid said, her tone disbelieving. Then her attention wandered; she crouched down, hands cupped.

"What is it?"

"Mouse magic." She stood, coming up with a mouse. It was alchemized; a blue spatter colored its tail, and it was the size of a softball. "Something the grumbles said . . . I guess I figure it out later."

"Astrid? Cleaning up? Taking a meeting?"

"Right." She held out the mouse. "Can someone find a cage for this little guy?"

"I'll do it," said Janet, taking it. "Good plan, Forest."

"Uh . . . thanks."

"You're off to the baths?" Mark asked.

"I'll be there in a few minutes," Astrid said. "I need to catch up with a couple projects."

Janet grunted. "You need to learn to delegate."

"Delegate," Astrid agreed, her eye following the mouse. Then she shook off whatever thought had grabbed her. She headed for Bramblegate, moving, Will noted, as though her body ached.

CHAPTER TWENTY

"WILL FOREST IS IN the little conference room." Juanita murmured the message into Roche's hearing aid.

She had been off duty and trying to meditate, to grab a few minutes when she wasn't at Sahara's mercy or Roche's whims.

It hadn't worked out so well. She liked the idea of meditation better than the practice: she knew she should take it seriously, but something—early childhood conditioning, maybe?—resisted. She'd relax, start breathing, and right away an inner voice piped up, snarking about how she was grasping at straws if she'd resorted to Prayer Lite.

She'd cracked an eye open to check the clock, and Forest—a spooky, see-through Will Forest made of dust and sunbeams—was standing in front of her.

"Sorry to interrupt," he'd said, "but I need a favor."

It was almost a relief. And at least she couldn't complain she was out of the loop, right?

"Forest is here?" Roche gave her a gimlet-eyed glare, but when Juanita didn't say anything else, he gestured to Gilead and followed her out of the courtroom and down the hall.

"In here." Juanita pushed open the door and froze: Forest had been joined by a ghostly Astrid Lethewood.

It was like seeing a movie star, or maybe the Devil. Gilead claimed Lethewood was to blame for everything: the release of magic, the end of the old world. Juanita had imagined someone flamboyant, with more stage presence than Sahara. But she looked profoundly ordinary—almost distracted.

Gilead eyed her like a cougar stalking a rabbit.

Roche broke the uneasy silence. "Your children, Will?"

"They're in dreams."

"You betrayed me for nothing, then."

"They're safer there," Will said. "Arthur, I had to try. We were getting nowhere. But I regret . . . I am sorry—"

"Save your breath." Roche struggled visibly with his anger while Gilead glowered at Astrid. "Why are you here?"

Will said, "Someone's dumped an injured man in Indigo Springs. He was a trial witness."

Oh no, thought Juanita. This was about the guy Sahara'd possessed and tortured.

Gilead's face was a mask, unreadable. "Is he dead?"

"He's been contaminated, like Wallstone. He thinks he's Sahara Knax."

Roche asked: "Then Alchemites did it?"

If I'd never slipped Sahara any chantments . . .

"They gave him tainted blood," Astrid said.

"Sahara's blood," Gilead growled.

She nodded. "Can you help him?"

His face was rigid. "There's nothing to be done."

"There's gotta be a treatment."

"Purity comes from fire, Lethewood. Like you, he'll burn."

"Death by fire?" Astrid seemed to be tasting the idea. Her hand rose, tracing her throat. Gooseflesh rose on Juanita's arms.

Will interrupted: "We didn't come to exchange threats. Your friend—"

Gilead's voice was toneless. "He burns."

"Son—," Roche said.

Will shook his head. "Turning over your man so you can barbecue him isn't what we had in mind."

"Lucius will pray for salvation."

"This is nuts," Astrid said. "He's only cursed because of your spell. Break it. The guy doesn't have to fry—"

"The guy—my *brother*—" Gilead's diction was as precise as that of a Shakespearean actor. "—will welcome death."

"You'd just write him off?" The words were out before Juanita realized she was angry. The men started, as if the desk or curtains had spoken. Astrid grinned.

Gilead spoke through clenched teeth. "It's what he wants."

"You've asked him?"

"Juanita, Lucius is—"

"Is this woman telling the truth, Gilead? Your magic's what's messed him up, and now you're going to burn him for it?"

"Sahara Knax has violated him."

She said: "You can't punish Lucius for that."

"Punishment . . ." He made a sweeping gesture, a hokey illusionist's move, nothing up my sleeve. Suddenly there were unstoppered glass flasks in his hands. He poured three potions down his throat, hurling the test tubes away.

"Observe your future, Lethewood." Blue candle flames flickered under his fingernails. They spread down his wrists and arms, moving over the surface of his skin like wildfire. He reached for Forest, raking his fingers through the dust forming Will's illusory body. Motes danced and wheeled, sparking.

"You're angry—," Will began.

"Professional empathy won't save you," Gilead said. Smoke roiled between the embers of his teeth.

"The person we're trying to save is your brother."

"Tell Lucius," Gilead said, "tell him the Alchemites felt the heat of my vengeance."

The defendants.

Juanita lunged to block the doorway, but Roche caught her arm, wrenching her off balance. "Let it play out, Corazón."

Cold air gusted over her face—the a/c system, kicking in as the room heated. The flames on Gilead's skin brightened from orange to incandescent white. Juanita yanked free of Roche, but it was too late: Gilead was gone.

Roche slammed the door behind him, trapping her inside.

"Are you insane?" Juanita demanded.

"Think! His brother's been tortured. Nobody will blame him for going crazy."

"Arthur!" Will protested.

"Sahara dies, the problem's half-solved, Will."

"It's true," said Astrid. "Gilead burns Sahara."

"Arthur, you ass, Caro's in there." The grit and dust forming the illusory Will lost coherence, collapsing into haze. Juanita saw a new Will rising from the floor on the other side of the glass door. He was running after Gilead.

"He doesn't burn her now," Astrid said. "What?"

Juanita hit her radio. "Gladys, lock down the courtroom. Lock it down now! You—Lethewood. Can you stop him?"

"Maybe," Astrid said a little dreamily.

"What's wrong with you?"

"Oh." Astrid clutched at her stomach. "It's going to be terrible."

Juanita bulled past Roche, sprinting after Will.

The courthouse doors were already burning, the security barrier ablaze. One of the marshals beat at the flames. Beyond the flaming doorway, Juanita heard screams and gunfire.

She darted inside . . . into a standoff.

No sign of Judge Skagway, was her first thought: maybe court was out of session. But no—lawyers and journalists were fleeing to the outer walls.

Gilead was facing the bench, his whole body a torch. Fire followed him like a cloak, spreading across the floor as he surveyed the room. Frightened spectators scrambled for cover: crouching behind seats, under tables, pressing themselves against walls. One of her marshals was hammering on the sealed emergency door near the jury box.

Gladys was protecting another exit, one that was still open. A single line of observers filed behind her, escaping as she fired on Gilead. The bullets had no effect.

The Alchemite prisoners were clustered in front of the bench, protecting Sahara.

"Have faith." Her voice rose from their midst. "I will not die today."

"Are you certain?" Gilead said, belching smoke.

Sahara tried to push her human shield away—halfheartedly, Juanita thought. "We do not fear you, Burning Man."

"Do not fear, do not fear," the Alchemites chanted.

"Funny, you sound scared," Gilead said.

Will Forest, still a ghost, stepped between Gilead and the defendants. "Landon, this is my fault. The Alchemites captured Lucius because I knocked him out."

"Your time will come, Forest."

"You don't have to do this."

"Believe me, I want to," Gilead said.

Overhead sprinklers kicked in, spraying Juanita with icy water. She saw Caro Forest's face as she recognized the dusty simulation of her long-absent husband . . .

By the exit, Gladys was reloading.

White flame gathered around Gilead's face, a lion's mane of fire.

"Stop!" Juanita yelled. "Gilead, stop!"

But he raised his hands, cupping his mouth, and blew. Fire streamed out, engulfing one of the prisoners, Arlen Roy.

Time slowed. Roy shrieked, danced, and fell. The stench of burnt flesh and hair filled the room. The people crouching behind the chairs and benches began to scream and retch.

Gilead drew breath for another attack.

"Praise Sahara!" An Alchemite threw herself into the stream of flame.

The ghostly simulation of Will staggered.

Dear God, that was Caro Forest.

Gilead moved on to the next defendant. And Sahara wasn't playing brave anymore; she had her fingers hooked into the jumpsuit of one of her followers, shielding herself as she backed away.

"Somebody stop him!" she roared.

Gilead burned the remaining defendants down, one after another, advancing until Sahara was exposed.

She had reached the edge of the defense table, and as Gilead drew breath for another blast, she grabbed a lawyer, hauling him up and using him to shield herself.

It's that same old guy she almost vamped to death before, Juanita thought. She felt a giggle building, even though it wasn't funny. *I'm losing my mind.*

Two of the jurors were in motion now. It was the pair Juanita had identified as probable Alchemites. They were each dragging someone, a hostage, attempting to bolster Sahara's human shield.

"Well?" Sahara demanded. "You gonna fry innocents, too? Show some balls, big guy."

Her gaze flicked past Gilead to Juanita. Expecting her to grab a hostage too, probably?

Horror at the prospect paralyzed her.

"Club Gilead." The spectral Astrid Lethewood appeared at Juanita's side. "Use something solid—big and solid."

Juanita grabbed up a chair and took a running start, using it as a battering ram. It burst into flame, billowing smoke, adding the reek of burned fabric and foam to the charnel house air—as she slammed it into Gilead's body.

He pitched to the floor, practically landing at Sahara's feet. Juanita upended the defense counsel's table on his head, setting the exhibits afire.

"Get Prisoner One out of here!" she yelled.

Gladys, bless her, reacted fast. She dragged Sahara through the side door as Juanita struck Gilead again. The flames on his skin didn't go out. Searing heat boiled off him, and she couldn't get close enough to cuff him. For now, he lay atop the charred bodies, apparently dazed.

Bodies. She was standing among the burned.

What about the judge?

"Clear the room!" she coughed, making for the bench. "Please, please . . . *Madre de Dios*, there's his chair . . ."

He was behind the bench, sheltering one of the clerks with his body, a letter opener at the ready in his hand. When he saw Juanita, his wide face lit up.

"Everything's all right, Billie." He dried the clerk's tears with the sleeve of his robe, pointing her at the exit behind Gladys. "No, go, don't look back. It's all right."

"Are you okay, Your Honor?"

"*Corazón*, you're never *ever* getting another day off."

She covered her mouth, fighting a sob. "All those people."

"Hush, Corazón, I know. Just get my chair, will you—"

A roar made them both jump. Down on the floor, Gilead was burning brighter than ever. There was that whumping gas-stove sound, and he became a ball of flame. Rising up to the ceiling, he burned his way out, up, rising into the sky and vanishing.

The fires were everywhere. Juanita pulled an extinguisher off the wall, spraying down the floor between the bench and the ramp to the exit.

The spooky Will Forest crouched near his wife's charred remains. He was made of cinders now, of all the bits of fire rising from the floor.

Lethewood tried to speak to him; he brushed her off, vanishing. As her eyes came up, Lethewood focused on Juanita.

Oh, no. Not you too, Juanita thought.

"Are you all right?" she asked.

"Leave me alone." How had she become the go-to girl for all these freaks and murderers?

"We can help each other, Juanita." She gestured at the back wall, and an archway grew there, a doorway of twisted thorns, green shot through with red and purple. Blackberries?

"I told you to go," Juanita said.

"Think it over." Lethewood disappeared. The arch stayed.

"Let's keep it orderly, people," boomed the judge. He had lifted himself back into his chair, and his voice calmed the remnants of the crowd.

Juanita scanned the room. The civilians had mostly evacced. The sprinklers had stopped the spreading fires, and Gladys had returned and awakened the unconscious marshals. A few MPs had even turned up, too late to do anything but pick up the pieces.

Pieces. All those bodies. She'd been standing . . . She had ashes on her shoes.

"Corazón?" The judge handed her a folded white handkerchief.

She took it automatically, staring past the crisped defendants to the main exit, where a chalky-faced General Roche was helping people limp out through the gaping, burnt doors. "He ordered me to let it happen, Your Honor."

"We're ants among giants, my dear," Skagway told her, wiping his own face with the back of one immense hand. "And the giants are in no way wise, but mere children wielding magnifying glasses."

CHAPTER TWENTY-ONE

HIS WIFE WAS DEAD.

Will shook off Astrid's attempt to comfort him, making for his room.

Caro screaming, suffering—it had been quick, but by no means painless. Would the reporters air that? Was the execution already on the Internet?

Throwing herself in front of that wretched woman, tossing her life away, not a thought for Carson and Ellie . . .

He should tell them. Bramblegate would take him into dreams; he could meet with Carson.

Instead he sat, brooding. It was hours before someone got up the courage to knock on his door.

This is your fault, he was going to say. *It was you, you who made Sahara a monster.* But when he opened up, he found Olive Glade, looking like she understood and holding a brandy flask.

"Is that whiskey?"

"I got Astrid to make a bottomless barrel of my great-granddad Elmo's carrot wine."

"Carrot wine."

"I know—sounds mild. Don't worry, it's pretty much moonshine. Might make you blind, but it's pleasantly sherry flavored. Elmo would throw any old thing that might ferment into a vat when he was making liquor."

"I'm not sure I want company," he said, nevertheless standing aside to let her enter.

"I get it, I really do." She poured two cups and held one up in a toast. "The fallen?"

"The dead." He clinked.

Sipping, she sat on the edge of his bed, eyeing the bits and pieces he'd accumulated since his arrival: toy elephants for Ellie, a couple pairs of socks, empty picture frames.

The alcohol was barely sweet and strong enough to burn a hole in a steel wall. They'd drunk two glasses before either of them spoke.

"It was over between us," Will said finally. "She'd come to hate me. I was working on acceptance. . . ."

She looked amused. "Really?"

"Okay, I'd meant to work on it. Things have been . . ."

"Insane. Yeah. I'd been divorced twelve years, remarried too. But when Astrid killed Lee . . ." She pressed a hand to her chest.

Lee. Another Fyreman who had failed to kill Sahara. And Olive had lost more than one ex-husband. She was Albert Lethewood's widow, Astrid got her son shot. . . .

He laughed harshly. "This is minimizing the body count?"

"Alchemites tortured that man, Will, not us."

"Lucius. They only got him because I knocked him down."

"You saved the strike team."

"I didn't join this crusade to kill people."

"Who've you killed? That Fyreman murdered Caro."

" 'That Fyreman' who is Lucius Landon's brother?"

"So it's all your fault?"

He eyed her sourly.

"Or perhaps it's Astrid's?"

"Astrid broke the magical well open. Astrid unleashed Sahara, murdered Lee, got Jacks shot—"

"And her father stuck her with the well, and Jacks's father killed Albert. Will, you didn't make your wife join Sahara, and you certainly didn't fry her."

She said it kindly, but the word *fry* brought up the memory of Caro in flames. Shuddering, he gulped wine.

"What am I going to do, Olive?" He held out his cup.

She poured. "Believe Astrid when she says it'll be okay."

"It's not even slightly okay."

"No, it's not—but what can you do?"

"Turn back time," he said. "Bring the old world back."

She toasted him with mock cheer. "Good luck with that."

He bit back a heated response . . . and then his skin tingled. Vitagua was powerful. . . . It made anything imaginable a possibility, and he was a chanter now. Why not turn back time?

What if he changed the past? Say he saved Albert Lethewood—that would delay Astrid's takeover of the magical well. If Albert lived, if Sahara never returned to Indigo Springs . . .

His heart raced. He'd tell Albert it was Lee Glade hunting him. Albert had been fifty-four when he died—he might have lived to seventy or eighty if he'd known.

Astrid had told Will all the details of the magical spill. Albert, Jacks, Lee—he could save everyone. Caro might leave him, but she wouldn't die a fanatic. . . .

If he changed the past, they'd never brainwash his daughter.

"Where'd you go just now?" Olive asked.

"Ellie," Will lied. "I need to find that padlock chantment, reverse the brainwashing so the children can come home."

"Good idea."

"I'll start by becoming a better chanter," he said.

"Do us a favor and sober up first."

"You have me there," he said. "Good night, Olive."

She took the hint, leaving him to totter to bed, where he fell into a nightmare about the Roused, trapped in the frozen magic. He'd be betraying them too, not just Astrid and her volunteers. But they were asleep, peacefully asleep—safe. They could wait.

He saw Teoquan, black eyes burning with fury.

He awoke with a hangover, went to the bathroom to splash water on his face, and remembered anew that he had no running water. Instead of cursing, he croaked at the tuning fork hanging at his chest. "Pike, I need to start chanting things—toys."

"Top of the mornin' to you too," came the reply. "Your workshop's near the Chimney."

"I have a workshop?"

"I make things happen, remember?"

"Thank you, Pike."

He gated to the plaza, and stood for a moment blinking at

Astrid's bizarre little empire—the borrowed sunshine, people moving through Bramblegate, alchemized spiders spinning silk-screens to police the contaminated pollens, and everywhere the heavy flower-shop scent of liquid magic. People from every corner of the globe traveling to and fro, all of them giving him space because they knew his wife had died. They'd even shut down the plaza TV, going elsewhere for their fix of trial news.

Intolerable.

His "workshop" was on a new curl of fill on the other side of the Chimney, an open patio that overlooked the pooled vitagua in the ravine. A cluster of toys lay on its floor, and a huge glass punch bowl had been mounted on its edge. The bowl was filled with vitagua.

Will dipped a fist in the punch bowl, and the vitagua quailed away.

The ring. Easing it off, he was blindsided by memory: Caro, slipping it onto his finger at their wedding.

Caro, hat pulled low over a bad haircut.

Caro, burning.

Blinking hard, he began chanting toys.

He fell into a rhythm. Dip a finger, chant something, dip again. A shampoo bottle shaped like a TV cartoon character, a toy phone, a set of jacks, a stamp that made gold stars, a bracelet with bells on it, a toy gun, a plastic stove, a fake stethoscope, a pretend radio, a stuffed frog . . .

His hangover burned away. Clarity returned, intensifying his anguish over Caro, but giving him the strength to focus on his plan. Change the past. Get the old world back.

Volunteers turned up, bringing new toys, carting the chantments off.

Keep improving, Will told himself. *Don't let Astrid know you're planning anything.*

He should find her—reassure her that all was well.

Forcing himself to slip the ring back on, he went in search of her. She was conferring with her head scientist, Katarina, inside the town's Anglican cathedral. The building had been buried under the mulch of vitagua-infected wood, but the interior was sealed. Astrid had chanted its pipe organ. It was this—and a round-the-clock shift of musicians, who ran the communications center—sending out messages to volunteers via tuning forks and penny whistles.

The women were deep in conversation with an orange-haired, mustached stranger of about forty years, with a slouched posture and a shabby coat. The only thing at all notable about him was a red knitted scarf around his neck. *From somewhere wintry, then,* Will thought, summoning enough curiosity to consult the personnel wiki.

No answer. Will frowned. He'd gotten used to knowing everyone's bio at a glance.

"Hey," Astrid said before he could greet the stranger. Her voice was gurgly.

Something was off here. Astrid's eyes were a solid, glowing blue, flooded with vitagua, and she wasn't wearing the healing bangle that fought off the sea-glass poisoning. He lay a hand on her arm. Her skin was cold as frozen steel.

"Astrid?" he said warily.

"How are you doing?" it—whatever *it* was—asked.

"My wife is dead, my kids are . . . How do you think?"

"I never knew, Will." There was no tongue inside that mouth, nothing but a blue cavity. "Caroline's portrait wasn't in the ballroom."

"She couldn't be saved," Katarina said.

He stepped back. "What is this?"

"Mouse magic," the orange-haired stranger said. He took off the red scarf, handing it to Katarina, and just like that, turned into Astrid. The other Astrid, the vitagua . . . clone? . . . froze to statue-stillness.

"This is my true self."

"Astrid prime," Katarina said. "Touch her."

It wasn't necessary: he could see that this Astrid was sick, could see too the healing bangle on her arm and the letrico flowing through it, keeping her alive. "I don't get it."

Katarina spoke: "Sahara's possessing people using contaminated blood. It makes me wonder: Perhaps vitagua can act as a storage medium for human consciousness? It makes sense, if you consider the grumbles in the unreal. Astrid is in constant contact with the well, so—"

"Sahara copies herself using other people, and you . . . This is a copy of you?"

"Yeah. I didn't want to infect anyone with my blood—"

"Because . . . ewww," Katarina said. She tapped the frozen Astrid, nudging open the collar of its shirt and revealing a frozen, alchemized mouse.

Like the Roused, Will thought with a pang of guilt. If he rewrote the past, they'd all be like that, as they had been for so many centuries already.

"Small chordates have skin cells, hair, brain cells, nerves, vocal cords," Katarina said.

"Vocal cords. That's why this copy of Astrid can talk?"

"Not just talk. I can see with this thing, Will. I can hear, and think. . . . It almost feels like me."

His skin crawled. "Can it chant?"

"No." Unexpectedly, she grinned. "But you can. You've made what? Twenty chantments today?"

"I wasn't counting," he lied. Each chantment took him closer to rolling back the calendar, restoring the world, saving Caro. . . .

Pike's voice rang from the pipe organ: "Boss, they're ready."

"Be right there."

"Ready?" repeated Will.

"The pipeline," Katarina said. "Ribbon cutting's today."

"Right." The Serbian mine engineer, Ilya, had used a tunneling chantment to sink a shaft down to a depth of forty feet. He'd beelined seventy miles northeast to a long-abandoned coal mine and flooded it with vitagua. There'd been no discernible effect on the already-contaminated forest.

Next they had eased a shaft outside the contaminated zone. They'd let five thousand gallons of vitagua seep into the rock, forty feet down. Again, there'd been no ill effects.

The underground dumping smacked of desperation to Will, but what did it matter if he was going to rewrite the past?

Pen.

The voice at his ear was so clear that he turned, looking for someone who wasn't there. His stomach flipped; sweat broke out on his forehead. One of Astrid's grumbles?

The time-travel chantment will be a pen, Will.

"You don't have to come," Astrid said. Her clone said it too, multiplying his sense of wrongness. "Everyone will understand if you need some time off."

The sideways mention of Caro's death brought grief to the surface again. "I'm fine."

Both women nodded politely.

Let the Roused sleep, he thought. *I didn't trap them there.*

He followed the women across Bigtop, crossing with them to a clearing at the edge of the lagoon. Here, a single tree had survived the race to the sky. A red-barked arbutus with glowing, vitagua-veined leaves, its tangled limbs stretched up, impossibly high, to the canopy of the magic forest.

Will had imagined oil pipelines when this project was initially conceived: miles of concrete or steel pipes, snaking around the country. But Ilya was just digging a channel for an underground river of vitagua. A serpentine irrigation ditch had been carved into the downward-sloping forest floor, a streambed for liquid magic to flow into the hillside. It vanished into a keyhole-shaped opening under the arbutus roots, a monster-mouth bordered in long grasses and leading down into the earth.

"Oh, this is going to be a lot of magic," Astrid said, catching Will's hand.

He returned the squeeze, feeling almost soiled. None of this was going to happen. And it would be better for Astrid. Her life since Albert died had been a disaster. Jacks would live, Ev would be sane. . . .

We'll never meet, he thought, and was surprised by an upwelling of feeling, a sense of loss.

"What if this gets bombed?" a volunteer asked.

"We bury eventually." Ilya, behind them, was surveying his work with satisfaction. "Dirt and stone from tunnels can become protective wall—we close up overtop. Nothing is wasted."

Will examined the tunnel. The trench where the vitagua flowed was about two meters deep, and its banks were lined with sandbags. The banks themselves were wide enough to accommodate two adults walking side by side.

Ilya stepped into the dry irrigation channel and waved for silence. "One team dug west to sea," he announced peremptorily. "Spirit blood now travels under ocean in coral pipe. Very brave crew calling itself Mermaids, led by Chakeesa, will build pipeline on ocean floor through coastal islands, up to Alaska, eventually to Siberia."

The volunteers applauded the overalls-clad Chakeesa and her crew. Tunneling was claustrophobic enough, but working underwater, with all that pressure overhead . . . If something went wrong, if the letrico ran out before they could Bramblegate back, the Mermaids would be crushed before they could drown.

Ilya indicated the rest of the miners. "Land tunnel heads southeast, bound for Florida. We get more volunteers, more digging chantments, we start channels in other directions, try for Hudson Bay and South America."

It was a simple enough plan. If magic could simply seep into the soil, it would free the Roused while—they hoped—changing the real less radically than would an open-air release.

Ilya looked expectantly at Astrid.

She bowed her head. "Concentrate, Will."

Will closed his eyes. He felt the vitagua within the ravine shifting suddenly, flowing toward them in a trickle. A thin blue line of magic dribbled into the tunnel entrance.

"Now the tricky bit," Astrid said. He sensed her attention moving to the Chimney, the break between the real and unreal, felt the vitagua melting around Jacks. All that ice . . .

"Think about warmth," she murmured, squeezing his hand.

Will tried to pull, sucking his lips back against his teeth. *Fire,* he thought, and the image of Caro going up in flames surfaced again. There was a tremor.

"Nice and slow," Astrid said. She was there with him, wherever *there* was, steadying him. Will imagined fishing, reeling in a line steadily, one turn of the crank after another.

That's it, think heat, now you're cooking with gas. . . .

He ignored the Teoquan-flavored grumble, reeling his imaginary fish. The trickle in the irrigation ditch doubled, trebled, and then became a steady stream.

"You did it!" Astrid said.

Will shrugged, feeling insulated from it all. He'd be setting all this to rights soon enough.

Solemnly, Ilya checked a gauge. "Rate of outflow is one thousand cubic gallons per mile of tunnel per hour. Every day we dig one more mile."

The watching Springers burst into wild applause. *What the hell,* Will thought, and joined them, cheering this latest stage of the end of the world.

CHAPTER TWENTY-TWO

"THIS WAS ONCE A village."

Eliza stood atop an outcropping of blue rock, a crescent-edged cliff that had defied the glacier, jutting above the ice that stretched to the horizon. It was a decent vantage point; Ev could see the Roused city and—looking the other way—the curved roof of the earth lodge at Pucker Hill.

Ten feet below the cliff's edge, the glacier's surface was particularly clear. Frozen within were trees, cedars by the look of them, caught in the frozen vitagua. They curled at the tips, hooked like the spines of leaping fish. A few branches had snapped and begun to fall in the split second, centuries ago, when the vitagua had frozen. They hung in the ice, suspended in midfall.

Here and there within their branches were people, caught in the attitudes of surprise that reminded Ev of Pompeii.

The witch-burners came with the missionaries," Eliza said. "They started on the East Coast, bringing plagues that killed millions. They murdered medicine women and chiefs, shamans and leaders. They looted graves and stole our farmland. As they moved westward, banishing magic, people fled here, to the realm of the spirits. They had time to have babies, grandbabies. This was, for a time, a thriving town."

"Thriving," Ev echoed, wondering why she felt the need for a history lesson. They were here to free people who would see things Eliza's way: patient, sensible folks who could oppose Teoquan's plan to blast his way into the real.

Not that he was going to say that aloud. In her infinite wisdom, Eliza had brought more than fifty of the Roused with them. With their whiskers and fur, their forked tongues and other mutations, the rescuers resembled the cast of some animated kids'

show—bright-eyed critters awaiting the first round of some winter game. Ev had no doubt that at least one would be spying for
Teoquan.

Maybe the speech was for them.

Eliza put her raccoon hands on her hips and huffed. "They're
elders, Ev. The Pit was the battlefield; the people there are warriors."

Oh. Now he got it. Warriors equaled young hotheads, who
tended to follow Teoquan. Here they'd find more mature and
moderate minds. Ev didn't know much about aboriginal culture,
but he had seen that many of the People, as they mostly called
themselves, had a deep respect for age and experience.

Eliza raised her old-fashioned skirt and began tapping her foot,
like a square dancer.

Nothing happened at first. Then there was a shiver underfoot, a crackling sound. Ev clapped his hands over his ears. His
skin buzzed with the vibration; his teeth locked. He had time to
admit to a stab of fear. . . .

Quiet returned.

He opened one eye. The glacier had settled and become
opaque—Eliza had ground it to powder. The hooked cedar tree-
tops sprang free of confinement, spraying fine, cobalt snow. A
suspended branch completed its centuries-delayed fall, landing
with a puff of displaced blue crystal.

"Now what?" Ev said.

She laced her delicate fingers into a basket, raising them slowly.
The snowpack shifted, and the trees quivered.

"*La!*" A frozen figure rose from the snow. He was caked in ice
about an inch thick, and his hands were thrown out defensively.
A woman with the face of a mountain sheep skipped down the
cliffside, pulling him up the treacherous path, passing him to the
others.

More people were rising to the surface of the still-settling
snowbank. The Roused rushed to get them up the cliff.

"Will they waken?" asked a girl of maybe twelve years with
penguin feet and feathers.

"We're just chipping them out," Eliza said. "They need to go to the Pit, where it's warm, to thaw."

A bone bridge had been erected at the cliff's edge; the rescuers lifted each of the newfound people, carrying them over it and vanishing. Eliza, meanwhile, assigned others to shovel the pulverized vitagua into buckets, carrying it up to the clifftop, where a trio of seal-men and an alchemized penguin girl were molding it into bricks, starting a wall.

"What's with that?" Ev asked.

"The snow has to come right off the glacier," Eliza explained. "Otherwise we're freeing some at the cost of burying others."

"Of course."

"Come on. I'm going to crush more ice," Eliza said. He followed her away from the others, out of earshot.

"So . . . ," Ev murmured. "Elders. Mellow elders?"

"Being older doesn't mean they automatically oppose Teoquan. But I used Astrid's chantment to shuffle a few radicals out. Stirred the snow around."

"Will it be enough?"

"It'll tip the balance. The wisdom of these villagers was legendary, Ev. The others approve of freeing them."

"You can't just rescue moderates. Teoquan's not stupid."

"Don't worry, I'll be subtle."

He felt a pang. Rationalize as he might, this was wrong. What had Astrid called it? Vote-rigging.

Eight hours of hard labor later, they had excavated the tops of the trees, exposing high platforms and blue-stained tools along with the village's former inhabitants. Eliza was crumbling ice along the perimeter, making more snow, no doubt concealing the occasional would-be troublemaker in some other glacier. The crew tasked with making a snow fort had constructed a number of igloos near the cliff's edge. Now they were laying the foundation of a bright blue tower.

They'd sent several hundred people to the Pit when a shaft of fiery gold light shot skyward.

Everyone stopped sweeping and cheered.

"They must've opened the pipelines," Ev said. "The underground tunnel and that pipe on the seafloor."

"Right on time," Eliza said. "Want to see how it's going?"

They returned to the city and found the rescue operation scrambling. The far edge of the Pit was melting so fast, it was a real waterfall now, not just a hint of one. The ice roof over Jacks had melted away. He glowed, too bright to look at.

The revived elders stood amid an emotional, cheering crowd. Even by the standards of the unreal, they were impressive. Their bearing spoke of grace, confidence, wisdom. There was a woman with the teeth of a shark and flat, frightening eyes; two men, twins, with the talons and wings of eagles; a mountain lioness with her cubs.

A shaggy buffalo sought Ev's eyes. Sensing one of his own, he crossed the throng. "Is there . . . Can I do anything for you?"

The other shook its great head, speaking the Roused tongue.

"Sorry, I don't understand."

The buffalo rumbled laughter and clasped Ev by the upper arms, exuding goodwill, before lumbering into the crowd.

There was no sign of Teoquan.

Don't pick the scab. Go back to the dig. Instead of taking his own advice, Ev trudged up to Patience's suite.

Teoquan was there, all right. "The more of us Astrid melts free, the sooner the People see things my way," he was saying. "A few old folks won't change that."

"I'm an old folk, Teo, " Patience replied. "And just because you can bust into the real doesn't mean you should."

"I should stay here, behave, do everything Eliza says?"

"You're all attitude and no plan."

"Oh, I got plans."

"Don't start that again. The real's dangerous, Teo."

"You could be a goddess, Patience. Real worship, instead of hollow celebrity. Ain't you tempted?"

He could make her a goddess? Ev swallowed.

"What would that accomplish?"

"Anything you want! I'll give you power over life and death. The two of us and a committed war party—"

"Are you bulletproof, Teo? Are you so sure you're unstoppable?"

"Eliza and Astrid can't keep us here forever."

"Astrid's speeding things up; what more do you want?"

"She has a live Burning Man. I want him."

Patience sighed. "I'll tell her."

There was a sound that might have been a kiss. "Think about my offer, and give Ev my regards." Then Teoquan brushed past him, vanishing into the honeycomb.

Ev gave it a minute, then slipped into the room.

"Don't say anything," Patience said. She was coal black, of medium height, and heartstoppingly beautiful.

He swallowed protests: warnings about Teoquan being dangerous, reminders that Astrid was doing her best.

Instead, he put a hand on her shoulder.

"Dammit, Ev, I am nothing but bones. I'm a restaurant dishwasher, not some emissary to gods and psychopaths."

"You were a beauty queen," he said. "A celebrity."

She turned into his arms, and his heart pounded. "I look good, but I'm damn well sixty-eight today."

"You're more than bones."

"He's going to break into the real, isn't he?"

"Teo will be okay," he said, trying to be generous. "If anyone can take care of himself—"

"Hang Teo, Ev."

He squeezed her, cursing the arousal that came with this proximity . . . yet enjoying it too, the desire, the feeling of physical rightness, of being who he was meant to be. "The magical spill was always going to be a terrible mess."

"Mmph." That cranky grunt. God help him, it was sexy.

"You know, you've been working seven days a week."

"You're one to talk."

"You say it's your birthday?"

"You gonna bake me a cake?"

Something penetrated. "Did you say . . . hang Teo?"

"Ev Lethewood, you may be the dumbest man I ever met."

He kissed her. It was a stupid thing to do, he knew it. But before he could draw breath to apologize, her hands were on his face; she was responding, passionately.

Ev felt the tightness in his chest break. He swept her up, off the floor, and carried her to bed.

"Happy birthday to . . . Lord, you're heavy."

"Save your breath, old man." Giggling, she yanked him down after her. "You'll need it."

⚜ CHAPTER TWENTY-THREE ⚜

JUST AFTER SHE ESCAPED government custody, Astrid had camped in a salvaged pup tent in a clearing she, Mark, Patience, and Ev had carved out between the vitagua well and the Grand Hotel. The rubble of downtown provided objects to chant, and she'd used them to mulch the overgrown forest around the hotel. The others immediately insisted she take a room inside the building, for safety. Now they'd gone even further, moving Astrid's real body, the one Katarina called Astrid Prime, into a so-called bomb shelter, a hole Ilya's tunneling crew had dug below the hospital.

She hated being underground; it reminded her of jail. A volunteer with a healing chantment was always hovering, just like a guard. It was a reasonable precaution, she knew, given the seaglass caught inside her. Still, having a babysitter chafed.

At least she could concentrate on the mouse magic while her real body was lying around on magical life support.

She'd started with that first flawed copy of herself, the one Will had met. That doppelganger wouldn't have fooled anyone at a distance, but with practice, she'd been able to make the copies—ringers, Mark had dubbed them—identical to her.

Now there were only a few ways to distinguish between a ringer and the real Astrid. They were icy to the touch, for one thing. For another, the muscles of the small animals at the core of a ringer were weak. They struggled to lift anything heavier than a pencil, and they couldn't make chantments.

Once she had that first perfect copy, Astrid tried making a second.

She hadn't expected to be able to control two. To be in more than one place at once, to look out at the world through multiple sets of eyes and hold multiple conversations. . . . She should have been hopelessly confused.

But the ringers were surprisingly autonomous. They weren't puppets exactly: they were Astrid, or she was them. They went about her business while Astrid Prime lay in the bomb shelter. Astrid remembered everything they did, every conversation, every decision, as if she'd done it herself.

It was a little like being in a noisy bar, of standing on the edge of a number of overlapping groups, each engaged in intense discussion. The ringers joined in; Astrid Prime heard it all.

She had tragedies to prevent, lives to save. When controlling two of the ringers got easy, she worked her way up to six.

She was working on a seventh when Olive appeared in the cave, with a sack in her hand and a forbidding look on her face.

"Know the only thing worse than having you running around barking at people?"

"I'm not running anywhere. I'm cooped up here."

"Copies of you everywhere barking at people."

"I don't bark. I'm not a barker."

"Can't you task one of these ringers with relaxing? Take it to Disneyland or something."

"If I wanted to bark, I might have reason, but—"

"Don't be defensive," Olive said. "Nobody's making you stay down here."

"Guilt," Astrid sighed. "Works better than Roche's handcuffs."

"Is guilt why you're living like a monk? Look around! All you need is bread and water, maybe a flail. . . ."

It was true: aside from vitagua lanterns, letrico, and a hospital bed, the cavernous chamber was empty. Maybe it was what she deserved, Astrid thought, remembering Sahara, the pile of burned bodies in the courtroom. Caro Forest. "What are you suggesting, Olive?"

"Ilya dug you a big damn hole here."

"It's still a hole."

"You can make anything you want of it. Make a mansion."

"I should live it up while everyone else is camping?"

"Make a mansion with guest rooms." Olive gave her a shake.

"Now? Katarina's trying to teach me quantum physics, and I'm going over priorities with Pike."

"The point of the ringers is that they can just keep on doing that, right?" Olive said, "I'm telling you, Astrid, make this place habitable."

Astrid slid off the bed, stifling a moan. That was another thing about the ringers: They felt chilly, cold as if they'd been caught in a hard winter rain, but at least they didn't hurt.

She pulled letrico through the healing bangle, tamping down the pain.

Olive upended the sack over the bed. Construction chantments tumbled out. "This magic thing can be fun. Remember fun, Astrid?"

"Fun for me is being outside."

"Then this is an opportunity for personal growth."

"No, it's a waste of power."

"Your being a grouch is bad for morale."

A flicker of shame. "I didn't mean to be grouchy."

Olive put an arm around her, an embrace that felt both motherly and unfamiliar. Astrid caught a glimpse of an imaginary life that might have been, if she'd married Jacks after all, if Olive had been her mom-in-law. Her father alive, Ev female, a grandmother.

She wished she'd let herself be happy with Jacks, instead of mooning over Sahara.

Sahara had held that old lawyer in front of her. She'd have let Gilead burn everyone, just to save herself.

And it wasn't vitagua madness; it was who she was, deep down. All these years, Astrid had been in love with a Sahara who'd never existed.

It was too late to tell Will now that he was right, to apologize or say she got it. When Gilead burned Will's wife, he'd burned all her hopes. The grumbles had to be playing with her. How could Will love her now, after all that had happened?

So Astrid grabbed on to the illusion of might-have-been, just for a second: an ordinary existence, a life with Jacks. No magically flooded towns, no memories of murder, no air force raids trying to kill everyone she knew.

"Olive, I'll be nicer," she said. "But Teoquan is after me to locate Lilla Skye, and nobody knows how to help that injured Fyreman. And the curse on magic, we still have to break that."

"You're working on that six times over, boss."

"Boss, right." Like a queen bee in a hive, Astrid thought, seemingly in charge, almost a slave. She picked up a silver spoon that shaped stone like modeling clay. "You really want me to turn this hole into a prettier hole?"

"It's important," Olive said.

"I keep ending up underground." Roche had kept her in a fake apartment, drywall and plastic plants, a façade of normalcy. She shuddered. Re-creating that . . .

"Fun," Olive reminded her.

"I'm trying." Fun. Speeding on the highway with the radio on, horseback rides, cycling, gardening, boating on Great Blue Reservoir . . .

Jacks had taken her caving once.

Drawing letrico, she started with the ceiling. She remembered a bowl-shaped cavern with a jagged seam of quartz crystals on its roof; now she copied it, dragging the crystals in a rocky bristle that meandered across the chamber.

"Oh—" Olive paled, covering her mouth.

"He took you there too?"

"Pictures. Of the two of you, I—" She fisted a tear away.

"I didn't think—"

"Don't get mushy, Astrid, and don't stop."

Embarrassed, she turned to her rudimentary bathroom, molding the stone floor into a trio of deep pools, one steaming, one with icy water, the two nested around each other like a yin–yang symbol and overflowing to mingle in the third basin.

She built up a privacy screen of tumbled pebbles around the hospital bed, then turned to the far wall, digging out sconces for the vitagua lanterns randomly scattered on the floor. The process made a fair pile of rubble. She mashed it all into a massive table.

"You're *not* building a boardroom," Olive warned.

"People keep saying we don't have anywhere proper to talk."

"Put in a garden, young woman."

"Yes, ma'am." She molded the stone floor, creating columns and walls, building up raised containers, paths, alcoves, stone benches, and a grotto.

Even as she played around with the cave, one of her ringers was in the hotel lobby, working with Pike. Now she asked: "Olive's got me redecorating the cave. Can you send someone down with uncontaminated topsoil and seeds?"

"Aye, done. Need sunshine?"

"I'll make something. Someone scavenged up a cheesy suit of armor; maybe that? And some chairs . . ."

"Armor, furniture," Pike echoed.

Armor. The idea quirked her sense of humor—

"You're smiling," Olive said. "Does it hurt?"

"Yes, okay, you were right. Why don't you Versailles this place up?" She passed her an ornamental gavel made of brass. The volunteers called it the Midas. It turned rags to silk, pennies to gold, costume jewelry to real gems. They used it to make things they could pawn, when they needed money.

"Really? You want gilt?"

"If I'm gonna be trapped like a genie, it might as well be in a cave of wonders. Go crazy."

With a whoop, Olive whapped the privacy screen around her bed, turning it to jade and turquoise. Volunteers appeared, carrying cheap pine chairs and bins of topsoil. As the chairs came in, Olive converted them to oak thrones, positioning them around the big table.

"Don't stop," she told Astrid.

"I hear and obey." Astrid turned to the three pools, cutting a stream of fresh water into the floor and making a water garden on the opposite side of the chamber. Someone brought in the suit of armor, and she chanted it so that fresh air blew from the dyed horsehair plume of its helm. They set it in the center of the shelter, and she grew a stone dais underneath its feet, raising it halfway to the ceiling. She chanted a bicycle wheel so that sunshine emanated from its spokes, then pinned it above the knight with a single tall stalagmite. The room warmed.

Her spirits rose.

Volunteers stepped in to run the chantments and fill the garden plots.

"We bringing in a TV?" someone asked.

"No." The last thing she needed was the news mumbling and flickering at her all day. "Ilya can dig another chamber for that."

Outside, in town, Astrid's ringers were busily working. Her physics tutorial with Katarina was wrapping up. In the seers' silk tent, volunteers worked steadily on locating people for the Lifeguards to save. Things were quiet in the Octagon—there had been no bombing runs in a week. Mark was using the downtime to set up a "proper" center for gathering and analyzing world news. He was already calling it the Doghouse.

One ringer sat in the old Anglican church, watching the communications volunteers send messages through the magic pipe organ. Another was with Ilya at the far end of the pipeline, watching his team plot the route for their underground tunnel, for the river of magic.

"Astrid?" Katarina said. "Are we still having a science briefing with Astrid Prime?"

"When's it supposed to be?" She'd lost track of time.

"Any minute now."

"Yes, come on down," she said to Katarina. To Olive, she said: "I need a clock by the big table."

"On it." Rummaging in a bin of furniture the scavengers had brought, Olive raised a cheap cuckoo clock to eye level and started tapping it with the gavel. Letrico flicked through her, and an ornate wooden grandfather clock grew from the plastic original. It ticked resonantly, standing against the wall.

"Is that enough decorating for now? I have a meeting."

"Yes. Go back to multitasking yourself to death." But Olive was teasing now.

Not by fire, not by poison, not by overwork.

Even the grumbles were giving her a hard time.

Relieved, Astrid healed herself yet again before taking a seat at the limestone table.

Katarina gated in, trailed by a dozen scientists. She rolled a map of the West Coast out onto the table. Hand-drawn lines showed the two pipeline routes: Ilya's tunnel heading east from Indigo Springs, and the Mermaid team's route as they inched toward Vancouver Island underwater, moving at a rate of forty feet per day. Ilya's team was faster. They were well out of the contaminated zone, crawling toward Denver, undulating to skirt the towns in their path.

A murmur filled the cave: chatter about vitagua outflow rates, contamination, carbon uptake.

Will should be here, Astrid thought. But Will was at the Chimney, grimly chanting toys. Trying to get better at it, as he should. He had been distant since his ex-wife's murder.

It was hardly a surprise, though she couldn't help but feel hurt by his withdrawal.

She drew on her sense of After, and the future felt the same. The kids, safe and laughing . . .

Katarina said: "In the towns nearest the pipeline route, people have seen ghosts. There are reports of cows having two-headed calves. Seven ostriches on a Washington farm starved themselves to death last week."

"Good things are happening too," someone put in. "The patients in a pediatric cancer ward in Pendleton went into remission. A number of murderers have turned themselves in."

"Alchemites are taking credit, of course," Katarina said.

"Even though the Fyremen are torching them willy nilly?"

It had started in Cleveland, with a nurse. The victim didn't have any chantments; she was just a woman who had bought Sahara's line about the Age of Miracles. They flattened her house, dragged her atop the wreckage, and lit her up.

Gilead Landon had been there, whipping up the crowd, recruiting. Attracting a mob of angry young men, he'd preached destruction of everything magical, issuing a public challenge to Roche: Work with me, or get out of my way.

"Astrid? You with us?"

"I'm great," she said.

Twenty pairs of eyes regarded her dubiously, and there was a roil of pain within her stomach, acid hot, that subsided as she drew letrico into her healing bangle, raising it up so they could see her mending herself.

"Let's move on to climate change," Katarina said. "We have volunteer in Northern BC who's asking—could we use timed heat draws to kill infestation? Some insect . . ."

"Mountain pine beetle."

There was a surge of activity at the pipe organ—a lot of messages, coming through fast. In the hotel, Pike cursed.

The Astrid ringer, beside him, said: "What's up?"

"That Fyreman's grabbed Janet and run into the forest."

Astrid drew on the vitagua in the mulched lagoons, chasing a pulse of body heat. She rolled in its direction, washing over a contaminated squirrel. Drawing liquid magic over the struggling animal, she formed another copy of herself around its small body. Squirrel skin grew over the ice-Astrid in a sheath; silky hair broke through its new scalp. The eyes took a minute to grow, but she was getting better at this.

She was naked . . . but only for a second. Pike pulled letrico through a hat rack she'd chanted for the purpose, spinning the ringer a T-shirt and jeans—generic-looking but lightweight garments that wouldn't tax her mouse muscles.

Her mouse self in the Octagon was joined by Mark. "Eyes on Janet," he said. They peered at the bamboo screen, but nothing happened.

"Janet's Sketch is in the ballroom, in Limbo." Jupiter said, voice tight.

Astrid said, "I made a blanket that pulls people to it—"

"Will destroyed it grabbing his kids, remember?"

She took a doppelgänger to Will's workshop, cutting in on his chanting session. "Lucius is loose—we need you."

"To do what?"

"You're the expert, you tell me. Talk him down?"

"Maybe we should let him go." He set down a chanted toy, a plastic teapot, as if it weighed a ton.

"He's got Janet."

He turned toward the nearest gate. "Where?"

"Outside town. What do we do, Will?"

"Talk to him. See what he wants."

"He wants us all dead."

"It's time we figured out what to do with him." His tone was neutral, but Astrid thought she picked up a whisper of accusation. "Is he a patient? A prisoner?"

"We let him go, his big brother will toss him on the nearest bonfire."

"If that's truly his choice—" He let his words trail off as he stepped through the gate, joining the ringer already making its way deeper into the forest.

"Over here!" Igme waved from between two overgrown trees. Beyond him stood a long ranch house encircled by a quake-rattled fence, a lawn surrounded by a mesh of tangled tree roots and overgrown forest. The yard within the fence was uncontaminated, its grass dead.

"I don't understand," Aquino said. "Why isn't it enchanted?"

"This was Chief Lee's house," Astrid said.

Will sighed. "It's protected against magic?"

"What do we do, Will?"

"In a hostage situation, we hope the subject wants to live. The threat of getting shot gets him talking."

"This guy's pretty much suicidal."

"That's more dangerous," Will agreed. He raised his voice. "Lucius?"

It's like he's humoring you, innit? Her mouse selves shivered as the grumble said, *You hide things from him, right? Deception's a two-way street.*

"I made that shovel," she said suddenly. "If they used that ropey glass stuff to protect the house, it'll break through."

Aquino startled, and Will went poker faced.

I must have barked, as Olive put it, she thought, but she couldn't stop: "How did we miss a patch of magic-proofed ground so close to Bigtop?"

"The forest's practically a hedge," Aquino said.

"It's sloppy." She glowered, feeling like a bully as he wilted.

"Lucius isn't talking," Will said.

Igme was sprinting toward them, brandishing the shovel.

"If I do die," Astrid said, "you'll just sit around making toys in a funk until the army burns you out."

Instead of answering, Will plunged the shovel into the dirt at the base of the fence. Letrico shimmered; green shoots spiraled through the dead lawn, working themselves into the protective chains surrounding the house. Vitagua soaked into the parched sod.

"We've broken through."

Astrid shook off a restraining hand—she wasn't sure whose— and walked toward the house.

"Astrid—"

Straining her squirrel-weak muscles, she pushed open the door . . . then froze. A line of salt, glass, and gunpowder had been sprinkled over the threshold.

She tried to step over it, failed.

Pulling on the vitagua within the forest, she drew liquid magic over the threshold, thinking to wash the barrier away. Instead, there was a crackle and a burst of smoke. The glass and the vitagua immolated.

Vitagua destroys sea-glass; sea-glass destroys vitagua, she thought. This was what Jacks had been telling her. If she immersed herself in magic, the glass within would be destroyed. . . .

The linoleum, where the salt and glass had been, was pocked and burned. She rolled another wave of vitagua over the floor, watching the little explosions, imagined that happening to the sea-glass inside her body.

Upstairs, Janet cried out.

Astrid looked back, to Will. "What do I say?"

"What do you want to tell him? Don't bite my head off. What?"

She raised her voice. "You don't have to die, Lucius. You're contaminated, you're . . ."

"Scared," Will supplied. "Angry."

"Freaked out and mad at me, at Sahara's people. . . ." She stepped over the threshold, passing one of Jacks's early paintings: trees, a lake, a campfire.

Lucius growled from atop the steps. He was holding a pistol to Janet's head.

"Let her go," Astrid said. She saw Sahara in there, in the flash of hatred, the edgy, quicksilver smile. "Killing her won't get you anything."

"No?" He shoved his hostage, propelling her over a line of salt. Janet stumbled, tripping over Astrid, who went down too. Her mouse muscles weren't up to a tackle.

"Third time's the charm, medic," Lucius crooned, scooping salt off the floor.

"You okay, Janet?" Astrid asked as they disentangled themselves.

"Don't fret." Janet bared bloody teeth. "Been through worse, remember? How 'bout you?"

"Help me up." They regained their feet, facing . . . "Lucius? Sahara?"

"What's your plan, princess? They keep you on life support forever?" Lucius undulated in a dance Sahara had incorporated into her religious ceremonies. "You're getting weaker."

"Is Lucius Landon in there?"

"Nobody here but us goddesses. Lucius couldn't resist my charms."

"Then why come here, to Lee's? Why put up barriers?" She kicked at the salt. "You love magic, Sahara. Why lock it out?"

"Darling, don't be tiresome. We need to talk."

"You need to talk to the . . . Who am I? The Filthwitch?"

"That's just about branding; don't hold a grudge."

"I'm not interested in this," she said wearily.

"No? Truly? You used to find me irresistible."

I used to believe in Santa Claus, too, she thought. "I thought you were all the things I couldn't have."

A long, furious-sounding bird trill. "Lucius saw this future, you know. And he's seen you dead and burning."

Down in her cave, Astrid Prime's flesh crawled. "I don't die by fire."

"Says who? The grumbles? They didn't tell you Jacks was gonna get shot."

With a jeer, he hit the button on Lee's dusty, battery-operated answering machine. Lucius's voice echoed: "Uncle, it's me. Listen—don't go to the chanter's place alone."

She snapped it off. "He called just before you killed Jacks's dad. Too late, of course. Remember that feeling? Trying to change what's meant to be. Lucius felt it too."

"Sahara, do you remember the chantment you used on Ellie Forest? It's a padlock."

"Wouldn't you rather know about the curse? That Fyreman curse on magic you're obsessed with? Lucius knows all about it. Twelve old men in a cave, reciting Befoulment. Sowing madness into magic, reducing higher forms of life to low . . ."

"Quit with the games and tell me about the chantment."

"You'd really choose Forest and his brats?"

"Their mother died for you, Sahara. Show some respect."

"If you break the curse, you might yet save me."

"The kids, Sahara."

"Will Forest doesn't want you, darling. Cut him loose." Sahara's fist spasmed, pouring a handful of salt on the floor, closing the circle around her. Her posture straightened, and he raised the revolver.

"Lucius?" Astrid asked.

The contaminated Fyreman nodded.

"I'm sorry this happened to you."

"Sahara spoke the truth. You're doomed." He scratched at the spiral kudu horns in his forehead. "I've seen you burn."

"Help us with the Frog Prince curse, Lucius," Astrid said. "We could cure you."

He drew a visibly pained breath. "If you stopped releasing the magic, all this could be over."

"The magic's releasing itself."

"You know your power. Even now, it's not too late."

"I won't sell out the Roused," she said.

"They'll never know. Reverse the flow of vitagua and freeze them all."

"They're people."

"The evil must be expunged—"

"You guys weren't burning witches back in the sixteenth century because you thought magic was evil. You did it so you could have all the power yourselves."

"We birthed the modern world, Lethewood! Do you think the Internet and the space shuttle and automatic dishwashers would exist if the laws of nature had remained subject to the whims of sorcerers? Order, consistency—that's what people need."

Astrid shook her head. "Magic didn't stop the Romans from building roads and aqueducts. There were clockworks—"

"Magic won't stop my brethren from burning you."

Another fanatic. "I stopped the Chief, didn't I?"

"You slaughtered him."

"Is Sahara right? Are there Fyremen out there keeping up the curse? Is it just a matter of shutting them up?"

He shrugged, poker faced.

"If they stopped, you'd be a man again?"

"With Sahara within? I prefer to go to the fire."

That she could almost understand.

"Lethewood, did you ever think maybe it's you who has the Messiah complex, not Sahara? You're destroying the world."

"Sure, I've wondered," she said. "But then your brother sets some poor nurse on fire, or the Alchemites torture you, and the doubt leaks away."

"My brother is going to kill you," he said. "He is going to

throw you on a pile of wood and burn you like the sinful piece of trash you are."

Down in the Cave of Wonders, her throat was dry. "What happens to you, Lucius? Do I give you to the unreal?"

"Don't you know?" He fired Lee's pistol. The bullet struck her ringer in the hip, exiting in a harmless spray of blue ice.

She washed vitagua up the steps, flooding the salt circle he'd laid, filling the air with the stink of burnt flowers and floor varnish.

Pouring vitagua around him, Astrid forced it into his eyes, ears, nose. His transformation accelerated—the kudu horns spiraled out to their full length, and bird feathers fluffed out from his neck.

"Astrid," Janet murmured.

"It's all right. He can't hurt anyone in this state. Maybe if we break the curse, he'll recover."

Lucius had other ideas. He turned the Chief's answering machine back on. Then, before his hands could change into hooves or talons, he raised the pistol to his head.

"At least I can kill the witch within," he said.

"Wait!" Astrid said, but it was too late.

The shot was loud, terribly loud, and there was a spray—

Red blood, blue magic, Astrid thought. *No, no.*

"Don't look, honey," Janet said, physically turning Astrid away.

The sound as Lucius collapsed was soft, not quite a thud.

"And that's it for me, isn't it?" The answering machine broke the silence with the months-old recording of the dead man. "But, Lethewood, you're still gonna burn."

CHAPTER TWENTY-FOUR

NONE OF THIS WAS going to happen.

Will was in dreams, snatching a few precious minutes with his son while Ellie was elsewhere: he assumed she was with an Alchemite, but couldn't bear to ask. They had dreamed up the real world. Carson was driving a blue convertible along an empty oceanside roadway.

Carson was happy; he clearly had no idea his mother was dead. If Will could change the past, undo all of this, there was no point in telling him.

"Caarrrr, where are you?" Ellie's voice cut into the music playing on the stereo. The convertible came to a dead stop and Carson leapt out.

"I'll try to get away tomorrow, Dad."

"Maybe we'll try a fighter plane."

"That'd be cool."

Will accelerated away before his daughter could catch them.

Stepping through Bramblegate, he headed to the hotel lobby. "Where's the globe, Pike?"

"Burned out, lad—overuse."

"How do I catch up on the news?"

Pike handed him a nickel-sized disk of vitagua-infected hardwood. "We've upgraded."

"What's this?" It looked like a coin—a tree was carved on one side, a tiny, intricate map of the world on the other. There was a faint hum of life within, a sensation that reminded him of a moth he'd caught in the kids' room one night, dim electric charge of vitality, clasped safely between his hands.

"Doghouse is up and running in London," Pike said. "Give it a second, you'll have everything you need to know."

"Thanks," Will said, warming the coin between his fingers.

U.S. news came to him first: At Wendover, the trial was dead in the water. Journalists had moved on to tracking the spate of Fyreman executions of Alchemites, all while debating whether Juanita Corazón had done a good thing or not in preventing Gilead's attempt to execute Sahara.

Across the world, governments were getting jittery. Astrid's volunteers had been spreading contamination outside North America for long enough now that it was getting noticed. Contaminated crocodiles had been spotted in Africa. The Australian police had arrested a fugitive Alchemite and were extraditing her to Texas, where the attorney general had a capital murder prosecution all warmed up for her.

A burst of tactical information wrapped up the bulletin: Sahara Knax remained in custody. Gilead Landon's whereabouts were unknown. Alchemites had been sighted in Elko, Nevada. Roche was in Washington, D.C., meeting with the joint chiefs and the president.

The sooner he remade the past, the better, Will thought.

". . . ideally, a combat medic." Janet's voice pulled him back to the here and now.

"I'll get our People Peeps on it," Pike said cheerily.

Will asked: "Hiring a replacement?"

"An assistant, anyway," Janet said.

"Nobody would blame you if you wanted off the strike team." Her smile was a little worn; for the first time, she looked her age. "After Lucius grabbed me, you mean?"

"You got hurt in Atlanta too. And Sahara's threat—"

"Implied that next time I won't be so lucky. Boss ask you to trauma-counsel me?" She led him out into Bigtop, past a crew that had gathered up a few thousand plastic water bottles. They were filling them with liquid magic—part of some dispersal plan, presumably, that Will hadn't heard about yet.

"Astrid didn't send me, Janet. We're friends, remember?"

She plopped down on a log bench. "I'm still in Limbo, Will. Yesterday's excitement didn't move my portrait to the Big Picture."

"We still have time to save you."

"Maybe."

"You're saying you don't care?"

"Of course I care, Will. I'm not looking to die."

"Sounds to me like there's a *but* coming."

She shrugged. "I had a son and daughter, you know, same as you."

"Had?"

"Brad hanged himself in '93. As for Sally . . . Last I heard, she had a conservative husband and an SUV and four lovely children. We're not speaking."

"I'm sorry."

"Don't mean nothing," she said.

"People get out of Limbo, Janet. Ev did. Olive—"

"This isn't a counseling session, right? We're just two friends hanging out?"

"Of course."

"Your youngest thinks you're Satan, Will Forest. You saw your wife burned to shit. You're having an on-again off-again romance with the closest thing this earth has to a deity. You feel like talking about that?"

He felt his jaw dropping, tried to pass it off with a chuckle. "You're telling me to back off."

"I'm a tough old bird, and I'm committed to this fight. Getting grabbed by a lunatic patient—"

"Watching him commit suicide," he interrupted.

"It hardly comes up on my radar."

"Still," he said. "If you could rewrite the past."

"I wouldn't change a thing," Janet said. She reached into her satchel, pulling out a black cashmere sweater. Bunching it, she pressed it to her face, inhaling—then passed it over.

Cautious, Will sniffed. The sweater smelled of laundry fresh from the dryer, and he flashed on a summer backpacking trip across Greece. He was twenty, standing at the temple of Delphi in the pouring rain, kissing a Danish girl in a cotton dress. The rest of the tour group had fled the storm.

Every sensation was as vivid as it had been that day: the warm rain sluicing over their bodies, caramel-colored mud spurting everywhere—the way it felt to neck with a stranger in the navel of the world.

"Wow," he said.

"No offense, but I'll take magic over therapy," Janet said. Having reclaimed the sweater, she strode away.

Will was about to follow, when Astrid joined him on the bench. She had gotten so good at the mouse magic that he had to lay a finger on her to check . . . but, yes, her skin was cold.

"If it looks like me, it ain't," she reminded him. "I'm only allowed out in disguise."

"Right." By disguise she meant a magic scarf that made her look like a nondescript middle-aged guy.

"You've been keeping to yourself," she said.

Guilt intruded on his magically induced bubble of cheer: it was one thing to plan to wipe out this bizarre empire, another to lie to Astrid's face. "I've been making chantments."

"Powerful ones, some of them."

"Maybe, but it's still only toys that have sparkle."

"You're doing what my father did," she said.

She meant that Albert Lethewood had kept his vitagua exposure to a minimum. The grumbles brought disorientation and knowledge of the future. It had scared Albert, and Will could certainly sympathize with that.

But Astrid was right: Albert had never been much of a chanter. It was getting drenched in vitagua that had accelerated her development as a well wizard.

"Grumbles can't guide you if you don't listen," she said.

"It's like chatting with a lion who's planning to eat you," Will said.

"They're not that hostile," she said.

"Okay, I'll take on a bit more." None of this was going to happen, after all. He would be changing the past.

After removing his ring, Will drew fluid from the forest floor, letting vitagua seep into him. Cold magic filled his nose and throat. Choking, he yanked his hand back. "Alchemites are asking us for sanctuary."

"When?" Astrid said.

"Ugh, this is awful." He groped: "I think . . . now."

Thrashing in the forest beyond the ravine, followed by a scream, interrupted them.

Clouds of wasps formed around the periphery of Bigtop. As Will watched, Astrid raised the level of vitagua in the mulch, transforming the forest floor to impassable swamp. Spotlights shone down from a dozen umbrellas hung in the forest canopy, swiveling to focus on a single point.

Mark and Jupiter appeared in the beam, marching a young woman between them. Vines bound her arms; she was barefoot and had a bad burn on one shoulder. Her clothes were tattered, her hair matted and dirty. She'd fallen in vitagua more than once: she was changing into a pigeon.

"Just a girl," Astrid murmured. "Come on, Will—let's follow them to the hospital. We'll test this doppelgänger trick of mine on a stranger."

"Okay." He suppressed an interior shudder: he found her ringers creepy.

They trotted to Emergency, where Janet, clad in the magic cashmere sweater, was examining the girl. It was hard to be sure, because of the pigeon features altering her face, but she looked about fourteen.

"Is she carrying any chantments, Will?" Astrid asked.

Will closed his eyes, trying to sense magic, and felt nothing. Instead, he frisked her. "Just this hairbrush."

"Can you tell what it is?"

"It let her wiggle through the growth—it's how she got through the forest."

An orderly glowered. "We're treating Alchemites now?"

"Shut up, Bernie. She's a kid," Janet said.

The girl was staring at Astrid.

"You gonna call me the Filthwitch to my face?" Astrid asked, but her voice was gentle.

She struggled against her bonds. "They're frying everyone, all of us."

"You shouldn't have tortured that fellow you captured," Jupiter said. "Pissed 'em off."

"That wasn't me," she said. "Please, there are Fyremen everywhere. Wherever we fly, they're waiting."

Mark laughed. "You're asking us for protection?"

"Wait here with the medics, okay?" Astrid pulled the men aside. "What do you think? Can we help her?"

"Are you serious?" Mark said.

"One of these Alchemites must know where that padlock chantment is. They give it up, we can fix Will's daughter."

Will was surprised by the flare of hope. Had he given up on Astrid too soon?

"It's risky," Mark said. "If we give them access to town, to Bramblegate and the plaza—"

"No, we can't just bring them here. But I want to stop the executions."

"You don't owe them anything, Astrid," Mark said.

"Of course not," Will said. "Why would she?"

"If they all come to the forest, it allows the Fyremen and Roche to focus on us."

"If we don't, Landon will fry them all."

The words stirred up the memory of Caro, her fine blond hair afire, her mouth open in a scream. All for Sahara . . .

"Nobody's touched our satellite bases in Europe," Mark said.

"We're talking thousands of Alchemites." Astrid frowned. "They'll have to be nearby if we're going to protect them. We don't want them having a lot of chantments. And they'll be praying to Sahara."

"I don't want that in my face."

"No," Astrid agreed. "We can't ask the volunteers to suck that up."

The volunteers, Will thought. *Not her?* Something had shifted in Astrid's feelings toward Sahara since the massacre at the courthouse.

Maybe seeing her childhood crush object use a sick old man as a human shield stripped away her last illusions.

"Astrid," Mark said. "They'll vamp us all and pick our bones."

"This is a chance to stop them vamping altogether," Astrid said. "We'll make them forget the cantation."

"Even if you do, they can't stay in town," Will said. "Mark's right—we'd have riots."

"I agree. We'll set them up in the forest, close to here."

Mark said. "Astrid, talk sense. The Alchemites hung their own asses out—"

If it doesn't work, I can still rewrite the past, Will thought. "Didn't you tell me there was a ghost town nearby? Cabins, running water, that kind of thing?"

"Tishvale," Astrid said. "Good idea."

Mark groaned. "You'll bring the Fyremen down on us."

"Time we should go after the Fyremen," Will said.

Astrid shrugged. "Go after them how? Our seers can't find 'em. . . ."

"Do it the old-fashioned way," Will said. "Investigate."

"Wow! We never thought of that," Mark said.

"You don't have to be sarcastic," Astrid said.

"Will, we've got people going through Chief Lee's house," Mark said. "Scavengers are searching for the fire hall."

"Sahara's people might help there," Astrid said. "They know things about the Fyremen. If we shelter them, they'll have to tell us everything."

"So who does what?" Will said.

"Alchemites won't talk to me," Astrid said.

"Will's the negotiator," Mark said. "Let him wheel and deal."

"Sounds good," Will said, ignoring his snarky tone.

"I'll set up the ghost town," Astrid said, and another full-grown ringer, blue in color, crawled out of the ravine. Clothes and skin grew over its nude body, and red curls spilled over its torn right ear.

Shuddering, Will focused on the Alchemite.

CHAPTER TWENTY-FIVE

WENDOVER HAD A PERPETUAL smell of spent jet fuel and scorched grass, a sere, acrid atmosphere that, along with the heat and the glare of the sun reflecting off the salt flats, made the whole place seem inhospitable, like the surface of the moon. At first, the base staff seemed to marvel at its novelty. Now that the judge had declared a mistrial—what else could he do, with seven defendants dead?—people had been going out as little as possible. They blamed the heat, but Juanita sensed something else: a feeling of impending defeat, perhaps, like the surrender of an injured animal that curls up in a patch of shade, waiting to die.

She had taken to running around the barracks and administration buildings, escaping from the desperation pervading the base while she contemplated her own diminishing options.

Gilead was on the loose, out running up his body count and playing to the press. But he hadn't killed every Alchemite at Wendover, and once the survivors pulled themselves together, Juanita knew she would be back under their thumb.

She couldn't handle that anymore.

Which left Astrid Lethewood and her offer of help.

Would Lethewood do any more good than Gilead? What if she was another murderous magician, like Sahara? Even assuming she could protect Juanita's family, what would she want in return?

Will Forest trusted Astrid. She had tried to release Lucius Landon.

But she too had killed someone.

She also confessed, took responsibility.

If that was true: Gilead called her a Lady of Lies.

Gilead is a homicidal maniac.

Does that make his facts wrong?

Facts? What facts? False prophets, remember?

"Corazón!" Judge Skagway's voice broke her out of the mental tailspin. He was in his sports chair, volleying a tennis ball off the barracks wall.

She trotted to his side. "Your Honor."

"I've been trying to get us out of here—you, me, the rest of the Federal Court staff. Roche is stonewalling."

Out of here. Could it be that simple? No, Sahara would chase her in dreams no matter where she went.

"What about the trial?"

"I'd order selection of a second jury . . . if Roche could guarantee their security from beasts and mad wizards."

"I'd have thought he'd want us out of here."

"Us, maybe. Since we'd be taking Knax with us . . ."

Of course. On paper, Sahara wasn't in military custody; that was why Juanita and the other marshals were here. "He doesn't want to give her up?"

"He wants her dead." He smashed the ball, racing to catch it on the rebound. "I told the Attorney General this could work. Told him we could try her openly—that American law could handle this magical outburst."

"It was a good try, Your Honor, we just . . ."

The judge caught the whizzing tennis ball, wheeling to face her as he braked his chair, as graceful as a mountain lion. "What if we did take her out of here?"

"Pardon?"

"You're a resourceful woman. If we transfer Sahara out, can you hang on to her without military backing?"

She was ice cold. "No."

"If she was drugged . . . unconscious? Come on, Corazón, take a chance for me. I refuse to believe a bunch of cultists, however well armed, is invincible."

"I . . ." the words caught. "I'll have to think about it."

He beamed, bathing her in that affectionate, fatherly glow she found so irresistible. "That's all I ask."

She bit her lips against an urge to tell him everything. Then, as temptation receded, she found she felt less burdened. Now she *had* to see if Lethewood could help. It wasn't selfishness at all.

Skagway went back to his workout. With a farewell wave, Juanita jogged to the darkened, soot-walled tomb that had been the courtroom. The arch of thorns was waiting.

She put a hand past its chilly boundary, holding her breath. No wussing out now.

"Beam me up," she murmured, and stepped through.

She found herself in the ruin of a bus or train station, amid a throng of commuters, many visibly contaminated. Hundreds of people were crossing the terminal, vanishing into a blue glow emanating from the stone columns at its edge.

Step into the light, she thought. *This is crazy.*

The people were cheerful and chatty, walking in pairs and clusters, calling greetings across the station, occasionally pausing for handshakes or hugs. Many carried egg-shaped rocks, and others bore stranger objects. She saw an old lady with a garish motorcycle helmet, a long-limbed, bearded fellow with a plaster gargoyle strapped to his back, a teen with a faintly glimmering paella pan.

A glassed-in TV on one side of the terminal was tuned to one of the news channels, updating a handful of viewers on the stalled trial and Gilead's reign of terror. Her own face flashed onscreen, raising goosebumps on her arms.

Alchemized trees rose above her, cathedral tall, a branched roof of blue-tinged light.

"Welcome to Indigo Springs." She jumped. Astrid Lethewood, the Devil herself, was at her side.

Juanita backed toward the archway, bumping against the flow of the crowd.

"That gate's the 'in' door," Astrid said. "But I can tell you how to get back to Wendover."

Embarrassment at having shown fear sharpened her temper. "What the hell do all you people want from me?"

"You came to us."

Juanita studied her closely. Lethewood wasn't a tall woman, or a charismatic one, but there was something solid about her, and she seemed . . .

You're going to trust her because she seems nice? That can be faked, the inner voice sneered.

Could it? All these people here, they trusted Lethewood. Could she fool them all?

I'm here for the judge, Juanita reminded herself, forcing her fists open, but what she said was: "The Alchemites are threatening my family."

Astrid's hand came up, and a startled titter broke from her lips. "I'm sorry, I . . . Wow. I should've picked up on that. I'm sorry, I'm not laughing. It's like shock."

Sorry. An apology was the last thing she was expecting.

Astrid regrouped. "We can . . . yes, we can protect them. Since Wendover, I've been making chantments for hostage situations."

Juanita felt a rush of tears. "Too little, too late."

"I know. But maybe not for you." Astrid pivoted, moving in the same direction as everyone else, drawing Juanita after her. The crowd parted for them as they crossed the plaza.

"Hold on. What's your help going to cost me?"

"We'll call it even for you saving Sahara the other day."

"She wouldn't give me a dollar to save you."

"Well, I don't want her burnt," Astrid said.

"That's very forgiving."

"Oh, I'm no saint." Astrid's words came weighted heavy, like stones from the heart.

"After all the trouble she caused, you don't—"

"She dies, I die," Astrid said.

Juanita stopped short. "Do me a favor and can the prophecies. I'm not a believer and I don't want to hear it."

If Astrid was offended, it didn't show. "Okay."

"I don't want to be in debt to you."

"You won't. I've tried to keep Sahara from . . . I should have realized what she was up to."

"You're just saying that."

"Okay, try this." Astrid's cheeks dimpled. "I'm prone to crushes on tough athletic girls."

A champagne bubble of amusement threatened to crack Juanita's mask. "Are you flirting with me?"

"Would you mind?"

This time she did smile. "I don't date magicians."

"That's really quite wise."

They shared a self-conscious smile, and suddenly being here didn't feel so weird. Then a familiar face behind Astrid on the plaza broke the spell.

"Everything okay?"

"I just saw my Sunday school teacher."

Astrid scanned the crowd. "Stella? She's one of our science types—" She paused, wearing that trying-to-remember expression Juanita had seen before. "She's studying the reproductive cycle of alchemized foxes."

"How does that help whatever you're doing here?" *And what are you doing?*

Astrid shrugged. "Do alchemized animals breed? What happens to their young? Sooner or later, we'll need to know."

"What if it's later?"

"It's what Stella wants to do," Astrid said.

"Yeah? Everyone here's doing what they want? You included?"

"I'm granting wishes," Astrid said. "Today, that means protecting hostages."

Juanita bit the inside of her cheek. "I should probably mention that I have a lot of relatives."

"No problem." They dodged around a gaggle of Japanese women dressed as stewardesses. Then Astrid led her between the cold blue columns . . . and out into a golden haze.

Juanita blinked against a curl of sun setting over a sea, trying to figure out which one it was. The Mediterranean? They were behind a farmhouse that looked like it had been plucked straight out of a chick flick. As her eyes adjusted, she did a slow circle, taking in a grape arbor that ran the length of one stone wall. Ripening oranges and lemons hung from trees planted up the hillside.

Interspersed between the trees were steel sculptures, figures of welded-together metal. Juanita recognized their constituent parts—clockworks, a lawn mower blade, spark plugs. They were the sort of abstract sculpture you saw in public parks in bad neighborhoods. Largely incomprehensible, they were both inoffensive and hard to vandalize.

One piece was vaguely representational—a two-meter-high figure, male, made of steel staves. Its fists were raised in a fighting pose, and it wore silk shorts and mismatched boxing gloves. In the salad bowl that stood in for its head, a jumble of dried beans somehow evoked green eyes, blood, and brains.

A woman sat next to the statue in a rocking chair, flicking thin jolts of electricity into the statue's navel from a crystal in her lap.

"Juanita, this is Tonia. Her son makes the sculptures."

"*Buonasera,*" the woman said.

"Hi," Juanita said. "What is this?"

"He's a bodyguard chantment." Astrid patted the boxer. "We tell him about people who need protection, Tonia feeds him magical power—" She pointed at the luminous chunk of stone. "If anyone attacks them, they get bopped on the nose."

"That's insane."

"It works." Astrid was gazing at the orchard with a professional eye. "Whisper a name in his ear—whoever you're most worried about."

Juanita stepped close to the thing. "Mamá," she breathed.

It came out a sigh, a chorus of names, all in her own voice: Ramón, her sisters and nieces, Judge Skagway, her school friends, her last two girlfriends. Everyone she loved, caught in a single exhalation, a tremble of air that seemed to hang suspended in the boxer's rib cage of steak knives, making this cobbled-together collection of parts the most beautiful thing she'd ever seen.

The statue suddenly meant as much to her as anyone she'd ever known. She wanted to enfold it in her arms, like a baby.

"Abracadabra," Astrid said. "Your loved ones are off the Alchemite menu."

Juanita stared at the sculpture, mesmerized. "They're safe? You're serious? Just like that?"

"Granting wishes, remember?" Astrid said. "That's what genies do."

"If you're screwing with me . . ."

"Cross my heart, hope to die, stick some sea-glass in my eye." Astrid ran a finger over a ripening lemon. "We have someone here day in, day out. Twenty-four/seven, as they say. It'll stop 'em, don't worry."

She looked at the thing. "Chantments burn out, don't they?"

"We use this one sparingly."

"What about my brother? He's caught in dreamland."

"Alchemites can't hurt him there. Sorry—is something funny?"

I didn't expect to like you, Juanita thought. "I thought you'd be more like . . ."

"It's okay, you can say her name. More like Sahara? Like her how?"

"Scheming, pretending to be some kind of martyr."

Astrid wrapped her fingers around the lemon, tugging, but seemed unable to budge it. "Till the other day, I'd hoped the craziness—some of it, anyway—might be an act."

People burning, Sahara cowering behind. "It's no act."

"No."

"The Wendover shrinks throw around the word *narcissist.* Sometimes—*malignant narcissist.*"

Astrid fingered the lemon. "I lie awake, wondering when she lost her mind. If there was any point where I could've cured her. Mark says it started before the vitagua, years ago. . . ."

"If anyone would know, it's Mark Clumber."

"He cheated on her; I told myself he was making excuses."

"Both things could be true," Juanita said.

"What does it say about me that I never noticed?"

"That you cared for her. That you didn't judge?"

Astrid's eyes dulled; her attention was suddenly far away. "Alchemites are attacking Wendover."

"Didn't I ask you to can the prophecies?"

"It's no prophecy," Astrid said. "We're watching the base."

The judge. "How do I get back?"

Astrid gestured at the arch of thorns. "Across the plaza, into the glow. Think about where you need to be."

"Thanks."

"Anytime, gorgeous." The lemon broke free, falling into Astrid's hand. She dropped it immediately, body jerking as if it weighed a thousand pounds.

Juanita sprinted through the gate, cutting through the throng in the plaza, running to the weird light. No hesitation this time; she came out in the courthouse foyer. The smell of scorched upholstery, stronger after the clean Mediterranean air, assailed her.

She'd traveled around the world in less than a second.

Tense voices echoed in the corridor.

"Knax doesn't give a damn about her followers." It was Skagway. "She let them burn."

Roche, replying: "She knows right from wrong, so what?"

Keeping an ear tuned to the conversation, Juanita peered out at the airfield. A jet touched down, leaving rippling waves of heat in its wake. Business as usual.

"Arthur, the attorney general promised me you'd follow the letter of the law on this."

"What can I do, George? The president's assurances to the public have been useless. We look like idiots."

"Assassinating Knax won't restore your credibility."

Juanita tensed. Two milky-blue scorpions, each the size of a truck, were emerging from the pilot's lounge.

"I tried it your way and failed," Roche said. "I lost Will Forest, the defendants, I may have to work with Gilead Landon—"

"How you must miss the murderous pyromaniac."

"Don't be sarcastic. I need to start posting some wins."

"This isn't soccer, General, and you're not committing homicide—"

The scorpions were drawing gunfire. Bolting the door, Juanita sprinted toward Roche and Skagway.

"—I may have no choice but to work with the Fyremen—" Roche stopped in midsentence. "What do you want, Corazón?"

"Alchemites are attacking the base, sir."

"A rescue attempt? They're getting desperate. Here." Roche slapped a jade pendant—a carved fish—into the judge's palm and drew his sidearm. Juanita saw a small black tassel dangling from its trigger guard.

"Why don't you give that one to Corazón?"

Roche flicked the judge an irritated glance.

"We don't want our prisoner getting accidentally shot."

"It's legal to shoot her if she's trying to escape," Roche said.

"She can't run, remember?" Skagway said.

Was that why Astrid put the bottle cap in her, Juanita wondered, to keep Sahara from getting shot escaping custody?

"Fine." Roche slapped the gun with the tassel into Juanita's hand and took out a laminated baseball card.

"I have a weapon," Juanita said.

"This one's a chantment," Roche said.

"What's it do?"

Roche flicked the tassel with a finger. "Trick shots. Call yourself Annie Oakley. You won't miss."

"Until I pass out from exhaustion?"

"Doesn't take that much juice—you already know how to shoot. You'll run out of bullets first."

"Unless they kill us."

"Pah," Roche said. "Every time they try this, we end up with new prisoners and more of their toys."

And a bunch of MIAs to show for it, Juanita thought.

They edged toward the cells as concussions shivered the walls. The doors banged open, but what came through wasn't mutant scorpions: it was Heaven and a pilot.

"Help!" Heaven's leg was bloodied; she was leaning on the airman, limping.

Roche made a disgusted noise, buying it, and lowered the baseball card.

"Annie Oakley, huh?" Juanita raised the pistol. Angles and trajectories filled her mind. She spotted a hoop of plastic in Heaven's hand, a mandala pendant that might be a chantment.

She squeezed off a shot, watching as the bullet seemed to bounce in slow motion off a light fixture, shattering the pendant before passing harmlessly through Heaven's sleeve. There was a spurt of blue.

Gotta admit it, she thought, *that was cool.*

Heaven's partner in crime dropped the pretense of supporting her weight, throwing out an arm. A hailstone the size of a bowling ball shot toward them.

Juanita turned, shielding the judge, but the ice ball stopped short. Roche had the baseball card up again.

"Arthur!" Skagway had reached the door to the cells. Roche tossed him the keycard, deflecting another hailstone. Juanita fired at a third, shattering it into snow.

Skagway got the door open, wrenching his sports chair through. They followed him, locking the door again.

Sahara was out of her cell, patting down a semiconscious Gladys, who lay on the floor, thrashing weakly, her face blue-white, apparently suffocating. Sahara was murmuring quietly.

"She's vamping her," Roche said.

Juanita fired, sending the bullet just past Sahara's cheek, close enough to burn. Sahara shrieked.

Juanita closed the distance between them, catching her by the throat and squeezing. "She dies, you die."

Gladys whooped, drawing in air.

"Let me guess—you thought this'd be your big escape?"

"You are going to pay and pay for this," Sahara rasped.

"Where's the chantment, Sahara?"

Before she could answer, hailstones pounded the door out of its frame. Heaven darted into the corridor, arms extended, hands streaked with vitagua. She was making straight for the judge.

Before Juanita could shout a warning, a golden boxing glove appeared out of nowhere, pasting Heaven . . .

. . . bopped on the nose, just as Lethewood promised . . .

Heaven fell, shrieking: "Letter go, letter go, nownow*now*!" She sounded like one of the starlings.

By the doorway, the pilot was firing hailstones at them . . . and Roche was looking tired.

Move, Juanita thought. She shoved Sahara into a cell, caught Heaven by the arm and pulled her in too. That gate of thorns had flowered on the wall. What would Astrid Lethewood think if she just dragged them through, made Sahara her problem?

"Gladys," Juanita bellowed. "Get up."

Fingers clamped around Juanita's ankle. Her throat, where the sea-glass pendant hung, began to throb.

She looked down, horrified. Heaven was clutching Juanita's leg with her blue-streaked hand.

Contaminated, she contaminated me, Sahara's laughing . . .

A sound like a thunderclap. Heaven passed out, the Alchemite pilot fell, and the judge lurched in his chair, huffing and red faced. Jade dust—the remains of the pendant Roche had given him— trickled through his fingers.

Roche snatched up a radio. "Where's my tac squad?" He was cradling his arm, as if it hurt.

A tinny voice. "Sorry, sir. Scorpions have us tied up. What's your six?"

"Prisoner's secure, that's what matters." He was shivering. "See, George? You really think your marshals can hold off the Alchemites?"

The judge was panting—he looked at least seventy. "Corazón. The little cook's an Alchemite?"

Juanita nodded.

"What tipped you off?"

"I—"

He must have seen something of the truth in her face. He tried to wheel away, forgetting he was braked— *He never forgets he's braked,* Juanita thought. Then he was gone.

"Let him go," Roche said.

She hadn't realized she was following. "He needs to eat something."

"You, on the floor—go after His Honor." Gladys struggled to her feet. "Make sure he's okay, then report to the infirmary."

"Yes, sir." Gladys tottered away after the judge.

"He guess right?" Roche asked. "You one of them?"

Juanita stepped out of the cell, locking Sahara in. "I slipped her three chantments. One hides the other two."

"You don't seem like the true-believer type."

"They got to my family. I'm sorry."

Roche sat, cradling his arm. "They were bound to threaten someone."

"Are you hurt?"

"Just a scratch." He opened his fist. There was a scrape there, tinged with blue.

Juanita showed him the contamination on her ankle.

They sat, glum and silent. Finally Juanita indicated the unconscious Sahara: "She'd say it makes us blessed."

"Landon would say it makes us firewood." Roche sighed. "I ought to arrest you."

She unclipped her key ring and weapon, holding them out. "Can I pick my own cell, sir?"

"Don't be a drama queen. Confine yourself to quarters and wrap your head around doing some media interviews. You're the only PR card I've got left; I'm not telling the nation you're an Alchemite stooge." With that, Roche heaved himself to his feet, heading for Security.

CHAPTER TWENTY-SIX

PATIENCE SLEPT ABOUT AS gently as a prizefighter: she rolled and murmured, lashed out with her legs, giggled. She'd fall into a silence and Ev would doze, only to jolt back to alertness when she shape-shifted or began to snore. Since they'd begun their affair, he had been going without sleep.

It had to be exhausting, he'd realized, feeding energy into the shape-shifting when she couldn't control it.

If Teoquan really could make Patience a goddess—whatever that might mean in this already altered world—would that help her? What had he offered her . . . power over life and death?

Hot air, Ev decided. Teo was, fundamentally, a loudmouth. *I was jealous of him, built him up into some big threat.*

A low chuckle against his chest and Patience shivered, shapeshifting again. For one wistful moment, he remembered that Albert had slept like a corpse.

He kissed the top of her head. She relaxed against him with a contented huff, sliding deeper into sleep, he hoped. Now, if only he could get drowsy himself, he might be able to follow.

Closing his eyes, he reached out, fingering the wooden coin Astrid had sent from Indigo Springs. Dogtags, they'd been dubbed, and as he toyed with the thing, it filled him in on bits of news from the real world and from the town itself. Closing his eyes, he let the image of a map form in his imagination, bringing up the routes of the two contamination pipelines—the one digging eastward from Oregon toward Colorado, the carefully reinforced sea pipe stitching northward under the coastal islands. With a thought he pulled back, expanding the view so he could see the whole of the world. Tiny sites of vitagua contamination dotted all the continents. Astrid's volunteers had moved gallons of the liquid magic out of North America, secreting it in glaciers, spilling it into lakes and watersheds, misting the corners of the world's inaccessible wild places.

Blue blotches marked the cities where the strike team had clashed with Alchemites: St. Louis, Saskatoon, Manchester, Tijuana, Manila, Atlanta. Centered within the map, Ev's hometown and the forest around it were a bright, roughly circular patch of cobalt.

Drops in a very large bucket, Ev thought. Even with the pipelines, they weren't moving fast enough.

A soft cough brought his eyes open, and he saw a vitagua-contaminated mouse staggering toward them across the floor of the earth lodge.

"Hello?" Ev whispered. The mouse trembled, tongue hanging. A few of the Roused were almost completely transformed, but they didn't have this wide-eyed, feral look.

Was it a contaminated animal? How had it gotten here?

A glob of vitagua flowed over the mouse, growing to human size and taking a familiar shape.

Astrid. Ev pulled the blanket over himself and Patience. By now the mouse had been engulfed, and the Astrid form was as big as a ten-year-old. Gray fur sprouted from her waistline and her collarbones, forming a Tarzan-esque fur bikini.

She—it—coughed, twice. "Pop?"

"That is creepy, kid," Patience said, waking.

"I didn't know you'd be asleep; it's nearly noon."

"No day or night here, remember?" Ev said.

Skin grew over the vitagua shape, and suddenly—to look at, at least—it was his daughter. She took in the sight of them in bed, added it up, did the sum again, and let out one of those shocky titters of hers. "I didn't mean to barge."

Patience yawned. "What's up?"

"Ma—Pop called. Said it was an emergency?"

"What? No."

"Your sense of time gone screwy again?" Patience asked. "Maybe you're going to call, Ev."

Which meant there would be an emergency. Great.

"No," Astrid said. "I'm not confused about the time."

"What about the sea-glass?"

"Poisoning hasn't affected my sense of time."

Ev said, "Hell, kid, you aren't cured yet?"

"I figured out how, but—"

"But you're scared?" Ev asked.

She raised her hands. "It's okay, I know it doesn't kill me. Not by poison, the grumbles say. But—yeah, I'm afraid."

Not by poison. "Astrid—do you know what does kill you?"

She shook her head. "It's confusing, Pop."

"I don't want to lose you."

"You won't . . ." A frown—*the* frown, the one that meant the voices were throwing half truths at her.

"Ev's right, sweetie. Unpoison yourself, please."

"Soon, Patience."

"Today," Ev insisted.

"Okay. But if you didn't call me, who did?"

"I called." The words came from outside: Teoquan.

"Be right there." She headed to the exit. "Pop, Patience, sorry about . . . you know. Interrupting."

Ev leapt up, then was pulling on a robe and heading after her.

Teoquan had been remarkably little trouble since Ev and Eliza began their shell game with the rescued Roused. As the pipeline drained the vitagua glaciers into the real and the population of moderates grew, the Pucker Hill letrico mill had been expanded. Food-spinners set up a factory, turning the energy into food, shelters, supplies. Astrid's science crew sent a surveyor to figure out glacier volumes and calculate the land mass beneath them. Eliza had people counting the frozen Roused.

The elders' village was thriving, too. A spring of uncontaminated drinking water had been found flowing out of a fissure in the cliff at the edge of the village. The soil there was richer than the gritty sand that covered most of the unreal. The trees excavated from the snow were waking from dormancy.

Eliza kept grinding the ice into blue snow, and teams of

Roused were making bricks of it, building up towers to stack the displaced vitagua where it couldn't trap anyone else.

Peace had reigned, morale was high, and Teo had kept his head down.

"Cute trick with the fake body," he was saying as Ev caught up. "What happens to my little cousin?"

"Sorry?"

"The mouse?"

"It dies after a couple days," Astrid said.

"Figures."

"I only take animals who are on their last legs."

"I'm supposed to say—what? That's sweet?"

"It was Pop's voice I heard calling me."

"I'm a gifted mimic."

"Why didn't you call me yourself?" Astrid asked.

"Who am I to you? Nobody."

"I'd have come."

"Maybe." Teo was surveying Pucker Hill, the earth lodge and food-spinners, the wind farm. Ev felt a surge of pride, as if he'd created the settlement himself.

"What's the emergency?" Astrid demanded.

He knows, Ev thought, and Teo shot him a piercing glance, as if he'd spoken the thought aloud.

"The emergency is I want that Fyreman."

The vitagua Astrid tilted her head. "For what?"

"You're getting above yourself, missy—that's unreal business, none of yours."

"You want someone to punish."

"That your opinion, or your profiler boyfriend's?"

"I'm sorry, Teoquan," she said. "Lucius died."

Teo let out a long growl. When he spoke, his voice was an inhuman chatter of stones. "You ignore me at your peril."

Ev swallowed. "We all want the same thing. The Roused freed, the magical balance of the world restored . . ."

"Small change, Everett. I've spent centuries under ice, and someone's gonna pay."

"I'm not a killer," Astrid said.

Teo smirked. "Come on, sweetie pie, we all know that ain't true."

"I've given you chantments, power to run them, and more people free each day. I draw the line at human sacrifice."

"If you won't hand over my enemies, dear heart, I may have to start on your loved ones."

"Teoquan." That was Patience, her voice iron. She was barefoot, wrapped in a blanket. "Even if the unreal is calling for the blood of its enemies, nobody Astrid loves has wronged us. Not Jacks, not me, not Ev."

"No?" Teo's eye fell on Ev, and once again he had that sense of being seen, known.

"If it's a matter of needing blood, the actual substance—" Astrid looked thoughtful. "We could steal medical waste."

"Kid," Ev protested, repulsed.

"Low-end hospital leftovers?" Teo looked affronted. "I said the blood of our enemies."

"You want a Fyreman, Teo, get your own. I'll bet you're capable."

"That's twice now you've denied me," he said. "Want to go for three? Where's my chanter?"

"We've located Patience's niece, finally, but Patience is right— Lilla's contaminated. She can't become a chanter." Ev caught a look of relief on Patience's face.

"Was that your doing, Astrid?" Teo asked.

"Of course not," she said.

"I'll get you another name."

"The grumbles mentioned that judge, Skagway. He's . . . Haida, is it?"

"That old man? I want someone with a bit of punch."

"Punch?"

"He wants someone short-tempered and easy to manipulate," Patience said.

"I want a warrior. Not some airy-fairy pacifist who'll act only on Astrid's say-so."

"You're asking me to go find some random violent jerk with a grudge?"

"Hundreds of the People are in prison, I hear," Teoquan said. "Why not start in Winnipeg?"

Astrid's jaw worked. "There has to be some middle ground."

"That's what I thought you'd say. You know where this is going?"

Ev's chest pounded—he was holding his breath.

"Do you?" Astrid said. "I don't think you and I ever come to blows, Teoquan."

"Maybe you haven't let yourself remember yet." With that, Teo walked away.

"Where it's going?" Patience demanded when he was gone.

"He's bluffing." Astrid waved that away. "I've told you where we end up. Magic loose in the world, people using it, the Roused free, everything getting better. Will and his kids together, after all this . . . blows . . ."

"What is it?"

She was turning in a slow circle. "Here. We'll be here, on Pucker Hill. This is where our cottage will be. This is where I see Jacks again. . . ."

The relief on her face was unmistakable.

"There is a whole lotta room for bad between now and the dream house, kid," Patience said. "Teo's after your ass, you get that? Couldn't you give him the Fyreman?"

"The guy'd already been tortured once," Astrid said.

"How much time do we have left?" Ev interrupted.

"Pop, I don't know, okay? We'll talk more later: this mouse is finished." With that, the vitagua Astrid froze solid.

"Ducking the question," Patience said. She poked the ringer. "Sucks when someone you love's keeping secrets, huh?"

"She's going to die. Teo's going to kill her."

Patience's scowl broke. "Ev, no. Happy ending, remember?"

"Those damned grumbles." He shook his head. "She'll get that day with Will and the kids, but . . . how do we stop him?"

"You think I know?"

"You know something. Who is he? Why isn't he cursed?"

"This isn't just about your daughter, Everett Lethewood."

"Who's holding out on who now?"

Whatever she might have said next was drowned out by a crash from the direction of the elders' village. They ran to the bone bridge, stepping out into calamity.

It was Eliza.

Part of the cliff had broken free above her. She was dead, a raccoon smear with shattered glasses, her blood puddling among the fallen rocks. The crack in the mountain had widened where she fell; the bubbling spring had become a torrent, ice cold and filled with salmon.

"Tragic," Teo said.

He was at the edge of the crowd that was forming around the rockfall. Haughty youngsters, half-human teenagers with sharpened claws, surrounded him. He looked from raccoon's body to the flow of water. "See the renewal?"

"I see it," Ev said. "So?"

"The unreal demands the blood of its enemies, remember? Poor Eliza must have been a little corrupt."

"That's enough," Patience said. For months, she had been unable to control her shape-shifting, but now she became herself again, an old woman with arresting features and blazing eyes. She scanned the crowd, seeming to poll the villagers.

The buffalo nodded: "Walk away, Old One."

Teo's nostrils flared. "We'll be down in the Pit—with Miss Astrid's Fyreman boy toy."

He sauntered away, leading the entourage of young warriors, leaving the elders with the corpse.

CHAPTER TWENTY-SEVEN

THE ROAR OF A plane brought Astrid's attention to the canopy of the alchemized forest, and the sight of the jets blasting a fireball into the woods near the edge of the Big Blue Reservoir. Plumes of blue smoke were pouring skyward.

She wasn't worried: another Astrid was in the Octagon, watching Mark and his defense crew as they brought rain down to quell the flames.

She had a ringer down in the sea pipe, too, reading maps for Chakeesa and her crew as they worked in their bubble of letrico-pressurized stone, force-growing coral to extend the vitagua pipeline. They'd tacked a hand-lettered sign reading *Hawaii or Bust* on a hook-shaped stalactite. Bramblegate, on the chamber wall, offered a quick escape route back to town in case of emergency.

The only place she didn't keep a ringer full-time was the unreal: many of the Roused, not just Teoquan, found her use of animals to construct the dopplegängers offensive.

One of the Astrids was in the so-called Doghouse in London, surrounded by newshound volunteers as they watched a visibly uncomfortable Juanita Corazón take reporters' questions about Sahara, Gilead, and the slaughter at the courthouse.

"The air force is in control of Wendover," Juanita said. "Sahara Knax remains in government custody."

It was barely true; according to the seers, the Alchemites had almost flattened the place in the recent battle.

"We should reach out to Juanita again," she said to Olive. "Any ideas?"

The mouse within her ringer in the Octagon wasn't going to last much longer. Its heart fluttered; pains shot through her fingers and toes. She took it to the plaza, heading into the glow.

Katarina's ecologists had pinpointed a number of remote, inaccessible wildlands, prime sites for contamination. Choosing one, she stepped out into the humidity of the Laotian jungle. Ambling through the woods, she let the substance of her vitagua body turn to mist, leaving the barest traces on flowers and vines. Smaller plants didn't overgrow as conspicuously as trees did. When she spread the contamination thin and kept away from human settlements, the effects usually went unnoticed.

Her sense of illness intensified. She focused in on Astrid Prime, stretched out in bed within the cave.

Janet was holding her hand. "How's the battle?"

She tried to sit, and couldn't. "Rolling downhill. Can you send for Will?"

"Of course," Janet said, touching the tuning fork that hung around her wrist.

Sinking into the pillows, Astrid reached out to the Chimney, drawing liquid magic through a channel in the rock, filling one of the stone basins she'd created when she and Olive were remaking this bolt-hole into a cave of wonders.

"Astrid?" Will's voice brought her back. They were both healing her now, beating back the pain. Letrico poured through them. So much power, just to keep her alive . . .

"It's time to get the glass out."

Janet frowned. "I'll call—"

"Just you two," she said. She didn't want a hundred witnesses to this. The feeling of being owned—by the volunteers, by the Roused—made the hurt more intense. "I want it done without fuss. It's not gonna kill me, I promise."

They exchanged a long glance, wordlessly debating.

"What do we do?" Will asked finally.

She held out her hands. "Get me up."

Janet put a hand on her back, helping her sit, and then Will lifted her. Astrid tried to resist, to step down, but she was weak, too weak. "The tub."

He carried her around the jade privacy screen that hid her bed. The basin waited, brimming with vitagua.

"Put me in," Astrid said. "The vitagua and the sea-glass will destroy each other."

His arms tensed around her. "Are you serious?"

"Janet's ready with the healing chantment."

"Astrid, this is risky."

"If we don't believe in a Happy After, Will, how can we expect anyone else to?" She met his eyes and was shocked: there was no answering belief in his face.

He said carefully: "So it's a leap of faith?"

"It's only a leap if you drop me."

"That'd make it a dunk of faith," Janet said.

Okay, he wasn't sold. There'd be time to convince him. *Don't cry,* she lectured herself. *Sound* sure. "Put me in, Will. It's all right, I swear."

Still he hesitated.

No more waiting. Astrid stretched out a toe.

Her body, ever the sponge, drew the fluid in. Pain flared in her hand, and she screeched as blood flowed. A second later, part of her knee was gone, just gone. White bone shone through a gory hole.

Will tried to pull back, but Astrid twisted out of his grip, collapsing, pitching into the vitagua. She grabbed her neck, clamping her hands over the big veins there.

Red blood and blue magic, she thought, *is that now?*

Exsanguination. Now there's *an ugly word.*

More pain as past and future jumbled. She was Before, kissing Sahara with blood on her hands, she was five years old and playing with one of Dad's magic toys, she was having sex with Jacks, with Will, with her first real girlfriend, Jemmy. She was standing by the wreckage of the power plant in the unreal, she was bleeding, she was on trial, she was flirting with Juanita Corazón. She was fog, drifting through a big mall in Alberta. She was upside down, like a bat. She was helpless, she was dead and burning, she was watching Jacks take a bullet.

Let go of the reins, rip the Band-Aid, poison the world, warmth-Will-think-warmth-Boom . . .

Agony, a thousand cuts, stench of burned flowers . . .

Will pulled her out of the pool of magic. Janet healed her, one last time. New flesh—pale, unfreckled, and hairless—grew over her wounds. The stink of burnt vitagua hung in the air.

Sandblasted crater with a bone-shaped mountain at its edge . . . Roused, Fyremen, and Alchemites at each others' . . .

"Throats." She released her neck. "Is this the part where we find the fire hall? All Chief Lee's stuff, the potions . . ."

Janet shone a light in her eyes. "Astrid, snap out of it."

"It's just the grumbles." Will lifted Astrid again, carrying her to the Chimney. As he stepped out into Bigtop, volunteers mobbed them, their voices mixing with the grumbles:

"What happened?"

"Is she dying?"

"Is she cured?"

"Where you taking her?"

"To the fire," Astrid answered.

Will shushed her. "Astrid, just make chantments."

"Janet healed everything," she said, twisting the barbell she'd had pierced through the web of her right hand.

There was no pain.

Teoquan slugging it out with Lucius's brother, warriors pouring out of the cracked, bloodied Chimney . . .

"Chant, Astrid," Will repeated, and she realized she had almost wandered off.

She stared at the objects, baffled. Fear spiked through her: had she forgotten how, lost her connection to the well?

But no, that hadn't happened yet. A sagging Victorian footstool caught her eye. When the unreal popped, someone named Parminder would use it to keep back a storm surge that would otherwise have destroyed Galveston.

She reached out, thinking of disaster prevention—tornado deflectors, firebreaks, chantments to strengthen buildings that would otherwise fall in quakes, chantments to turn those that *did* fall into harmless dust. Something to carve channels for lava—because there would be eruptions: when the unreal popped, more than one mountain would go boom too. Storm shelters, lifeboats, something to capture debris in Shanghai before it became shrapnel in the rising wind. Spotlights to lead people to safety, something to calm panicked animals, a horn whose shriek would drive people inland before the tsunamis could take them, air bubbles for sinking ships . . .

Diggers for tunnels, more routes for Ilya's spillway . . .

The volunteers were whooping. "Three cheers for the boss!" someone shouted, and she could see relief on their faces as they embraced, as they reached out to touch her.

Will had her by the arms. "Better?"

He's looking for a pen . . . , one last voice said before the grumbles subsided.

"You're looking for a pen?"

He stared through her. "How are you, Astrid?"

She had forgotten what it was like not to be in pain. Her mind was sharp, and she was bursting with energy.

"Astrid," Pike asked. "Is it true—you're okay?"

"I feel . . . I feel amazing."

"Rumor's spreading that Will cured you. People are calling . . . Plaza's got a thousand people in it. Your ringers have frozen over. Nobody knows whether to panic or party."

"Tell them I'm cured."

Turning to the diminishing pile of scavenged objects, she chanted a bubble gum machine. Each turn of its crank would bring her another sick, contaminated animal.

Around her, tuning forks and pipe whistles hummed: a general announcement going out to say she'd been cured.

She reached for her doppelgängers, splitting her attention even more easily now that the pain was gone.

"Sometimes this is so easy," she told Will, cranking up a new mouse for another ringer. Clothes and skin grew over it, and she grinned into her own face. She could go everywhere.

"You're okay?" Will said.

Astrid caught his hands, trying to twirl, but he resisted. She grabbed for a random volunteer instead, and the growing crowd lifted her to their shoulders.

"Did someone say they found the fire hall?" she asked.

"You. But if it was a grumble talking, the timing could—"

Pike interrupted: "Astrid, scavengers just found the fire hall."

"Ha! Get the strike team together, Pike."

"Hold your horses," Janet said. "You aren't going anywhere near that place."

"I'll send a ringer." A parade was forming beneath her; people bobbed and sang. "I'll send a dozen."

"Won't that defeat the purpose?" Will said. "The idea's for people to take them for you."

She stuck her tongues out at him. "Spoilsport. Race you there?"

She found the fire hall untouched by the quakes and overgrowth of the forest, as Lee's house had been. It sat atop a crumbling ridge south of town, encircled by blue-tinged roots and foliage, a brick edifice crowned by a six-story fire tower.

"Dad brought me here as a kid," she told Will when he appeared in the cleared patch of woods. "We'd watch the men run up and down the tower with their tanks and hoses. Middle of summer, full gear, sweating in the summer heat."

"It's a demanding job," he said, still remote.

"I came back when Jacks was training, to watch him. Took a picture, but never developed it."

"You must have been the last person on earth without a digital camera."

The scavengers had cleared a ten-foot perimeter of forest around the hall, binding yellow tape around the property that marked the point where the magic stopped. Glimmering letrico crystals had been piled just outside the tape.

"Where's that magic shovel?"

"Here." Igme shoved the blade into the ground, and willow roots, thick and vital, plunged into the ground around the building.

Astrid's ringers glanced around. Everywhere she looked, the

letrico supply was surprisingly robust. "How much juice did it take to keep me alive?"

"It took what it took," Clancy grunted.

"Meaning?"

Janet said, "Thunder put in that second power plant."

Astrid shivered. All that energy, just for her . . .

"Thar she blows," Igme said.

The fire hall seemed to sigh. It doors buckled inward. The ground danced, dirt pluming as the buried primer cord ignited. They stepped over the threshold, the ringer first, Igme last.

"Look for test tubes," Will said, voice tight. "When Gilead Landon killed Caro and the rest, at the trial, he drank potions."

"For a second, I thought he was doing shooters," Astrid said. She walked past the trucks, into a narrow hallway that led to a kitchen and a gym, and came face-to-face with a portrait of the fire department from the year before. Six uniformed men grinned into the camera. Lee Glade had an arm around Jacks.

Jacks looked happy.

Whatever their differences, the father–son affection was evident in this picture. Astrid remembered anew how it felt, swinging the block of ice at the Chief's head, the rage . . .

"*Hola!* Found an office," Aquino called.

The Chief's furniture was old-fashioned but ordinary enough: a bulky desk and chair, steel file cabinets, a fifties-vintage electric fan. A laptop sat atop the desk, looking out of place. Framed news stories about past fires hung on the walls, their paper yellowing.

"Potions," said Janet, pulling a bunch of test tubes filled with variously colored fluids from the file cabinet.

"And here's a gadget," Clancy announced. A peculiar oven sat on a shelf in the closet. On its hearth was a chantment, a wallet Astrid remembered making as a child.

"What you suppose it's for?" Janet said.

"It finds lost change."

"The oven, Astrid, not the wallet."

"Laptop battery's still got a trace of a charge," Igme reported.

Will opened a book. "Anyone read Latin?"

"Me." Clancy settled a pair of glasses on his nose, flipping pages. "You burn chantments in it and collect the ash here, in the flask. Vitagua ash . . . *purificado,* it's called. It's part of their magic cocktails."

"All magic's bad except our magic." Astrid flicked a tube with a nail. "Hypocrites. They use liquid magic, same as us."

"This is why they tried to burn the unreal," Will said. "To make magic with the ash. I wondered why they stopped trying to control enchantment and moved on to destroying it. But destruction *is* control."

"Gotcha!" Igme was going through the desk—he waved an index card with a list of passwords in front of the laptop. He typed furiously. "Okay, Glade was searching the Web for references to magic. He had a bunch of fake identities. . . ."

Astrid peered over his shoulder. "Sahara and I chatted with someone who claimed she was on the run with chantments. Marlowe. She taught us the cantation for heat draws."

Igme nodded. "Yes, here's the message they sent."

"They?"

"Looks like Lucius Landon was helping—he and Chief Glade were your Marlowe. Why would they teach you how to draw heat?"

"To build trust," Will said.

"Yeah, and they were tracking us. The drops in temperature are conspicuous. Storms make the news. Where it's coldest, where the fog's thickest . . . that's where the chantment was used."

"Devious bastards," Igme said. "There was a chanter in Nevada, in the mid-nineties, looks like they got him that way."

Astrid nodded. Sahara's followers had found a cache of chantments in Nevada; she had assumed there must have been a chanter there.

The search continued. Janet found a file cabinet full of news clippings: pieces about UFO sightings and unexplained occurrences, stapled to articles about people who had died in fires. More chantment users, probably.

It was easy to piece together how the Fyremen worked. Some odd event would attract their attention. They would trace the culprit, kill them, then steal their chantments to burn for potions.

Recited prayers seemed to be the key to making the potions. They mixed purificado with other ingredients, praying over the formulations for hours, even days.

"Putting in the energy up front," Janet said. "No casting without cost."

Astrid turned to Clancy. "Is there anything in those books on the curse?"

He flipped pages. "Curses, let's see. Ruination, Befouling. There's mention of a Lady of Lies and Atlas—"

"An atlas of where?"

"The mythical Atlas . . . Boss, it's not a cookbook."

"Sorry."

He kept scanning. "Near as I can tell, what Sahara told you's right—there's a bunch of guys somewhere reciting this 'Befoulment.' Been at it nonstop since the 1300s."

"The Befoulment's the curse that makes the contaminated insane?" Astrid asked.

"And Frog Princes them," Clancy affirmed. "Looks like it's just a matter of finding the circle and shutting 'em up."

"Oh, is that all?" Janet said.

"Where are you going?" Mark, in the Octagon, spoke to the ringer Astrid had installed in the bank vault.

"Pardon?"

"Astrid Prime—your body—you're on the move."

She had been about to duck out on the celebration in the middle of Bigtop, which was getting wilder by the minute.

"I need a little air, Mark."

He said, "Fine, but get back to the shelter soon, okay?"

"And do what?"

"Is it too much to ask that we get to protect the one Astrid we can't replace?"

"Roche kept me in a hole underground."

"Roche had a point. You aren't even in disguise."

"Dis—" Oh. He meant the red scarf that made her look like a middle-aged guy.

One of her ringers passed through the plaza, stepping out to stare in amazement at the skyscrapers of Delhi.

Imprisoned again, maybe, but she was free at the same time.

"Okay, I'll go cloister myself," she said, adding, silently: *for now.*

CHAPTER TWENTY-EIGHT

JUANITA FLOATED UP FROM sleep to find herself stretching and curling her hands, like a cat kneading a blanket. Fisting her hands, she peered around the room. It was voices that had wakened her . . . but there was nobody in the room.

That Fyreman finds out you're contaminated, he'll burn you.

She glanced at the gateway of brambles between her closet and the bathroom door. It had been following her, a constant temptation to escape. But she was facing the consequences of her actions. Showing the judge, if he happened to care, that she had some integrity.

The gate wasn't the only sign that Astrid Lethewood had an eye on her—Juanita's birthday, a week before, had brought an unexpected flurry of cards and good wishes via the mail. Some she'd expected. Others . . . there'd been a note from the Sunday school teacher she'd seen in Indigo Springs, the one who was studying contaminated foxes: "Wanted to let you know life is great! I'm happy and busy, hope you are too." There'd been an email from her aid worker cousin, enthusing: "I'm doing so much good here—for the first time, we aren't just spinning our wheels as people suffer. . . ."

A note came from the blackjack dealer who lived across the street from Ma: "Everyone in Reno safe and well. Take care of yourself."

And half a dozen others just like that, mixed in with the family cards and packages. Innocent messages of well-being, reassurances, nobody asking a thing of her. It was sweet, almost hokey. Why risk exposing themselves like that? Roche had to be scrutinizing her mail.

Nerves drove her to the bathroom mirror. The blue stain of

contamination on her ankle had long since vanished, and she looked like herself: ordinary, human. It might be months before her appearance changed.

You don't have months, the voice said. *Fyre Brigade's coming—*

Her gaze dropped to the counter, where Gilead's sea-glass pendant rested in a pool of gold chain. It burned to touch it; he'd see she wasn't wearing it. That was all he'd need.

So don't touch it, sister.

After retrieving a cellophane wrapper from the trash, she laid it over the crudely carved lick of red flame, then pressed a finger to the plastic. Was that heat? No, she decided, just her body warming the glass.

No burn.

So there it was. Live—or die?

Using the cellophane as a barrier, she pinched up the pendant and slid it off its chain. Her sister-in-law had sent her a gift basket full of cosmetics: manicure kit, powder, lipstick. It sat unopened on the counter. Now she dug into it, finding a vial of clear nail polish.

Sitting on the toilet, she began varnishing the sea-glass. While it dried, she did her nails, picking apart the rest of the basket. Nail file, blush, mascara—what was Rosalia thinking? She tried it anyway, playing with her face as she waited for the pendant to dry, tarting herself up for nobody, then applying another layer of polish to the pendant.

She caught herself enjoying the nail file, the feel of it rasping over her nails. She imagined them digging into something, Sahara maybe . . .

With a start, she realized she was purring.

She set down the file and closed her eyes. "Please," she murmured. "Please, I—don't want to burn."

Praying. She braced for a mocking comment from the voices, for her own cynicism to kick in. But there was nothing, just a spreading pool of interior calm. What could she do now but ask for help?

By dawn, she had painted six careful layers of enamel on the

pendant. It was shinier than it had been, but that might go unnoticed. It was glass; it looked like glass.

First threading it back onto the chain, she dangled it over her
knee, then lowered it to her skin.

No burn.

Weak with relief, she put it on.

Dress for work, the voice said. *Roche is coming. . . .*

"You really need to shut up now." She flexed her hand, resist-
ing an urge to claw the countertop.

She was buckling her belt when the knock came.

It was Roche, all right, as crisp as ever, no sign of contamination on him, either.

"Another dog and pony show, sir?"

He shook his head, holding out her gun and base ID. "Prisoner transfer. You're to bring her to the airstrip."

"Aren't I under secret house arrest?"

"President ordered me to work with Landon." A strained
smile. "I'm not sure who's in charge, or what constitutes a burning offense at this point—"

Her stomach clenched. "But?"

"Better if you're a guard, not a prisoner." He looked away, as if
embarrassed.

"You didn't tell him about me," she said.

The barest shake of his head.

"That's . . . kind of you, but the judge'll tell him what I've
done."

"I sent George Skagway home to Reno."

She felt a twinge of loss, ridiculously, amid the rush of relief.
"Why the change of heart?"

She didn't expect Roche to answer. He was contaminated too.
Wasn't that enough? But after a second's contemplation, he produced a photo from his pocket, passing it over.

The shot showed a younger Roche with Caroline and Will
Forest. They were standing at a trailhead, clad in hiking gear,
shaggy and exhausted, fists raised in victory.

"I knew you and Forest were friends," she said. "Didn't realize it was all three of you."

"I'd almost forgotten myself."

"I'm sorry."

He took the photo back, standing stiffly. "Good luck with the prisoner."

"Yessir."

She found Sahara circling her cell, limping within its confines. When Juanita appeared, she bared her teeth. "Finally. Judas shows her face."

"Surprised, Sahara, or just sulking?"

"I don't sulk."

"It's not my fault your prophecies turned out to be so much fertilizer."

"You're at my side in the coming battle," Sahara said, but her voice lacked conviction. "You promised to stay with me."

"You better hope I don't. Step back and prepare for transfer."

Sahara put her hands behind her head and turned from the door as Juanita unlocked her cell and began the ritual of cuffing her: waistband first, wrists, then ankles. "The tumbleweeds are screaming, Juanita. They're burning the contaminated growth."

If this was true, it was news to her. Still, she grunted: "Scorched earth."

"Won't help. It's in the roots, dust, pollen, all the bits of green. . . . They'll never get it out now." She swayed, her restraints clanking. "It's crumbling, like a cookie."

"A cookie, huh?"

"Like a broken dam," Sahara amended. "My bonds crumbled under the water's onslaught, praise the river—"

"Works better than cookie," Juanita said.

"You think building a religion is easy?" Sahara said. "Creating rituals, expressing ancient truths in fresh ways?"

"Making shit up?" They started down the corridor.

"I have done great works."

"You used chantments. That's nothing special."

"The magic springs from me," Sahara said.

"Even the faithful will expect a real miracle in time."

Sahara stumbled, and as Juanita caught her, their eyes met. "Part the Red Sea, virgin birth, that kind of thing?"

"Now you're a virgin?"

"Rise from the dead," Sahara mused, regaining her balance. "That's the big god trick, isn't it?"

"Big god trick? I'm actually offended by that."

"Ah, darling Juanita. Against your will, you continue to inspire me."

"You are pure huckster, aren't you?" Beyond the courthouse, the formerly overgrown sagebrush and tumbleweeds had been scorched black. Flamethrowers whooshed, baking the air, all but drowning the keening of a wounded animal. Natural gas and burnt sage choked her as camouflage-dressed men reduced the vegetation to ash. Helicopters hovered like wasps over the smoke.

The burnt air made Juanita tear up and cough. When she could breathe again, she saw Heaven.

The Alchemite chef was dangling over a stack of wood, hung like meat from the business end of a front loader. It was her shrieking . . . around a bloodied gag.

A tall man in a fireman's jacket was watching her struggle. Gilead.

Juanita's heart slammed in terror. But as he turned, his eye fell on the doctored sea-glass pendant. He smiled.

"Think," Sahara muttered. "It's okay, think, come on . . ."

I don't want Sahara to burn, Astrid Lethewood had said. Juanita stepped in front of her prisoner.

It was an empty gesture. Gilead had the airfield, the soldiers, the bonfire, the president's seal of approval. As for running . . . Juanita scanned the field, looking for the gateway to Indigo Springs. There: on the back wall of an outbuilding. Too far. Gilead must have disenchanted the landing zone.

"He's not here to burn me." Sahara had regrouped. Her voice was resonant, her Goddess voice.

"I do burn you," Gilead told her. "It's foretold."

"You want the Filthwitch, you need me," Sahara said.

"What makes you think I need help?"

"Had any luck getting into Indigo Springs?"

"My resource base is expanding, witch; yours is spent."

"I'm the key to the locked door." Sahara batted her eyelashes. "I bet that's foretold too."

"How?"

"Astrid wants to save me," Sahara said. "It's her Achilles' heel."

"If you got in, you'd ally with Lethewood against us."

"And people say I'm paranoid. Astrid won't work with me."

"Then you're gambling you can overthrow her and betray us."

"Right now we're both on the outside." Sahara's expansive gesture was jerked short by her restraints. "You want a shot at the magical well, you'll have to risk it."

"What you're risking is your last followers in a battle you cannot win."

Sahara didn't blink. "Sounds like a good deal for you."

"Astrid Lethewood has visionaries too."

"Astrid won't let foreknowledge or common sense get in the way of her crusade to save everyone. Come on, big guy, teeny-tiny little reprieve? What's your book of prophecies say?"

"Ruination and Befoulment," Gilead intoned. He laid a glowing finger on Sahara's forehead, and she gagged. The chantments Juanita had given her dropped from her mouth—first the stamp, then the amber bead. With a heave, she brought up something else—a rusted, blood-tinged bottle cap.

"Gilead—," Juanita said.

Sahara trilled as her face shifted, eyes darkening to shoe buttons, mouth stiffening into a beak. The contamination, no longer arrested by the chantment embedded in her chest, was changing her back into a bird-woman.

That could be me, Juanita thought, dry mouthed.

"No more disguises," Gilead said. "You're Befouled; now you look it."

"My true self restored," Sahara said. "You burning me now, or not?"

"Not you." Gilead nodded at one of his minions.

Juanita lunged, but it was too late. The wood ignited and Heaven caught fire, her body going rigid with agony as flames enveloped her.

"You had no right to do that!" she bellowed.

"It's all right," Sahara said. "Heaven's honored to be sacrificed in my place."

Juanita pulled away from them both, forcing herself to look at the pyre as Heaven fought and wailed. *Please, let her pass out fast.*

She watched until Heaven became a still, dark shadow amid the flames.

"Juanita," Gilead said.

She dashed at her eyes. "Neither of you is anything special. You know that, don't you? You're a couple of fucking serial killers."

Sahara cackled.

Gilead's voice, when he replied, was gentle. "Get your prisoner onto the chopper, Marshal."

CHAPTER TWENTY-NINE

THE PADLOCK CHANTMENT WAS a heavy iron antique, heart shaped and covered in rust. It lay in Will's palm, ice cold . . . and securely locked. Whoever'd made it had that in mind when he chanted it: a heart, closed against something it loved. He sensed the dark intention within the thing. The vicious personality of its chanter, long dead, lived on in his works.

The lock had come in with the latest Alchemite refugee, a lanky woman with a Southern accent who was in the final weeks of pregnancy. She lay unconscious on a gurney in the Indigo Springs hospital as her rescuers searched her for chantments and members of Janet's medical team checked for illnesses or injuries. All the new arrivals got this treatment—volunteers checked them for everything from influenza and cancer to magical contamination.

"She's okay?" Astrid's ringer asked.

The medic on duty nodded. "Utterly healthy, no contamination. They set her house on fire, but we got her before she breathed in much smoke—"

"Chantments?" Astrid asked.

"Just the one."

"Can we move her to the ghost town?" Will asked. "I want to find out about the padlock."

Astrid frowned. "Is the baby okay?"

"Fine," the medic said. "She could deliver any time."

"Are we set up for that?"

"It's doable."

"Astrid, you're procrastinating," Will said.

"I just . . . We're missing something."

"What do the grumbles say?"

She tilted her head, listening. "Nothing new."

"I'll interview her myself, if that helps."

"Okay." Visibly dissatisfied, Astrid nodded. The medic raised a silver martini shaker, shaking a lone drop of vodka into the woman's mouth. Sahara had taught her followers the words to the vamping cantation, the one they had used to suck the vital energy from people. The magical shaker jumbled up the memory so they couldn't do it anymore.

"Let's go," Will said.

After new arrivals had been searched and doctored, they were taken, still unconscious, to a silk tent pitched within Tishvale, where the rescued Alchemites were encamped. Ten miles of dense, enchanted forest lay between the ghost town and the Bigtop, barrier enough in its own right, but Mark was taking no chances. He'd had dense, thorny hedges planted around the perimeter of the new town. They were wound through with scavenged barbed wire; like any refugee camp, this one doubled, in essence, as a prison.

Setting it up had sparked the first genuinely acrimonious fights among the volunteers. Clancy and others like him wanted Astrid to stick to the original agreement they had all made; they didn't want anyone locked up, under any circumstances. Mark had argued, successfully, that Alchemites were the enemy, that they couldn't be trusted.

A freshwater stream ran through the campground, and Thunder's engineers had put up a small dam and a waterwheel, a turbine that could produce enough power for the Alchemites to spin food and necessities with the few chantments allowed them.

As Will and the pregnant Alchemite reached the tent, volunteers spun her a set of clothes and allowed her to waken. Now in exchange for protection, she had to tell the Springers everything she knew about the Fyremen, and about Ellie.

The Alchemites' intelligence about the Fyremen was sparse, but they too had learned the curse was a live thing, that somewhere there was a circle of elder Fyremen reciting a cantation, day and night, to keep it functioning. As long as even one person was reciting this Befoulment, vitagua would damage everything it touched.

Nobody knew where this prayer circle, as they called it, was located.

Will stood as the woman was ushered into the room and lowered herself carefully into a chair.

Caro had moved like that when she was nine months along. . . . He tucked a magical lie detector, a carved wooden turtle, into one palm, fisting a chunk of letrico in the other. "What's your name?"

"I was born Mary," she said.

"Not a typical Alchemite name."

She shrugged.

He indicated the padlock chantment. "You were carrying this when we rescued you. What can you tell me about it?"

"Caroline gave it to me for safekeeping."

"Do you know what it does?"

"Our beloved Sahara said it would help Caroline retain custody of the Children of the Well."

"Carson and Eleanor, in other words: Caroline's children."

She nodded.

"Was the padlock part of the Nevada stash?" Sahara and her first followers had found that cache of nasty chantments in Yerington.

"The First Trove," she affirmed.

Sahara had apparently told her followers she'd set aside the Nevada stash decades earlier, as a contingency. The Alchemites believed Sahara had salted away other caches of magical items, leaving them for her followers after her arrest. They'd told him she was *still* hiding magical items for them, equipping them from prison.

"How do we open the padlock?" he asked.

Mary stretched her neck. "Caroline made a thin braid of your daughter's hair. By drawing the hair through the lock, she made a key. Look inside."

Raising it, he saw a fine web of gold wound into the mechanism.

"You need the key to break the lock," Mary said.

"Who's got the key?"

A toothy smile. "Passion."

Will glanced at the wooden turtle in his hand. It had its head and legs pulled into its shell. Mary was telling the truth.

Passion. Most zealous of the Primas. She would never accept Astrid's aid.

He let his mind drift to the world beyond Indigo Springs. If Passion had been sighted, the newshounds in the Doghouse would know. But no: witnesses had put her at Wendover, coordinating the failed Alchemite rescue of Sahara. Afterwards, there was one possible sighting, in Mexico City; she'd supposedly caused a palm tree to bleed sap that turned, by moonlight, into rubies. Nobody had seen her since.

Gone to ground, Will thought, *but where?* Her fellow Alchemites were fleeing to Indigo Springs. Those who didn't were easy prey for the Fyremen. A cell of them must be loose, using magic to hide from Gilead's people.

Why had he believed this might work? He touched his tuning fork. "Pike, I need someone to take over this interview."

"Boss thinks there's something up with that one."

"Ask the seers."

"Astrid says—"

"Is someone free to take this interview or not?"

"I'll need a minute—"

"Never mind. You can go, Mary," he said. Whatever she was or wasn't up to, it wouldn't matter, if he rewrote the past. He gestured at the tent flap, the entrance to the ghost town. The Alchemite heaved herself upright with a *whuff* and headed outside, to an exultant cry of welcome.

Will took Bramblegate to the plaza.

Even with Doghouse up and running, a few die-hard newshounds had the plaza TV on. In Washington, Arthur Roche was spinning what was essentially a demotion into a new partnership between the military and the Fyremen. "The terrorists have fled into the contaminated forest," he said. "We are seeking

Congressional approval for an offensive against Indigo Springs. This battle will be over soon."

"Light at the end of the tunnel," muttered a volunteer, triggering a smattering of nervous laughter. Confidence wasn't as high as it had been a few months ago. Why should it be?

Will pushed on. It was time to bring down the curtain, to close this farcical show before anyone else got hurt.

One of Astrid's ringers caught up with him. "What did you learn? Is she—?" He brushed her aside, stepping into the glow and coming out in the Bigtop . . .

. . . where another one of her was waiting. "Will—"

"Passion's got the key to the padlock," he said shortly, heading for his workshop. Only an hour ago, he had chanted all the toys the scavengers had been able to find. They'd found more, but it was a small pile, maybe a hundred objects.

She trotted to match his pace. "This is good. We can—"

"What? Bring her here?"

"Why not?"

"Passion's not going to cower here with the rank and file."

"Sahara returns to the magical well," Astrid said. "Where she goes, Passion follows."

"If Sahara comes to town, you both die. You're pretty sure of that, right?"

"Everything comes out all right."

"Even you can't still believe that, Astrid." He thrust his fist into the Chimney, letting liquid magic saturate him.

"Will, what are you—?"

Biting open his lip, he sprayed vitagua into the toys, cars, trains, dolls, the baby lamps, science projects, the stuffed animals, building blocks, rattles, and noisemakers. As he did, he heard the grumbles suggesting uses for each item. He picked and chose among them. He kept his eyes open for a pen, a toy pen perhaps. . . .

No luck.

But today's the day, today you learn to grant wishes. . . .

There were no more toys. Bursting with energy, he drew more vitagua, as much as he could, and returned to the plaza.

"Will—," a ringer protested.

"Manhattan," he said, stepping into the glow. "FAO Schwarz."

It was noon on the East Coast.

Will walked the aisles of the mammoth toy store, avoiding the shoppers, pouring vitagua into everything he saw, making magic toys.

The rush was incredible. He had thought he'd gotten used to the constant sense of physical well-being, but this was a high. His senses were razor sharp. He smelled baby powder, three different perfumes, the cleanser they used on the floors, a light layer of dust in the air-conditioning system, the distant burnt smell of New York smog. His memories sharpened, carrying back childhood discoveries and disappointments, joys, sorrows, scares and surprises, all the emotional sediment of his past.

Rounding a corner, Will saw the whole place now sparkled, and it wasn't just the toys. The customers' jewelry glimmered with possibility, as did their handbags and neckties.

He could chant anything. But could he choose what he made?

There—

He snatched a heavy silver pen from a customer service desk, lifting it to his blue-tinged lips, kissing it.

Wishes, he thought, fusing magic to object, and he'd done it, it had worked. He'd made himself a magical time machine.

"Security!" someone called.

Will dashed outside, fleeing into a hotel lobby, then a bathroom. He whispered a cantation for a power draw, pulling electricity directly from a socket on the wall, filling the room with letrico threads.

Will gathered the power in his hands, pressing them into a crystal.

"Before," he whispered, and the lights flickered.

CHAPTER THIRTY

THE ROUSED ENDED UP building a cairn for Eliza's sad scrap of a raccoon corpse, laying her to rest not far from the spot where she'd died. That hadn't been the initial plan: villagers had excavated the fallen boulders from atop her remains and then, after she'd been washed, dressed, and endlessly sung over, had attempted to freeze her into a glacier. But vitagua rolled off the body, like water off a waxed car, making it impossible.

There was no talk of cremation; fire was the enemy.

In the end, after sky burial and sending her to the real for interment had been rejected as possibilities, they'd laid stones over her in a waist-high pile. They'd watered the white grit around the cairn, and anemic grass sprouted around it. Eliza's broken granny glasses, resting atop the cairn, were left as a wordless memorial.

Since her death, the mood of the Roused had been uneasy. Teoquan and his followers were down in the Pit, trying to force a route through to the real. The glaciers were melting fast, freeing more people every day.

At Pucker Hill, the gendermorphed Roused kept weaving letrico and making food. At the cedar village, the stream continued to bring forth salmon; a careful harvest was under way. The snow fort kept rising on the drylands. The elders were scraping ice from the bodies of the trapped; with Eliza gone, it was a slower process, but the work continued.

Ev had been keeping to himself, spending his days in consultation with the scientists Astrid and Katarina were sending to the unreal, trying to catch up on everything they were learning about magic. The discovery of the fire hall had led to a flood of information about the magic the old witch-burners had wielded, about the nature of the curse.

Pike had sent some wooden coins—dogtags, they called them—to the unreal, and the bulletins from the news center caught him up with world news and Astrid's various projects. Everything was in motion: The population of the Alchemite refugee village in the ghost town, Tishvale, was burgeoning. Gilead Landon had "disenchanted" the White House and Congress with rosarite. The Danish government had confirmed vitagua contamination in two separate lakes. All the grandparents in attendance at a recent Irish wake had been transformed, overnight, into newborn infants. Fyreman and National Guardsmen working together had raided a house in Tulsa but failed to find Passion. . . .

"You're avoiding me, Ev Lethewood."

Startled, Ev looked up from a list of Fyreman potions they'd found in the Indigo Springs fire hall.

Patience had retained control over her shape-shifting since Eliza's death. She was her true self—a Native woman in her late sixties, in other words—a coiffed and healthy version of the run-down old beauty queen who'd lived on Ev's first mail route. Even now, even angry, she was heart-stoppingly beautiful.

"I've been . . ." He waved the bundle of science stuff, but she wasn't fooled, and he'd resolved to tell her the truth anyway. With a gesture, he invited her to sit.

"Ev, what is it?"

Taking her hand, he murmured: "I knew what Eliza was up to. . . . It was my idea."

Her lip curled. However much he might deserve it, the contempt on her face cut right to Ev's heart.

"I can't make up for it, but I'll admit it to Teoquan."

"Don't be idiotic. He'd kill you. Oh, Ev—what possessed you?"

"I thought—"

"Don't tell me. You were scared for Astrid." A hint of compassion now. Not forgiveness, but he'd take it.

"What should I do?"

"Do you know where Eliza stashed Teo's . . . allies? Finding them's the first step to making it right."

"I might work it out," he said. If the radicals got melted, Teoquan and his buddies would bust into the real that much faster. . . .

"Work it out how?"

"Everett Burke. The hyperobservant mailman."

"That was a delusion."

"Yes, but it worked."

She frowned. "Explain."

"I did solve puzzles as Burke, Patience."

"Puzzles—you mean mysteries?"

"Minor crimes, anyway. It wasn't just knowing what was in letters. I found a couple stolen dogs, caught Len Stiger cheating on his wife, talked one of the local girls out of suicide when nobody could've guessed she was thinking it."

"Becoming Burke again . . . it'd be dangerous?"

"If I don't, I owe some kind of blood debt to the unreal. Isn't that how it works?"

"Teo would say so."

"See, that sounds dangerous too."

She scowled. "Ev, your gift for understatement was never one of the things that attracted me to you."

"I love you too," he managed, and she kissed him. "Still mad?"

"Absolutely," she said. "But it'll pass."

"Can you get me into Eliza's place?"

"You get your own self in. You're not persona non grata, you stupid man."

"You're sexy when you speak Latin."

"I'm always sexy. So . . . it's only me who knows this?"

"I think Teo has a pretty good idea."

"Be glad what he knows and what he can prove are two different things. How'll you do it, become Burke?"

He flexed his hand. "The dime that lets me gendermorph people—"

"The one keeping you sane?"

"It's embedded here."

"You're not going to cut that hand off?"

"Definitely not."

"Then how?"

"It'll be easier to show you." He pulled his tool kit off a salvaged shelf and led her toward the bone bridge. He felt electrified, nervy—and more than a little relieved. She'd forgive him. Not today, maybe, but she would.

Eliza's chambers were at the base of the honeycomb, close to the Pit and the rescue effort there. Her beeswax walls glowed with vitagua; she had carved animal masks around the perimeter. Their stylized eyes seemed to stare at Ev in accusation.

"Now what?" Patience asked.

Ev opened his kit, revealing a brittle glassine rope—rosarite.

"What the hell?"

"According to the Fyreman notes, it negates magic—chantment magic, anyway," Ev said, pulling on a pair of work gloves. "Katrina's had her brainy types investigating how it interacts with magic and the Roused."

"You filched it?"

"I asked for some," he said, irritated.

"Pardon me for impugning your honor."

He laid the beads on his forearm, wrapping the rope around until there were three coils on his wrist. "They put this around buildings they want to protect from magic—they call it disenchanting. If my hand's encircled, it might affect the magic dime in my hand, stop it from working."

"Sounds like you're playing lab rat."

"Someone has to." He gestured at a spool of copper wire in the kit. "Tie it off?"

"Okay." She wound the wire, cinching the improvised bracelet shut. "Does it hurt?"

"Tingles," he said. "Like my arm's asleep."

He felt a rush of feverish heat, a stretching sensation in his forehead. For an instant he was afraid he was reverting to a female body, but then his beard tickled, the way it had the first time it broke through the skin.

That's right, Ev thought, *I was turning into a goat.*

Mumbles assailed him: *She's dead, baby girl's toast.*

And another . . . *It'll work out, Ev, I promise.*

"Jacks? Tha-at you?"

Patience rubbed the sore spots on his head. "You're growing horns. Happy now?"

He met her angry gaze. "Ma'am, if you are happy—"

"Cut that out and get to looking for the hotheads."

"Right. Things to do, mysteries to solve." Everett turned to the mess that was the murdered woman's lair, taking it in. Answers . . . the answer would be here. He started poking through things. Paper was his forte, but Eliza wouldn't have written anything down. He sorted through her possessions.

A twinge of paranoia. His—or Eliza's? She'd wanted the hotheads sunk deep, to be the last to escape when the unreal, as Astrid so frequently put it—

Popped. And . . . was that Astrid's voice? Was she one of the grumbles? Did that mean she was already gone?

Ghost me's been here all along, Pop. In the future, looking back, in the past, looking forward.

Whatever that meant.

Time's funny here.

Fingering a thumb-sized chunk of rebar, of all things, that Eliza had hung on a rusty scrap of chain like a pendant, he thought of building foundations, building blocks, and then the blocks of ice forming the snow tower above the elders' village. The spires were meant to be solid ice, silos of vitagua, a means of maximizing the number of people rescued at the Pit. They were huge. They were meant to melt last.

Hard to get to too, all those people stuck in the center of an expanding structure . . .

"Got it," he murmured

"You're sure?" Patience said.

"There's a chamber inside the ice towers."

"Let's get that thing off you." She had found a pair of snips in his kit; he extended his arm, and she cut the copper wire.

Ev dropped his hand, but the glass beads declined to fall. They clung to his wrist as if stuck there. His skin pulled, like it had been glued. Heads bowed, they examined the intersection between the flesh and glass.

Crystal teeth, dozens of them, had grown from the beads and sunk into his skin.

CHAPTER THIRTY-ONE

WILL HAD RUN OFF.

He'd come back, Astrid knew, and forcing the issue would be a mistake. She still heard the four of them up ahead in the future—her, him, and the kids. Chattering, getting along. Happy.

It didn't help the hurt she was feeling now. He'd dumped her. Walked away, like Sahara. And she should've seen it coming—he dumped Roche, didn't he? He was a dumper.

Maybe I should seduce that marshal. It was an entertaining thought: Why restrict herself to one lover, after all? *I'll get a harem.* The idea provoked a halfhearted giggle.

Her true self, Astrid Prime, was aboveground for the first time in weeks. Since recovering from the sea-glass poisoning, she'd let Mark bully her into remaining within her cave of wonders. They'd expanded her chanting operation there, and she'd kept making objects that could save lives. Olive and the Lifeguards were recruiting more and more volunteers to forestall disasters when the unreal popped. The pile of portraits in Limbo was shrinking by the day; everything seemed to be going well.

But Will had left her.

It wasn't working out anyway, was it? His wife dead, one disaster after another . . . and now Teoquan knows about my stupid conspiracy with Pop and Eliza.

Time was running out. Soon Teoquan would lead the Roused into the real, worsening an already-messy situation.

She had been working round the clock, chanting everything the scavengers could find, everything the volunteers could buy or steal. Her ringers roamed the world beyond the protected cave, meeting with experts, slipping contamination into remote woodlands, checking on their many dispersal projects. The newshounds' contamination map showed more and more blue spots, slowly spreading pinpricks of blue, scattered worldwide.

Right now, Astrid Prime was testing her scarf chantment, the one that hid her identity. Disguised as a scruffy middle-aged guy, she was heading into the Alchemite refugee camp with a basket of fruit and vegetables.

She found a prayer circle on the lawn, a bunch of petitioners begging Sahara to forgive them for accepting the protection of the Filthwitch. Everyone not praying was improving the camp: building sleeping quarters, a dining area, planting a garden. A cluster of Alchemites around the waterwheel Thunder had erected were weaving letrico for the few chantments the Springers had allowed them.

It was impossible not to feel a kinship with them. This was what Astrid had done in those early days with Mark and Ma and Patience: figure out how to live among the giant trees.

"Nobody's recognized you so far." Mark was speaking to a ringer back in the Octagon.

"One of the women has burn scars on her face."

"She got them in a clash with the army. Medics offered to restore her, but she refused. Says they're relics of the holy war." He touched the ringer's arm. "Astrid, we did the right thing."

"Using them as cannon fodder?"

"What were we going to do, fight the U.S. Army? Stop beating yourself up. Sahara isn't, I guarantee you."

"True, she wouldn't."

"Go on, talk to someone," Mark said.

Astrid mingled with a crowd of refugees, angling for the pregnant woman, Mary, who was waiting to use a chantment.

"Bored?" she asked.

Mary shrugged. "Hoping that when I get up there, I don't just get to make a sandbag or wood-chip a dead tree. Is that fruit?"

"Help yourself. Can I ask—?"

"Go ahead."

"Why line up at all? Why not organize work crews, and let everyone else do their own thing?"

Mary selected a peach, touching it reverently. "Alchemy is worship. It's prayer. Working miracles is touching the Goddess."

Astrid frowned. "Using magic is part of your religious practice? Like a Communion ceremony?"

Mary nodded. "So we take turns using the chantments."

"But you'd rather not make sandbags. It doesn't feel holy?"

A struggle worked itself out on the woman's face. "All Works are holy."

"What if you had something more inspiring to do?"

A smile. "I'd meant to go cure AIDS patients in Kenya. . . ."

"Would you still?"

"Pardon?"

"If someone turned you loose in Africa with a curing chantment, would you do it?"

The woman blushed. "There are others ahead of me for that honor. Besides, the Fil—Lethewood would never permit it."

Astrid shrugged. "She's always looking for—well, you'd call them miracle workers."

Mistrust shaded Mary's face. She put her hands over her belly. "I can't leave here."

"Astrid, you can't recruit these guys as Lifeguards," Mark said.

"It's okay, Mary, nobody's kicking you out." To Mark, she said: "Why not? Give them beneficial magic, scatter them, get more people out of Limbo and onto the Big Picture?"

"They'd run off and do whatever Sahara told them. Or the Fyremen would pounce on 'em."

"Still . . ."

"Why don't you come on back?" Mark said. "It's obvious none of them recognizes you. Successful experiment."

"You don't like my idea, so it's back to my cave?"

"Are you invulnerable? Are you a god?"

"Don't be silly."

"Well, mortal, accept that you deserve protection."

"Deserve," she echoed. She wasn't sure she deserved any of this, the good or the bad. She'd done so much damage. Will had left her. *Everybody dumps me.*

With a last look at the praying campers, she headed back through Bramblegate.

In the tunnel where Ilya's diggers were extending the spillway, her ringer's hands tingled painfully. Signs of imminent failure, Janet called it. The mouse within was dying. She took the ringer back to the plaza, walking into the glow.

"Death Valley," she murmured. She stepped through, into a furnace, laboring to breathe as her iced body began melting.

"Mouse six is finished," she said, this time via a ringer in the science wing. A biologist noted it: she was tracking Astrid's ability to extend her consciousness through the vitagua.

"You're living every woman's dream." Katrina came up behind her. "Doing a million things at once."

"Thirteen things, anyway," Astrid said. Out in the screaming heat of California, she took a last look around. Alchemized locust nymphs were hatching from vitagua-soaked sand. Cobalt grass grew at the edges of the blue-stained puddle she was leaving as she died. Birds, spiders . . . she'd never have thought a desert could be so alive.

The researcher produced another contaminated rat for her, dropping it into a tub of vitagua. A new Astrid coalesced around it. Once dressed, she'd gate back to Ilya's crew.

"It feels harder right now," she reported. "Maintaining the split focus."

"Maybe because Astrid Prime isn't chanting. The rush keeps your concentration sharp, right?"

"That makes sense."

"We'll set up a proper experiment." The researcher made a note. Astrid took the ringer back to the end of Ilya's spillway.

She stepped through . . . into chaos.

Red blood, blue magic: the first thing she saw was Ilya, bleeding into the underground river of vitagua. Tilde, the volunteer who drove the tunneling chantment, lay half in and half out of the fluid, features shifting as contamination turned her into a muskrat. The others were under guard; armed men covered them with rifles.

One of the soldiers had been watching for her. He fired, embedding a bullet in her blue iced skull.

Astrid let the ringer fall into the river. There were more popping sounds now; they echoed weirdly in the vitagua, and she sensed bullets moving past her.

A flare: the liquid magic was afire.

"It's the pipeline, there's an attack, the whole pipeline could go up," she said, all her duplicates at once—to Mark, to Katrina, to Pike and Olive, to the London intelligence center, to the scavengers and Chakeesa down in the sea pipe.

The digging crew was in danger. Rising again from the vitagua, Astrid pulled more fluid into herself, growing huge, seven feet high, eight feet. Flames licked her ankles, and her rat nose filled with a stench of burnt flowers and hair as she reached for the soldiers.

It worked. They turned, pumping more bullets into her but missing the rat, whose heart was stuttering under the strain of so much liquid weight.

"Pike, tell the miners to run through Bramblegate, now!"

The pipe organ hummed and the Springers stepped back, against the wall. One, two, three. Everyone but . . .

"I can't get to Tilde," she said.

"Tilde's dead, boss," Pike answered. "I'm sorry."

The fire was spreading—she was the fire. Astrid felt a terrible sense of dislocation— *Is this it? Is this when I burn?* Then relief: if this *was* it, it was just another mouse death.

One of the Fyremen was gathering the smoke. They would use it to make purificado for potions. . . .

"Astrid, can you seal off the tunnel?"

"Yes," she said. They had taken precautions: a row of sandbags lay on the bank of the channel, innocuous and well out of the flow. Now she washed vitagua upward, soaking their contents: not sand at all but a mixture of live things. Grass, seeds, mushroom spores, dirt, bamboo shoots, and earthworms began to grow and mutate, filling the confines of the tunnel, digging roots into the rock, devouring space, oxygen, and moisture. Here and there, the fire began to smother; in other places, the exploding vegetation began to burn.

A Fyreman's bullet finally struck the rat at the heart of her ringer, and it collapsed.

"This is the Doghouse." The announcement boomed out over all the musical instruments posted in town: "The pipeline is shutting down, repeat, pipeline is shutting down. Ilya and Tilde are dead. The rest of the tunneling crew is at the hospital. It's the Fyremen. . . ."

Vitagua was still burning. She focused on the Spillway, reaching out, freezing everything solid—then did the ravine too. Iced vitagua didn't ignite.

The flow of liquid magic from the unreal slowed.

For a terrible second, she thought it wouldn't work. But the fire burning its way down the pipe slowed as the chill took hold and the sandbags filled the tunnel with organic matter. Soon the tunnel was an impassable mass of frozen roots and magical fluid.

The ground shook: the unreal, pushing against the slowing of the vitagua flow. She sent a ringer straight to the source: Teoquan, of course, down in the Pit.

"What gives, bitch?" Teo usually wouldn't deign to speak to the ringers: he was offended by the way she used dying mice and other animals to sustain them. And they never lasted long here—even as he locked eyes with her, the ringer began to ache. "Daddy finds my missing people, so you shut off the flow?"

"We've got a problem here," she told him.

The survivors of the digging crew were with the medics. "They drilled into the pipe," said one. Others were sobbing, mourning Tilde and Ilya.

Crew leaders were converging on Astrid's cave. "Chakeesa," Mark asked, via tuning fork, "How's the sea pipe?"

"No sign of trouble," she replied. "We're gonna keep going."

"I'll arrange more security," Mark said.

"What do we know, Mark?" Astrid said.

"Those guys were definitely military."

"The Fyremen teamed up with the U.S. Army. They're not working at cross-purposes anymore: they're focused on us."

"I told you taking in the Alchemites would lead to this!"

"Mark, enough. How do we deal?"

"Take 'em out before they get to us," he said.

"They may be an army, but we aren't," Astrid said. "And I have to get the vitagua flow reestablished before Teoquan claws a doorway from the unreal into the Chimney."

"What if we kill two birds with one stone? Let the raging bloodthirsty lunatics out of the unreal and see how they make out against the pyromaniacs?"

"The Roused are nobody's sacrificial lambs."

"But the Alchemites were?" That was Olive.

With Will gone, they could discuss this openly. She clamped down an urge to cry. "The Alchemites were going after the army anyway. All we did was arm them."

"Well, they're out of the game now. Either the Roused go after the Fyremen or we do," Mark said.

"Meaning?"

"Come on, Astrid. Every time you come up with one of these warm fuzzy vitagua-dispersal programs, the bad guys smack us down. It's time to rip off the Band-Aid."

She was alarmed to see people nodding. "No, it's not that time yet."

"Are you sure?"

"Mark, what are you suggesting?"

He pushed his nonexistent glasses up his nose. "Take that shovel you made and fry their rosarite. They're hiding in the magic-proof circles they've made, their precious zones of disenchantment. . . ."

"And where are we supposed to start?"

"Do the world. Blow *all* their defenses. Expose them, and we can go after the source of the curse."

"Mark, a global-scale chanting—we don't know if it would work. Even if it did, it would take so much power. . . ."

"We'll draw heat."

"That much cold air would do a lot of damage. The storms—"

"So we shelter people."

"All of them?"

"It might make a good dry run for Boomsday."

"You're talking about an enormous storm. And the Fyremen won't sit idly by while we destroy their defenses."

"It'll be dangerous," Mark agreed. "It's time some of our butts were on the line."

Ouch, she thought. "I bet you've got the butts all picked out?"

"Excuse me?"

"You ban me from the strike team, guilt me into hiding down in a cave, and now you're accusing me of cowardice?"

"I didn't mean—"

"It's all very well to push people around a map in the war room, Mark. But how do I pick who lives or dies? You talk of newbies, nonessential personnel—"

"Tilde and Ilya are dead," he snapped. "Is it any better because you didn't *choose* them?"

He was right. She should have done something better, something more. "The cold snap you're proposing to trigger . . . innocent people will get hurt."

"Who dies if we keep doing this piecemeal?"

"We can't just—"

"You let Will roam off without so much as a by-your-fucking-leave, Astrid. Either you're in charge, in which case grab some guts and do this, or sign off on it."

Again, that disturbing sense of agreement from the others. "Who? Who are you asking me to kill, Mark?"

Mark's mismatched eyes widened. "Do you still believe in your Happy After prophecies? Aren't they worth dying for?"

"Thunder, maybe? No, he's too important. Olive—wait, that's not fair, she's paid a high enough price, what with Jacks dying and all, and Lee, and Dad—"

"Don't drag me into this," Olive said.

"We might *all* die." Mark reached up, touching the bridge of his nose, pushing up the glasses that weren't there anymore. "I'm not on the Big Picture yet."

"There's time. I can save—"

"Goddammit, Astrid, your hang-up about saving every last soul is what got Jacks killed."

She heard people gasp.

"You're right," Astrid replied, stung. "If I'd handed you over to the cops when I had the chance, maybe he'd be here now. Then I'd have someone who was actually—"

"Don't stop now."

"Someone who had my back, no matter what."

Mark's lips curled back. "Maybe. But you'd be short a punching bag, wouldn't you?"

He pushed away from the table. Thunder put out a hand, and he slapped it away.

"I'm fine," Mark said, and the magic glasses embedded in him told them all it wasn't true, he was lying. He vanished through Bramblegate.

Astrid buried her face in her hands.

It was Olive who spoke first: "He'll chill."

"He's not wholly wrong," Thunder said. "We need to deal with those maniacs. The thing keeping us from releasing the magic into the open air is the curse. Bust that, and—"

"Happy After," Olive said. "It's got to happen sometime."

"This is the Doghouse," boomed a nearby timpani. "There's a riot in progress in a New York toy store. A power blackout is spreading across the East Coast. Someone's drawing power directly from the grid."

"Mark?" Thunder asked.

"Mark's in the Octagon," Astrid said. "Giving my ringer there the silent treatment."

"A Fyreman trap," Olive suggested, "trying to lure in Alchemite looters, maybe?"

"Toy store," Astrid said, her heart heavy. "It's Will. He's not just off sulking somewhere. He's lost faith."

CHAPTER THIRTY-TWO

WILL HAD ALWAYS LOVED time-travel stories, and he knew well enough that his own romantic ideas, gleaned from those books and movies, were the reason he'd seized upon rewriting the past as the solution to his current problems.

Time travel seemed elegant and clean; it let you do things over, do them better. It was 20/20 hindsight and an opportunity to act on it.

The summer *Back to the Future* had first come out, he saw it a dozen times in the theater. He bought a skateboard and dislocated his shoulder trying to ride behind the back of a truck, just like Marty McFly.

When he decided to travel back and save Albert Lethewood, he imagined himself materializing in the past, in the pre-Spill world he missed so much. He had envisioned looking at graffiti-painted walls covered in gang signs instead of Alchemite symbols. Of seeing the pale, uncontaminated sky.

Now the time had come. He thought himself back using the magic pen . . . and immediately felt a bone-deep sense of wrongness. He squeezed his eyes shut, thinking this was stupid, he was in New York with magically spun clothes. No wallet, no ID, no money . . . What was he going to do? Hitchhike to Oregon?

Next, he thought: *Awfully quiet for New York.*

Opening his eyes, he saw his bedroom in Boise. He was staring at a ceiling-mounted poster—the Violent Femmes, *American Music*. His shoulder throbbed, and the broken halves of his ill-fated skateboard lay on the floor.

A tarnished silver pen was clenched in his fist.

"Oh, no."

The dusty mirror above his dresser confirmed his guess. He

hadn't physically shifted in time. He'd just taken up residence in the body of his eighteen-year-old self.

"Mouse magic," he muttered, as if it were a curse.

He'd run away, he remembered. Out of the blue, one summer afternoon. He was already reaching for a scrap of paper, thinking about the kind of note a kid would leave, something so the police wouldn't take his absence for an abduction, something to make it seem minor. He was of legal age. If he did it right, they wouldn't look for him.

He had been gone for days, he remembered, and when he came back, he'd said he didn't remember anything. Nobody believed him.

His wallet was on the dresser, and inside were his driver's license and a checkbook. His account wasn't exactly full—he'd bought a car three months earlier—but there was gas money, enough to get him to Oregon, especially if he raided the fridge.

That would be smart, wouldn't it? It would bolster the runaway thing. Loading up on sandwiches and fruit, he hit the bank, emptied his account, and got on the road.

He had to stop several times, because staying in the past took so much energy. He would lock himself in a public washroom and draw electricity from the power grid, weaving letrico, triggering blackouts, and driving on.

On the radio, the pop stations were playing the soundtrack of his youth, all the cutting-edge punk stuff he'd loved. The songs were oldies now—how weird was that?

Twelve hours into the drive, he found himself swearing at everyone who passed him. He was furious, he realized. He'd meant to stop in Portland on the way to Indigo Springs—watch the kids heading off to school, just get a look.

They wouldn't be born for years. He hadn't meant to come back so far.

Cheated again, he thought, turning up the radio.

Forget the kids—how could he approach Albert Lethewood? If Will scared him, Albert might run.

The point was to keep Albert alive and working. Astrid

wouldn't take over the well, Sahara Knax wouldn't be contaminated. . . .

If Astrid's dad survived, she'd have a better life.

We'll never meet, he thought, and that hurt now, but it wouldn't soon. He would never know what he'd missed.

Astrid, eyes sparkling as she chanted one thing after another. The weird imagination that went into the chantments, and her forthright honesty. The way she clung to everyone, Jacks, Ev, Olive. Even Mark, whom she didn't especially like.

Loyal to a fault. Will's expression, in the rearview mirror, looked guilty. *Can't say that about myself, can I?*

"She deserves better," he said to his teenaged self. "Maybe this way she'll get it."

It was strange to see Indigo Springs before it had been flattened. The bank was intact, the town square a bit run-down. The Indigo Springs Grand Hotel and the hospital stood at opposite corners of a well-manicured lawn. Up on the ridge, the copper roof of the fire tower gleamed in the sun. People went about their business, never guessing that in a few decades their homes would be rubble.

Not if I succeed, Will thought.

He found Albert in an antique shop, picking through stuff, dressed in jeans and a grubby T-shirt. Looking aimless, he weighed the cost of two magically receptive items.

Albert had always been broke, Astrid said.

Will dug out a twenty. "I'll buy them."

Albert pushed the money away. "Why would ya?"

"For an hour of your time."

"You're looking for drugs, kid, I ain't that guy."

"Buy the doodads," Will said. "They've got a certain sparkle."

Albert flinched. "You shouldn't be here."

"No choice."

Snatching the twenty, Albert bought the antiques, then headed out to a beat-up pickup truck parked on the street. He fiddled with the keys as Will got in. "Where to?"

"The house on Mascer Avenue?"

Albert started the truck. "There's a Burning Man working the area, son."

"I know who he is."

"Think that'll save you?"

"It's Lee Glade," Will said.

"Jesus!" Albert was caught off guard as he was shifting gears. The truck bucked, almost stalling. "I'm going to be married to the Chief's ex-wife."

"And his son is going to fall for your daughter." It was almost fun, being the know-it-all for a change.

At the mention of Astrid, Albert bristled. "Why are you here?"

"Lee kills you," Will said.

"No. He gets me, he gets Astrid too. He doesn't get her, I know that, because . . ."

Because the well opens, Will thought. *Because you've seen the future.* "He doesn't recognize you. You have a chantment, a coat . . ."

Albert swallowed. "Keeps people from recognizing me."

"Lee shoots you, but he doesn't make the ID. You die of sea-glass poisoning."

"He doesn't figure it out?"

"He thinks you're a drunk, Albert."

"Then Astrid's safe," Albert said.

"Nobody's safe if he shoots you," Will snapped. "Not you, not Astrid, not even Lee. It's going to go terribly wrong."

Albert parked behind the house, the one Astrid would one day inherit. Will had seen it destroyed on TV. Here and now, Patience Skye was puttering next door, cleaning her front window with vinegar and newspaper.

Will suppressed a pang of guilt. Patience had caught a lucky magical break, a new lease on life. Magic, and Sahara, had helped her.

Magic and Sahara burned Caro, Will reminded himself. *Maybe if Patience Skye gets carted off to an old folks' home in twenty years' time, Jacks Glade and my wife will live to ripe old age.*

"Come on." Albert led Will indoors. In the front room, a blue smear marked the wood floor in front of the fireplace; a roll of pink carpet lay nearby, awaiting installation. Albert fussed with it for a second. When he turned, he was wearing a girlish silver pendant around his neck, a feather. He spoke, his voice suddenly compelling: "Why are you here, son?"

"I'm in love with your daughter," Will said.

He spoke without thinking; he couldn't stop himself. *The feather,* Will thought. *Sahara called it Siren. She used it to control other people. . . .*

"My daughter is five," Albert said.

"I will be in love with her, when she's grown," he amended. *Or I would have been,* he thought, *but I'm going to make all that go away.*

He felt that electric jolt of grief again.

Albert tilted his head. "How's that brought you here?"

"I'm trying to prevent the magical spill," Will said. "To take Sahara Knax out of the equation."

Albert slipped off the feather with a sigh. "That's not what happens."

"Don't give me the fixed destiny crap."

"I never went to college, kid, and I'm no philosopher, but you know what I figure destiny is? Stuff you can't change. Winter comes after autumn. Everybody dies."

"I've heard this. You tell it to Astrid, and she tells me."

"Listen this time. You can't keep the magic from busting into the real."

"How can you be sure?"

"Free will doesn't mean we control it all. We just get to shape what is. We all die, but how? Sometimes we go to war, sometimes we destroy ourselves with drugs."

"Sometimes we don't give up."

"Sure, fight. Diet and exercise, pay the best doctors, buy time. Hold it off, at best make the end less painful. . . ."

"There's nothing wrong with less painful, Albert."

"Think about heart transplants, son. You need a heart transplant, someone else has to die."

"If you need a kidney, they don't. Don't be simplistic. Every dead organ donor saves more than one life."

"That's just it. The recipients still die. Just . . . not of that." Albert sighed. "This is why I failed debate. What's your name?"

"Will Forest."

"Look, Will Forest—grumbles say this well's the last well. They say it's gonna blow, that Astrid lets the magic out. She kills hundreds, or thousands . . . or millions. They tell me this when Astrid's not born; I'm barely married. And yeah, at first I figure to keep it from happening. I ask my sister to take over for me. She freaks, moves out East.

"I try to bring her back. It's a fight. Now my sister hates me. Any kid she has I never get to meet, so I can't recruit them. Also, I showed her some family heirlooms, chantments, and she stole 'em. All I did was create a new problem.

"Oh well, I figure. I got a cousin I can initiate. And I'll make him better than me, more powerful. But—"

"But he had leukemia," Will said. "Astrid told me."

"Initiating him causes more problems. He gets the greeds, trying to cure himself. We almost get caught. He makes stuff I can't get rid of, dangerous stuff. That damned pocketknife, remember? He spends the cash Granny set aside for us. And being so broke, it works a hell of a number on my marriage."

"I'm sorry, but—"

"You gotta work with the grumbles, son, not against 'em. I hadn't figured that out. I tried again. New apprentice, a friend. Maybe if he's even more powerful, I think. So I make him more powerful. Oh, he's golden—till someone murders him."

"Lee," Will said. "Lee murdered him."

"Lee Glade," Albert said, "I can't believe it."

"You'd better if you want to live."

"Well. I turn to my daughter, do the thing I tried to wriggle out of with all that free will. By then the magic trick I'm best at is making chanters. I turn Astrid into this power, this typhoon. . . . Of course she's gonna remake the world."

Will squatted next to the fireplace. The crack between real

and unreal was here, hidden within the hearth. He examined the bricks, looking for a fake, and Albert popped it out. A pinprick of blue welled through the crack.

"You're not initiated; don't touch it," he said as Will was about to put out his hand.

"Right." He sat a respectful distance away. "I could kill Lee Glade."

"You're a stringbean of a kid."

"I have a powerful motive."

"Sweet little Jackson Glade," Albert said after a second. "Wouldn't hurt a fly, am I right?"

"So?"

"What happens if his daddy's murdered? Maybe some nice uncle type, another Burning Man, comes to town and says 'Witches killed your pop.' Convinces him to start looking for me?"

"There's Sahara Knax."

Albert teased a plastic bag out from under the roll of carpet, coming up with a kaleidoscope. He handed it over. "Look east. What you do is—"

"Astrid told me how it works." He cranked its eyepiece to the left. The wall and intervening houses melted away. A puppet theater had been set up in the town square. A female Ev Lethewood was there, with Astrid and Sahara. Olive sat nearby with a baby on her lap.

"There's what, fifty kids there?" Albert said.

"So?"

"Any of 'em could become Astrid's new best friend. Any of them could do more damage than Sahara ever thought of. For that, you're gonna attack a six-year-old?"

"She gets my wife killed," Will said, but there was no force in his voice. "She's destroyed my daughter's mind."

Albert put a hand on his shoulder. "Fight the grumbles and it gets worse."

He said, through a tight throat: "You give Jacks a magic watch, you hypocrite. You try to save him."

"We all have our moments of weakness," Albert said.

Will felt a wave of fatigue—he was out of power again. "I don't suppose you've got electricity at this place?"

"Can't afford her."

"Could you at least buy a bulletproof vest?"

"I'll talk to the grumbles. If it's a good idea . . ."

"Even if Astrid inherits the well a few years later—"

"Maybe Lee woulda got me next week if you hadn't come." With a weary grin, Albert closed up the fireplace.

"At least let me teach you how to draw power—"

"I think you're about out of that yourself." He stretched, joints popping. "Let yourself love her, son. Do you both good."

A rush of spots before Will's eyes, a sense of dizziness, and suddenly he was in the bathroom of a New York hotel, hiding in the pitch black of a power outage.

Before he could look for Bramblegate, he found himself reclining in a leather chair in the Indigo Springs bomb shelter.

Astrid was there, whipping off the scarf she used as a disguise. She snatched the magic pen, snapping it in half. "Would you have done it? Unmade all this?"

He clambered to his feet. "What do you expect? Passion's never going to give me the key to that padlock."

"Sahara'll be here soon. Passion will follow her."

"I'm tired of waiting for soon and someday, Astrid. If I'd succeeded, your father would be alive. The Chief, Jacks—"

"And Caro. You'd be unhappily married."

"Is that what matters here? You're jealous?"

"What matters is trust." Her words were clipped. "After Sahara . . . do you know how hard it's been?"

"You've just figured out believing's hard?" he asked. "You expect me to buy in to your happily ever after."

"I never pushed you! Not on being a chanter, not on us."

"Why didn't the grumbles warn us Caro was going to get flash-fried?"

"I don't know, Will, I don't."

"Maybe they wanted her out of the way. If my becoming your concubine is their idea—"

"So don't get involved with me, then."

"Thanks for that, Astrid, I won't."

The ground shivered. She turned, fighting, as he'd seen her fight before, to tuck the hurt beneath her poker face.

I did that. I hurt her.

Let yourself love her, Albert had said.

Cobalt blooms of vitagua roiled through her eyes. Was she losing control? Was there more emotion there than he'd guessed?

Closing his eyes, Will reached for the magical well, imagining a deep pond, a reservoir without ripples. The ground stilled. They stood in silence, two chanters working together to stabilize the break between worlds.

Okay. Try again. Stay calm. "Astrid—"

"You were right, you know." She braced herself against one of the planters. "My feelings about Sahara when you got here, they were still tangled. I'd loved her my whole life. I knew she'd never come back to me . . ."

He thought again of Caro. "Giving up on someone entirely is very tough."

"Know what I saw that day at the courthouse? The Sahara I loved wasn't even real, just someone I imagined. Another pattern, I guess. You've always been kind to me, but . . ."

Cool waters, no ripples, everything still and serene. "I'm imaginary too? Is that what you think?"

"If all I've ever been to you is the way back to your kids, Will, it's okay. I get it."

A thrum underfoot. "Now you're saying I'm the one who doesn't care? Astrid, you're not even attracted to men."

"Then you must be a woman, Will, because—"

"You want a man? Go back to Jacks."

"Jacks develops a thing for Katarina." She giggled, sharply, a little shocked. "Katarina . . . I didn't know . . ."

"Dammit, Astrid, we're talking about *our* relationship."

She stepped close to him, wrapping her arms around his waist and staring upward with vitagua-tainted, unblinking eyes. Will tried to pull back, but she hung on. He paused, balked, wanting and not wanting to shove her. Frustration simmered outward from his chest; the ground shook again, and this time it was him losing control. The space between their bodies warmed, and she just held on.

You're going to fall in love today, she'd said when they first met, but how could he love the end of the world, the bringer of so much destruction? It felt like betrayal, even though Caro had left him, even though she was gone.

Astrid's body, lithe and muscular, her lightly freckled skin warm against his. All that power and passion, and the ground bucked beneath them.

"This is all your fault," he said, and with that he let go of something—he couldn't have said what—and bent to kiss her.

CHAPTER THIRTY-THREE

THE ROSARITE COILED AROUND Ev's wrist sank its teeth deep
into his flesh over the next several days. It didn't hurt or impede
the use of his hand. The arm was heavy; that was all.

He might have ignored it, if not for the coarse hair coming in
on his legs, the ache in his forehead where the goat horns had
broken through . . . and the madness.

Being the imaginary detective Everett Burke wasn't so different from being Ev Lethewood. They were both mailmen, both
parents—the hyperobservant mailman from Ev's favorite novels
had a son, Peter, who was Astrid's age.

Astrid. My child's name is Astrid. I can hang on.

That was what he kept telling himself, right up to the moment
when Burke took it into his head to have a chat with Teo.

He stepped off the bone bridge and found Teo waiting, his
long hair unbound, a predatory smile on his face. Contaminated
warriors were arrayed behind him. Hostility poured off them
like skunk musk.

Jacks, an angel of fire, burned at the edge of the Pit, melting
the underground river that poured into the Chimney.

"Your people are hidden in the ice towers," he said. "I can
show you where."

"Looking for a thank-you, Harry?"

"I'm past expecting anything from you." It was petty and he
knew it, but Teo's lip curled.

"Where's Beauty?" he asked. "She losing interest now you're
devolving into an old goat?"

"Patience has things to do."

"Like avoiding her crazy-cursed she-male of a sweetheart."

"You're trying to pick a fight," he said, trying to breathe through the sting of Teo's words.

"I should know better. You Lethewood girls wouldn't show an honest emotion if—"

"It's Burke, young man."

"Your daughter's gonna fry, you know. Your woman's drifting away, your sanity—well, that's moth-eaten already, and as for this delusion that magic has made you one of the boys—"

"That's enough."

"Gonna shut me up?"

"No," Ev said, but his arm—the heavy one—disagreed, straight out from the shoulder, *bam*, and he'd done it, he'd punched Teo in the nose. There was a crunch, as of plaster breaking, and a fall of red sand, a dry nosebleed that mixed with the bone-colored soil at their feet.

The warriors hooted in triumph. Teo grinned, baring his teeth, and fell into a crouch. Ev's gut clenched around a dawning awareness of having been foolish.

The light coming off Jacks flickered then, and diminished. The vitagua river froze with a series of loud, icy snaps.

Teo took Ev's hand with surprising gentleness, turning it upward to reveal a split knuckle. He smeared Ev's blood on his fingers, taking a deep whiff.

There was a crackle in the air, like electricity.

"What's that?" he asked.

"That's me, shoving my head into the crack between worlds," Teo said.

"Stop!" One of Astrid's ringers rose from the pooling vitagua. Teo rounded on her. "What gives, bitch? Daddy finds my missing people, you shut down the outflow?"

"We've got a problem in town."

"What sort of problem?"

"Pop—were you fighting?"

"Oh, kid," Teo said, flicking red sand away from his face. "You so aren't the boss of him."

Ev laughed, surprising himself.

"What's this big problem you're having?"

"Fyremen hit our pipeline. I lost two of the tunneling crew."

"Boo hoo. Dig another hole."

"And have that burned out too?" she said. "Teoquan, we need time to work out a new vitagua-dispersal scheme that'll have a minimal impact on the real."

"Minimal impact," he mocked. "This could be all over in minutes if you wanted."

"I'm not the one who trapped you here."

"You aren't getting us out, either." Teo rubbed the smear of Ev's blood on the bricks at their feet. A jolt beneath them; Ev grabbed his hand, wincing at a sudden flare of pain.

Astrid's mouse face pinkened. Vitagua gushed upward, backwards, out of the real and back into the Pit. Jacks dimmed to an ember glow. A roar, a huff of steam, and the air filled with blue mist. Astrid waved a hand, congealing the last of the melted vitagua into a pool of slush at Jacks's feet. As a chill ran through the chamber, Teo's feet were caught in ice.

She pushed back, Ev realized. Reversed the well's flow . . .

"You're right, Teo. It could be over in a minute—one way or the other."

One of Teo's warriors took a run at her, and Astrid caught him in a wave, freezing him solid.

"Oh, sweetie pie, you want to play with me?"

"To hell with you, Teo," she said. "You complain, you moan, nothing's good enough. Do it faster, do it better . . ."

"For that, you'll toss us all back in the freezer?"

"To save lives—"

"You'd leave Mommy and Auntie Patience in here to freeze?"

"He's got a point," Ev said. "You can't keep turning the flow up and down like the volume on a stereo."

Petey and Teo both startled, as if they had forgotten he was there.

"This isn't some whim, Pop. Ilya's *dead*. The river's gone."

"Then blow the well, like he says."

"The curse—"

"Break it," Ev said.

"Pop—"

"Break the Frog Prince curse, Pete—Astrid."

"Attaboy," Teo said. "Listen to Dad, Petey."

"As for you, Teo," Ev said. "Grab a little perspective. You want to ignore the logistics of moving half a million Roused in the real? You need to listen when Patience says it's not that easy."

Teoquan's lips pulled back, again revealing the points of his teeth. "Okay, not now. But when we run out of letrico—outta food—you start the open-air release, curse or no."

It was obvious she didn't want to agree, but after a long moment Astrid nodded. "Okay."

"One other thing," Teoquan said. "I see another of these mousey Popsicle abominations of yours, I rip its head off."

"I understand," she said, putting out a hand. Teoquan ignored it, leading his entourage of warriors away.

Ev took a long breath as she watched him go. Bulletins were coming in on the dead tunneling crew, on a power blackout in New York, on a big Fyreman recruiting push—practically a draft— under way in California. In Memphis, pet owners were reporting that their dogs were refusing to leave their homes; cats wouldn't come in.

Tuning in calmed him, washing out some of the confusion that came with being Everett Burke.

The ringer turned. "Brawling, Pop? Are you crazy?"

"Let's get to Pucker Hill before he changes his mind."

"What did you think you were going to accomplish?"

The urge to tell her to butt out warred with the weight of parental responsibility. Did he really have to be a good role model anymore? He was fifty, and Astrid was . . . still his child.

"You're right, of course, I shouldn't have hit him. But we just snatched three or four days you didn't have," Ev said. "He might've busted through now and taken all the vitagua with him."

"Open-air contamination, worldwide, with the curse . . ."

"Break it," Ev repeated. "My horns hurt."

"Right. Like it's simple. Like any of this is simple." She rubbed her eyes, looking so much like her poor father that confusion whirled in Ev.

He put a hand on her shoulder. "Do your job, kid. The future will take care of itself."

"You believe that?" Little-girl eyes, like she was six.

No, Ev thought. *We only have your word that it'll all be okay, and if you aren't sure . . .* "You promised, right?"

To his surprise, she burst into tears. He held her chilly body awkwardly. Albert had been so good at this. . . .

"The letrico will run out within days," she said. "I was hoping for decades."

"Decades of getting carped at by the likes of Teo?"

She sniffed. "Well—"

"Maybe it's like having a baby," Ev said. "You don't get to pick the time." Memories of being in labor clashed with his Everett Burke persona, leaving him queasy. His core, the person he really was, was eroding.

She let out a shaky breath. "I've burned this mouse out."

"Talk to you later, baby." He kissed her on the forehead, and the ringer froze in place, a mannequin Astrid, too much like the Albert statue for comfort. Ev turned his back on it, shaking out his knuckles as he headed back to the earth lodge.

CHAPTER THIRTY-FOUR

IN SLEEP, ASTRID LOOKED like a completely different person.
The frown of concentration unkinked itself from her brow. With
her ball cap off, the corkscrew whorls of her hair spread across
the pillow, copper wire against snow white linen. Fairy-tale stuff:
her cheeks pinkened, her lips pursed. Freckles sprayed random
constellations on her skin.

As Will watched her sleep, he flashed on a night years ago,
him and Caro with their backs turned to each other. There had
been a fight brewing, yet another fight . . . He couldn't remember
what. Ellie had been in trouble at school, maybe? Neither of them
had the energy or the desire to push it to actual yelling. They had
turned in, silent, furious, and—in Will's case—desolate.

Was this his future, he had wondered, endless nights of suffocating silence?

He woke later with the sheet twisted around him, a stretch of
cotton across his windpipe. For the barest of instants, he had
been convinced his wife was strangling him.

Paranoia, nothing more, but right then he'd known their marriage was ending.

He would tell the kids the truth, and organize some kind of
memorial service for Caro. As he made the decision, another of
his internal knots untied itself. Astrid drew in a noisy breath
that was almost a snore.

Oddly at peace, he slid out of bed. Stepping into the scalding
embrace of the spring-fed hot pool, he washed, then wove himself some clean clothes. Feeling as neatly pressed as Arthur in a
full-dress uniform, he stepped out of the living quarters onto
one of the garden paths . . . and came face-to-face with one of
Astrid's ringers.

"Hi."

He started. Behind the screen, Astrid was asleep. Yet here they were, nose to nose.

"What's up?" He spoke before the ringer could kiss him.

"Mark's run off to expose the Fyremen."

"When you say run off—" The questions forming in his mind triggered a flow of information from the news center: Mark had drunk one of the potions they found at the fire hall, something that hid him from the gaze of their seers. He'd disappeared through Bramblegate with the magic shovel. Apparently there'd been an argument while Will was gone. Mark had wanted to use the shovel to go after the Fyremen's rosarite and, hopefully, find the source of the curse.

"Did he take letrico?"

"Not enough," Astrid said. "He'll do a heat draw."

"He'll hit the far North or the South Pole then," Will suggested. "Or maybe one of those Canadian forests with the invasive beetle problem."

"You know how big those forests are?" Astrid said. "He could be anywhere."

"We can track him when the storm starts."

"If he hasn't frozen to death by then." Her flat agreement gave him a chill.

"Why would Mark, of all people, hare off like that?"

"He thought I was procrastinating," she said. "And . . ."

"What?"

"By running off, he . . . I didn't have to send anyone off to die."

"You think he's being noble?"

"Why not?"

Will scratched his head. "When Mark first learned about magic, he got the greeds."

"That was a long time ago."

"Yeah," he said. "It was."

They stepped into the Bigtop, into a gathering of hundreds of volunteers. Igme was passing out chantments.

"If Mark succeeds in exposing the Fyremen," the ringer said, "I'll send people out to try breaking the curse. And—"

And not all of them would come back, Will thought.

"They'll have a better chance if you go too, Will. You could chant things as they're needed."

"Of course I'll go."

Her smile was forced. "I think the Happy After is quite close now."

"Maybe you should focus on being happy now."

"Is that possible?" The anxiety she usually hid was on the surface.

"We'd better hope so." He said it lightly.

"What about you?"

"If you try for happy, Astrid, I'll try too."

"Deal," she said, sticking out her hand, oddly formal. Will put his arms around her, hugging carefully. Her skin was cold.

"Wait for me, dammit." Janet was pushing through the crowd, which parted sluggishly, as if reluctant to let her go.

Will nudged the ringer. "Time for a speech . . . boss."

"Not again." She was watching Janet.

"Part of the job." He pushed through the throng, drawing the ringer with him to the patched-up combat trolley, *Overlord*. The murmur quieted as she stepped aboard.

"I suck at this."

"We know." The heckler was a stunningly beautiful woman from Indonesia; she'd been mangled in a childhood car accident. Whole and healed now, she was looking at Astrid with a passion that bordered on worship.

"You sure you want to go on another mission?" Will whispered to Janet.

"I ain't dead yet, Forest."

"I never wanted this to be a battle. But we've been at war, in a way, for a while—" Astrid stopped, biting her lip.

Great, Will thought—*she's choking*. He looked at the crowd of expectant faces, seeing excitement, hope, and terror.

"Mark's risking everything so we can break the curse," she

said, and people nodded. "With that done, we'll release the magic, free the Roused, and start putting the world right."

That got a cheer.

"Seers are getting a location!" Jupiter's voice rang from a tree-mounted saxophone: "The Fyremen are on Crete."

"Mount up, people!" Clancy bellowed, ringing the bell on the trolley.

Astrid's ringer shifted, whispering in Will's ear: "If any of the Fyremen die, can you send them to the unreal?"

He looked at her, shocked.

"Teo's an inch from gutting Ma. Giving him a few bodies . . ."

"To desecrate?"

"It's awful, I know, but if it helps buy more time . . ."

Instead of answering, he gave her a quick kiss. Then, to Clancy, he shouted: "Get us to Crete before they regroup."

Overlord trundled forward, and suddenly they were blinking away daylight, rolling to a stop beside a shattered length of Fyreman chain. Beyond it was a stark white house with a blue door, built on the edge of a cliff wall. It was a remote, hard-to-reach spot; the trolley was teetering.

Igme put a tin whistle to his lips, blowing, burning letrico. Music poured out: orchestra and chorus, then one high soprano note. The cottage windows shivered and rained down in shards. Hopefully, any flasks containing Fyreman potions would shatter too.

Bramblegate grew on an outcropping of rock as volunteers took positions on the cliff.

Men were emerging from the house, their bodies aflame—they'd had time to throw back at least a few potions, then. Linking arms, they marched, creating a wall of fire and coming straight for the Springers. Machine guns clattered; one volunteer fell. Igme brandished a domino mask, and the rest of the bullets flew upward.

Janet ran to the injured woman's side.

Clancy waved the diamond bracelet they had taken from Ellie. The machine gun fire thinned as Fyremen fell asleep, vanishing into dreams. The walkers, bodies aflame, kept coming.

Behind the volunteers, the cliff was crumbling away.

"Chant," Astrid's ringer said in Will's ear. She stepped out, near the edge of Igme's shield, drawing their fire.

Will slid off his ring, selecting a carved wooden swan. He chanted it, thinking of dance floors, grace, ballrooms.

"Here." He handed it off, and the swan took flight, swirling and dancing behind them, its volunteer drawing up letrico. The cliff was falling out from under them, but polished mahogany floorboards were growing underfoot, providing support wherever its feathered skirts happened to sweep.

With room to move now, the volunteers spread out. Janet had healed the girl who'd been shot. Astrid's ringer had the machine gunners—those who hadn't been knocked out—distracted.

Will grabbed up a rubber mallet, chanting it and then handing it off. A volunteer smacked the mountain with it, knocking away the house and a good portion of the hillside, exposing a tunnel and a dozen men armed with swords, some gaping comically, others fainting into sleep and vanishing.

The rest charged.

Will slipped his ring on and moved to the fore of the melee. The air was cooling; fog rolled down the mountain, drawing wind downward. Soon they'd be blown off the cliffside, mahogany platform or no.

The tunnel crumbled further, revealing a low-ceilinged cave, a chamber of twenty-five or more men, gathered around a stone altar, surprised Cretan faces . . .

There was a minotaur on the altar. Withered, weak, with mad eyes and burns on its arms and legs . . .

Heat wafted over Will's face; he heard shots, a scream. The dance floor was burning.

Janet scooped up a dropped plunger, swinging it overhead. Silence fell—the men, whose lips were still moving, clawed at their throats. She stepped forward, her white mitten extended toward the creature on the altar.

Half human, half animal—part of the Befouling spell, Will

thought, and then—*No, this is it. Igme uses a coiled toy snake to sweep aside the ring of old men, but one clings to the altar. . . .*

A scimitar-wielding Fyreman ran at Will. He ignored him, leaving his magic ring to rebuff the assault. Janet had reached the minotaur, was pouring letrico into him, feeding vitality into his body through the white mitten.

"Watch out!"

Too late. Behind her, an old man rose up, fighting the wind. He shot Janet in the back with an ordinary-looking pistol.

The minotaur rolled to its feet, snapping the shooter's neck. Janet dropped the healing chantment, grabbing for the altar, sagging.

Beneath the volunteers, the dance floor cracked and swayed.

Roaring, the minotaur hurled the Fyreman's body away, plunging into the fray. Two Fyremen jumped on the Astrid ringer, chopping into her false body with swords.

Bramblegate was ablaze.

"Pull out!" Will shouted. "Everyone run!"

Igme lunged into the spreading fire. He caught Janet before she could fall, dragging her through the gate. Others followed, grabbing up the wounded and beating a retreat.

Will held them off as Bramblegate erupted into flames.

Alone now, Will drew the last of their letrico into his ring and reached out, embracing the crush of Fyremen as they tackled him.

He thought, longingly, of Jacks and the unreal. That was what Astrid had done, the first time she'd gone there. She'd wished herself out of the real. . . .

The light changed, and he was at Jacks's feet, ankle deep in a puddle of magical slush. Fyremen, maybe six of them, were trying to overwhelm him. He was out of letrico: the ring was draining him. . . .

Then Teoquan and his warriors came pouring from the nooks and crannies of the Pit, burying the flaming men under the weight of numbers.

He crawled free, out of letrico and weak with fatigue. The Fyremen were screaming.

"Pike, how'd we do?" he panted aloud. "The curse down?"

No answer.

He tuned in to the news center. Casualties were arriving at the hospital. Mark had destroyed the brand-new rosarite circles around Washington, D.C. Seers reported that Roche and Gilead were launching a major offensive against Indigo Springs. Sahara Knax's whereabouts remained unknown. Juanita Corazón's whereabouts remained unknown. Gilead Landon's whereabouts currently unknown. Will Forest's whereabouts were unknown—

Will touched his tuning fork. "Doghouse, Octagon—I'm safe, I'm in the unreal."

"Will Forest is unharmed and in the unreal," the briefing amended. "Four volunteers have been lost in the assault on Crete. A massive windstorm has sprung up in central Africa, assumed to be magical in nature. . . ."

Mark Clumber had probably performed his heat draw there when he destroyed the Fyreman disenchantment circles, Will thought.

"The curse is not broken. Our seers are actively searching for other Fyremen who might be reciting the Befoulment."

"I said bring them corpses." An Astrid ringer had materialized next to Jacks, staring in horror as the Roused warriors wrapped up their massacre of the Cretan Fyremen.

"The corpses weren't kicking our asses," Will told her, dragging her out of sight before Teo caught a glimpse of the ringer, drawing her back into the real.

CHAPTER THIRTY-FIVE

THE CHOPPER TRAVELED WEST to an airfield on the coast, south of the contaminated forest in Oregon. From there, they transferred to a sixties-vintage troop transport.

Juanita scanned the area as they trotted across the airfield to the plane. The place was a-bustle: camouflage-clad young men, thousands of them, were doing combat drills under the direction of bright, flame-licked drill sergeants.

As she stepped aboard the plane, the murmuring voices at the back of her mind hushed, all at once, like candles being blown out. The muscles in her hands—the ones she kept clenched against the urge to knead—relaxed.

Disenchantment? She took a careful look around, spotting a web of rosarite strands wound through the cabin. It would be a lie to say she wasn't relieved.

They lumbered into the air and were soon out over the Pacific, bound, they told her, for Hawaii. Gilead sat up front, conferring via radio—with underlings or superiors, she didn't know which. Sahara was under guard in the rear. The arch of brambles was nowhere to be seen, and the voices remained silent.

It was as close to being alone and unobserved as Juanita had been in two months. Even in sleep at Wendover, the Alchemites had had her under siege. But Sahara couldn't invade her dreams anymore. She closed her eyes.

When she awoke, it was dark. She prayed again, expecting to feel dumb—hypocritical, maybe—and instead discovered an odd certainty, as if she were eight again and her dad was still alive, as if the clock on her faith had been reset to those last unquestioning days before his death. Somehow, she was in the right place, where she needed to be.

She took a minute to savor the sense of gratitude building within, then turned her mind to the mess unfolding here and now.

All these factions. Gilead. Sahara. Astrid Lethewood. Only Astrid had helped her without asking anything in return. She wanted to protect people . . . protect everyone, from the sound of it. She didn't want Sahara torched. *I'm not saintly,* she claimed, but that seemed pretty big of her.

What about me? Juanita wondered. *Do I want Sahara burned?* She considered the Alchemite's threats against her family, Ramón locked in dreams, the fellow marshal they'd executed while she watched. She remembered Heaven, going up in flames.

That debt's been paid, she decided.

But how to save herself, let alone Sahara?

"Hey." Gilead, off the phone at last, handed her a cup of steaming coffee. Without waiting for an invitation, he sat across from her, long legs crossed on the floor. "What are you thinking about?"

"Inner peace," she said. "You?"

"Attack's a go. We have the green light from Washington to burn the contaminated forest and everyone in it."

"How soon?"

"Roche is positioning support squads—new guys, borrowed from the marines."

"Guys only?"

"Not necessarily." His eye fell on the sea-glass pendant still hanging at her throat. "My uncles have blessed your name—you're one of us, if you want to be."

He didn't know she was contaminated, then. But—"That's not an option."

"You're sure?"

"Gilead, as far as I can tell, you're the most liberal guy in this fraternity of yours—and you're a homicidal maniac."

"Don't you think that's overstating?"

"Believe me, I wish."

"I'm not the monster you imagine."

"I didn't *imagine* you burning Caro Forest to death."

"I released her," he said. "She'd been condemned to life as Sahara's plaything."

Her lip curled. "What you did was repellent."

She thought that would end the conversation, but he sank back in his seat, looking pensive. "If we're to save the world, a few people must be sacrificed. You must see that."

She snorted. "Who's the next 'sacrifice'—Sahara?"

"Not necessarily." He glanced toward the rear of the plane, where Sahara sat with her guards. "Before he was . . . abducted, Lucius was studying a particularly confusing prophecy. Sahara's destiny is to return to the Hive of Befoulment—it's there that she meets her fate."

"Hive of—you're taking her with you to Indigo Springs?"

He shook his head. "I don't know how to breach Lethewood's defenses. But Sahara believes she'll get in."

I don't want her burned, Astrid had said. Might she simply let Sahara through that gate of thorns?

"What exactly does your big book of prophecy say?"

"Don't mock." His lips thinned. "Lucius believed Sahara's return to the Hive would trigger a battle for control of the well. There's a passage—'the slow fouling of the world ends. The Brigade will be tested, then transformed.'"

She sipped the coffee, which was bitter and grainy. "Transformed?"

"Victory's a kind of transformation, don't you think? It goes on: The survivors offer peace to our enemies, the traditions of centuries will be overthrown—"

"Habits," she said. "Secrecy, torching people?"

"Excluding women."

"I'm not signing up for this."

"Don't you see, Juanita?" His eyes shone. "When we've won the well, there'll be no need for the pyre."

"You've spent your life planning to burn every single chantment and contaminated person. You expect me to believe that if you win, you're gonna come over all warm and pacifist? How naïve do you think I am?"

He patted the book. "You know I believe in this. When you see, Juanita, that it's come true, you'll believe too."

"Believing in what's proved isn't faith," she said, quoting something the judge had told her. What he'd think of this . . .

Inspiration struck. "You want me in?"

"I do."

She pushed the coffee away. "Put the bonfires out."

A startled laugh broke from his lips. "The prophecy says peace comes *after* the battle."

"Promise me you won't burn another living soul," she said, "and I'll get Sahara Knax into Indigo Springs for you."

"You? How?"

"I'm a resourceful woman, Gilead."

He mulled it over as they flew inland, over the smoking red maw of an active volcano, over a wall of jungle and into a perfectly cross-shaped compound shaved from the bamboo. Smoke poured from the center of the compound, and as they circled it, Juanita saw a pyre.

"No," he said at last. "Knax and Lethewood die, the well falls into our hands. Then we transform."

"That what it says? First one, then the other? Show me this so-called faith of yours, Gilead, and I'll take Sahara to Lethewood."

"That's nonsense."

"How do you know? It's all euphemisms and symbols and what did some guy who died three centuries ago mean by 'transformed'? Or Lady of, what was it? Masks?"

"Lady of Lies. And you don't believe any of it."

She crossed her arms. "You need Sahara Knax to go home."

They touched down, bounced, touched down again.

"I'll think it over," he said.

"Think fast." The plane juddered to an abrupt stop. "If I see one more person hit the barbecue, Gilead, this offer expires."

His jaw worked for a second. Finally, after he'd failed to stare her down, he went up front.

"All the damn pyres!" she shouted up the plane. "I don't care if they're in Timbuktu."

A cracking noise drowned her out; a second later, tendrils of plant root pushed in, breaking the windows. They were growing fast, winding themselves around the rosarite in the fuselage—and burning in the process. Glass shivered and broke; a smell of burnt candles filled the air.

The catlike urge to knead returned.

Juanita pressed her hands against her lap, waiting while Gilead argued on the radio in Latin. She couldn't fool him for long; she had to get out of here, get Sahara away. . . .

Finally Gilead cracked the airplane door open, letting in a rush of moist, humid air.

"Lethewood's people have attacked one of our bases in Europe. You expect us to lie down and take it?"

She cocked an eyebrow. "Do you think I can't distinguish between self-defense and executing helpless people? What about the bonfires?"

"We've suspended the cleansings," he said. "Tell me how you're going to hold up your end."

"Okay," she said, peering out at the runway. Something had happened to the rosarite all around the compound—the ground was churned up, the chains broken by willow roots. Men scrambled to and fro, stowing gear and humping weapons—it had the look of an evacuation.

The bramble archway had grown in about twenty feet from the runway. "Uncuff Sahara and bring her here."

"Are you kidding?"

"I'm blessed, right? I'm in the gang?"

"There's a loyalty oath."

"Yeah? All those marines of yours take it yet?"

"It can wait." With a half smile, he handed her three glass flasks. "Welcome to the . . . Brotherhood."

She pocketed them quickly, before he could see them burning her hand. "Sahara, Gilead."

He gestured, and the guards brought Sahara. On the plane,

she had reverted to a more or less normal appearance—the rosarite had arrested her transformation. Now it was broken, she
was shifting back into a bird-woman.

"You can't save her, you know," Gilead murmured.

"My prisoner, my problem. Why don't you focus on offering
peace to your enemies? Of all the crap you've predicted, that's
the part I actually like."

Taking Sahara by the arm, she coaxed her down the boarding
steps. Camouflage-dressed soldiers stared as they passed. Torches
raised, they radiated hatred.

"You don't really believe they'll start beating their flaming
swords into plowshares, do you?" Sahara whispered.

"At least I've given him a chance. Would you prefer to stick
around and see how long it takes them to torch you?"

"When Gilead figures out you're bluffing—when he figures
out you're contaminated—"

"Who says I'm bluffing?" They had reached the arch. Juanita
walked through, clutching Sahara's upper arm as if her life de-
pended on it. What if Lethewood had lied? What if she was as
crazy as the others and didn't care what happened to Sahara?

Please, Juanita prayed, *let me be right, let Lethewood be okay
with this.*

The light changed . . . and she still had Sahara.

Instead of the train terminal she'd arrived in before, they
were in a blue-lit tangle of brambles, a dim and apparently endless thicket that stretched in every direction.

"What the—what in the name of the Blessed Earth is this?"
Sahara demanded, shaking brambles from her growing wings.

"It's your big escape," Juanita said, and as Sahara turned, talons raised, bird eyes black with rage, she added weakly: "Tah dah."

CHAPTER THIRTY-SIX

ASTRID'S EARLIEST MEMORY OF Mark Clumber went back to first grade, to her first fire drill. She had evacuated with her classmates, but Sahara had dragged her off somewhere—she couldn't remember why—and somehow they got mixed in with the kindergarten kids waiting, by the swings, to go back indoors.

She had been worrying they'd bring down the wrath of Teacher when Sahara said, "You have funny eyes."

She'd turned to see Mark watching them.

If Mark had been hurt by the comment, it hadn't shown. Instead he had held out one pale hand, opening it to reveal a bit of found treasure—a glittering crystal prism, the sort of thing that fell off hotel chandeliers. He'd raised it to the sun, letting rainbows splash out on the sidewalk.

That same hand lay before her now, half-buried, tawny desert sand whisking over its palm in the wind. Its fingers and wrist were unmarked, as they had been that day in the playground, but the rest was burned flesh, a charred skeleton with a pair of glasses fused to its skull. The smoking remains of the shovel chantment lay beyond its grasp.

"Is he there?" That was Pike. "Should we send medics?"

"No," she said. "The Fyremen got him."

"I'm sorry, lass," Pike said.

We weren't friends. Her mouth formed the words, but she didn't say them aloud.

"Katarina says it should be about a hundred and nine degrees where you are."

She held out an arm, testing the air. "I'd say it's thirty below."

They had never done this before. She'd done a couple big heat draws when she first built Bramblegate, but she'd gone to

Antarctica and the far North for the power, places where it was already cold, where climate change—according to the scientists—had damaged the permafrost and melted icebergs, where cold was the normal state and the animals had thick fur. They got less letrico in subzero temperatures, of course, but the idea had been to minimize their impact.

"Thirty's survivable, and the desert's not exactly teeming with people," Pike said. "Maybe all Mark's killed is bugs and plants."

"Maybe." She bent, laying a hand on the burnt remnants of the skull. "I'm sorry, Mark. I can't begin to . . ."

Information was pouring through the news center and the Octagon: rosarite destruction had unveiled Fyreman bases in Rome, Kiev, Juneau, Hawaii, and Rio de Janeiro. The sites were being evacuated, but the curse was still in effect. The Fyremen were concentrating in California and Hawaii, and there were hundreds of them now reciting the Befoulment. . . .

"Any sign of the bad guys there in the desert?" That was Jupiter, in the Octagon, speaking to her ringer there.

"I have the place to myself." She looked around the ocean of sand. It was cold, but the air rushing down from above was hot. The chill Mark had put on the desert would not last long.

Spying a shape on the horizon, she trotted after it, loping up and down the dunes with the wind.

One of her other ringers caught a whiff of baking beans, and nostalgia overtook her. Sahara was such a meat-and-potatoes kid, she remembered.

An Astrid doppelgänger was in the hospital too, watching as the medics worked on the volunteers who'd fought in Crete. Tragedy had struck there too: Janet, an ex-marine named Jimmy Dean, and a couple other volunteers were dead. The doctors were sober and busy, using work to keep grief at bay.

"Jupiter," she said, speaking through the ringer in the Octagon, "it looks like all the Fyremen are reciting that Befoulment now."

"They're massing in one place," Jupiter said. "We might get another chance to shut them up."

"Mark won't forgive us if his death doesn't matter."

"Gilead Landon's been located in Hawaii."

Back in Emergency, she said to Will: "Landon's at a Fyreman base in Hawaii—should we go after him there?"

"Damn right," Igme said. "Press the advantage."

"Excuse me, what advantage?" That was Thunder—he was sitting with Janet's body.

"Igme's right," Will said. "We should go immediately."

"You nuts? At best, Crete was a draw."

Bad morale, Mark would've said. *Poor Mark,* Astrid thought, *always so big on the armyspeak. . . .*

"You don't want to come, Thunder, don't come," Will said.

"We aren't soldiers, Forest—"

"They're on the move," Jupiter said.

He was right—the bamboo screen showed the Fyremen standing around a willow-strewn plane, downing potions in a grim parody of a drinking binge. They turned to bright, white-hot figures, whirling in place until each man became a column of smoke. Merging, they swirled into the bamboo.

Aquino said: "Oh, there's a lot of them, isn't there?"

"They're all together now," Jupiter said. "They're merging with the group in California."

By now, Astrid's ringer in the desert had nearly reached the speck, which turned out to be an acacia tree with a camel tethered to it.

"If it lets us get them all at once . . . ," Jupiter said.

"Thunder's not wrong about us getting our asses kicked in Crete. They're fighters—we're just not," she replied.

The camel wasn't quite dead—it was hunched over, head bowed, and it was frostbitten, shivering. Astrid reached for the animal and it flinched.

"Shhh," she said, fumbling with her mouse muscles to untether it. If she could coax it through Bramblegate, one of the healers might—

She wasn't strong enough to undo the knot.

The camel wheezed, seeming to plead with her.

Astrid reached out again, bleeding herself of everything but a bubble of vitagua around the mouse. She flowed into the camel, contaminating it, and brought down the temperature of the liquid, chilling the last of its body heat. Its pulse slowed. The great body shuddered; the animal died.

Astrid, toddler-sized now, was left staring up at the ice blue corpse, wondering whose camel it was, whether they could survive without it.

Are you sure? people kept asking her, and she said yes every time. This was the right path. But the bright certainty she had felt in the beginning had dulled, worn threadbare by the doubts of others, by setbacks and losses. She'd been sure she could prevent Mark and Janet's deaths. She'd been sure she could save Will's kids, Sahara, even herself.

Had all this been about saving her own life?

"I don't want to hurt anyone," she told the dead camel. "And I don't . . . I don't want to die."

Give in, a grumble said. *It's the only way.*

"Right," she said aloud. "Like I'm gonna fall for that."

She was so far down this road now. And the good outcome was still in there, audible despite all the other voices: her and Will and the kids together, a future of teaching children how to chant, an ongoing set of talks, politics, and negotiations—

"But how? If I die, how?"

No answer.

Let it unfold, she thought. *Stop pretending you're in control of the flood.*

Wind-hurled sand bit into the corpse of the camel, carrying away minuscule bits of magic, embedding some into the tree, which was already starting to grow.

Something was scratching underfoot.

Astrid pressed her ear to the sand. The dune was hard here— not frozen, just a solid wall. Inside, barely audible voices were speaking—she assumed—Arabic.

"Jupiter," she said, "did Mark take any chantments with him besides the shovel?"

"A rubber gas mask, I think."

"I never made anything like that."

"Will did," Aquino said. "It shelters people. It weaves a . . . a life pod, I guess . . . with water, some food . . ."

"So Mark protected the people in the freeze zone?"

"That's the way we do things, right?"

Down in her cave, she felt tears on her face. "Yeah."

Jupiter stiffened. "Fyremen are in the forest."

"Where?"

"Edge of the Big Blue Reservoir."

"So the good news is we've found 'em," Aquino said. Their bamboo screen showed a blue-black funnel cloud twisting at the edge of the reservoir, that spot Roche was always bombing. The funnel had ignited the contaminated trees.

"It's feeding off the burnt magic—what did they call it?"

"Purificado." There were faces in the funnel, dark masks whose lips were all moving in unison.

"They're making for the Alchemite refugee camp."

"Can you use the rainstorm chantment to fight them, Jupe? It'll take a lot of letrico."

"That's what we have power reserves for, right?" His laugh was edgy.

"Hurry," she said, and there was a rumble of thunder. Her outdoor ringers turned their faces up into a downpour.

"It's slowing them down," Jupiter reported.

"They're too close to the Alchemites," Aquino said.

"We could arm them," Jupiter suggested.

"They've done enough fighting for us," Astrid sighed. "Evacuate them. Give 'em chantments, send them out to save lives."

"What if they object?"

"I'll talk to them," she said.

Jupiter frowned. "We get the Alchemites out of harm's way, the Fyremen'll come straight here."

"There's time yet to deal with that," Astrid said, hoping it was true.

CHAPTER THIRTY-SEVEN

THE ALCHEMITES WERE PRAYING as the hedge around their village burned.

Will and Astrid's ringer found Sahara's followers, thousands of them, sitting cross-legged on the grass, arranged in a rain-soaked spiral and holding hands as they sang praises.

As the two of them stepped into the clearing, the prayer stilled.

"You sure about this?" Will murmured.

"These are our people. They just don't know it yet." She squeezed his hand with her icy one, and he tried not to grimace. The ringers might resemble Astrid, but he was uncomfortably aware of the dying rodents within.

"Hello?" Astrid began, a little uncertain.

Hostile, staring silence from the Alchemites.

"Leadership, Astrid," Will whispered.

Astrid's back straightened. "A large force of Fyremen is in the forest. You know what'll happen if they get here—they'll burn the chantments, the vitagua used to create them, and, well . . . all of us."

"It's you they want," one of them muttered.

Astrid nodded. "Sahara's right, you know—I'm a gardener, not a god. I set up a community here in the forest because I needed advice and help. I don't have all the answers."

A ripple of uncertainty.

"I'm the Filthwitch, you don't like me, that's fine. I'm not asking you to change. But whatever you think of me, the volunteers in Indigo Springs believe in the same things you do—clean air, clean power, magic for everyone."

"We believe in the goddess Sahara," came a voice.

"Sahara says the magical well is sacred, and it's in danger."

She paused, letting it sink in. A few Alchemites glanced at the approaching fire.

"If the Fyremen get through, the future will be witch-burnings. Magic will never be anything but potions made of dead, burnt vitagua. Take a breath—what do you smell?"

"Gasoline," someone replied.

"Fire," said another.

Will felt a burst of pride. She had them.

"There's your choice. A garden or the fire."

"That simple?" someone scoffed.

"Sometimes it is that simple," Astrid said. "We need people to go work magic, to save lives. That's why you joined Sahara, isn't it?"

"We'll do it." The pregnant Alchemite, Mary, wobbled to her feet. "As long as we don't have to deal with you personally. No offense."

Will opened his mouth to protest, but Astrid bowed her head in assent.

"Thank you," she said. She turned, strolling off.

When Astrid was gone, Mary turned to Will: "May we assist in defending the well?"

"We're asking you to take chantments out into the world. We're expecting earthquakes, storms . . ."

"What's to keep the witch-burners from hunting us down?"

"For one thing, we're pretty sure they're all here."

Mary cocked her head, as if listening to the breeze. At length, she nodded. "Fine."

"Are you all ready to go?" Will said. "Do you have anyone with mobility issues?"

"In the Age of Miracles?" She scoffed. "Sahara was lamed so the slow might walk, the blind might see . . ."

Will remembered it rather differently, but instead of arguing, he said, "Pike?"

His tuning fork buzzed. "Aye?"

"They're on board."

"We've cleared Astrid's ringers from the plaza," Pike replied. "Draw them through."

Reluctantly, Will put out his hand. Mary took it, reaching back for the next woman in the spiral. Following his lead, they filed through Bramblegate and into the plaza.

Olive's crew was waiting, standing before a chalkboard—a list of endangered areas—and a crate of chantments.

Will had a strong urge, suddenly, to see Astrid Prime. Leaving the Alchemites with the Lifeguards, he walked into the glow and stepped out into the cave of wonders.

She was hard at work, of course, chanting everything her scavengers could throw at her.

"You're still chanting?"

"Getting magic out to people is the most important thing." She couldn't quite hide her fear. "Contaminated animals are fleeing the forest; they're going to end up in the towns closest to our borders. People need fresh water—"

He pulled her behind the screen, into her makeshift bedroom. "I don't trust the Alchemites."

"We can't leave them to burn."

"True," he said. Unlike the ringers, this Astrid was warm— the real thing, alive and well.

"They'll be back in the world soon enough." She kissed him, visibly savoring it. "Will, we have to talk."

"About what?"

"About before and about after." She drew a line above the bed, a shimmering blue boundary of vitagua, silk thin.

"You're afraid we can't beat the Fyremen."

"The grumbles insist it'll be okay. You, me, your children—in the unreal. Happy After, I can still hear it."

"But?"

"But there are contradictions."

"We can't afford your euphemisms now."

"I'm not on the Big Picture—Olive would say I'm still in Limbo."

"You might still die."

"Not by poison, not by fire, the grumbles say—but yes. I have no idea what it means."

"You saved Olive and Katarina."

"But not Mark, not Janet."

He cupped her face in his hands. "The obvious answer is they kill off a ringer. That's why you made them, as decoys."

"Maybe—"

"Astrid, I'm not going to let you die." He remembered Caro burning, the anguish of being helpless. He snatched up the scarf that made Astrid look like a nondescript older man. "You should have this on."

"Fyremen can't get me here. No door."

"They just hopped from Hawaii to California to here. Disguise yourself."

"Okay," she said without picking it up.

She's ready to die, he thought. Or was that a grumble?

"Astrid, you're entitled to your life."

"I've done a lot of harm, Will. Mark, Janet, the Chief—"

"You're allowed to live. You have to fight."

"I will, I swear," she said. "But—"

"No buts!"

"You have to be ready to take over."

"If they kill you, I'm not going to have a choice."

"That's . . . talk," she said. "Promise that whatever happens, you'll keep the well open."

"I made this commitment months ago."

"Did you?" She swallowed. "When all's said and done, wouldn't you rather have the old world back? You tried to rewrite the past—"

"Going back to see your dad was a mistake."

"The Fyremen might still make things the way they were."

He kissed her. "They'll kill everyone here. I'm a chanter. What are they going to do, let me escape?"

"You're being practical. I'm talking about what you want, Will, not what you think. Vitagua is about desire."

"My desire . . . I want you to live, Astrid. I want my children and I want a real life, not one where we're crouching in caves fending off bombs and assassins. If that's not the answer you want . . ."

"Well, it's honest." That faint smile, the one that said she was trying to find the upside.

Time to change the subject. "What about your exes? What becomes of them in this glorious After?"

"When . . . if I die, Sahara burns."

"And since you're not going to die?"

"Dunno."

"Jacks Glade?"

"The grumbles tell of him blazing, looking at me with eyes of flame. Later—like I said, there's Katarina. For a while."

"Everyone burns, Astrid? That's your best-case scenario?"

"The grumbles don't come with an index; I can't just look stuff up."

Their tuning forks buzzed.

"Sorry to interrupt," Pike said, "But that Alchemite gal's gone into labor in the plaza. There's about five hundred of 'em won't leave her."

"I'll see if I can hurry things along," Will told Pike.

"Thanks kindly, Will."

He hugged Astrid tightly, fighting a rising feeling of dread. "I'll be back to help with the chanting."

"It'll be okay," she said.

"Of course it will." *They'll get a ringer,* Will told himself. *Ringer dies, prophecy comes true, Astrid lives in peace. Check and check.* "But put on that scarf, just in case."

He gave her a last kiss and headed for Bramblegate.

CHAPTER THIRTY-EIGHT

"TIME'S UP." TEOQUAN TURNED up at Pucker Hill as the last baskets of venison and blueberries were emptied. He was dressed in a frayed yellow zoot suit—God alone knew where he'd gotten it—and his two-tone shoes were polished to a glow. Clasped loosely in his left hand was a bone knife. He wore the bright, delighted smile of a kid on Christmas morning. "Your girl around? I wanna talk to her."

"She's right . . ." Ev turned an expectant eye on the ringer standing at the base of the Pucker Hill wind turbine, but the figure of his daughter didn't move. "Astrid?"

No response—the ringer was frozen. Condensed water beaded on its face, dripping down her chin.

"How anticlimactic," Teo said. He was all but purring.

Using his good hand, the one not weighted by the shackle of rosarite, Ev tapped on the statue. "Petey? Sweetheart?"

Nothing.

"What do your super-deducto skills tell you about this?"

"Something's wrong in Indigo Springs," Ev said.

"Or we've been forsaken," Teo said.

"Astrid would never do that," Ev said.

"You sure? If she had to cut someone loose, wouldn't we be the logical choice?"

"I believe in her."

"You're obliged. You're her mommy, aren't you?"

"Yes," Ev said mildly. "So now what?"

Teo glanced around. "Where's Her Ladyship?"

"Here." Patience came out of one of the huts. Her old-lady mouth was drawn tight, and her hair was up in a bun. She was radiant. "Teo, if I asked for more time—"

"No," Teo said shortly.

"If I asked *nicely*," she said.

"You turned me down, gorgeous," Teo said. "Flow's stopped, time's wasting, and I got responsibilities."

"And it's just busting you up inside," she said sourly.

"I am what I am, Patience." He tap-danced in place.

"Let's get this over with," Ev said.

"Works for me." Teo bowed, gesturing at the bone bridge.

They crossed into the Pit. Ev put an arm up out of habit to protect his eyes from the blinding firelight of Jacks. But Jacks was banked, cool.

"Baby girl shut the flow down, remember?"

A step behind him, Patience retched. Ev's stomach did a slow, uneasy roll as he smelled rotting meat.

Lowering his arm, he saw a moist pile of flesh, pieces of body, clothing and hair, abuzz with giant insects—fully transformed Roused. The corpses were arranged in a circle. Blood pooled in the center of the grisly mound, forming a mirror-smooth surface whose edges were lined with grass.

"Fyremen," Teo explained. "From the battle in the real."

"You bloodthirsty bastard," Patience said. "Why—?"

"Building materials." Teoquan shrugged.

"For what?" Ev asked, and was sorry he'd asked. Whatever the answer, it couldn't be good.

"A better bridge." Teo led them to the lip of the Chimney. Human bones were lashed together there in a crude boardwalk that pointed straight down. Planks made from femurs, ribs, and spinal columns were bound by a winding, multicolored cord of hair. Skulls, gathered at Jacks's feet, were arranged so that what little vitagua there was flowed through their eyes and teeth.

Teo sauntered to the edge of the walkway. "Come on, Ev, time to pay your blood debt."

"Teo," Patience said. "You're not doing this."

"It's all right," Ev said.

"It's *not*."

He kissed her. "We're not supposed to die, remember?"

She shook him, furious. "That doesn't mean you can't be hurt, Ev Lethewood, or lose what's left of your marbles."

One of the Roused warriors gently broke her grip.

"After you," Teo said, sweeping out one yellow sleeve.

With a shudder, Ev stepped onto the bridge. It was more substantial than it looked; there was no crunching underfoot.

"What now?"

"Strike up the band!" Around them, drums started beating. Unreal voices, human and animal, rose in song, and the assembled Roused began to dance. Ev's ears rang.

Teoquan drew his blade over Ev's breastbone, releasing a thin trickle of blood.

Ev closed his eyes, thinking of Astrid. *Me for her,* he thought, offering himself to anyone who would listen.

"Down zee daisy," Teo said. They stepped over the lip of the Chimney, but instead of falling, Ev just stumbled. His stomach lurched, resettled. He stood on the bridge, which led to the vertical brick wall of the Chimney, pointed sideways but as steady as if he were on the ground.

Teo clasped his shoulders, turning Ev to face the Chimney, the wall separating real from unreal. "Dig."

Ev put his hand on the rough bricks, feeling a bit of crumble within them, shifting his hand to pry out a loose bit of stone. His nails shredded immediately. Gritting his teeth, he pushed harder, scraping the pads of his finger, then a knuckle. The blood seemed to soften the stone, so he kept digging, worming blindly through brick and iced vitagua, groping for home as the pain in his hands worsened.

The song rose around him, and soon there was nothing but the pain in his hands and the pounding of the drums.

A chunk. A sense of give. The bloodied tip of his finger broke through to hot air on the other side.

"You're doing great," Teoquan murmured in his ear, and Ev raked his wrecked hands along the sides of the channel he'd made, digging up to daylight, or possible ruin.

"Hang on, Pete," he murmured. "Pop's coming."

CHAPTER THIRTY-NINE

THE PREGNANT REFUGEE, MARY, was screaming her throat raw.

Will found her on hands and knees in the plaza, head down, fists pressed against the stone floor. Alchemites surrounded her, holding off a medic who'd come to assist. They were cursing the Filthwitch with enthusiasm.

Will flashed on Mary's intake interview; he'd been distracted by the padlock, the question of Ellie. Astrid had suspicions, but he hadn't cared, he was going to change the past—

"Something's wrong." It was a man's voice, behind him.

"He's here!" Mary moaned.

The letrico in Will's pocket sparked and shrank, a sign his ring was drawing power, defending him from danger. A teenaged volunteer—Suri from Afghanistan, the wiki told him, she'd been defusing bombs in Kabul—pitched over.

Volunteers began passing out all over the plaza.

Mary screamed, with joy this time. Her belly expanded, ballooning within her silk maternity dress. Her outstretched hands began to crack, then crumble, falling to pieces like dried clay. Then she was silent, and from the dead, steaming crust of her body stepped Passion, Sahara's right-hand Prima, her chief torturer.

Passion was covered from head to tattooed toe in magical objects, rings and bracelets, caps, trinkets, a host of chanted gewgaws. Alchemites were swarming to grab them.

Will sprinted to the glowing columns of vitagua, thinking about the Octagon.

"Alchemites have taken over the plaza," he said as he stepped through into the steel vault.

"Shut Bramblegate down," Jupiter said.

Aquino slid the pin into one of Mark's toy grenades, setting it on the blackjack table as he released its striker lever. "Good news, they're stuck. Bad news, with our transport hub out, so are we."

"Boss, come on," Jupiter said, addressing the ringer sitting next to him. But Astrid was frozen solid, caught in openmouthed surprise. "Pike, I need Astrid."

The pipe hummed. "She's not answering, Jupiter."

"Eyes on Astrid," Jupiter said.

The bamboo screen shimmered, revealing the plaza.

With Bramblegate shut, the Alchemites were hemmed in on all sides by impenetrable, overgrown forest. Some tried to find a way out, examining the frozen archway, probing for exits in the wall of greenery and between the columns. Others were tying up the unconscious volunteers in the plaza. Once restrained, each prisoner was jerked upward, drawn by invisible forces so they dangled, head down, above the plaza.

"What's with that?" Jupiter said.

"A precaution," Will guessed. "If we attack whichever Alchemite is holding them up, the hostages fall on their heads."

"Fantastic."

"Doghouse, send out a bulletin," Aquino said. "Alchemites have taken the plaza. Bramblegate is closed, repeat, Bramblegate is closed."

Pike broke in. "Astrid's out there."

"What?"

"There." Aquino pointed. "The guy with the red scarf."

"Didn't take them long to make a move," Jupiter muttered.

"Igme," Aquino said, breathless, as they hoisted another hostage. "Oh no."

"Astrid got him onto the Big—" Jupiter fell silent when Aquino shot him a glare.

"They're drawing a lot of letrico," Will said. "Will we run out?"

"With them gassing and hanging people and us burning power to hold out the Fyremen? Reserves are already dropping."

"Octagon, we have a call from Passion," Pike said. Sure enough,

Passion was brandishing a tuning fork, holding it to her mouth like a microphone.

"Put her through to me, Pike," Will said.

"—said, anyone there?"

"This is Will Forest," Will said.

"We've got your people," Passion told him. "Unless you want to see them hurt, you'll make me happy."

Time to dust off the old skills. He took her in—body language, posture. Was she scared? Angry? "What is it you want?"

"I want the gate reopened."

"That's going to take a minute. . . . You've overdrawn our power resources."

"So?"

"It takes a lot of juice to open Bramblegate."

"How long?"

"I'll get an estimate from our engineers," he said. "It would help if you lowered the prisoners—"

"Forget it," Passion said, sounding distracted. The image of her frowned; her eyes fluttered.

"She having a seizure?" Jupiter said.

"We should be so lucky," Aquino said.

Will tapped the screen. "The goal in a negotiation is to prolong things. Longer the talking goes on, the better the chances everyone escapes."

"If we run out of letrico, or Passion figures out she's got Astrid . . ."

"Yeah. Our clock's shortened."

Passion's apparent confusion resolved itself. "You don't have a gate problem. Open it, or I start killing your people."

"Is that what you do for Sahara, Passion—execute people?"

"Wanna test me?" She raised a scalpel to Igme's throat.

Aquino sucked in his breath, but Will lay a hand on his shoulder. "Where is it you want to go, Passion?"

"That's not your problem."

"If we reopen Bramblegate, what do we get in exchange?"

"There's no exchange. You do as I say—that's the whole deal."

"We do things by committee here," he lied. "Give me something to work with."

She flapped a hand derisively, eyes fluttering again.

"If it's not seizures, why is she gapping like that?" Jupiter asked.

"She's talking to someone," Will said. "Relaying what we tell her. Getting orders?"

"Passion only takes orders from Sahara," Aquino said.

Jupiter groaned. "Eyes on Briarpatch."

On the bamboo screen, a field of brambles appeared. Dozens—no, hundreds—of Alchemites were entangled in it.

"They don't want out, they want in," Jupiter said. "All those Alchemites, stuck. Look—there's the lady herself."

He was right: Sahara was trapped along with all the others.

"Let her rot there," Pike said.

"Is this something you can work with, big guy?" Passion dangled a fine golden key in the air. "I'm prepared to let you have your chicklets back."

His heart slammed.

"Will," Jupiter warned.

"Open the gate, Forest."

Pike protested: "Ye can't leave the boss hanging there!"

"What's it gonna be? You sold out Wendover—you gonna betray the Filthwitch too?"

Jupiter said, "You can't!"

"It's a deal, Passion," Will said.

"Dude!"

"They're my children," he said, and before Aquino could weigh in, he said, "Passion, untie Igme. . . . He's the man—"

"Oh, I know all your names," she said.

"Give him a tuning fork and the key to that chantment and let him walk to the columns. Then move your people to the Bramblegate side. I'll open the gates. Igme leaves, your people get in, simultaneously."

Jupiter made a grab for the Bramblegate grenade, but Will had chosen Igme for a reason—Aquino held him off.

Pike's voice thrummed through the guitar. "Lad, if anything happens to Astrid—"

"Astrid promised us that everything's gonna be okay."

"*Now* you believe her? That's convenient."

"Who would she choose, Pike—herself or them?"

By now, Igme was at the columns, the key in his hand.

"Where's Sahara?"

"More distance between you and him, Passion."

She sneered, but the Alchemites moved, clustering against Bramblegate.

"You better know what you're doing, lad."

"Igme, whatever you do, don't lose that key," Will said.

He pulled the pin on the grenade.

Igme sprinted into the glow as Alchemites poured through Bramblegate. Sahara was the first through. She was thin and dirty, her hair rat-tangled. She looked very much the part of a terrorist on the run.

"Home, sweet home," she said.

A crack, like a rifle shot. Smoke billowed up from the crack in the marble floor of the plaza. A thousand new fissures ran through the stone, breaking it into wedges.

"Oh," Jupiter said. "This is bad."

"Why?"

"Because this vault is in the train tunnels underneath—"

Before he could finish his sentence, the whole of the Octagon roof crisped away in a mirage-ripple of searing heat. Jupiter and Aquino collapsed. Will lunged to scoop letrico crystals from the safe deposit boxes with his free hand.

Then he was staring up at Sahara as she peered down at him . . . and backed off.

A moment later, Juanita Corazón started down into the Octagon with a resigned look on her face.

Will was stunned. "You're an Alchemite? You?"

"I'm a real joiner," she said. "Look, Sahara wants your ring."

"Why doesn't she come get it?"

Juanita's eyes flicked, meaningfully, to his hand.

Mark's toy grenade. He remembered Astrid standing right here, saying it would come in handy, that he'd use it to bluff—

He made a throwing gesture, and there was a cry above, the sound of shuffling retreat. Juanita flinched.

"It's okay, Juanita—it's plastic."

A flicker of surprise. She took another step down the incline, and then stumbled, hooking the wall with badly bitten, retractable claws.

"You're contaminated?"

The barest of nods.

"Are you hearing voices?"

She nodded. "Now we're here, it's gotten pretty bad."

"I want Caroline's ring, Forest!" That was Sahara. He let his gaze rise, but apparently the Alchemites thought he was holding a real grenade. He and Juanita were, effectively, alone.

"Actually," Juanita said, and he could see how much it cost her, pushing down her pride, "I could use some help."

Will nodded slowly. "A chantment, embedded within you, would treat the contamination, stop the voices."

Juanita flushed: "In exchange for what?"

"No price," he said. "And only if you want."

A pained smile flickered across her face.

"Did I say something funny?"

"No. Go ahead." She held out her hand. "And, Forest?"

"Yeah?"

"Thanks for giving me a choice."

"You'll need to scratch me," he said. Clumsily, he pushed the magic ring off his finger, working it around to his palm. He reached for Juanita, and the claws dug in, drawing blood. He remembered what Astrid had said: it was like pressing the chantment into warm butter.

Juanita's eyes shifted, becoming normal. Now she was the one drawing vitagua . . . and Will's eyebrows were singeing.

"Here," he said, scooping another letrico hunk off the blackjack table. "You'll need this."

She tucked it away, then cursed, loudly, in Spanish.

"Juanita?"

She turned her face upward. "The ring's vanished. He put it in my hand, but—"

Sahara trilled in frustration. "Can you disarm him, at least?"

"I let go of the grenade, the gate closes!" Will shouted. "You want that?"

A pause. "Fine, Forest, hold the gate open. Juanita, get him up here."

"We can't leave these guys to burn," Will said. He rolled Jupiter off his chair and onto his shoulder with a grunt. Juanita picked up Aquino. The two of them scrabbled up the incline of rubble, climbing to the plaza and lowering the unconscious men to its broken marble floor.

"Superman no more, eh?" Sahara said. She grasped Will's jaw, squeezing until his teeth ground. Her talons were like knives. "You're *my* prisoner now. How do you like it?"

"Beloved Goddess." Passion held out a yellow poker chip.

Sahara's face glowed with the affection a sane person might reserve for their newborn child. Shoving Will away, she scooped up a hunk of letrico, then flipped the chip like a coin.

Chantments dropped from above, falling off the bound, hanging volunteers. Alchemites dived after the items eagerly. The scarf around Astrid's neck untied itself, whisking downward to the cracked marble . . . and as it fell, Astrid became herself again.

Sahara trilled happily. "Passion, wake the hostages."

The dangling Springers opened their eyes. Some cried out; others struggled against the ropes holding them. As Sahara approached Astrid, a hush fell.

"Beloved Goddess," called an Alchemite. "The Fyremen are about a mile from the plaza."

Sahara pivoted beneath Astrid, so they were nose to nose. "Bet you weren't expecting to see me again, hmm?"

Astrid's face was turning red. Will swallowed. No chance she was really a mouse.

"Hello, Sahara."

"That's all you have to say?" Sahara walked a slow circle around her, flicking her talons through Astrid's curls. "No declarations of undying love, no apology for turning me over to the man?"

"Would you accept an apology?"

"Don't be tiresome."

"You should go, Sahara. It's not safe here."

"Is that supposed to be clever?"

That got a flicker of weary resentment. "I'm not clever, Sahara—that's your thing."

Sahara reached up with one misshapen talon, stroking her hair. "Sarcasm doesn't suit you."

"It wouldn't, would it? I'm too solid, too unimaginative. Isn't that it? You're the one with the flash."

"Right. You're substance and I'm . . . what? Vapor?"

"You might still escape."

"Running, Filthwitch? When I'm finally where I belong?"

"Sahara, you can't fight the Fyremen."

"I fought the U.S. Army to a standstill." Her voice rose. "My few, my followers, using troves of chanted weapons—"

A hoot from one of the captured volunteers. "You kept them off our backs."

Sahara wheeled, infuriated. "Who said that?"

"Don't—," Astrid said.

"Troves of chanted . . . ," Will repeated.

"I created the war chests," Sahara trilled. "I told my Primas where they were. I told them what to do, where and when to attack. All from jail, I might add. What did you do in jail besides suck your thumb and mourn Jacks Glade?"

"My God, Astrid, you armed them," Will said.

"Yes," Astrid murmured. "This is where he finds out. . . ."

Some of the Alchemites exchanged uneasy glances.

Oh, he'd been blind. "It wasn't a chantment here or there to keep them from doing too much damage. It was *everything*. Everything they used against Roche in the battle with the army."

"Not the lock they used on your daughter," said Astrid. "I swear, Will—the stuff from Nevada, they stole that themselves."

"Nobody armed us," Passion said scornfully.

"You've been conned, Passion," Will said. "We all have."

Astrid's eyes were locked on his. "They were going to go after Wendover anyway, Will. Roche had Sahara."

"You *gave* him Sahara! And you used me to do it!" He laughed. "You asked what Astrid was doing in jail, Sahara?"

"She was crying her little Filthwitch eyes out."

"She apparently found time to set us all up. She set the Alchemites on the army—using you as bait."

"Silence!" Sahara bellowed.

"Try to understand," Astrid pleaded. "The people she would have killed—the soldiers, cops. Lowering the body count—"

"And if the pesky Alchemites kept you off Roche's agenda, that was . . . what? A side benefit?"

"What was I supposed to do, Will, take 'em on? Me, Ma, Mark, and Patience? All Roche had to do was drop one nuke on the well. I needed time, and the Alchemites wanted to fight."

"My wife was an Alchemite!"

"I didn't know she'd be killed!"

"You're just like the grumbles. Always a card hidden, right? What was it your dad said, magic grows best in the shade?"

"Darlings, darlings." Sahara tried again: "Charming as it is to have ringside seats on your first lover's spat—"

Will spun, confronting the dumbfounded Alchemites. "It never made sense, did it? All those chantments waiting, none of them lethal enough to give you an outright victory."

"The Goddess respects life!" someone shouted.

"All so fragile, so easily burned out . . . Astrid didn't want you getting too powerful."

"My Primas sacrificed themselves for magic, not for the Filthwitch!" Sahara bellowed. "They fight for me. They died for me."

Astrid sighed. "And that's something to be proud of?"

Sahara's face darkened. "See how you like it."

With that she spun, slashing a razor-sharp talon across Astrid's throat.

There was a spray of red blood and blue magic.

CHAPTER FORTY

"DING FRIGGING DONG," SAHARA said, "the Filthwitch is dead."

Silence smothered the plaza: everyone—Alchemites and Springers, Will, Juanita herself—was taken aback by Sahara's sudden murderous turn.

Astrid's mouth flapped open and her body jerked, the muscles of her bound arms flexing. Red and blue fluid poured over her upside-down face, running through her hanging curls . . . and then froze into a stalactite as blue ice, like glowing antifreeze, caked to slush over the wound in her neck.

Just a woman, Juanita thought, *not a monster at all, and Sahara slaughtered her. . . .*

"You think a little compress will do the trick?" Sahara said, tapping a talon on the ice. Astrid's body stiffened, then went limp.

"See how easy that was?" Sahara said, addressing hostages and believers alike as she let her bloody hand drop.

"Please," one of the dangling Springers said. "It's not too late to heal her."

"You all just hang tight—hang tight, get it?—and watch her die. It'll be a good lesson." Sahara's gaze roved over her assembled worshippers, pausing on an Alchemite who wouldn't quite meet her gaze. She tipped up the girl's chin. "Something to say, Chalice, my love?"

"No, beloved Goddess," she stammered.

"Tsk, darling, I know that's not true."

The woman struggled to gather herself. "What she said—the troves. Did she . . ."

"Are you questioning Sahara—?" Passion's voice was choked with rage.

"Hush, Passion." Sahara put up a placating hand. "Chalice needs to see that I don't need the Filthwitch to work miracles."

"She's right," someone said: Will Forest. "Do you believe or don't you?"

The words meant something to the prisoners from Indigo Springs. Their weeping stopped. Several had seemed to retreat inward after the attack on Astrid, into personal shells of fear or shock. Now they revived, drawn back by Will's words.

Looking up at one of the bound Springers, an ancient-looking black man, Forest said, "May I?"

"Be my guest."

Using his right hand—he was still clasping the grenade in the left—Will lifted the old man's walking stick off the plaza floor. The movement opened the scratches Juanita had made in his wrist; blue fluid seeped from the wounds into the wooden cane. Moving with an odd formality, Forest offered it to Sahara.

Wary, she nevertheless accepted it, taking a deep whiff of the wood. "What's this?"

"You wanted the well," he said. "Presumably you're not planning to let the Fyremen take it from you?" He pointed at the edge of the plaza. Smoke was pouring into the clearing; it had formed a column with flame-bright eyes.

"It's a trick," Passion said.

"No," Sahara said, examining the cane. "This does . . . fight fire."

She turned, striking a fencing pose, extending the cane's tip into the column of smoke. A flowering of light, shimmering and multicolored—like the northern lights, Juanita thought as it grew higher and higher—blossomed, expanding skyward. The column of smoke thinned; the flaming eyes dimmed.

Bathed in radiance, wielding the cane like a sword, Sahara looked every inch the avenging angel.

Passion shouted: "Praise the Goddess!"

Others took up the chant. Juanita looked from one Alchemite to another. Ecstasy shone in more than one face, but there was uncertainty here and there.

Of course. They'd seen Forest make the chantment.

Sahara claimed to be the source of the magic. She'd preached that the Filthwitch had usurped her, assured everyone that she would possess the well once Lethewood was gone. Now here she was, taking freshly made magical objects from Astrid's supposed puppet.

Were some of the sisters looking past the spin?

A snap, a fizzle. The radiance surrounding Sahara dimmed. The sparkling reserves of power—letrico, Forest had called it— were shrinking.

Passion clapped her hands. "Draw heat."

The cantation rose from a dozen throats at once. Small bolts of power flickered to the edge of the plaza.

"More!" Passion shouted.

Again, the light show surrounding Sahara wavered. People shivered as the temperature dropped. And there were more frowns now. Each failure of the showy aurora kindled more doubt.

"Lowering the prisoners will save power," Passion said.

"Fine." Sweat was running down Sahara's forehead. The captured Springers began to drift to the concrete floor of the plaza. They seemed less afraid than their captors.

"I could make something to protect you from the cold," Forest offered.

"Silence!"

As the prisoners came to rest, there was a rush of power toward Sahara. Her aurora brightened, but the smoke didn't lessen. If anything, it was coming in faster now, drawn by the drop in air pressure. Air was rushing out as it cooled, but smoke was pouring in from above, lots of smoke. . . .

Passion saw it too. "Stop the heat draw!"

Too late: hot air gusted over them.

"The turbulence is fanning the flames," Will said. "This is the part where the woods really catch—"

"Don't you *dare* start with Astrid's 'I'm so confused, what time is it?' crap!" The shimmer around Sahara faded again.

Chalice, the Alchemite who'd questioned Sahara, shot a quick look in Forest's direction. She wasn't subtle enough—Passion yanked her to her feet.

"Something on your mind, sister?"

"Leave her be," Will said.

"He made the cane. I just thought . . ."

"It's all right," Sahara said. "Come here, child."

The Alchemite rushed forward, eager to please, and Sahara put out her free hand, as if in blessing. The girl grasped it, bowing, a prayer on her lips.

Sahara was speaking too, murmuring words, and suddenly the aura around the cane was blazing again, blinding and beautiful, illuminating Chalice's face as it became pale and drawn. She grew thin, then skeletal. By the time she'd realized she was being vamped, she was too weak to pull away. Bony, aged, and dried out, she dropped to the ground without a murmur.

"Any other doubters?" Passion turned her gaze on the other Alchemites. One, foolishly, backpedaled. Two of the sharper faithful seized him, dragging the man to their goddess's waiting, deadly grasp.

I have to stop this, Juanita thought.

"I thought the Goddess respected life," Forest protested.

Sahara shot him a scornful glare. "Wanna be next?"

"I go, the well closes."

"The power comes from Sahara!" Passion whirled, knocking him on his ass with an inexpert but effective punch.

"You wouldn't be trying to shut me up, Passion, would you?"

She stood over him, fists raised. "You need to remember you're not invulnerable anymore."

"If Sahara can't beat the Fyremen back, they'll burn the well and everyone here."

"I am beating them back," Sahara said with obvious effort. "Passion, get me another sacrifice."

"Him." Passion chose another Alchemite.

As they dragged him forward, he shrieked: "Goddess, if you took a little from each of us—"

"Shouldn't you be ready to give her everything?" Forest said.

He was provoking them, as Astrid had, Juanita thought. These people needed lessons in diplomacy.

"At least take the prisoners first," the proposed Alchemite sacrifice pleaded.

"Yeah," Will said. "There's commitment. There's belief."

Belief, Juanita thought. It wasn't the Church she'd been missing all this time. It was belief itself. Divinity, the life of the spirit . . . call it what you would, it was what the Alchemites were missing, too. Why else had they followed someone as transparently opportunistic as Sahara?

"We will go to her embrace willingly," Passion said.

"Listen to me!" Forest shouted. "Even if Sahara turns back the Fyremen, she will suck every last one of you as dry as Chalice. You've seen she's as human as you are."

Sahara said, "These people will gladly die for me."

"Show of hands, folks," Forest said. "How many would like to get fried by Sahara here and now, and how many would at least prefer to see the hostages go first?"

"We are not voting," Passion said. "That's the stupidest thing I ever heard of."

"You said you'd die for her," he said.

"I need another offering!" Sahara bellowed. She had reduced the man to a husk.

Juanita yanked Gilead's lick of fire off her throat and crushed the glass between her palms. There was a tickle, a sense of heat. A wave of fatigue spread through her: Will's magic ring was protecting her from the sea-glass.

She looked at the Alchemite next to her, speaking just loudly enough to catch Passion's ear: "Wanna make a run for it?"

The Alchemite flinched away, and Passion pounced.

Struggle, Juanita thought—*make it convincing.*

"Beloved Sahara, I beg you, take this life."

Passion shoved her forward. Juanita faked a stumble, landing on her knees at Sahara's feet. She put up her hands, as if in self-defense.

Sahara beamed. "You believe now, don't you?"

"Funnily enough," Juanita said. "You were right about everything."

Then Sahara was reaching for her.

CHAPTER FORTY-ONE

IT WILL ALL BE okay.

It was the ultimate promise of every faith, Will thought as he watched Juanita play Passion, as the Alchemites dragged the former marshal toward Sahara. Everything would be all right in the end. First the apocalypse, then paradise.

But things weren't okay. Astrid was dead; her body lay ten feet from him. He'd promised he wouldn't let her die, and then exchanged her life for those of his kids. Now, if he couldn't turn this around, they were all finished.

"That aurora's very flashy." Pike interrupted his reverie, buzzing words at him through the tuning fork.

"I lifted it from a movie I saw ten years ago."

"Thought I'd seen it. Boss dead?"

Grief cut through him. "Sahara murdered her."

"We're a hair short of screwed, then, aren't we?"

If something happens to me, she'd said, *you have to be ready to take over.* He owed her that much, at least.

Sound sure, he thought. "We're gonna come out of this, Pike."

"Glad to hear it, lad." Pike's cheery lilt seemed forced. "Bigtop's afire—we have to evacuate through Bramblegate."

"No other way out?"

"Fyremen've burned our back door. Also—perhaps ye've noticed—the well's in danger."

"There's something developing here that should make for a distraction. Give it ten seconds and have everyone run."

"Ten seconds," Pike agreed. "Nine."

Juanita was on her knees, face peaceful, lips moving . . . in prayer? Everyone watched, spellbound, as Sahara reached for her. The aurora splashed color around them, Vegas razzle-dazzle.

Juanita lifted her hands . . . protecting her face? Sahara took them, beaming, murmuring the vamping cantation.

Her expression changed. She trilled, tried to yank back. Suddenly Juanita was the one holding on.

Passion lashed out at Juanita and was blown back, slamming into a barrier of trees by the plaza.

Caro's ring, Will thought. *It's protecting Juanita as she does . . . What is she doing?*

Whatever it was, Sahara had dropped the cane. Now nobody was holding out the Fyremen. Before anyone could take it up, the chantment caught fire, filling the smoky air with a scent of scorched lilacs.

A *whump,* like gas igniting. The column of smoke expanded. Dense, alchemized foliage above the plaza turned ember red, wisping away in cinders. Ash rained onto the plaza from above.

Above the burning canopy, Will saw the sky, the flat disk of the sun obscured by a pall of violet smoke.

"Fyremen have reached the plaza!" a volunteer shouted.

"Three, lad."

Sahara leapt upward, beating her wings, breaking Juanita's grip. Cackling, she rose over the plaza, ten feet high, then twenty. She fled upward, blood dribbling from her hand.

Sea-glass poisoning, a grumble said. For a moment, Will thought he recognized its voice.

"Two."

"Pike, tell everyone to run, run now!"

Volunteers began pouring through Bramblegate. A few sprinted across the plaza and into the glow, vanishing between the columns. Most stopped to cut free their imprisoned friends. A few Alchemites attacked them, but with Passion stunned and Sahara wounded, most were fleeing the approaching Fyremen.

"Get out!" Will shouted. There were hundreds of men, bodies white-hot, igniting everything they touched as they marched through the plaza. "Run!"

He pushed through the throng to Juanita.

She was staring upward, openmouthed with horror, at Sahara. "What have I done?"

"Stopped a massacre," he said. "Unfortunately, they seem to be coming in waves.

"Can we bring her down?" Juanita asked.

"Leave her," Will said.

"Astrid didn't want her burned."

"Juanita, listen. That ring won't protect you forever."

"You gave me one of your magic batteries."

"Batteries run out. The ring'll suck you dry, just as Sahara did Chalice." He pointed at the oncoming Fyremen. "If they attack you—"

"Attack me?" Juanita laughed bitterly. "I just poisoned Sahara Knax for them."

Pike appeared at his side. "Will, lad, we have to get you out of here."

"Too late," he said. "Now's when the Fyremen surround us."

There were more Alchemites and volunteers than Fyremen in the plaza, at least for the moment, but Astrid's recruits were still bound, and the Fyremen seemed impervious to magical attack. They formed a perimeter around the old train station and the clearing they were burning around it. The roof of forest above them, tons of alchemized vegetation that had protected them for so many months, was ablaze.

A distant hum—choppers—hinted that reinforcements were on the way, just waiting for someone to create a landing zone.

"Search everyone!" Gilead Landon shouted. The Fyremen turned their attention to shaking down the Alchemites, none too gently, confiscating chantments, incinerating each object with their bare, fire-hot hands, and slurping up the smoke.

"Will," Pike whispered. "What happens if they burn the Bramblegate grenade?"

"I don't know." He let vitagua bleed out of the scratches on his palm, forming a shell of iced magic around it, then bringing down its temperature so the model grenade was locked and the gate open. Crouching slowly, he tucked the chantment under the edge of a toppled bench.

"It'll melt eventually," Pike said.

"Best I can do for now."

Sahara was flapping awkwardly for the small break into the trees, trying to flee from the Springs as she had done once before. But Gilead Landon strode to the middle of the plaza. He raised his hand, revealing a glob of bright molten glass. Blowing on his fingers, he formed it into a glassine javelin.

He threw it gracefully, piercing Sahara's wing.

Shrieking, she crashed to the plaza floor. Fyremen surrounded her, hauling her to her feet.

Juanita bellowed: "You promised me no more pyres, Gilead!"

The Fyreman turned to face her. "Just these two."

Pike stepped in front of Will, fists raised.

"He means Astrid, Pike," Will whispered.

Fortunately, Juanita had Gilead's attention. "I gave you everything I promised. You control the town. You have Sahara. You swore, Gilead—you *swore* you'd stop burning people."

"Juanita, be reasonable." The Fyremen were making a pyre of burning logs in the crater where the Octagon had been.

"Are you a homicidal maniac or aren't you?" Juanita demanded.

For a moment, Landon seemed to waver. At last he shook his head. "This has to happen."

"Why, because it's foretold?"

"I'm sorry." He shoved Sahara into the midst of the blaze, pinning her by her wings, using the glass javelin. Then, bending, Gilead picked up Astrid's limp body, flinging it so she fell at Sahara's feet.

"Boss," Pike whispered.

When she burns, I burn, a grumble said.

Will batted the voice away.

Astrid lay unmoving as the flames rose around them—a mercy, Will thought, remembering Caro.

Sahara was alive and conscious as her wings burned. Pinned

atop the pyre, she became a writhing, bird-shaped torch. Her screams rose over the deafening rush of the flames and the wails of her worshippers.

By now, the Fyremen had the plaza surrounded, corralling fleeing volunteers and shattered Alchemites alike. The approaching helicopters were closer, and there were flaming figures atop the forest canopy, ready to catch anyone who tried to use a chantment to fly away.

With every moment they packed in tighter, driving the crowd inward to escape the growing heat.

Find something to chant, Will thought as he was jostled to the middle of the pack. He scrabbled at his pockets. Empty—no, wait. His fingers closed around a silk elephant he'd been keeping, all these months, for Ellie.

What could he make? Power was low. And the Fyremen had taken potions anyway, Will thought. Magic probably wouldn't affect them.

We're past that now, the grumble said.

A chill. It was Astrid's voice, but she was . . .

A grumble, he realized—she's in the vitagua. Had she been there all along?

Always a card to play, she said. *I didn't even tell myself.*

"They're gonna burn everyone," he whispered.

No, love. Now's where we stop them.

"How?" An Alchemite bumped him, and he nearly fell. Volunteers bore him up. The Springers were clustered around him—protecting him, as Caro had tried to protect Sahara.

Sahara Knax let out one last howl, a starling shriek that tore the air as she collapsed within the burning logs.

"Our work is unfinished—the well remains open!" Gilead boomed. "Lethewood must have initiated another chanter."

All these months, we've been easing the magic out. Astrid might have been speaking in his ear. *But Teo is right—we can yank the tooth.*

"Do things the hard way, not the easy way?"

Are you kidding? A laugh—not the sly, teasing laugh of the unreal, just an ordinary Astrid chuckle. *What part of the last six months has been easy?*

"What do we do?"

Think about warmth, Astrid Lethewood said.

"Heat up the vitagua? How much?"

Warmth, she repeated. *Not heat, not cold. Bathwater, sun on your skin, lying under a comforter in the wintertime. Affection and kindess.*

"Warmth," Will murmured. The knot of volunteers tightened around him.

The Fyreman began to mutter something, a low cantation that spread through the encircling wall of his fellows. One word, repeated over and over.

"Was that *hut*?" Pike asked.

"*Hut* like in football?"

Forget them, Will, Astrid said. *Think about warmth.*

"It's *huff*," Katarina gasped. "As in huff and puff and burn your house down."

Smoke roiled from the witch-burners. Eyes watering, Will met Gilead's flame-red gaze. Huff, huff, huff.

Okay, he agreed. *Warmth.*

Curling up on the couch with the kids to watch old cartoons, waiting on cooling mugs of cocoa. Ellie dozing with a stuffed elephant tucked under each arm . . .

That's it, Astrid said. *Here comes the Small . . .*

"Huff! Huff! Huff!" The air clogging, unbreathable. Everyone about to suffocate . . .

"Huff, puff," Will said. "And boom."

A world unfurled beneath him.

CHAPTER FORTY-TWO

ASTRID HAD BEEN IN a dozen places at once when the Alchemites made their move.

She had been in a hammock behind an abandoned garden cottage in Northern England, waiting for a dying ringer to slip away. She was climbing in the canopy of the forest, watching the Fyremen and chatting with Katarina about vitagua sequestration and contamination levels. The tiny ringer in Africa was roaming the desert, contaminating whatever it touched. She was with Pike in the hotel lobby, with Jupiter and Aquino in the Octagon.

Astrid Prime was in the shelter, making chantments for the Lifeguards and the poor troublesome Alchemites.

"Astrid," Pike had said, "the Unreal's claiming their deadline has elapsed."

Deadline, she thought. *Such an ugly word.* There was nothing to do but go plead with Teo for a few more hours.

She touched the scarf, her magical disguise. *I decide to go in person,* she thought. *I have a ringer stashed at Pucker Hill, but Teo's offended by the use of the mice. He'll kill it, and if I send another copy of myself across the plaza, all those Alchemites will start screaming Filthwitch. . . .*

Mark would have a fit. There was a tinge of unease in the thought; this was risky. "Olive, how's the body count looking?"

"Death toll's dropping substantially," Olive reported. "Sketches are coloring in Faster than we can post them on the Big Picture."

"Any significant changes?"

Euphemisms, the grumbles chortled, but Olive understood. "You're still in Limbo. Sorry."

"Sahara?"

"Her too."

When I burn, she burns, she thought. "Thank you, Olive."

Have a little faith, kid.

She stepped into the bathing grotto, dipping her hands into the hot pool. She splashed water onto her face, tugged a comb through her curls. She put on a clean, pressed-looking pair of jeans and a new red shirt. She fluffed the pillows on her bed, pulled the blanket straight.

There was nothing left to tidy. She owned nothing else.

She stared into the mirror for a second more before putting on the scarf. Her features changed, and she took Bramblegate up to the plaza.

As she arrived, her head began to ring.

All the Astrids frowned, as one. "Something's wrong," she said, to Pike and Jupiter and the plaza and the songbirds in England.

Then she was swooning—that was the only word for it.

And I must be unconscious, she thought, because she, they, all of her were icing over, leaving her to peer at the world through blue filmy eyes, to listen with the slush-clogged ears of rats and mice.

She strained to take in as much as she could. There was so much going on: Alchemites in the plaza, Fyremen burning a path into town, Igme fleeing with a golden key. Sahara, home at last, mutated and deranged. All of her gone but for that insatiable need for worship. Magic had devoured her friend whole, taken her as it had taken Jacks and Mark and Dad.

And you, a grumble said.

Yes, Astrid replied. *It's almost that time.*

She felt a last pang of fear. In its wake came sadness: she hadn't broken the curse, hadn't cured Pop, hadn't released the Roused. So much unfinished . . .

It'll be okay. Was that her own voice, mouthing hollow reassurances from the future?

No, Bun, really, it will.

Daddy?

Happy After's just up ahead. Believe a little longer.

Could she do that? Maybe. Yes, she thought. A little longer.

A vague stir of consciousness: they'd brought her around. She was hanging by her heels, staring into a once-beloved face. "Hello, Sahara."

And then we argue, don't we?

She saw, in a flash, that she had to break Sahara's grip on the Alchemites. They wouldn't leave, wouldn't save anyone, if they stayed with Sahara to the end. They'd be slaughtered.

Get this one last thing done . . . tease her, undermine her. Plant that seed of doubt.

Juanita was staring at her, incredulous. *Don't provoke her,* she seemed to be pleading.

Too late, said the grumbles.

Sahara whirled. Dancing? There was a sticky burst of heat and Astrid realized she was bleeding. She tried to draw vitagua to her throat, close up the wound . . .

Let it bleed, Astrid thought, and then . . . black edges, black hedges, blacking out. *Not by poison, not by fire, not some sacrificial ringer. Sorry, Will, that's how it goes.*

Exanguination, she told an earlier version of herself. *There's an ugly word.*

She sank into the cold.

That's it, she thought, *I'm trapped in the glacier. All that work, and I've ended up with the Roused. If Will lets the well close, we're here forever.* Was this the end? Was she trapped in the ice, left with the taste of having screwed up?

No. The Happy After will come.

Her confusion lifted. Eleven pairs of eyes opened.

She was with Pike. She was in England, in Africa. All the unreal was wound within her belly, yearning to get loose, to spring forth. All she needed was heat.

Warmth, she thought.

Nothing.

Heat!

We can't do it now, Bundle, we're dead, the grumbles said, and it was her own voice, and Dad's, and Eliza's, and her granny Almore's too, all the Indigo Springs chanters telling her what she'd always known.

She needed warmth. Needed a well wizard. She needed Will.

CHAPTER FORTY-THREE

"BOOM," WILL FOREST WHISPERED.

For a second there was no reaction. A tremor underfoot, maybe, nothing to distract the stamping Fyremen who'd encircled the plaza, nothing to keep them from suffocating everyone caught in their human cordon.

Warmth.

He could feel, rather than see, the first blue fronds of magical steam as they rushed from the Chimney. A blue plume unfurled from the ravine, sprouting skyward, staining the sky like squid ink.

Gilead saw it first. His fire-lit face tipped upward, and Will saw fear and exultation in equal measure. The Fyreman reached into his coat, producing a stoppered vial. . . .

More, Astrid said. *Quick, before he ignites the well.*

Warmth. He clung to that memory of his children. Reading to them both in bed on sleepy winter nights . . .

Wind lifted his hair, and there was a bite of grit in its caress. The cloud of choking smoke blew off the edges of the plaza. Clothing flapped. Everyone staggered, save for Juanita Corazón. She grabbed two nearby volunteers, supporting them against the gale. Moving into the crowd, she got the prisoners and Alchemites to link arms.

Making a human chain, pushing them toward the gate, Will realized. Could it break through the line of Fyremen?

Not your problem, Astrid told him. Her voice seemed clearer in the magic-drenched air.

Right. Warmth, affection. He sensed Jacks Glade, smoldering amid the bergs and drifts of vitagua. "More, Jacks."

Gilead's flask blew out of his hand; he crawled after it. His followers were picking themselves off the ground. Volunteers and a few Alchemites pushed toward the columns. The line of Fyremen blocking their escape was getting ragged.

The oversized trees groaned as the wind continued to rise. Wind stripped every leaf, every twig. The branches that hadn't burned were ground to dust by debris howling in from the unreal. The edge of the ravine was crumbling.

Will felt the ground give beneath him, but he did not fall. He was borne aloft on a geyser of lukewarm vitagua, rising to the epicenter of the gale. Below him, the Chimney yawned, disgorging a profoundly contaminated Everett Lethewood. Patience followed, chasing him into the storm.

Roused were rushing in now, sprinting over a bridge to attack the Fyremen in the plaza.

Olive Glade clung to a pillar at the edge of the glowside, shouting instructions to the human chain of escaping Alchemites and volunteers as they got away: trying to save lives, even now.

Juanita, meanwhile, had turned her attention to the wounded, to anyone who couldn't run away. She struggled to turn an oak bench that had fallen across . . .

Passion, Will saw, it was Passion. Juanita extended her hand, offering to help her up. Passion slapped at her, crawling instead to the pyre where Sahara and Astrid's bodies lay smoldering.

Will felt a future—Ellie in his arms, the warmth of her . . .

. . . warmth . . .

. . . her head pressed to his chest. He remembered the first time he'd held his son, the sense that the whole universe was burning through his eyes as he looked in wonder at Carson's face, this miracle made of, by, for him and Caro . . .

Passion screamed at her fleeing sisters, trying to draw them into the brawl developing between the Roused and the Fyremen. Gilead had recovered his potion, and had lit it, like a Molotov cocktail, trying to get a bead on—

On me, Will thought—*which makes sense, doen't it? I'm the well wizard now, the last well wizard . . .*

Try putting that on a business card, son, someone said, laughing. Albert Lethewood?

Astrid was right. Gilead wasn't his problem. Will let his memories drift forward to a camping trip, years from now, Carson grown, the three of them in sleeping bags, deep within the alchemized forest. Astrid talking about dogwood.

But Astrid's gone, he thought. *Just another vitagua ghost.*

Dead, Will. Not gone.

"Astrid?"

Here. She was within the cloud bank, rising upward to the troposphere. Condensing as she rose, she was raining into lakes, streams, extending foggy toes into fields. She would spread herself around the globe, avoiding fires, avoiding the seas.

Not dead. She had survived somehow; they had thought the ringers would present her enemies with alternative targets, but they hadn't been decoys at all. Backups, he thought, with a strange laugh. She was okay. She was fine.

"Abracadabra," he murmured.

Below, Passion crawled to the pyre, to her goddess. She stretched across a fallen log, laying her hands on Sahara's bloodied face.

She licked her fingers.

Gone mad, Will thought, but Passion's face changed, and she cried out with Sahara's voice. Whirling birds threw themselves out of the storm, alchemized starlings, shrieking as they made for Gilead.

The flask in the Fyreman's hand erupted into flame, burning the birds to ash. Passion kept calling them down as her body withered, drawing every last calorie, every dram of vitality.

Then Fyremen swarmed over her, silencing her for good.

More?

It was Jacks Glade asking.

Will looked down, seeking Juanita. It seemed she had rescued everyone she could. The Roused and Fyremen were still fighting, but the volunteers and Alchemites were gone, into the glow. It seemed distant. How much time had passed?

Will held himself in check, imagined pulling the reins of a

runaway carriage, counting a hundred precious seconds. *Just a little grace period,* he thought, *that's all this has ever been about. Calm between storms. I hope we made good use of it.*

Juanita found one last unconscious woman, hauling her bodily to the exit. Bramblegate itself was falling. . . .

More? That same query.

"The more, the merrier, Jacks," Will replied. "Melt it all."

A puff of steam heralded the destruction of everything around him.

CHAPTER FORTY-FOUR

EVERETT BURKE, HYPEROBSERVANT MAILMAN, was digging in an open grave with his hands. Whose grave it was he didn't know, though surely he had already deduced that.

Wet clumps of flesh at the ends of his arms pounded at the bricks blocking his path. A bracelet of glass and burning chemicals cauterized the blood as it flowed from his right arm; the left bled freely.

The passage he'd made was big enough for a child to pass through, and small animals—birds, lizards, and bugs—were sprinting over him, busting out at long last.

Far away, he could hear a woman pleading: "You've got your crack between worlds, you sadist—finish the job yourself. Let him stop—"

"No."

Romantic rivals, the Everett Burke voice noted. *Teo has a motive to let our hero die.*

"Hush," he murmured. "The girl loves me, that's settled."

A breeze ruffled his beard.

"Wind's rising," he called. The others kept arguing. Beyond them, the Roused were dancing, beating their war drums.

Wind meant a flow of vitagua out of the unreal. It meant the turbine at Pucker Hill would be turning again. It meant letrico and food and water.

Not this wind, said a voice. *This one flattens everything.*

He was knee deep in liquid magic now. Above him, the murdered boy, Jacks, was getting brighter. Had anybody noticed?

"Nuh-ah-ah, folks . . ."

The brick wall crumbled. Ev pitched into a hole, then rose, falling *up* the Indigo Springs ravine. He threw out an arm, catching himself on Teo's awful bridge of bones. Getting his feet under him again, he half ran, half stumbled out of the chasm, into the midst of . . .

Of hell, he wanted to say, but that was too florid, even for an old-fashioned pulp hero like Burke. He was caught in a windstorm that had blown away everything between town and what was left of the old train station. The Roused who'd preceded him were brawling with Fyremen. People fled, as best they could, toward the glow, the way out.

A plume of blue mist curled upward from the ravine, growing sky high, shining like sunlight through the ocean. Around it, the ground crumbled, forming an expanding crater.

Everett's heart slammed. Was that Petey? Wind batted him down when he tried to rise.

"Ev!" Patience, running flat out, shot over the lip of the ravine. "Ev, are you all right?"

The girl loves me. "We're in trouble."

"Oh, you think?"

Animal howls, behind them. Twenty, fifty, a hundred Roused raced out of the widening Chimney, crossing the bone bridge. Predators now: bears, wolves, lions, eagles.

Teoquan was with them. He scanned the chaos with satisfaction, the expression of a man who's achieved his life's ambition. Then one of his warriors, a panther, swiped at the phosphorus-bright form of a Fyreman . . . and burned to ash with a howl and a stench of burnt meat.

Teo's smile widened. "Stay out of trouble, lovebirds." Strolling up to the glowing figure, he opened his mouth, letting out a low hum.

Ev felt a pinch in his chest.

The Fyreman blew out, collapsing as definitively as a china doll getting hit by a truck.

"Ev, we have to get out of here."

He forced himself to concentrate. "Patience, do you have any chantments?" It came out *cha-aan-ant-ments.*

"No." She shook her head. "If we can cross the plaza—"

"People need help," he said.

"Look at us, Ev Lethewood—we need help."

It was true. His bloodied fingers were stiff and clubby, with thick, splintered nails. Hooves? "I gotta-ah find . . ."

Who? Who did he need to find?

"Come on," Patience said. Clinging to each other, they could just move against the wind. They staggered to the edge of the plaza, skirting a pile of garbage—medical stuff, it turned out: crutches, bandages, scrubs. Rubble, from the hospital—

"Wait!"

A movement within the pile caught his attention. He pushed aside a gurney and found a girl, Alchemite from her dress. Her leg was broken.

"Here." Patience fished a wheelchair from the debris.

The girl struggled as they loaded her into the thing. "They burned Sahara," she said dully. She had a chantment with her, one of Astrid's first, an aluminum rake that wove fruit baskets.

Ev bent to face her. "What about Petey?"

"Astrid Lethewood," Patience corrected.

"I think . . . I think the Goddess *lied*," she said.

"She's in shock, Ev." They managed to get the chair rolling, leaning hard and bumping toward a relatively unbroken stretch of marble floor. They struggled on, bent against the wind, with its aromas of burning plastic and heated flowers.

"Over here!" Patience shouted. Ev raised his head, hopeful, but she was waving at a stranger, someone he distantly recognized . . . from TV, he remembered; she was one of Sahara's jailers. She strode across the plaza, a chunk of letrico in her fist, ignoring the smoke and flying debris. She was helping people reach the glow, he realized, getting them through the wind to the columns.

The marshal threw an arm around them, and the wheelchair rolled faster.

"Ev!" Olive was up ahead, at the Gate.

"He's hurt!" Patience shouted.

Olive tapped Ev with a tongue depressor, hitting his shoulders as though he were being knighted. Ev's hands stopped bleeding and his mind cleared, at least temporarily. He was still hairy as a goat, but for now he knew who he was.

"I can't do more—Juanita needs what's left of the letrico to get people out of here."

"Does that mean we're not winning?" Ev asked.

"Wind gets much worse, even they may have to stop fighting." Olive pointed at the combatants. "That's about the best-case scenario."

"Oh, the well's blown; the wind'll get worse," Patience said.

"You need to get out of here," Ev said.

"Me?" Olive smiled grimly. "I'm on the Big Picture."

"Tell *them* that."

"I doubt the Fyremen will last much longer," Patience said. "The Roused will outnumber them soon, and Teo—" An ear-shattering sigh heralded another Fyreman death, finishing her statement for her.

"What about Astrid?" Ev asked. "Is she okay?"

"Ev, look around. Nobody's okay."

Dodging the question. His heart punched at his chest. He rubbed his clubbed hand over the horns on his forehead. "Where's my daughter, Olive?"

Olive's eyes flooded. Her gaze flicked past him, to a pit of burnt branches and blue embers. "Gone, Ev."

"No." He shook off their hands, holding himself upright against the wind.

Gone.

"It was—"

He cut Olive off before she could torture him with details. "Teo said he could make you a goddess, Patience. He offered you power over life and death—"

"Oh, you're gonna pimp me off?" Teoquan was just then shattering another Fyreman, a kid with a buzz cut. "To that?"

He slumped. "I'm sorry."

"Listen to me. If that power ever existed, it's Teo who'd wield it—and he's not your daughter's biggest fan."

"I know it's hard, Ev—," Olive began.

He ran from their kindess and sympathy, fleeing to the edge of the fire.

There were two bodies.

One was pinned upright, in a standing position. It slumped forward, arms extended so its crisped hands hung downward, its elongated fingers seeming to reach for the slumped form at its feet. Burnt skeletal wings grew from its back: little Sahara Knax, Leona's granddaughter.

The other body was facedown, but its tangled orange curls were unmistakable.

"Oh, baby girl." Ev edged closer, into the heat, and pulled, yanking awkwardly until he had what was left of her cradled in his arms. "Albert, you bastard, this wasn't supposed to happen."

"Mr. Lethewood!" Juanita had come after him.

"Magic took everything I had," Ev said. The marshal's arm braced him against the wind. He got moving, carrying the weight of his child away from their hometown.

Just another murder victim, the Everett Burke voice said. *Some girl,* not Petey.

His hands, on the girl's burned skin, told Ev things he'd rather not know. The dead girl—she looked like her grandpa at that age—had her throat cut by someone she'd once cared for. Cremation was postmortem.

It had been fast, no suffering, not like Albert . . .

Albert who? Everett Burke said, and the pain eased.

Supported by Juanita, Everett bore the murdered girl to the glowing pillars. Nobody special, just another crime victim. She must have been someone to his love interest, the beauty waiting in the wind. She was sobbing through her hand.

"The pillars are crumbling," Olive said. "We gotta go."

"Yes, let's get out of here," he said.

"Where, Ev?" Patience asked.

"You decide," he said, used up now, and she put a hand on his shoulder and led him past Juanita, through the gate.

CHAPTER FORTY-FIVE

DYING, ASTRID REALIZED, WAS weirdly freeing.

She raised the magical fog bank to the heights of the world, beyond Fyreman reach, and climbed until the sky turned from blue to black. Her mouse brains registered the sight with wonder and terror.

She extended a tendril, far from Indigo Springs, touching down at the edge of Tacoma, Washington, and swirling eastward. She had to avoid the oceans, to stay away from the destructive salt water. She seeped into trees, lawns, buildings. People inhaled her in cool wafts.

The volume of escaping mist grew huge, harder to manage. She poured herself over sick cats and dogs, over half-dead rats. Each new ringer increased her control.

Forming bodies from iced vitagua, she went out into the streets to calm people, to help find those trapped in crashed cars, in earthquake-tumbled buildings. She joined rescues and ran messages.

Mostly, though, she simply expanded, pushing the magical fog bank east and south, gliding across the United States and Canada. Up north, down south . . . people infected by the vitagua were showing signs of Befoulment, but Astrid couldn't worry about that anymore. Either the curse could be broken, or it couldn't. At least Will was freeing the Roused. Rousing the Roused?

Soon she had eyes extended into night and daytime at once. She expanded to the edges of the North American coast, to the northern frill of the Alaskan border, up to James and Hudson Bay, down the edge of California and into Mexico. Forests and jungles drank her eagerly.

As she approached the southern cities, she found them shuttered up, the people hidden indoors.

That was fine; she wouldn't force contamination on them.

Magic continued to pour out of the unreal. Astrid arced high, riding the jet stream, and swept across China, infecting livestock and wildlife alike on the steppes. She seeped into moss, dripped into meadows and crops. She drenched the Gobi, moving west into Europe, south into Africa. She sent ringers into towns and cities, saw TV broadcasts tracking her advance in a hundred different languages. Blue light and storms heralded her approach. Volcanoes erupted. The ground shook. People brawled in grocery stores and rushed home to put on oxygen masks.

She made mistakes, of course. The earthquakes caused tidal waves, and more than one ringer got swamped in seawater. People shot at her. She ran into open flames: fires and lit cigarettes. She was flammable, so she had to smother the flare-ups with ice storms, burying the flames in frozen clumps of vitagua, smothering out the air—and occasionally freezing people too.

She stretched out, into lakes, jungles, and grasslands, contaminating animals, leaving tons of iced magic atop mountains to mingle with the snowpack.

And finally, finally, she was as stretched as she was ever going to get. She was out, all of her in the real; she'd kept her promise, and the Roused were free. She felt an elastic ping, imagined a bungee cord snapping. The unreal was empty, and she was shrinking at last, her volume diminishing as she seeped into the biomass of the living earth.

Will Forest was calling her name.

She groped after his voice, finding him in a crater of blasted, blue-stained earth. A few yards from its lip lay a wounded squirrel; she built a ringer around the creature and stumbled down the side of the hole, throwing her vitagua arms around him.

"How long have we been at this?" The night sky above them was black and full of stars.

"Less than a week, I think." He pulled free, running a finger over his chin—to gauge the length of his beard, she realized. "How much damage did I do?"

"Did *we* do?" She quashed an urge to lie. "There were quakes, floods, storms. People died . . ."

His face went slack.

She spoke fast. "Practically everywhere I went there was someone with a chantment, Lifeguarding. We saved a lot."

"The more, the merrier," he said, voice thready.

"We can check the Big Picture." She didn't want to see the faces of the dead, but if Will needed . . .

"I think it's been pulverized along with everything else."

Suddenly it sank in. This hole they were in was the magical well. The ravine was gone. The *town* was gone.

"You said it would be okay," Will said, stunned.

"It is," she said. "Will, it's over."

A shaky laugh. "And what do we do now?"

"Let's start by seeing what's left of the unreal."

He nodded, taking her hand with a slight flinch. She felt him—not her—make the shift, and suddenly they were there, in the remains of something that might have been the land of the fairies, centuries ago.

The white grit was gone. In its place was the piled-up wreckage of Pucker Hill: turbines and stone and the remains of the earth lodge, all Ev's work tumbled and sunk in bluish mud flats that smelled of gingerbread. The wind had been too much for it.

It was all but dark. Of course, Astrid thought, without that glow from the glaciers, it would be.

"Nobody left?" Will said.

"Some of the Roused come back," Astrid said. "And . . ."

He tilted his head, listening. "We end up living here, don't we?"

"You want to settle down, remember? And there's plenty to do yet: chanters to initiate, a whole world to rebuild."

"You're suggesting we get back to work this second?"

"You're the well wizard now. You get some say."

"I'm the well wizard? What are you?"

"The dregs of the well?" She wanted to kiss him, but they both knew she was a mouse inside all that vitagua.

He broke the awkward moment by taking her hand. "We'll figure something out."

"Yeah," she said. "Happy After, right?"

"Right," he said, and then: "I love you."

She met his eyes, showing him certainty. "I love you too."

They walked uphill, out of the muck and onto drier land.

"I've seen this," Astrid said. "We live here. With your . . . Will, where are your children?"

"Still in dreams." He pulled out the padlock. "Igme got the key, but Bramblegate's pulverized. I can't get to him."

"I hid our gatemaking chantment in Prague. Katarina has an oncologist friend there. Any idea where Igme went?"

"Back home? He's from San Fernando, right?"

"I'll look." She took a ringer to the Philippines, seeking out Igme's neighborhood and knocking on his mother's door with as much strength as her small muscles could manage. A cry, a scramble, and he opened the door, enveloping her in a gleeful hug. Aquino was there—they were watching the news and spinning a pebble of letrico from the ambient heat.

"Any idea how many of us made it?" Aquino asked.

She shook her head. "Pike will get communications up soon." *If Pike survived.* Nobody said it aloud.

By now she had also found Katarina. She and her doctor friend were arguing with a big grizzly bear—one of the Roused.

"Astrid." Katarina was clearly relieved to see her. "He says gates belong to these 'the People.'"

"Okay," Astrid said, and then, to the bear: "We need to be able to get around. We'll negotiate fares at some point, but can we get free rides for . . . oh, a while?"

"One moon." He dipped his shaggy head.

"Astrid . . ."

"We can't be in charge of everything, Katarina."

Katarina fished her old passport out of a drawer, radiating disapproval as she handed it over. The bear examined it, then vanished into the nearest wall. A minute later, gates—of stone this time, rather than thorns—began forming.

Across the world, one gate took shape within Igme's house.

"Where's Will, Astrid?" he asked.

"Pucker Hill," she said. Igme stepped through without hesitating, emerging a moment later beside her and Will.

"Your children." He held out the key.

"Thank you." Hands trembling, Will took the key from Igme, sliding it into the padlock. There was a scrape; then the lock popped, showering rust flakes into the mud.

Nothing happened.

"You'll need to go to sleep. Talk to Carson and Ellie, lead them out of dreams." Astrid looked around the mud flats dubiously. "It's pretty mucky here."

"I've been up for a week, it's not going to be hard to pass out." He hitched himself onto a relatively dry outcropping of stone, shifting uncomfortably, then closing his eyes.

Rather than watch him doze off, Astrid walked away. Her foot hit something solid sunk in the slime—a stone footlocker full of chantments. The infrastructure stuff for Pucker Hill, she guessed, straining her squirrel muscles to lift its lid. Yes, there was the turbine builder, the cottage maker, food spinners.

"Igme, look!" Then she saw dawn, glimmering on the horizon.

Jacks.

CHAPTER FORTY-SIX

EVERETT BURKE AND PATIENCE bore the murdered woman's burnt body to the Atlantic Ocean, to Assateague Island.

They weren't alone, of course—about fifty volunteers and several dozen Roused followed them, some carrying wounded Fyremen and Alchemites.

Mutated gulls swam on the surface of the sea, big and hungry looking. On the beach, the kelp beds had grown mattress thick, buzzing with massive sand fleas. Animal carcasses littered the beach, emitting the lilac-scent of the contaminated dead.

The girl's body smelled of it too.

Everett laid the scorched corpse on a flipped-over rowboat. Rain washed soot off her face, and he couldn't pretend anymore that it wasn't Astrid.

This was it: magic had taken everything he had.

He stared at her body, counting his dead. If he had known what Albert was up to, all those years ago. Messing with magic, training their kid . . . how could he not have known?

He'd have sat there forever if Patience hadn't screamed.

Teoquan had come out of the mist with a pair of knife-wielding fox-men. Patience was protecting an unconscious Fyreman, standing between them with her arms out.

Her eyes met his, pleading for help.

"What do you expect me to do? Teo doesn't listen to me."

"Ev Lethewood, get over here right now."

"You're the one kept saying Teo had a point," he said. "That the real world owed the People a debt too big to pay. What's another slaughter now?"

"Ev—"

"They killed my child." He covered Astrid's face, then crossed the space between them. "Give me one of those machetes."

"Please," Teoquan said contemptuously, but Ev walked up to one of the fox-furred changelings, a youngster who didn't look too happy to be standing, knife raised, over a helpless man. He wrestled the weapon out of its paw.

"What are you trying to prove?" Teoquan said, sneering.

"What are you? You're out; you said you wanted out. You want to chop up a helpless Burning Man, shouldn't I help?"

"Cry me a river, Ev, you and your crispy-fried baby, you think that's a fraction of the blood spilled, the pain caused, the debt—"

"Now who's whining?" Patience demanded. "Teoquan, you gonna just wipe out the Fyremen? As for you, Ev—"

"They've killed Albert and murdered my child."

"Sort of murdered, anyway," Teo said.

"Sort of?" Ev pointed at her corpse.

"What, suddenly you're stupid? That magical fog bank is moving. Who could do that but Astrid Lethewood?"

"Will Forest?"

"You honestly think the cop's that good?"

Ev's voice was thick. "You will not get my hopes up!"

"Have faith, old man," Teo said. "Call her."

Call her. As simple as that? He opened his mouth . . . and found himself afraid to try.

Patience whirled on Teoquan. "You want to play at being a leader of men, how about getting your people out of the bloody rain?"

Teo scowled. "Plenty of time for that."

"How would you know? Have you even looked? Eliza would have had them sheltered by now. You killed her, so that makes it your job. People! Let's spin up a little letrico. . . . Anyone have a chantment we can use to make food?" She stomped off, leaving Ev and Teo to murder the Fyreman, or not, as they chose.

Ev sighed. He dropped the machete into the sea.

Teo slumped. "It pisses me off that it's you she's in love with."

"Far as I can tell, everything pisses you off," Ev said.

He snorted. "I'd blame the curse, but—"

"But you're a fundamentally testy old bastard."

"Takes one to know one," Teo said. "Gonna talk to your kid, or what?"

Ev walked to the edge of a vitagua puddle, finding a mutated otter gasping for breath. "Petey? Astrid?"

Vitagua bled out of the air, obscuring its body . . . then forming the figure of his daughter. "Pop—you're okay?"

"Dammit, kid," he said, and the strength went out of his legs. He sat on the beach in the rising storm.

Astrid put her cold arms around him. "I'm sorry, Pop, I'm sorry, I'm sorry."

Rain lashed over them until one of the Roused came and said they had set up camp, and would they like to come in out of the wind?

CHAPTER FORTY-SEVEN

THE SLOW FOULING OF the earth had come to an end, all right, Juanita thought, remembering the prophecy Gilead had shown her. Too bad for the Brigade they'd never wondered if that might mean the contamination would speed up.

As for the Fyremen making peace with their enemies . . . well, it didn't look like there'd be any of them left to try.

Most were already dead, overwhelmed despite their potions by the sheer number of contaminated people darting across the widening chasm. A few were merely wounded, and Juanita got to dragging those across the remains of the plaza. Astrid's people—Lifeguards, they called themselves—were searching them for potions and then evacuating them to safety.

They weren't finding many potions. The Brigade had—pardon the pun—burned through most of its supply.

"Is that everyone?" Olive Glade shouted over the storm.

Together, the two women scanned the ruins of the plaza. The only remaining combatants were Gilead Landon and the gigantic native guy—Teoquan, someone had called him—who'd been slaughtering Fyremen with his voice. They were brawling, Gilead covered in flames, Teoquan dodging and murmuring.

"Any ideas on how to slow that guy down?" she asked Olive.

"You really want him to notice you?"

It was a good point. "I want to try to rescue Gilead."

"I'm kinda rooting for the other guy. See that?" Olive pointed at Gilead: "How his lips are moving?"

"He's praying," Juanita said. "So?"

"It's a curse. It makes the contaminated crazy, turns them into creatures. . . ."

She could feel the smile breaking over her face. "He shuts up, I stop turning into a cat-woman?"

Olive nodded. "If he's the last one, yeah."

"I'll take care of it."

"I think Teoquan's got it in hand."

"Really? Teoquan hasn't hurt him yet." Whatever potion Gilead had drunk, it must have been decades in the making. He was Superman; he was taking the other guy's attacks in stride.

"What can you do that Teo can't?"

"Lie to him," Juanita said. "Get him to drop his guard."

From her expression, Olive had doubts.

"If it saves his life in the process . . ."

A flicker of connection; she'd already figured out that saving lives mattered to this woman. "He's seen you helping us."

"Gilead knows I'm a bleeding heart," Juanita said. "I made him promise he'd stop burning people."

"He went back on that," Olive said bitterly. "Astrid, Sahara—"

"Oh, I haven't forgotten."

"Do you still have letrico?"

Juanita showed her the diminishing chunk of silvery white power clenched in her hand, just as Teo belted Gilead. He staggered back; then flames whooshed around him and he straightened, apparently unharmed.

Olive frowned. "This isn't some crazy attempt at self-sacrifice, is it?"

"Not my thing. Really, go. I've got this covered." With that, Juanita set off across the plaza. *Please, let this work,* she prayed, fighting fear, fighting a cough.

She had to shout to make herself heard above the wind. "Can I call a time-out here?"

Gilead goggled at her from within his wreath of flames. He was still mumbling in Latin.

"Time out? This isn't soccer, woman," the other man rumbled. Just the sound of his voice slurped power from her shrinking clutch of letrico. Juanita's mind crowded with horrors: blades, cutting flesh, mutilations, people thrown from helicopters, kids caught in explosions.

She made herself speak. "You guys have been pounding each other for a while. Nobody's won yet."

"His potion will wear off," Teoquan said. "All I gotta do is wait. Then he and his singsong are gone. Huff. Puff. Snuff. Like a candle."

"I know the Befoulment too," Juanita said. "I pass through that gate, I can have ten people reciting it by morning."

His eyes narrowed. "You're bluffing."

"Why would I?" She threw up her hands. "This fight's pretty much over, and I think whatever that is—" She pointed into the gale, at the sky-high blue geyser blasting grit from a widening chasm. "—we need to get out of its way."

"That," Teoquan sneered. "Your boy came here to burn that."

"Then nobody's getting what they want today, are they?" Juanita turned her back on Teoquan before her nerve went completely. She'd be having nightmares about him for the rest of her life. "Call it a day, Gilead."

He shook his head.

"It's over," she said. "That victory your big book predicted? It ain't happening today."

Gilead drew back, staring over her shoulder at Teoquan. Then he slumped. Juanita reached out. The flames on his palm guttered as they clasped hands.

With one last creepy half roar, Teoquan strode off the plaza, vanishing through the crumbling gateway.

"Time to bail," Juanita said. Gilead drew back from the gate, making a distressed face, still reciting.

"I know, it's the bad magic. You want to live or die?"

He nodded, surrendering to necessity.

Where to go? She led him to the pillars, thinking hard. Somewhere unfamiliar. Somewhere unpopulated . . .

Help, she prayed, and an idea came.

"Pripet," she whispered, walking into the glow.

They stepped out into darkness. The air was astoundingly

clean and still: no smoke, no burnt flowers, no windstorm. Her ears rang in the sudden quiet.

Gilead's face, edged by flame, looked at her meaningfully. His voice was hoarse. She could just make out the Latin.

"Want me to take over?"

He nodded, and she began to say it with him, haltingly at first. Once she had it, the vocal cadences drove themselves. It was catchy, damned catchy. When she had it, a thrum ran through her, a sense of electricity, her organs clenching.

Atlas, holding the world, she thought. Whatever this thing was, she was now the one carrying it.

With a sigh, Gilead bent over, hands on his knees, panting.

"This is a town?" He gestured toward the buildings ahead. Juanita nodded, keeping up the recitation.

"You did well, Juanita. You've earned a place among us."

She gave him a glare, to show she was unimpressed.

They started toward the city. Everything was dark. . . . Would he wonder why?

"Power must be out all over the world," he said, as if he'd heard her thought. The last flames on his skin were sputtering; better still, he looked exhausted. "Lethewood's infected everything. Befouled running loose . . . We'll have to rebuild the Brigade. Purification will take lifetimes. Open war—"

She smacked his arm—not hard, just to get his attention.

"Yes, I promised," he said. "But what can I do, leave it all to the witches? Juanita, I'll make it up to you. We'll be humane, drug them, something . . ." He rubbed his face. "It's not what I wanted either."

She heard hopelessness in his voice, remembered the feeling. The sense of purpose slipping away . . . like staring into a bottomless black well. She gave him a guarded but sympathetic shrug. Let him think he could win her over.

As they walked up a block lined by apartments and old black cars, Gilead's flames went out entirely, leaving them in darkness. "They must've evacuated. Place looks like it's been dead for a hundred years."

Was he catching on already? The road was crowded by over-grown trees; it was a bit like an alchemized forest, except that everything was stunted. Juanita's heart leapt as he patted his pockets . . . but what he came up with was not another potion, but a cigarette.

Sitting heavily on a cement stairway, he lit up. "We'll break into a house, find some paper and a pen so we can communicate. Someone always refuses to evacuate; we'll make 'em join the recitation."

She nodded, making a *stay put* gesture, and kicked in an apart-ment door, scavenging up a blanket and a pillow and bringing them outside. She held them out, mimed sleeping.

Gratefully, he stubbed out the smoke. "Sure this is okay?"

Don't overplay it. She waggled a hand, midair. *So-so.*

"I only need an hour, maybe two. Then I'll take over."

She kept up the recitation, pretending, for the last time. It was beguiling, this singsong. It might be hard to stop.

Gilead's eyelids were drooping.

Help me, she thought, and the strength came, a feeling that aid had been there all along, for the asking. Certainty, too. She was doing right. She'd been born to do this.

"Wish I knew where we've ended up. . . ." He pulled the blan-ket up and let his eyes slip shut.

Juanita took a deep breath, fought the song for a second, and then answered. "We're in Chernobyl, you murderous lunatic."

Gilead's eyes snapped open. He struggled to pick up the dropped song.

Juanita punched him in the mouth, as hard as she could.

The Latin slipped away, melting like a dream.

In the ruins of Pripet, all the surviving glass shattered.

CHAPTER FORTY-EIGHT

WILL SLIPPED INTO DREAMS and found his children among a queue of soldiers gathered at the stony archway.

He'd never let himself imagine this moment; it hurt too much to envision being a family again after so many months of separation and fear.

"Daddy!" Ellie ran to him, delight on her face. Carson, a step behind, sagged in exhausted relief.

Will wrapped his arms around them both. His chest burned as he fought to breathe; it felt as though some muscle he'd had clenched for months was being forcibly massaged out of stiffness.

He clung until Ellie started squirming. "Sorry, baby."

Carson jerked free. "Where's Mom? She hasn't been to see us in weeks."

"Son—"

"She's dead, isn't she?"

"Primas don't die," Ellie said. "Mommy is the Wind."

Will sighed. Together again, yes, but . . . "Mom's gone, son."

"Why didn't you tell me?"

Would Carson forgive him? How much Alchemite claptrap had Ellie swallowed? Astrid promised it'd be okay, Will thought, clinging to the idea. It was easier now.

"I'd hoped to save her, Carson. I should have told you."

"What happened, Daddy?"

"A very bad guy was going to hurt Sahara Knax, Ellie. Your mom—" It was hard to get the words out. "She tried to save her friend, and the bad guy killed her."

Carson wiped furiously at his face. "Did it work?"

How to answer that? "Yes. She saved Sahara that day."

"Passion says if you never arrested Sahara, none of this would've happened."

If. If Sahara hadn't had Lucius Landon tortured. If Albert Lethewood had survived . . . "Maybe she's right."

The line of MIA soldiers and the other prisoners of dreamland was moving fast, almost running, sweeping the three of them to the stone gate. A man in front of them trotted through, murmuring "Home," as he vanished into the chilly light.

"Home," Carson echoed before Will could choose.

They ended up on the muddy remains of Pucker Hill.

Ellie did a slow turn, looking in puzzlement at the muck, the wreckage. Her face was grave. "This isn't our house, Daddy."

"It's going to be," Will said.

"We're supposed to live here?" Carson asked.

"It's . . ." Will paused, hoping for a grumble, and finished weakly, "It's not going to look like this for long."

"What about school?"

"I don't know anything yet," Will said. School. Grief counseling. Family therapy. Could he make that happen?

Why not? People would return to the unreal. Astrid had recruited all kinds of help. . . . Why couldn't he?

"Sahara is going to make us into chanters," Ellie said.

"Is that what she told you?"

"She said we would be shapers of clay. She's the well of all magic, and me and Carson get to draw her power."

"Dream on, bratface," Carson grunted.

"You could be chanters yet—if you want," Will said. He was pleased to see curiosity on his son's face.

"What's this?" Ellie had found a reddish metal box sunk in the muck. They opened it, finding a cache of chantments and a few hunks of letrico inside. It was the kit Astrid had sent to Pucker Hill for constructing the power plant.

Will put out a hand, finding a slight breeze. Using a plastic gravy boat, he built a small turbine on the hill.

"Big deal," his son said. "You can use chantments."

"Ever try spinning power, son?" He began to demonstrate,

not waiting for a reply. After a moment, Carson stepped up to the mill, mimicking. Silvery threads of power wafted downward, webbing their hands. Will wound it into his palm, squeezing it into a crystallized lump.

He picked up a muddy, hand-woven welcome mat next, and fed letrico into it. Short, emerald green grass spread down the hillside, and an apple tree sprouted beside the empty banks of the brook. Next he took out an origami rooster, pointing it at the space beside the tree. A sod cottage grew out of the muck. It had a thatched roof and vacant, glassless windows.

"You expect me to live in that?" Carson said, but there was a thread of humor in his words now.

"We're magicians, we'll upgrade," Will said.

"Maybe I don't want to live in a dirt shack. Maybe I want my old bed and my books. Maybe Ellie wants her toys. . . ."

"I outgrowed my toys," his sister informed him.

Will hid a smile. "If I get your things, will you put up with the dirt shack for a while?"

"What about school?" Carson asked suspiciously.

"One thing at a time." Will reached into his pocket, closing a hand over the silk elephant he'd been carrying all this time. "Keep spinning, son."

CHAPTER FORTY-NINE

CHASING THE HORIZON SEEMED a fool's errand by the time Astrid had crested two hillsides' worth of the vitagua-slick mud, but for the first time in months, she had nothing better to do. Across the real, she had ringers engaged in rescues, pitching in where they could, reconnecting with her scattered volunteers.

Here, in the unreal, she felt comfortable and centered. There were only a few voices left among the grumbles, the murmur of the well's various chanters, Dad included. The clearest of the voices was her own. After a year with a chorus in her head, she was alone, mostly, with her thoughts.

She left Will to his kids, left Ev to his camp on Assateague Island, and explored the altered landscape.

Her first discovery was the statue of her father.

Dad and the other chanters had been columns of solid vitagua, but now he seemed to be made of white stone. He stood among a flock of intricately carved sparrows, tall and heroic. Astrid touched the statue, sensing him within. He'd been worried, both Before and during the Spill. That concern was gone now; affection and pride were what remained.

Nearby, a familiar form was melting liquid rills of stone from another block, carving out an image of Lee Glade.

"Jacks?"

He turned, coals banking in his eyes. The belly wound was there, smoking and glowing bright orange. A creature, no less a ghost than she, and Astrid's resolve weakened.

Then he smiled, and it was Jacks's old smile.

Astrid took a step, thinking to throw herself at him, but Jacks put out a warning hand. Extending one fingertip, he touched her. The contact sizzled painfully.

"Crap," she said, jerking back.

Jacks laughed. "So you died too?"

Joy swelled within her. "We all died."

"I was afraid it might play out that way."

Together, they stared at the mud flats. "Olive's on the East Coast with Pop. I'll bring her. She wants—she misses you."

He nodded, giving her that penetrating glance she remembered so well.

"I missed you too."

He beamed, leaning on his marble pillar. "What about Sahara?"

"We all died," Astrid repeated.

"Died like ordinary people, or half died, like you and me?"

"I didn't have a chance to save her; Will would've said . . ." She frowned. "You heard about Will?"

"You told me." He brightened a fingertip to molten heat, melting a rill of rock out of the sculpture. "You and he 'sort of have a romance going.'"

"It's complicated."

"Because you're dead?"

"More . . . I think his ex-wife got his kids to hate me."

"You, a stepmother."

"Don't laugh. I'm sure not having any kids of my own now."

"You always wanted children." His expression was clear: nothing hidden, no resentment. "It's okay, Astrid. With you and me in this state, we can't pick up where we left off."

And there's Katarina, she thought, remembering something she'd said . . . or would say. Her mouse heart triphammered. "I'm sorry, Jacks, about everything."

But he didn't seem angry, just happy to see her, and maybe a little resigned.

Jacks and Katarina . . . her and Will. But not forever, she thought. Jacks was fire now, she was fluid; the others were flesh and bone, and time would affect them all differently. "I mentioned it was complicated, right?"

Jacks mimed tweaking her nose, coming short of actual contact.

"We just blew the world to crap. Do you need to sort out our personal life right this second?"

"Still the voice of reason, are you?"

"Yep." He reached for a pile of stone chips, melting them to putty, adding them to his statue. "Relax, it'll be okay."

"You know that for a fact?"

"It's already okay, remember?" he said.

And it was. Across the world, at a hundred different rescue sites, Astrid's ringers stopped working, turning their faces up to the sky.

She had made it, despite everything, to After—and now that she had arrived, she even knew what it was. All After meant, she saw, was the point where things were going to get better instead of worse.

CHAPTER FIFTY

THE NEXT DAY, EV Lethewood buried his daughter's mortal remains, laying them in a rowboat and sending it out to sea.

Thousands came to see her off: Roused, a couple lapsed Alchemites, volunteers from the Springs, even strangers. The mood
was solemn but not funereal, and nobody made any speeches.
What did you say, after all, when the guest of honor might ooze
out of thin air at any moment to join the ceremony?

They gathered silently, and people threw flowers into the boat
until it was full. Ev used a chantment Will had given him to send
the boat on its way. Everyone in the crowd gave up a little of their
vitality, as a thank-you.

After it had vanished from view, they dug clams, made a bonfire, and danced until the tide went out. It was late when Ev
walked Patience to her tent.

He didn't stay. His transformation was too far gone, and he
was more goat than man. Olive kept healing him, pushing the
insanity back, but Everett Burke was lurking.

"Take care, old man," Patience said, kissing his forehead between the horns.

Tipping a hat he wasn't wearing, Ev strolled away.

He prowled the camp, listening to the snores and barks of the
contaminated, the rush of the sea. Sand slid underfoot. Without
a mailbag on his hip, his gait felt unbalanced.

He heard something—scuttling.

Ev followed the sound, rapid tip-tapping footsteps with—so
said his detective's instincts—a furtive tone to them. They came
from the camp's improvised compost pit, and as he neared it, he
heard clicks and gabbles.

Starlings.

A shaft of moonlight broke through the clouds, revealing hunter and quarry to each other. It was a woman. Short, stocky, and pale, she was clad in feathers and surrounded by flint-eyed birds. She had Sahara's hair and talons, and he'd caught her filching half-eaten corn cobs from the pile.

One of the Alchemites' blood sacrifices, Ev deduced: a contaminated believer who thinks she's Sahara Knax.

His gut clenched as he thought of the children of Indigo Springs—Mark, Jacks, Sahara, and Astrid herself. All gone.

"Do you still like pickles?" he asked her, on impulse. "I could scare some up."

It wasn't much of a peace offering, was it? Apparently not enough—the woman scuttled into the night, chirping.

Ev was about to follow, when something shifted under his skin. Heat washed through him, an unpleasant reminder of menopause. For a second, he thought he might vomit. Then the fuzziness that had blanketed him since Albert's death—the mulishness, the lost sense of himself, even Burke's sense of drama—dropped away.

Ev was himself, truly himself, for the first time in his life.

The rosarite band around his forearm quivered, then broke, falling in shivers to the sand. A second later, the goat horns fell too, leaving his forehead exposed and raw.

Across the camp, the Roused were crying out as their bodies shifted and became human.

Patience was out of her tent, calling for him. "It's the curse! Astrid must have broken it."

"Wasn't me," came a voice: Astrid's otter-ringer put up her head. "Olive put that marshal, Juanita, on it."

"A woman will break the curse," Ev said. "All this time, I thought it was you or Patience."

"I can't be responsible for every little thing, can I?"

"'Bout time you learned that." Ev clapped the ringer on the shoulder, nearly knocking it over. "What now?"

"Anything you want," Astrid said. "Will and I are rebuilding Pucker—"

A triumphant, inhuman shriek interrupted her.

Unlike the others, who were molting their feathers and shedding their fur, rubbing off their reptile scales to reveal human flesh beneath, Teoquan was growing. He stood flat-footed on the ocean, becoming bigger and bigger, a giant. His red skin became crimson. Colors shifted beneath it, and Ev was briefly reminded of an octopus.

Then with a howl, he was gone, rising to the clouds, staining water and sky alike with bloody color.

"What in the name of Sam was that?" Ev demanded.

"T'axet," Patience said. "Haida God of violent death."

"You knew?"

"I charmed it out of him one day."

"A god? How?"

"The curse turned the infected into lower forms of life. Humans became animals, animals devolved. Gods . . ."

"Became human?"

"Human-ish, anyway."

"Violent death? What's he going to do now that he's freed?"

"Relax, Ev," Patience said. "T'axet's a duality. Everyone's loose now, all the gods. His better half should turn up soon. Or he'll deify some nice girl and settle down."

"I'm not following you," Astrid said.

"There's a goddess of peaceful death. She'll balance him out."

"How many Native gods did the Small Bang release?" Ev asked.

"World's changed, Ev: we all have to adjust," Patience said. "But remember what you said to your kid? Teo's not your problem. Really, he never was."

CHAPTER FIFTY-ONE

THE FOLLOWING MORNING AT about sunrise, a squad of Ukrainian soldiers did a sweep through Pripet. Their captain was a stolid, sensible-seeming fellow, and he recognized Juanita from the broadcasts of Sahara's trial. When he offered to take Gilead off her hands, she agreed readily—what else was she going to do with him? If the various magicians or the American government decided they wanted him, they could extradite. In the meantime, Ukrainian jail was as good a place as she could think of for a murderer.

She packed away Gilead's book of Fyreman prophecies and his last two potions and hitched a ride south to Kiev, keeping her eyes peeled for blackberry archways that never materialized. A refugee camp came together outside the city: she bartered her first aid skills for a bed, shower, and a meal.

There were English and Spanish speakers among the displaced, and she was able to glean bits of news. The magical cloud had spread worldwide. Plants and animals were changing, but less dramatically—everything seemed less violent, less dangerous. People weren't turning into beasts anymore.

There had been earthquakes and tornadoes and fires, rains of spiders, stampedes by giant monsters and chemical spills, but many of these stories had the same happy ending. The danger had manifested . . . and then someone had stepped forward, armed with magic, prepared to blunt its effects. Dozens of Astrid's volunteers and more than a few Alchemites had died in the rescues. Others survived, along with the people they'd sheltered.

A dozen versions of what had happened that last day in Indigo Springs were spreading.

Lethewood saved us, Juanita thought. *I wish she'd lived long enough to know.*

That night, in dreams, she found her brother. He had abandoned the perpetual beach party and was queued in a long line of servicemen, journalists, and lapsed Alchemites who were moving through the endless, improbable lobby of a mostly Victorian dream-house. He lit up when he saw her.

"Nita!" He opened his arms.

She bounded into the embrace, fighting, as always, to be the one who lifted him. They tussled and then, dreams being dreams, ended up afloat above the pink flowered carpet.

"Gracias a Diosque estás salvada!"

"You been worried about me?" She laughed.

"Folks here talk," he replied. "Terrible things happening, disasters, our families . . . there's a thousand horror stories."

"It hasn't been as bad as it probably sounds," she said.

"It sounds horrific, Nita. I haven't seen anyone. . . ."

"What? Mamá, Lucinda, nobody?"

"Nobody."

The jolt of fear was enough to bounce her out of sleep. She rolled over, groping for her threadbare blanket, and caught a gabble of excited voices outside her tent.

"What's going on?" She went outside.

"Kiev airport is reopening," one of the other refugees told her. "We're packing up."

She said a quick good-bye to the head of the infirmary and joined the clot of foreigners trudging out to the terminal to see if it was true, if they could fly home.

She had gone only a few miles when someone walked up beside her: Astrid Lethewood.

Juanita stopped short—so fast, she almost fell.

"I startle you?" Astrid said.

"Depends. Am I still asleep?"

"Nope."

"I saw you die."

"I died," Astrid agreed. "Think of me as a kind of robust ghost."

"Robust?"

"Tough? Juicy? Potent?"

"You want to cut right to virile?"

"I'm not flirting this time, honest."

"Good, because I definitely don't date *dead* magicians."

"I still sort of have something going with Will Forest."

"Still only sort of?"

That got a rueful grin from Astrid. "We're a sorry pair, you and I."

"Sorry you died, anyway," Juanita said, deflecting. "So . . . you know what happened to Sahara?"

"You did the right thing. She would have killed everyone on the platform."

"I wasn't expecting hell to break loose afterwards."

"Boy, do I know what that's like," Astrid said. "Poor Sahara."

Juanita said, "You're very forgiving, aren't you?"

"I can afford to be. I won, remember?"

"Did you? You're dead."

"Dead-ish, yeah, but lots of other people made it."

"Silver linings, huh?"

"My dad was always big on looking for the upside. Besides, you forgave Sahara too, in your way."

She hadn't considered it. "I suppose I may have."

Refugees were sliding glances their way—everyone must know who Astrid was. "Any chance you'll get that gate thing of yours up and running soon?"

"The Roused took it over," Astrid said. "They've negotiated deals with a bunch of governments, including the one here. There's a gate at the airport. You can take it where you like."

"They want money?"

"They will, once the crisis is over. But you should ask them for a lifetime pass."

"Why, because you find me cute?"

"You are cute, but also because you broke the curse."

"Befoulment," Juanita corrected.

"That makes you a hero. So, where are you going first?"

"Home, where else?"

"Where else?" Astrid nodded. "I'm serious, you know. The Roused owe you—and they aren't the only ones."

"My brother's still caught in dreams."

"That gate's opening now."

"How's that work? Dreams are just another place?"

There was a pause, the look she'd come to associate with Astrid looking up information elsewhere. "The science guys are debating that one."

"Maybe it's a spiritual question."

Astrid frowned, not getting it.

"Not a scientific matter," Juanita prompted.

"Oh." Astrid shrugged. "Yeah, maybe."

"If you don't mind my saying . . . ," Juanita said.

"Say anything you want."

"Ignoring the sacred wasn't necessarily the smartest choice you made. Treating magic like technology . . . it's not right. It's not . . . *whole*."

"You want to be my spiritual adviser?"

"I'm not qualified. Besides, would you even want one?"

"Why not?" Astrid said. "Go check on your family. Think things over, and let me know if you reach any conclusions."

She was right, Juanita thought. She'd see Mamá and make it right with the judge, if she could.

Oh, and there's a little matter of figuring out what to do with the rest of my life.

It seemed wrong that after so much had happened, she still had to tussle with that one.

Her hand brushed Gilead's book. Spiritual questions.

The Kiev airport had been reorganized around one airplane hangar whose big doors had become a massive gateway. The gate wasn't made of thorns anymore, but a mixture of woods and stone, adorned with carvings and pictographs, symbols from a hundred cultures. Two queues—one of vehicles, one of people on foot—were inching toward the gate through improvised check-points. The guards were checking for weapons and scanning passports, but they weren't looking for hassles and were only too happy to send any foreigners home.

As soon as someone recognized Juanita as the American girl from the famous trial, they waved her through.

"I suppose all this will get normalized soon."

"Visas and immunizations and travel restrictions," Astrid agreed. "Business as usual."

"So the old world's not completely dead."

"No deader than me."

"I'm not sure that's funny," Juanita told her.

"When you decide, let me know."

People who'd made it through security tended to pause at the threshold of the gate, daunted by the cold air and blue glow. Juanita stepped through without hesitation.

She found herself at the bottom of a steep gorge walled by blue stone. Trucks and cars were rumbling downhill, lining up to pass through another checkpoint—this one staffed by Native Americans wielding magical items—at the exit. The line of pedestrians wound alongside the road.

Will Forest was waiting for her. "Going back to Reno?"

She nodded. "Find your kids?"

"Yes."

"That's good, I'm glad."

"Anytime you want to talk, call Astrid's name."

"I just want news of my family, Forest."

"That part of Nevada had some sandstorms, nothing too serious. Casualties in Reno were light." He walked her past the checkpoint, to the glow. "Think about where you want to be."

"No place like home, huh?" she said, stepping out into her mother's backyard.

She bolted up to the kitchen door, almost tripping over a profusion of children's toys. For a second, she thought the door might be locked, but no—it had always been sticky. She shoved it open. "Mamá?"

No answer.

Heart in her mouth, she poked through the house. It was obvious Lucinda was living here with the children again, obvious
too that the family had not been gone long—there was a half-
gnawed cracker with a smear of yellow fruit on it aging on the
counter. The smell of stale banana filled the air.

They were okay. She could wait.

She checked the card drawer. If any of her brothers had died
while she was out of touch, the telegram from the army and the
sympathy cards would be there.

Mamá's church earrings were gone.

She picked up the phone, got a dial tone, and tried Lucinda's
cell. It went to voice mail. Which meant nothing, with so many
towers down.

She dropped her bag, and went to rinse her face. The water
was off, and a basin by the sink filled with tepid water was the
best she could do. She washed up carefully: it felt important to
look her best.

Once she was satisfied with her appearance, she set out down
the empty streets. None of the houses seemed badly damaged.
She saw a collapsed deck here, a fallen tree there, lots of broken
windows.

Her feet brought her to her old church. As she climbed the
steps, she heard singing, a full house from the sounds of it. She
opened the doors, thinking to slip in unnoticed, lay eyes on
her family, and get out without a fuss.

Instead she collided with a young mother who'd retreated to
the foyer to soothe her baby. The kid screeched; heads turned.

Juanita flushed. Her eye fell on a banner behind the pulpit:
SERVICE FOR THE MISSING.

Great. She might as well have interrupted her own funeral.

Mamá cried out, running up the aisle, suffocating Juanita in
her arms.

"Sorry, Mamá," she whispered. "I didn't mean to worry you."

"I wasn't worried, baby. You're not on the list."

"No?"

"I knew you were alive," Mamá said, and there, in the rising heat, amid the crush of family, Juanita felt something powerful rising within her, a commingling of joy and strength.

"Come on," she said to her mother. "Let's find a seat."

CHAPTER FIFTY-TWO

WITHIN A MONTH OF Boomsday—Astrid had never been able to sell anyone on "Small Bang"—Indigo Crater and the forest around it had, unofficially at least, become an independent territory governed by the Roused.

The rush of vitagua into the real had brought debris with it—hundreds of tons of the gritty dirt that had lain under the glaciers. It had blown from the Chimney, carving the crater, and coalesced at its edge into a crag with sharp slopes and a jagged peak. Observers likened it to a snapped femur; people were calling it Blue Bone.

If anything remained of Indigo Springs, it was entombed beneath the mountain.

The Roused had been quick to exploit their monopoly on gate travel, making deals with individual airport authorities worldwide. Participating countries got gates: in return, the Roused agreed to follow international law as they moved people from place to place. Passports were stamped, visas checked, fees and duties paid.

Business as usual.

Arthur Roche and two aides came through the Blue Bone Welcome Center on a Wednesday morning. It was a shock, seeing him again: Astrid still thought of Roche as a petty tyrant who'd jailed her. But as he and Will shook hands, they exchanged a long look—of understanding, miles traveled together, old fights resolved . . . and she found the animosity slipping away.

He'd been through a lot, she realized, and he had less say in it than most of them.

"Welcome," she made herself say, and found she meant it.

He gave her the usual curt nod. "Am I the last one here?"

Will shook his head. "We're waiting on the Fyrefolk."

They escorted the government delegation to a sun-dappled meadow dotted with seats—stumps, rocks, a few proper chairs. Letrico boulders lay in the grass, and sunshine trickled down through a screen of leaves. Astrid settled on a mossy stump.

"This is your conference room?" Roche murmured to Will.

Will's hands moved, and the general laughed.

"I didn't know you knew sign language," Astrid said.

Will shrugged.

"He learned when I lost my hearing," Roche said.

The meadow was already occupied by representatives from other stakeholders: Patience's firebrand niece, Lilla Skye, was there speaking for non-Roused aboriginal interests, Jupiter for the Indigo Springs volunteers, many of whom were wanted for terrorism and war crimes. A trio of Roused—a warrior, an elder, and a Two-Spirited shaman, waited in the shade of an elm tree. The United Nations had sent an observer, which made everything seem shockingly important and official. There was also a camera crew.

As Roche took possession of a granite slab that might work, more or less, as a desk, Will beamed. "Told you we'd get them all here."

"Except they're not." As Lilla Skye approached Roche, Astrid sent a ringer to find Juanita Corazón.

Juanita was home in Reno, arguing with her mother in rapid-fire Spanish. The sound carried through the open window.

"I gotta learn more languages . . . ," Astrid muttered, straining her mouse muscles to push the doorbell.

A diminutive niece opened the door. "Grandma wants Tía to wear a skirt," she confided as Juanita rushed to the door, buttoning a pair of dress slacks. Her face fell when she recognized Astrid.

"Expecting someone else?"

"I guess not," she said. "Everyone waiting on me?"

"Pretty much. Your judge friend didn't show?"

She shook her head.

"I'm sorry."

"It's okay," Juanita said. "Expecting him to forgive me, let alone join the witch-burners, was probably a bit much."

"You're not witch-burners." Back at the talking meadow, Astrid's ringer raised its voice. "Fyrefolk delegation's on its way."

A chilly murmur. Getting the Fyremen a seat at the table had been a hard sell, even though Juanita had taken over the group, promising to focus their attention on spiritual issues.

Astrid let her gaze roam to the dancers and drummers awaiting the official opening of the talks. Negotiations would go on for years, Will had warned. She couldn't expect substantial progress today.

Elsewhere, in the unreal, a small hand tugged at hers.

Astrid had never finished high school, and to be heading up a class now felt . . . weird.

It helped that her classroom wasn't in a real school. There were no blackboards or desks; she'd chosen a space near a standing pool of vitagua, erecting a gaily colored silk tent bordered by gardens. Jacks's statue of her father stood half a mile away, down a path lined with Dad's favorite flowers.

Astrid's students ranged in age from eight to fifteen, and they came from across the globe. They carried books from more worldly classes—Will had recruited a math and science teacher, an English teacher, even a seasoned principal to run the school. The kids bubbled with energy.

Ellie and Carson Forest were among her students. Will's daughter bounced with barely repressed excitement. Carson, as always, was more guarded. Walls up, so much like his dad.

All of them had the vitagua-flecked eyes of the initiated.

"Let's start with a letrico circle," Astrid said.

They formed up around a windmill, reciting the cantation. Power formed in tufts, and they each crystallized a hunk.

"Good." She handed a chantment to Ellie. "Apple-spinning."

"Praise the Goddess," Ellie mouthed, raising the chantment and making fruit out of thin air. Apples for teacher.

Next, Astrid led the group to a shelf of random objects one of the Canadian kids had christened the Tickle Trunk, inviting each child to pick something with sparkle.

One after another, the students made chantments. They were minor items, imbued with random powers—only Ellie Forest seemed close to developing any control over what she made.

There was no rush; they had time.

In time, the students would return home to make chantments, improving the lives of their families and neighbors.

"Astrid." That was Katarina, speaking to a ringer in the new magic science center at MIT. "There's a quantum physicist in Sri Lanka I want on-site. Homeland Security's blocking his visa."

"Ask Pike to take it on."

"*Nyet,* I need him. Disguise or smuggle the guy."

"We can't do whatever we want anymore," Astrid said. Every hour, it seemed, imposed more rules on them. Laws on letrico use, agreements about chantment dispersal. Several U.S. states had already made vamping a capital offense. Humanity was fitting magic into a legislative framework, defining what magicians could do. Coming to terms.

She argued with Katarina, watched the Roused dancers opening up the peace conference, taught her class, and roamed the world. In Cleveland, Boomsday had caused tornadoes, but the electricity was back up, and most of the roads were fixed. Water was running. Life was getting, more or less, back to normal.

Olive was honeymooning in Cairo with Thunder. It was a working vacation—they were establishing a letrico mill.

In the talking meadow, Roche and Will were murmuring, feeling each other out on deals.

Roche: "We're asking you stop giving private citizens extraordinary powers. Firefighting, road building—that belongs to the government. Healing chantments go to licensed doctors, that kind of thing. Superheroes are fine for comic books, but you can't just go around sowing chaos—"

"We might agree to that," Will murmured.

"Astrid has to publicly accept our position that her U.S. citi-

zenship expired when her body died. She's no longer American.
And you renounce your citizenship too."

"Why?" she asked, startling them both.

"You two killed thousands on Boomsday. You can't be Americans anymore."

It hurt, strangely: the sense of rejection bit deep.

A rustle among the spectators drew their attention. George
Skagway was weaving his sports chair through the crowd. He
braked to a stop between Clancy and Juanita, nodding to them
both. Juanita was staring at the dancers, her jaw clenched. Fighting tears, Astrid wondered, or a smile?

An hour later, in her classroom, she sent the kids off to gym
class. She still felt a bit like an impostor as they filed out, chorus-
ing good-byes.

North and east, in Saskatoon, the Royal Canadian Mounted
Police were having a standoff with a man who had vamped seven
people. He was holding them off with a magical straight razor.

She asked: "Would you like a hand?"

"He's had every chance to surrender," one assented. Drawing
vitagua out of the prairie soil, she flowed into the house, overwhelming the guy, freezing him solid.

A thousand tasks, time for everything. She worked, watched,
wheeled and dealed, started learning Spanish. The day passed.

At dusk, she sent a ringer home to Pucker Hill.

Will was at the cottage with the kids, cleaning up dinner: corn
on the cob and baked ham, from the look of it. Carson's face
stiffened as she came through the door: he was polite in class,
but that did not mean she had won him over.

"Hey." Will came to the door, kissing her cheek. It was a
peck—he still found the ringers creepy.

"How's the world?"

"Changing," she said.

"What else is new?" He rinsed the plates and set them in a
rack to dry. "Carson wants to see what's left of our old neighborhood in Portland."

Astrid eyed him gravely. "Is it okay if I come?"

The boy nodded, his face unreadable.

They took Stonegate to Blue Bone, stepping through to Portland. The city was half in and half out of Roused territory; it lay on the edge of an area flattened by quakes and overgrown by alchemized forest. Overnight, it had become a border town.

Will's street had gotten a good shake. Heritage homes slumped in an untidy line along broken roadway and sidewalks, many cracked and slumping, none quite flattened. The trees around them had grown sky high, shadowing everything.

A trio of starlings flashed past, iridescent feathers glinting. Ellie waved: Alchemites who hadn't lost their faith on Boomsday considered the birds holy.

Flying rats, Astrid's father grumbled. He'd never much liked starlings.

"This is it," Carson said, voice strained. "Ellie, look."

Rhododendrons spilled over the porch of a three-story house. Will shoved the plants back, triggering a spill of red blossoms. Beyond the growth, the door was ajar.

Ellie darted in.

"Careful, baby." Will trotted after her, leaving Astrid alone with Carson.

"So . . . ," Astrid said before the silence could stretch. "You're looking for your old things?"

The boy shook his head. "Dad got them after Boomsday."

"Just wanted to poke around?"

No answer. She stepped back, letting him decide if he wanted to chase his father and sister indoors. His discomfort was obvious.

Maybe coming along had been a mistake.

Casting about for something to say, Astrid spotted a glimmer of steel at the edge of the garden, metal buried under leaves. She bent, struggling to unearth whatever it was, but her mouse muscles failed her.

"Here." Carson dug, coming up with a pair of ice skates, black leather boots with a touch of rust on the blades.

"It has that sparkle," he said.

"Yeah?" A glimmer of foreknowledge. "The first time I learned to consciously choose what a chantment I was making would do—I talked as I was chanting. I said what I wanted."

The boy shot her what she'd come to think of as his "wary dog" look.

"Your little sister doesn't have to be the class superstar," Astrid said, offering her hand, letting the tip of one finger soften to liquid magic.

After a second, Carson reached out, absorbing a bit of her essence. He bit his lip, bowed his head, and clenched the skates to his chest, whispering as the magic flowed into them.

"Any idea what they do?" Astrid asked.

He nodded, unable to hide a glint of triumph.

"It's what you wanted?"

"Yes." He hefted them. "Did you plant these here?"

"No," she said. "Want to give them a try?"

He sat, kicking off his shoes. "There's no letrico."

"The forest can spare a little heat."

Carson started spinning, just a little, and as the letrico coiled at his feet, he wound his hand in it, balling it around his fist in a cotton candy spool. He frowned that Will Forest frown, and Astrid's small heart pattered, expecting some hard question: How could she have let his mother be murdered? maybe. But he rose onto the blades, flexed his legs, and took off like a rocket through the trees.

The sound, the rasp of a knife cutting ice, brought Will to the porch at a run. "What's he doing?"

"Blowing off steam," Astrid said, fists clenched, unwilling to admit she was terrified the kid would slam into a tree.

He put an arm around her. "You are not going to become one of those permissive stepmothers who lets the children walk all over her, just for fear of being disliked."

"I don't know. Am I?"

"That wasn't actually a question."

"Rules, rules," she said, and he squeezed her as if she were still alive.

Ellie came out of the house with a stuffed elephant clutched in each hand. "Car-car! Let me try!"

"You'll accommodate," Will said. "We all will. We remade the world. How hard can building a family be?"

"It's the thing I never got right."

"It's going to work out, Astrid," he said, turning her so she was looking into his eyes.

"Do you mean that, Will?"

"I believe it," he said. Carson swooped past, bearing his sister skyward. Both kids shrieked with laughter as Will's breath began to fog on the steadily cooling air and he pressed his lips to hers.

ABOUT THE AUTHOR

A. M. Dellamonica is the author of *Indigo Springs,* a debut novel that won the Sunburst Award for Canadian Literature of the Fantastic. She has been publishing short fiction since the early nineties, some of which has appeared in *Asimov's, Strange Horizons, Realms of Fantasy,* and at Tor.com along with numerous anthologies. In 2005, her alternate history of Joan of Arc, "A Key to the Illuminated Heretic," was shortlisted for the Sideways Award and the Nebula Award. She also teaches writing courses through the UCLA Extension Writers' Program.

Dellamonica lives in Vancouver, British Columbia, with her wife, Kelly Robson, and two very spoiled cats.